Praise for _Death U..._

'Tense but patient, fast but substantial – this is a truly e... the next instalment _now_'   Lee Child

'I LOVED this. I found it totally immersive, and couldn't wait to squeeze some time from my day to return to it. The writing is very classy and the conclusion came as a surprise, which is always a treat'   Ann Cleeves

'Gloriously atmospheric and masterfully plotted with such a strong sense of place, this is a huge treat for crime fiction lovers. I can't wait for the next instalment!' Lucy Foley

'Stylish . . . a more than promising debut'   _The Times_

'Stylishly written by a skilled wordsmith, and an absorbing tale'   _Sun_

'A vivid, atmospheric debut'   _Daily Mail_

'A cosy crime read with an appealing protagonist'
                                                                            Guardian

'A pitch-perfect blend of psychological thriller and classic detective fiction, rich with smart plotting and characters so real we feel we know them'   Jeffery Deaver

'Brilliant, gripping, fantastic . . . I can't put it down'
                                                                          Chris Evans

'An atmospheric, often meditative, and beautifully written crime novel'   Vaseem Khan

'An outstanding debut'   Jeffrey Archer

DEATH
UNDER A
LITTLE SKY

Stig Abell loves detective novels above any other literature, films, plays or television. This is the first one he has actually written. Away from books, he presents the breakfast show on Times Radio, a station he helped to launch in 2020. Before that he was a regular presenter on Radio 4's Front Row and was the editor and publisher of the *Times Literary Supplement*. At one time or another he has written for almost every newspaper in Britain, and one or two in America as well. He lives in London with his wife, three children and two independent-minded cats called Boo and Ninja (his children named them, obviously).

X @StigAbell
@TheStigAbell

DEATH
UNDER A
LITTLE SKY

STIG ABELL

h

Hemlock Press
an imprint of HarperCollins*Publishers* Ltd
1 London Bridge Street,
London SE1 9GF

www.harpercollins.co.uk

HarperCollins*Publishers*
Macken House,
39/40 Mayor Street Upper,
Dublin 1
D01 C9W8
Ireland

This paperback edition 2024
1

First published by HarperCollins*Publishers* Ltd 2023

Map by Liane Payne © 2023

A catalogue record for this book is available from the British Library

ISBN: 978-0-00-851705-2 (PB b-format)

Typeset in Sabon LT Std by Palimpsest Book Production Ltd,
Falkirk, Stirlingshire

Printed and bound in the UK using 100% renewable electricity
at CPI Group (UK) Ltd

MIX
Paper | Supporting
responsible forestry
FSC™ C007454

This book contains FSC™ certified paper and other controlled sources
to ensure responsible forest management.

For more information visit: www.harpercollins.co.uk/green

*To Nadine, my partner in crime,
and in everything else.*

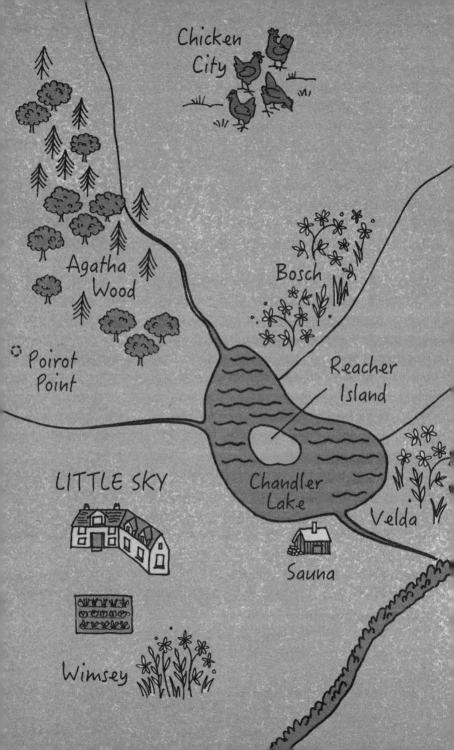

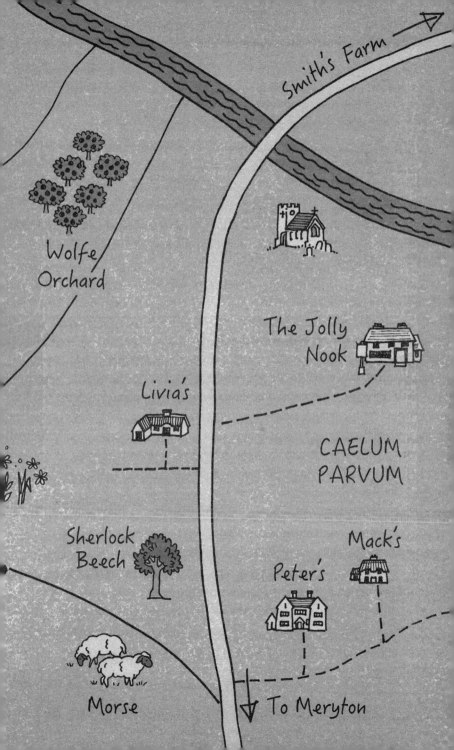

Reason thus with life:
If I do lose thee, I do lose a thing
That none but fools would keep. A breath thou art,
Servile to all the skyey influences,
That dost this habitation, where thou keep'st,
Hourly afflict: merely, thou art death's fool;
For him thou labour'st by thy flight to shun
And yet runn'st toward him still.

William Shakespeare, *Measure for Measure*, Act 3, Scene 1

PROLOGUE

It is a long way, as the heron flies, between lights in this part of the countryside. There is much silence and gloom in between, though the air is never completely still. Things rustle and murmur; creatures slink and scurry. Not just animals, but the occasional human too. The expanse is too forgiving for those with malign intent, and you can disappear into the twilit softness with great, alarming ease.

A woman stands atop old and crumbling stairs. There is pain in her eyes, but not fear, not quite yet. In a few moments, she will be crumpled on the ground below; the drama and striving, the passion and the pain of her life over. She has been watched all evening. In fact, she has often struggled to evade attention over the last few years, to find peace even in the wideness around her.

It is hard to separate some of the nearby men from the land itself. They work it – as she does – and it sticks to them, the smell of soil and growth and decay. She is surrounded; they are camouflaged. She strokes the downy hair on her arms, as a few goosebumps pimple her skin. The breeze is rising, she feels high in the sky.

She wonders if he is nearby, crouched furtive deep in a shadowy recess, watching and plotting. It is, sometimes, unbearable to imagine it. Her life here has been hard; she is an outsider, an invasive species. And yet she has found moments of solace in the thick land and silvery waters, in the sights and sounds of a natural world completely heedless of her needful fears. She has even found companionship with people on occasion. A friendly smile, an evening of carefree conversation.

But also constraint and fear. Dark, glowering eyes following her home, the physical threat of a man's unforgiving bulk. Not just one man, but several. A group, a gathering; a rape of men like a murder of crows. She had coped, and struggled, and made herself small, got herself lost in the open spaces. And then the blow had fallen, the cataclysm, the catastrophe.

Elsewhere, a man sits in his home. He doesn't love technology, but has become more adept with his camera over time: he used to have a darkroom, the sickly sweet toxicity of chemicals filling his nostrils and stinging his eyes, as the objects of his attention loomed back into ghostly existence. Now he is downloading images onto a computer, the screen-light dancing on a face that has been creased and hardened by the elements. He wonders if the people close to him know what is in his mind all of the time, the relentless throbbing of his senses, the things he is thinking when he stares at them. Of course they don't know, otherwise they would have stopped him. He looks out of his window to check he is not being seen.

Somewhere else, two men meet by an old tree. Their

cars are parked apart on the lane nearby, facing in opposite directions. The exchange is brief: two bags change hands, one of cash, one of product. They barely speak. They know that silence and security is essential. They cannot leave loose ends.

Lights flicker on in far apart houses. If you could swoop, quiet as a bat, and peer in through windows you would see family life in all its forms. The laughter between mother and daughter as bedtime approaches. The awkward stiffness between husband and wife who have run out of things to say to each other, and sit restless and aloof. The widow lost in front of a television screen. Two grown-up brothers who should have left home in pursuit of separate lives, but have been imprisoned by their own lack of ambition, their vitality and empathy drained year after year. One sneaks out while the other dozes in the corner, his dirty boots falling off his feet, the night outside preferable to these four walls. An old man at his kitchen in a dirty long shirt, painting the woman now standing on the tower. He can see her in the daylight of his imagination, the reflection of the water playing idly upon her pale skin.

The moon outside has glibly appeared, cold and sterile in the darkening blue of the dusky evening. As meaningful as a child's drawing, indifferent as everything else.

Beginnings

A country road. A tree. Evening. The taxi from the station, a wheezing old Toyota the same pale blue colour as the sky, had reversed into a gap in the hedge then chuntered away, exhaust rattling. He pauses to let the noise fade; he is hungry for silence. He has spent years – all of his adult life, in fact – in a big city, where it is never dark, never quiet, and he suddenly feels tired of the very idea of noise and brightness. The last hum of the car disappears, and he exhales slowly. There is not quite nothing left in his ears: the sigh of the wind rustles the leaves of what he supposes is an oak tree, the one visible landmark in the area. Two birds chirrup. But this is definitely a start.

All around him stand empty fields, thick and green, freckled with daisies and thistles and dandelions, unkempt like he always is. In his hand is the crumpled bit of paper that has the instruction: 'Get the taxi to drop you off at the oak tree; that's as close as you can get to the house.' It had not been easy convincing Josef, the driver, to agree to make a journey to a tree, but he had acceded with something approaching good grace. Family was important to Josef – he had pictures of a wife and daughter taped to the dashboard – and he clearly liked the idea of honouring an uncle's wishes. Jake had tried to keep his explanations to a minimum, not least because he is not sure himself why he has come here, his whole life so easily enclosed in a gym bag and a scarred black suitcase. In the back of the car, he had noticed, hanging forlornly on the suitcase handle, the airline tag from their last holiday, on their third recovery period. They had gone to Ibiza for some sun, had sat by a pool while he slowly, unwillingly burned, not talking much. He had started pale and milky, she always seemed effortlessly tanned. They drank a lot in the evenings, but stopped before their inhibitions made them say something they might regret. That poolside had a different type of quiet; the unhealthy, stilted, silted-up kind. The quiet of two people thinking busily, but unable to communicate. The silent dead thing between them again.

Jake breathes out once more, and picks up his bags and heads to the gap where the car had reversed. There is the faint outline of a track ahead of him, stretching out over the hump of the land. It is nearly six, so plenty of a summer's evening left; that most pleasant part of any warm day, the sun a faded glare behind him, beginning its descent towards the other horizon. Before he continues walking, he awkwardly shuffles both bags into one hand and pulls out his phone. No signal, no internet. He had been warned this would happen in the letter. In the last ten years, he can count the number of times he has been disconnected from technology, mainly when he was on a plane. He remembers how he and Faye used to message each other all the time. Little love notes, jokes, miniature revels in the banal. That was one definition of love, he had thought: taking pleasure in sharing the boring bits of life. What you'd had for lunch, something you'd heard on the radio, what the neighbour had said when he slipped on the steps. And that was one definition of love ending: when the boring stayed boring, when there was no point in talking any more.

Jake's hands tingle after a few minutes tramping up the incline. He is unused to this physical burden. As he reaches the modest peak, he peers downwards into a valley of more fields, a patchwork of green, mustard yellow and a deep brown. The breeze is stronger for a moment, and cools the sweat on his brow, bringing with it a pleasant earthy scent. There is life in the land, in the air around him. He cannot see his destination yet, but that is not surprising. The letter instructed him to find the path at the bottom of the pasture, and march east along it for a mile (there was a sarcastic parenthesis telling him that 'east' means left as he faces away from the main road).

It amused him that a man's last wishes could convey sarcasm, an eyebrow raised from beyond the grave. Uncle Arthur had never been a prominent presence in his life, but always a memorable one: visiting erratically in Jake's childhood, staying for a few days when he did come, the dining room converted into his living quarters, a mattress on the floor, clothes piled in the corner, the whole place filled with the exotic smell of cigars, the tortured sound of jazz trumpets coming from his portable stereo.

Arthur lived the rest of the year in America – Florida, the state of Disneyland and the ever-elderly, in Jake's imagination – and sent ironic postcards when the mood took him, and came and went with mysterious abruptness.

In Jake's teen years, his awkward, gangly, frustrated period, when his innards roiled with speechless frustration and angsty lust, Arthur was always a soothing presence. 'You don't need to talk about anything,' he would say, 'just sit down and read this.' He always carried a pile of books in his luggage, and left them with Jake when he departed: some big thick Victorian novels, some American new releases, classics and rarities. And lots of detective fiction, from all over the world. Jake once wrote to Arthur that he had started him on the road to the police force, and hoped it gave the old man satisfaction.

After Jake's parents' funeral, Arthur had visited only once. He had suddenly aged, Jake thought, his Florida tan scored with thick wrinkles like plough lines, his spryness stiffening into something more pitiable.

'I have got to the point in the world,' he confided one evening, as they sat outside Jake's student house, Arthur perching on a wheelbarrow with his cigar in one hand, Jake balancing on the only piece of garden furniture they possessed, 'when I can't really face things any more. It's all getting too much for me. I want to find some peace somewhere.' This struck a far more sombre note than Jake was accustomed to, even given the sombre circumstance of his own sudden orphaning. Arthur had loved life as much as he had loved literature. He had never married, but Jake always suspected the presence of romantic relationships somewhere, always felt that Arthur's pursuit of pleasure had taken him into other people's existences. That last time, Arthur had stayed for a few days in the house, and then performed his usual sudden departure. His remaining contact with Jake had come in the form of letters at indiscriminate intervals, some short and gnomic, others long and indulgent, reflecting on his own childhood and relationship with his brother, but never about his present circumstance. Jake always responded, to a postbox somewhere in one of those anonymous rural counties in the middle of England, and had always felt reassured of his uncle's interest.

The path meanders east, and Jake pauses again for breath, and to rest his aching arms. In the last half hour, evening has truly come, the shadows are long, the air settling into the cool of the night, the breeze dropping down to a decorous whisper.

He knows he cannot linger; there is so much he will have to do when he arrives. After twenty more minutes huffing along the path, he sees it ending abruptly at an old wooden stile, mottled with moisture and close to toppling, its base skirted with long grass. A small sign has been nailed alongside it. WELCOME TO LITTLE SKY, it says.

Home

Jake throws his bag over the stile and stands on it, to look down into what is now his property. He has been noticeably climbing again over the last few minutes, and has clearly reached the high point of the area. Beneath him now is a steep path through yet another field, descending into a valley. To the left there is a dark smear of purple-green, which looks like a wood, and further beyond something shimmers rose-gold in the final sunlight of the day. Some sort of body of water, like a lake or pond. The land is uneven still, rising and falling, a giant rucked quilt, and so the valley floor remains invisible. The gloaming has arrived, and with it the masking power of shadow. He had better move quickly now before he becomes enshrouded in darkness in the middle of nowhere.

Life had all seemed so straightforward at one point for him, he thinks: career, friends, marriage, children. Jake had finished law school fifteen years before, and been recruited to join the police as part of a special fast-track system designed to attract graduates with law degrees. He had met Faye four years into the job. She was a solicitor, who ate lunch on a bench outside the magistrates' court whenever she had a case there. He liked her red-brown hair, almost copper, and the way she wore Converse trainers with a work skirt. Jake's job brought him to the vicinity a lot, and he began timing his lunchbreaks to match hers, sitting on a nearby bench, pretending to read. In the end, she had approached him, when one chilly October afternoon the wind scattered her lunch wrappers, blustering them in his direction. He wasn't in uniform – that part of the job had been fast-tracked as well – but he still looked official, unrelaxed somehow. She knew he was a policeman, she said, because his eyes were never still, his body was taut even when he was trying to appear loose. She liked that about him, she often told him, even after they started going out; he was never sleepy or acquiescent. He was switched on like a light, and she relished never having to be in the dark any more.

They felt right together from the very next day when they shared her bench for lunch. After the third time, they both skipped work to go back to her flat, the thrill of breaking the rules a halo to the thrill of seeing each other's unclothed bodies. They clicked in the bedroom as they had on the bench. It felt simple and easy. And perhaps it was all too easy: the next couple of years, the compatible jobs, the shared friends from the big London law schools. They were married at thirty, a good age they told each other, life still very much to come, wandering freedoms stored where they should be, in the past. A shared desire to embrace life's encumbrances as they arrived. They pooled resources for a nice suburban house. Jake's parents had died before he graduated, shocking him into self-

11

reliance, giving him a financial push into comfortable adulthood. And now their own children would come, more encumbrances, more pressure, but also something to cherish and build upon.

Children never came. Only hope, then disappointment. Clutching her hand as the spasms racked her body. The trips to the hospital, after uncertain pains led to clouts of dark blood on the floor, a miniature crime scene. Doctors either brisk or baffled.

Everyone knows someone who has had a miscarriage before producing healthy children. The loss is awful, but not out of the ordinary; it is within life's reasonable expectations. But then a second miscarriage, then a third. The tests suggesting something not quite right. They didn't click after all. They couldn't fuse when it mattered the most.

As Jake descends into the dusk, the ground dark green in pools around him, he sees it: a farmhouse buried deep into the dip of the land, an L-shape on its side, with the broad front before him. It is dark brown in the dimness, splotched with ivy in parts, a huge birch tree to the side standing guard. He runs down the final part of the path, his heart suddenly racing. He can feel the house's emptiness like a palpable presence, something thick and unyielding. It is aloof to his existence, which is somehow reassuring. There is solidity here, he feels, something to cling to.

Crooked house

Jake reaches the door just as the sun disappears from the sky, the night now a hazy blue, with the white pinpricks of stars above him. You never see stars in the city, he thinks; and you seldom look above you to search for them. But now they are there, visible and aloof, part of the celestial furniture once again.

A couple of months ago, the letter had come. The envelope landed with a thud, a startling sound even against the background noise of the road outside and the planes overhead. Jake had hauled himself up, taken it to the kitchen table. It was a legal letter addressed to him, from a Dickensian-sounding solicitors' firm (Krunkles of Havencester; Jake still remembers it). Inside, it informed him that his paternal uncle Arthur had died, and he was the sole beneficiary of his will. It enclosed two further letters, both on thick, creamy, expensive paper. The first one was in Arthur's recognizably laconic handwriting and said this:

Jake,

This is my final letter to you. In a couple of days I will be dead, and it will be sent.

I always knew you and I were alike in some ways. But I spent all my life drifting around, living in the world, meeting people, getting into relationships and watching them dwindle. And then, after Jim died and we last spoke, I decided I'd had enough. I sold up the Midlife Crisis Mansion in Florida, liquidized my other assets, and looked for a place to bury myself. I found it, and that is where I have been for the last more than thirteen years. No phones, no internet, no noise. My place of renunciation.

And I want it to be yours. I paid someone over the last year to watch over you – sorry about that – and he tells me what your letters have sometimes said, your marriage is not full of joy. You are a fine detective and a good husband, but you, forgive me, seem to be nothing else.

I used to give you gifts, all those books, to broaden your horizons. Well I want my last gift to narrow them. I want you to have my place: Little Sky. It is all paid for, including the land and the lake. I have more than enough money to support your solitary life; and it is in the bank account I have created for you.

I am giving you the opportunity of a lifetime: let this all go. Bury yourself in the quietest place I could find in England. Find peace and happiness. Read books and learn to be practical. Stop the fight. Stop trying for something that doesn't exist.

Your friend and uncle,
Arthur

The other letter contained bank account details, directions to Little Sky, and some instructions about the house. Jake had kept both close by him, all the way through to the train journey this afternoon, and his early evening hike through the encroaching shadows.

The house is not locked, the door swings open loudly, and thuds into a wall before slowly repeating the curve back towards him. Inside, he can see almost nothing, just grey shapes, anonymous furniture. He feels loneliness like a sickness in his stomach. He has never in his life been this far from people.

And now he is truly alone, enveloped by a thick shroud of silence. He walks into the next room, allowing the door to shut behind him. He drags some cushions from a sofa that smells of age and disuse, drinks some water from a bottle in his bag, shrugs on a hooded top and curls up, a child in the foetal position once more. Tomorrow will show him what his life might become.

Wild swimming

The early light softens the darkness in the room first to pallid grey, then to a broader range of colours: the green of the armchair, the russet of the sofa, the cornfield yellow of the walls. Jake aches more or less all over, feels every one of his thirty-eight years. He can taste the bitterness of his own breath, smell that rancorous sourness of his unwashed body. His sleep – unsettled by the unwonted quiet, punctuated by mysterious, elemental noises he struggled to identify – has left him sore and shivery. The day is not yet warm, though holds the promise of heat to come, and he jumps up and down to get his circulation going. He now sees that his temporary sleeping quarters are a big living room, dominated by a fireplace thick with powdery white ash, with one other door – slightly ajar – leading down some stone-flagged steps. He follows them into what was originally a farm kitchen. There's a big wooden table near a huge black stove, emitting no heat at all. The other side of the room is a contrast: modern-looking cabinets, a teak-toned breakfast bar with stools, and a giant fridge, which is forbiddingly silent. Jake remembers the note saying: 'I have tried to live my new life minimizing my need to rely on other people. The power to the house comes from two sources. I got the local rogue – you'll probably meet him – to help me hijack the central electricity lines, but in case that fails there is a diesel generator too. The water is connected, and paid for in perpetuity. There is no internet connection, no phone lines, no radio, no cable television. The heating comes from fires in each room, and a central furnace for the water. The oven is wood-burning too. You'll have to keep up the wood supply yourself.'

The world is waking around Jake, and he pushes the back door out into the courtyard. The view catches his breath: beyond the perimeter of the house itself is a gentle sweep of longish grass at the end of which is a broad lake winking insistently in the dawn. On one side the water laps against thick clumps of trees; on the other, there is a gravelly beach acting as a margin against another field. The lake extends lengthways before him, and in the half-light he can glimpse a tiny, forlorn island in the middle, beyond which there is another beach of sorts, studded with long, white-green reeds which sway and hiss in the morning air.

He walks to the edge of the water, where there is a wooden pier jutting uncertainly into the blue. A small rowing boat bobs next to it. To his left, built from white plaster, is a thatched hut, containing boating paraphernalia and a pile of old crusty towels. Jake knows he should explore the main house properly first, but instead pulls off his clothes, and jumps into the lake. The cold water shocks him; he feels his heart beating peremptorily against his chest. He can do little other than bob about, flailing his arms to keep warm, kicking his legs hard against the water, before he remembers to put his feet down. They stick deep in the soft mud, and he finds he can stand. His body is goosebumped and pink, his genitals shrink-wrapped in on themselves, so he hurriedly pulls himself onto the pier and clutches the towels he has brought out. The whole process has taken less than five minutes.

Faye would have loved this, he thinks. Twice a week, over the last few years, she had left their house early to go swimming before work with two of her friends. There was a curve of the river near their home, which was clean enough to attract a broad group of mainly female swimmers most of the year. They wore bright gloves and shiny hats, swam fiercely in the cold water, and huddled together afterwards, sharing coffee and porridge and a sense of victory over the elements. Jake went along once, but was soon aware that his presence was unwanted. This was a ritual of friendship, and, he suspected, had some sort of deeper, gendered meaning too. It was a thing to be shared and fussed over, celebrated on Instagram, another part of the modern world left to baffle him slightly. But now he was connected to her, and it, despite being so far away.

His first reaction to Arthur's bequest had been to plan how to make the legacy work for both of them. A dutiful bid to make it fit in with their collective destiny. But he knew, and Faye knew, that they were reaching the end of their time: they were like swimmers – the metaphor was apposite – who were pulling themselves remorselessly down to the depths even as they believed they were saving each other. At first he did not want to admit it, then nor did she, but after two days they both believed it as an article of faith: if their lives were to have any meaningful joy, if they were to carry the shape of some sort of future happiness, it could not be alongside one another. Most people didn't get a clean break, Faye said, most people were entangled by money and property and the endlessly encircling tendrils of life. This was a simple escape, if he wanted to take it. At one level it was crazy: to leave your job and customary existence thanks to the intervention of a batty old man you had seen once in more than a decade. At another, it felt inevitable. Faye got the house, and the friends; Jake got whatever this was.

The lie of the land

Over the next two days Jake does little other than explore
the house and land, and establish what it will take to live
here in some degree of comfort. There are some pleasant
surprises. He soon finds the main power supply, and is
able to get light in every room at night. The place is
enormous, far greater than any one person could need, as
superfluous as his old family home had turned out to be:
draughty rooms scarcely furnished, with the musty taint
of old, unbreathed air in them. But at the bottom of the
foot of the L is a huge library, primarily of detective fiction,
the sort of books that had been given to him throughout
his childhood. All of the great English authors from the
mid part of the twentieth century: Agatha Christie,
Margery Allingham, Dorothy Sayers, Josephine Tey. And
long shelves of Americans, their gaudy covers gleaming:
Chandler and Hammett and Spillane (he and Arthur had
always argued about his questionable status in the canon),
then the sprawling modern series by Michael Connelly,
Kathy Reichs, Donald Hamilton, Donna Leon, John D.

MacDonald, Lee Child, Elmore Leonard, and so on. A Scandi Noir corner. A Tartan Noir shelf. Historical detective series, like the Cadfael books or CJ Sansom's Shardlake novels. It is the most wonderful room Jake has ever seen, and he knows instantly it will be the place he spends his winter days and evenings.

The whole room is wired with a sound system to play records, and Jake soon finds Arthur's jazz stash. He picks one at random: Miles Davis and John Coltrane, live in Stockholm 1960. But the discordant notes – to his baffled ears at least – are almost painful after his recent exposure to silence. He thinks he will try it again to see what the fuss is about: his rugged cop heroes like Harry Bosch loved Coltrane, Uncle Arthur did too; perhaps it is something that comes with time.

There is a trapdoor set in the floor – a happy crime thriller touch, Jake thinks – which leads into a vast basement that supports the entire house. Unlike the basements of noirish nightmare, it is dry and well-lit. There is an imposing furnace at one end next to a vast woodpile. One area is filled with dry goods: bags of flour, sugar, coffee. And tins of soup and meat. Nothing especially sophisticated, but nothing desperate either. It doesn't feel like a fallout shelter, just an underground cathedral to convenience. A cupboard behind the stairs contains Arthur's favourite cigars, and a block of what smells strongly of cannabis. Jake wonders if his uncle had turned to it as an analgesic in the dwindling days of his life. He had never mentioned smoking it before. There are racks of wine and beer, a couple of crates of Scotch, alongside an emergency supply of water.

In contrast to that largesse, there are some barren aspects

too. There are no carpets or rugs or curtains outside of the library. There appear to be no washing facilities anywhere in the house: no baths or showers, no washing machines or dryers. The weather stays fine and hot, and Jake has been wearing a pair of shorts and not much else. Each night he scrubs them in the lake and hangs them under the eaves. He reckons he can alternate two garments this way and pretty much survive the summer. In the chill of the evenings, he wears old pyjama trousers and a hoodie. He worries that he will start to smell at some point.

In the library there is also a box of local maps, and on the first day Jake pores over them. From what he can tell, Arthur owned the land on all sides of the lake going back at least a mile. The wood runs for that length before abutting someone else's farmland. The rest of the area is formed by grassy, ill-kempt fields. A stream trickles all the way through the property from the heights of the top paddock before disappearing north and eventually joining a river some three miles distant. The nearest settlement is the village that had clearly grown up alongside that river: Caelum Parvum. Little Sky in Latin. Had that drawn Arthur here in the first place? He was looking for shrunken horizons, after all.

A cry in the dark

Dusk on the third evening, and Jake is lost. For all his map-reading, he is still struggling to develop a proper sense of place. His sense of direction is compromised by the absence of recognizable landmarks, and he has wandered down a lane some distance from the property. The air hums with unseen insects, and is fragrant with the peppery smell of the hedgerow. The day has been hot, and the earth is still radiating warmth against the chill of the evening air. He is not unhappy. If he cannot find his way home, he'll walk until he is tired, and he'll wait for first light. Anxiety is an emotion he wants to leave behind in the city if he can. He has nowhere to be, so there is no problem with being nowhere he can recognize.

A darker patch looms in the distance; a substantial copse, he thinks, the trees crouched into a fixed position, their bark ridged like ropey muscles. No point in heading there, which is where the lane is taking him. Just to his left, there is a well-trodden pathway, long grass bruised and crushed by wheels, over a verge that leads to a gate.

Jake hops it, almost nimbly, before landing heavily on the unseen ground. A faint light glisters in the distance that could represent civilization. He knows that Caelum Parvum is a couple of miles in the other direction, so hopes for a farmhouse, or maybe a couple of cottages huddled together against the unremitting blackness.

A track of sorts threads its way on one side of the field, and he follows it. He can hear the comforting trickle of a brook hidden by the hedge, and he wonders if that might lead him back to the river that snakes and loops and meanders around the whole valley. Not all streams lead to rivers, he reasons, but this one might.

And after a couple of kilometres of his persistent, gentle loping, it does. The light is no more than a solitary lantern outside an otherwise deserted boathouse; its uncertain beam glimmers and fractures on the water flowing past it. But the building does have a name, and there is a crooked, mossy sign nearby that points in the direction of a road. Jake realizes that if he follows the river it will take him within striking distance of home.

He sits for a moment, his legs aching from the unaccustomed exercise, a gratifying breath of breeze cooling against his head. The silence mildly punctuated by unseen splashes, dusk now defeated by night. All seems at peace.

And then a shattering cry rings out, a jagged obscenity. Jake starts forward, nearly toppling into the water, saving himself by grabbing the thick reeds at the edge. He twists and turns, looking for the source of the sound, but there is nothing but the imperturbable puttering of the natural world.

He thinks the scream came from downstream, where he was heading anyway, and he jogs in that direction.

There are a couple of house lights he can now see, big places that must have land descending lavishly to the river. But there is no movement anywhere he can discern.

He slows to a trot, and then hears it. A low, keening wail, lifted into the breeze from somewhere he can't see. After a couple of minutes it stops. He hears a car door slam and an engine growl into life. And then nothing more.

Jake's heart is pounding, his senses alert, but no further sound comes. The night has gulped away the noise. He feels momentarily complicit: what are the chances of a stranger in this dark mass of countryside being an eavesdropper to someone's distress? But what did he actually hear anyway: a shriek of grief, of pain, of exasperation? He had heard no argument, no violent exchange. People scream and wail without being in serious danger. Such explanations bounce around his mind for a few moments, but he cannot be satisfied with them. Nor can he see an obvious means of actually doing anything. He is no longer a detective in a city full of lights and action. He is a tramper in the black, a wanderer in the anonymous countryside. A couple of hours later he is at home, curled up before a fire he has lit for comfort not for warmth.

Contact

At the end of the first week, Jake realizes he must establish contact with the village sooner rather than later. He needs things like toothpaste and toilet paper – which are not in the convenience cathedral – and he will have to establish some sort of supply of fresh food too. He wonders whether he might start a vegetable garden, though he lacks expertise.

At around six-ish, a weak light splashing through the window of his bedroom, he pulls on his shorts and his day-old vest, and looks down critically at his body. It is already showing the signs of exposure to the relatively gentle English sun: pinking on his collarbone and shoulders, but also perhaps darkening a little too. He has eaten little in the last few days, and walked a great deal, and he thinks he can see his stomach receding slightly. He has plotted a path around his property that measures around five miles and resolves to run it every day; he wants to feel lean and fit, and useful again.

For his whole life Jake has been tall – too tall – and

for the first thirty years he was too tall and thin. But in recent times, he has felt the thickening of his midriff, an unappetizing bulge whenever he leans forward. He likes salty snacks, and cheap chocolate, the cheaper the better, and doughnuts, which he remembers from his childhood as a reward for behaving during the weekly supermarket shop. The tongue-feel of grainy sugar, the deep, glutinous sweetness of the jam inside, the chewy comfort of the dough. For most of his life, his body had silently and efficiently burned all the excess away, a secret sin he did not need to acknowledge. That process seemed to work no longer. As if turning thirty changed the internal chemistry in a single day. Arthur had not stored much in the way of sweet treats, though he seemed to be partial to peanuts, so Jake feels he might be able to improve his diet somewhat. Self-isolation as self-improvement.

By ten, the morning is pleasantly warm, though there is a hint of dampness in the air that might suggest a storm to come. Jake's route to the village skirts the lake, before he crosses a field and follows the stream towards the river, a different section to where he had heard that scream. That noise plays in his mind, he can hear it when he pauses to think, but he can't work out what to do about it. It sounded tragic, desperate even, but had then dissipated into the forgiving ether, a mystery he cannot solve, so something to be put aside, nagging and troubling.

This morning he can't quite work out where his own land ends, so sticks to the pathway next to the trickling water. After a while he pauses for a break, and eases himself down the bank to soothe his feet in the water. He startles a heron, which had been standing sentinel midstream, its wings unfurling dragonlike – as if in slow motion – and lazily elevating it skyward and then away from him. Clutching his flip-flops, he follows its trail, the water icy between his toes, the bottom of the stream silky with rotten matter. After a few minutes, he hears a noise somewhere between a squeal and a giggle, and precariously hauls himself to the top of the bank. A dirty white blur clatters into his legs, nearly sending him sprawling back in.

'Stop that sheep!'

He clings to the creature's back, the wool thin and bobbled close to its body. And looks up: a woman's flushed face, brown skin framed by untidy black hair, smiling curiously at him. She is wearing jeans and a purple checked shirt, which is rolled up at the arms and half open, exposing a grubby white vest.

'Stop that sheep?' he says as his new charge writhes against his shins, warm and disconsolate, the farmyard scent rising up in the heat.

'Well, I don't want him falling into the stream. And you looked like a handy shepherd in an emergency.'

She walks up to him and, in a deft movement, forces something – a tablet, he thinks – into the animal's jaws, its eyes white, bulging and indignant, before nudging it back towards the field with a practised shunt of her legs. She huffs her hair out of her eyes and grins once more.

'We don't see many people wandering around these fields.'

'So my sheep-saving is particularly unlikely.' He holds out a tentative hand. 'I'm Jake. I live in the place behind the lake.' He wishes that had not rhymed.

'Oh, Arthur's palace. We used to call him King Arthur: you know, what with the lake and all. I've not seen him for months, though. He hadn't been well, and there was talk he needed to live somewhere closer to civilization. Did he sell up as well?'

'He died. I'm his nephew.'

'I'm Livia. I'm sorry to hear about Arthur. He was lovely. A bit distant, obviously. But a good thing in the world.'

She reaches out her hand and helps pull him from the top of the bank and onto the flat of the field. He is standing in the shade of a tree, but she is bathed in sunlight. Behind her is an expanse of green filled with sheep, determinedly cropping the grass. He can see a red bike pushed into the hedge, and a tartan rug to the left of an old stone trough.

'Are you a travelling sheep-botherer, Olivia?'

'Just Livia. Like the wife of Augustus, if that means anything to you. And I suppose I am: what is a rural vet apart from someone who roams the area bothering animals?'

'I used to be a travelling people-botherer then. A policeman. But now I don't know what I am.'

She leans forward, and pats his arm, which, he regrets, is tacky with sweat. 'Well, we might not quite know each other well enough to explore your crisis of identification.' She laughs, a welcoming, liquid sound. 'But I need a break in my sheep-bothering, so I could give you the lowdown on the place, and the people, such as they are. Now that we are neighbours of sorts.'

'I always imagined that a fragrant, classics-quoting vet would end up being my guide to the countryside.' They are walking across the field towards the rug.

'Vets are never fragrant. And nor – if you don't mind me saying – are sweaty ex-policemen in shorts and a vest.'

29

He starts away from her, and then the bubbling giggle emerges once more. 'Sorry, I don't get to speak to strangers much, as you might be able to tell.' She flops on the rug, and pats the area next to her. 'I bring this with me for my tea breaks. I'm out of tea, but, if you sit down, I promise I won't judge your smell any more.'

'Let's at least start by no longer talking about it.' He sits, the rug thick and radiating heat, noticing the slime on his feet and pushing them out onto the grass, which is lush and inviting, but pockmarked with sheep droppings.

'Deal. Right, so your brief, five-minute-because-I-have-thirty-two-more-sheep-to-see guide to the strange place that is Caelum Parvum. First, what we don't have: we have no school, no supermarket, no village green, no petrol station, no obvious place of entertainment, no offices. Hardly any children: though I have contributed one to the few we do have. For most of the modern world, you need to drive ten miles on questionable roads to Meryton. I take Diana, that's my daughter, there every day and it's a massive pain. Why don't I move away? I hear you ask.' Jake holds up his hands. 'Well, it is quiet here, and I need to be near the farms.'

'What *do* you have here?'

'Well, we have a general store that also serves as a sort of pub. It has a garden for summer and a cellar for winter. We have a few houses near the river. We have an old church, but no vicar. It gets the occasional enthusiast, but not much more. As I'm talking to you, I'm not sure how much there is to occupy a youngish policeman.'

'Maybe I could apply to be Assistant Sheep-Botherer.'

'Maybe.'

She lapses into silence. Questions crowd his mind, but

he doesn't want to be too nosy. Is she married? He presumes so. 'So tell me about the villagers.'

'It won't take long.' She pivots her body away from him, and sinks back onto the rug. The sky curves above them, blue to its very depths, so blue he feels he can see the tiny particles of the air coalescing in his eyes, miniature mosaics that combine to form the one true colour.

'So there is me, the youngish, mixed-race – if you can still say that, I never know any more – vet and single mum' – ah – 'and Diana, wise beyond her seven years, destined for great things. The shop – renamed *The Jolly Nook*, unsuccessfully for tourist purposes ten years ago – is run by Sarah. She's lived in the area forever. Used to be a farmer's wife, but he died; her kids now live in the city. She's suspicious, but kind enough when she gets to know you. Loves her food.

'Next to the Nook is Mary's place. She's in her eighties, and has two ne'er-do-well sons, Clifford and Martin, who live with her. They do odd jobs around the farms, but don't like regular work if they can help it. I wouldn't trust them if I was trapped outside my house in just a towel, put it that way.

'We have an old biologist, Dr Peter – the nearest thing apart from me to a medical doctor – who's interested in hedgerows, and spends most of the summer falling in and out of them. You'll like him; he's nice.

'His place has a small outbuilding, where Mack lives. He's the local handyman, carpenter, builder, farmhand, driver and anything else that needs doing. He doesn't talk much, smokes poisonous rollies, and seems to be able to do anything at all. I find him reassuring, like the existence of God might be to religious people.' She

31

pauses. 'I told you I don't get much conversation like this.'

'Anyone else? That sounds like more people than I was led to expect by Arthur.'

'Oh, it's pretty hard to bump into them, unless you come for a lock-in at the Nook or anything else. We get a few walkers and campers in a summer like this. And then there are the outlying farms, going towards the county border. But that's it really.'

Jake is tempted to tell his story, why he is here, what he has left behind, but he doesn't want to overburden a first meeting with too much emotional freight. He creaks himself into a standing position: 'I better go and see what this shop has, I might need. Maybe I'll see you here when I come back?'

'Maybe.'

He walks down the track, and turns once after a few minutes. Livia's shirt has become a purple speck, fluttering, the rest of her invisible as if she has been buried in the landscape. It is a hot trek, and he wishes he had brought a water bottle, so soon he is searching out signs of inhabitation. The river is becoming more and more visible, at first like a blue shoelace dropped on the land, and then something broader, the rich mingled marine colours of green, blue and brown. A few gulls squabble and shriek above him. Next to the river is a road, the first he has seen since his arrival, and a sign for the village. Coming off the road are a series of small paths leading to individual houses, all of which look like they have aged into their environment, old damp stone, and wood turned black with time. At the first bend, he sees the shop, which has a half-hearted display of tourist bait outside – a red shrimping net, a child's windmill and a pack of three tennis balls with Martina Navratilova on the outside – and a jaunty sign in effortful antique style.

Inside it is dark and airy, fragrant with cheese and meat. There is a cabinet of vegetables, their roots visible and caked with mud. There is a small shelf of household products. By the counter are rows of brown bottles and a metal barrel, which Jake presumes contains beer.

Standing guardian is a woman of indeterminate years, wide pink arms crossed, brown hair pulled tight in a bun. Her face is not hostile, but not exactly welcoming either. Jake starts picking up items and realizes he doesn't have a bag with him. He makes eye contact: 'Could I have a plastic bag?'

A sorrowful glance, and a shake of the head.

'Any bag?'

'People bring their own bags.'

'Could I buy a bag then?'

A long sigh, then she reaches down and brings up a taffeta shoulder bag, and rests it on the counter, as if daring him to ask for something bigger or better. Jake starts bringing his purchases up: deodorant, preposterously expensive toilet paper, carrots, tomatoes, some crisps, some honeycomb from a nearby farm, cheese and bread. He thinks he might bring a miniature picnic back for Livia. At the last minute, he remembers the water and lugs two litres with him.

Sarah, if it is indeed Sarah, wordlessly puts prices into the cash register, her thick fingers practised at the task. Jake pulls out a card to pay. She is expecting the move, already pointing to a handwritten sign, which she has been carefully concealing behind her elbow: CASH ONLY. Jake has not carried cash for years.

'Is there a cash machine near here?'

Another mournful shake of the head.

'So what do you suggest I do? I've got to tell you this seems a hard way to do business.'

A shrug that starts somewhere in the woman's stomach and ends with her shoulders in her ears. Jake feels slightly hysterical: he has had solitude, the flicker of a surprising connection with Livia, and now this. He feels sweat beading on his head.

The pause elongates. And then: 'Oh calm down, me duck. I was just having my little joke. You looked like you were expecting something a bit country when you walked in. I didn't want to disappoint you.' She frowns. 'The card machine is on the blink, though.'

'Well I can come back and pay another time. I've just moved into the area. I'm Arthur's nephew.'

'Oh, old King Arthur, how is he? I was worried about him the last time I saw him, though that was a while ago.'

'He died. I don't really know too much about his last few months. We used to be close, but he sort of sought out solitude in the end.'

She nods. 'That sounds like him. So nice, but not keen to get too near to you, which is fair enough. I'm Sarah.'

'Jake.'

'Well, Prince Jake, why don't I set you up an account and you can pay every month like the other lot who live here?'

They talk for a few minutes, before Jake leaves, happy he has set up a supply line. He ponders walking on through the village to the old church, but decides he might catch Livia if he hurries homeward. Carrying the bag on one shoulder, the big water bottle in the other hand, he heads

34

back the way he came, the slap of his shoes echoing in the quiet, puffs of hot dust rising as he goes. He is hot and damp when he reaches the field. The sheep are clustered in the shade of a big beech tree and eye him blankly. Livia is not there. He feels a pang of disappointment, which interests him faintly, and then sits down near the animals for a picnic, alone.

Routine

Jake settles into a pattern of life. Up more or less with the light, a run in the morning, fresh and free, before flinging off his clothes and shoes for a plunge in the lake. He swims its length and back, the water clear and cold and restorative. Occasionally, he sees the slinky shadow of a fish pass beneath him. After he dresses, he boils water for coffee, grabs a book from the thriller library, and finds a quiet patch and an old towel to settle on. He normally eats his lunch, of bread and raw vegetables, or cold meat from the Nook, in the kitchen, and then returns to his bedroom where he sleeps deeply and restfully. Then he finds jobs to do, a new man of the land. In the wood, he discovers a section of hewn stumps, where firewood has been collected, and starts the long process of felling a tree and separating it into chunks. It is a pine, rich with resin, sweet as maple syrup, and it makes the air heavy as he works.

The wood in the afternoon on hot days is ideal; it is dark and quiet, with abrupt stencils of light breaking through the leafy ceiling, the insistent murmurs of unseen and unidentifiable birds. He has taken to naming his local landmarks after detective stories: there is Poirot Point at the top paddock, where he first came in that evening; the three big fields are called Bosch, Wimsey and Velda (after Mike Hammer's assistant); there is Spenser Brook, Chandler Lake, Reacher Island, Agatha Wood. One evening, he draws a map with the new names on it, and is startled anew at the scale of where he now lives.

When dark descends – and it does quickly, and with a sudden plummet of temperature – he spends his nights as he thought he would do: in the library, a small fire sighing and spitting. At a rough count, there are more than five thousand books there, enough to keep him occupied for as long as he can imagine ahead.

His whole sense of time is changing; there is little to plan for beyond his physical needs; each day could be the same as the last. He has no idea what is happening in the world; no idea about the cases he left behind; no connection to officialdom or government. He feels this professional absence as both a loss and a liberation. A coil of worry has been removed from within him. But he is also haunted by purposelessness, and by the occasional remnants of past cases. The body of a child, his leg turned the wrong way, an obscene angle in death. The nagging memories of killers who had escaped justice, of deaths that had lingered inexplicable and unexplained to stunned families. Crime-scene photos an unwelcome slideshow as he closes his eyes to sleep.

He thinks of Faye less and less, apart from the odd stab of guilt, or the flicker of wonder at what she is doing. His phone battery has run down, and he doesn't bother to charge it. There are moments in the day when he feels he could be living in almost any century.

He has solved the washing problem, by scrubbing his clothes on the smooth stones of Chandler Lake. After a few minutes they smell of the water, a sort of musty dampness, not unpleasant he hopes, lingering even after they dry. His hair is growing thick on his head, an untidy beard a reassuring weight on his face. His body is unrecognizable, no paunch, reddy brown. He feels like Robinson Crusoe when he looks at his reflection shimmering in the water.

He has seen enough drunks in his time to be wary of drinking too much every day. Discipline is still important to him. His self-imposed, penitential runs make him disinclined to have a hangover. So he has the odd glass of wine or whisky on most nights, but little more. He wants to avoid the despair of drunkenness too. Some afternoons before his nap, he smokes a small amount of cannabis, without tobacco, though his native caution leads him to worry about doing this too often. His life is more or less monastic, inflected by the rhythm of the natural world.

Jake has not seen Livia in the weeks since their first meeting. He hasn't seen anyone much. There was the taciturn man who nodded to him outside the Nook one day – a face weather-beaten and rubicund – who might have been Clifford, the unemployed man living next door to the shop. Another time he saw a bald head peering into a hedge in the distance, but its owner had leapt on a bike and departed by the time Jake reached the spot. He feels he has wandered pretty far through the area, his mind pleasantly vacant bar the nagging desire to bump into the vet again. He wonders if she likes him, or is avoiding him.

One morning – he stopped counting the days after the first week – he has finished his swim, has waded out of the shallows, and is perching on the pier, feet clutching at the water weeds. He shivers, but the day is warm enough to stop him getting up for the towel. He hears a halloo of greeting, the first loud noise he has encountered in days. Spinning his head round, he sees Livia marching down the pathway, waving lustily, her face set in ironic pleasure at his discomfort. He is naked, his towel just out of reach, and he covers himself with one hand as he hops to get it.

Bones

A few minutes later, they are sitting in the courtyard on some wooden furniture Jake has dragged from one of the outbuildings, drinking coffee. He has a pair of shorts on; Livia is wearing black narrow jeans, a thin pink vest and thick walking boots, scuffed and muddied with use. The summer has deepened the darkness of her skin. Her eyes glimmer green against that background.

'I see you're making yourself at home.'

'Well, I'm trying to sort the place out a bit.'

'I meant not wearing clothes when you're outside.'

He flushes, but also feels unapologetic. 'I don't know. What's the point in returning to nature if I can't swim naked in my own lake? If I had known you were coming, I'd have put on some figure-hugging Speedos.'

She smiles, stretches her leg so her foot is resting on another chair. 'It's my fault for showing up unannounced, I accept that.'

'I have been looking for you, you know. I even brought

a picnic back that first day, but you'd stopped your sheep-bothering and sadly departed.'

'I thought our paths would have crossed by now, but this is a pretty empty bit of land, so maybe not. That's one of the reasons I stopped by; just to say hello.'

'And another reason?'

'Ah yes, local tradition. On Saturday, it's the hunt for St Aethelmere's bones. An annual event – we team up and seek out this relic, which has been hidden somewhere along the river. The people who find it are supposed to get a year's worth of luck.'

'Are they real bones?'

'What are you, a thirteenth-century monk? No, they're just a bag marked "bones". Sarah hides them, we all go looking, and then we meet for a fire at the end of the day. Some years nobody finds them. I've never found them yet and I've been here six years, so I thought you'd be my change of luck. Anyway, Diana and I would be honoured if you joined our team.'

Jake pushes aside the ignoble disappointment that her child is involved too, and allows himself a stirring of something like contentment. 'Sure thing. When is Saturday again?'

'You really do have it bad, don't you? The whole rejection of the outside world. It's the day after tomorrow. We meet at the bridge at eleven in the morning. You can tell the time somehow, can't you, or are you just going by the sun?'

He doesn't actually have a watch. 'I'll charge my phone especially. For you. Now, can I show you around? You're right; I don't have guests very often.'

'Just for an hour; I've got to get back to work.' She has come on her bike, which is resting against a wall.

He speeds her around the house, and she tuts at the idea of so much space for just one person. 'Diana and I live in a two-bedroom cottage, you know.' At the library, she confesses to never having read any detective stories, and so he makes her borrow a couple to get started with: *Murder on the Orient Express* by Agatha Christie, *The Nine Tailors* by Dorothy Sayers and a collection of Sherlock Holmes stories. He wraps them up in brown paper, and deposits them in the basket of her bike.

Outside, they survey the grassy area and he mentions his thoughts about starting a vegetable garden. 'But I've never done any gardening before, and I worry it will be just outdoor housework.'

'I can't believe you've never done gardening.'

'Well I can't believe you've never read Sherlock Holmes.'

'Maybe we can educate each other. Gardens and greenery are one of the reasons I came out here in the first place. Probably why I wanted to be a vet. There's something about the dark, mouldy, peaty smell of the soil. You know it? It reeks of spring and summer and life. I've always loved it. My parents gave me two loves, I think: science, and planting things. So here I am.'

'And where are they?'

'They died just after I left home. One after another, like the second one was hurrying to catch up.'

He feels her mind drift from him, so gently pulls her back. 'Mine died together in a car accident, and I've often thought that might have been lucky in a way. I could never imagine one of them growing old alone. So, we are orphans together.' She nods, eyes on the horizon, where a grey, plumped cushion of a cloud has started to appear. 'Plus,' Jake goes on, 'another thing we have in common: I wanted to be a vet for a while. I read the James Herriot books when I was a kid, and loved the idea of working somewhere beautiful and remote.'

Livia turns and grabs his hand, her face lighting up: 'Me too! I remember the Farnons, that dog Tricky Woo, and all those cows' bums. But I stuck it out and you didn't.'

'I realized in the end I was in love with the books, not the job. And then other books came along that were even more persuasive. Which is probably why I got into becoming a detective.'

They walk her bike to the path by the lake. 'How do I know you won't be naked next time I visit?'

'It's just a chance you'll have to take. I have no phone, remember, so you can't warn me in advance. Maybe just avoid first thing in the morning.'

'Maybe.' She grins, throws her leg, smooth and silky, a piece of living fabric, over the bike, and wobbles off slightly encumbered by the books in the basket, calling over her shoulder: 'The bridge, eleven o'clock. Don't be late.'

Legacies

The grey cloud shifts from the horizon over the next hour, bringing the first rain since Jake's arrival. He doesn't mind. The renewing smell of dust and water, the sense of outdoor jobs deferred. Cutting the tree has been pleasant, but more difficult than he would have imagined: it half-fell to the ground, but its messy labyrinth of roots clung stubborn and hard to shift, and the trunk itself was impervious to all but the hardest strokes of the axe. He wonders if he is doing it wrong, but doesn't know who to ask. It is a problem now for another day. He sits at the kitchen table, studiously rolling a joint, which he smokes in five puffs standing under the overhanging eaves, watching the water pound into the earth and pitting the lake beyond.

The rain continues in sporadic deluges all the next day. Swimming in a downpour is especially pleasing, once he has warmed up. He feels enclosed in one watery element yet exposed to another, the sense of being both within something and outside it at the same time. It is a curious, vivid sensation; the thrumming patter of raindrops a reassuring sound. Back inside, clean and glowing, he brushes the kitchen floor, and washes up (he eats mainly with his hands off wooden boards, so only has to keep his mugs and cups in check). He worries a bit about winter: will this all get claustrophobic? Might he be tempted to take trips back to the city? He feels there has been a tacit deal between him and Arthur, that he is attempting to change his life completely in return for all of his uncle's generosity. But it is not binding, it was not a condition of the legacy.

He recalls his visit to Arthur's solicitors, two weeks after he had received the letter. He and Faye had spent the time disentangling their affairs, living more or less separately from one another. He slept on the sofa; she in the bed. They didn't text each other what they were doing or when they would be home. Jake was putting in long hours at work, trying to clear his desk of his current cases. He had been working in what everyone called the Fridge, the floor devoted to cold cases, which new information or improved technology had brought back to life. Jake had been there for the last three years, after he discovered his own skill in prolonging narratives, in picking up the pieces of old investigations and making them fit a new story. He seemed to have some knack of reading a file, and then producing a plausible evidential arc. He wasn't always right, but he was known for developing leads worth pursuing.

Jake enjoyed the job, though spent too little time contemplating its impact on him. There was something police psychologists called 'psychic scarring': a sort of PTSD experienced by those who investigated serious crimes. You could find a child-killer or a rapist, you could close the case, but the life and death you'd encountered did not simply dissipate into a faint memory. It stayed, taking its chunk out of you, leaving its mark.

When Jake had encountered death in his own life, in particular the miscarriages – the loss of those potential children, those lives he and Faye so desperately wished to nurture – he found it hard to process: sometimes the pain was distant, like it was happening to somebody else, and he seemed aloof to Faye; at others, it was overwhelming and it left his whole body shaking, as if all of his nerves had been exposed. He wonders if he would have dealt with the deaths differently if he had been a lawyer or a teacher, if he were free from all the other damages wrought on his psyche. But some things damage you whatever your past history; and some things do more than scratch and scar over. They obliterate.

Krunkles was indeed Dickensian, as far as solicitors' offices went. An old Victorian building, mottled and mumped from the weather, on the corner of a cloister in a quiet English town. Inside, the air felt dry with the accumulation of cases and precedents, all those lives trapped in paper; the walls bore their thick leather-bound volumes with heavy ostentation. Jasper Krunkle was a small man, dressed in black, with a shock of ginger hair, and the habit of wringing his hands as he talked. He made Jake think somehow of an animated question mark. Krunkle had explained that Arthur had come to him five years before – without recommendation – and set up his will: the whole house and land to Jake in perpetuity. There was also a bank account – now Jake's – which could be used for household expenses, but could never have more than a thousand pounds removed in a lump sum on consecutive days.

'He wanted you, if I might put it this way, to live this legacy, not to control it. He has handled all of the death duties, all of the costs and legal contrivances, so you have to do very little. He was a rich man in the end, and used his money to get his own way.' Arthur's occupation had always been something of a family joke: he had left school at sixteen, and been taken on by a stockbroker firm that liked characters rather than formal education. The money he made was then multiplied, secretly and vigorously, by his own investments and deals. By the time Jake was old enough to ask, he used to say: 'I'm a gentleman of leisure, purchased at great expense.'

A separate bank account had been set aside and contained enough to support Arthur in his old age. He envisaged at some point needing permanent care, especially after he had been diagnosed with lung cancer. And, indeed, a little over four years after coming to Krunkle, he had signed himself into Valhalla, a quiet establishment for supported living. He had died there, his last few days made peaceful with jazz music and morphine. Krunkle shared a note from one of the nurses, who had provided a kind, clearly rather affectionate account of the end.

Jake, bemused by all this information, had sat silently, and then shaken the solicitor's hand, whose skin was papery and rasping. He returned to the city, placed most of his things in permanent storage, and sought to draw a bold line under his life. That last night with Faye had been curiously light-hearted, as if the central burden of their shared existence had been shed. They drank a bottle of wine, ate their favourite pudding from the delicatessen down the road, and promised always to have each other's best interests at heart. He couldn't say that they would see each other much, if at all, again; nor could she. They didn't undertake to be friends, or occasional lovers. This was an ending, an inevitable one. They hugged, he spent one more night on the sofa, and he padded out of the house at dawn, his keys left where she could see them on the kitchen table.

Bridging

The day of the bone hunt dawns bright, the land made fresh by the rain, thick green once more, bursting into hungry bloom. Summer is beginning its inevitable wane, future chill looming, a definite presence in the air. Jake feels the unaccustomed pressure of the later appointment, and is slightly more careful with his morning ablutions: he picks his least sun-damaged shirt and shorts, puts deodorant on for the first time in a week, carefully trims his finger- and toenails.

He gets to the bridge early, and wanders down towards the church. The clock there says 10.30, and he feels pleased at his promptness. The churchyard is cool, the gravestones mossy, their legends worn down by the elements, jumbled lines of old hewn stone covered by looming yew trees that keep most of the outside area in shade for the whole of the day. Jake hears a rustle, and realizes he is not alone: scuffling in a leafy corner is a man of indeterminate age, bald head gleaming with sweat, woolly tufts matted above his ears. He looks across and waves a hand that is holding a jam jar.

'Hail fellow, well met.' He bounds towards Jake, stepping heedlessly on the tombs. 'You must be the new chap, old King Arthur's nephew. They call me Dr Peter, but you can call me just Peter. People never do, though, no matter how many times I tell them. I'm not a real doctor, just your common or garden PhD. Actually I have a garden PhD more or less: I study the ecological imprint of hedgerows. Don't run away! Young Livia tells me you're something of a horticultural virgin, so we can pass briefly over the life-cycle of the bramble, or the pollinating prowess of the humble bee. You're more interested in humans, I expect: living and dead.' He pats the grave Jake is leaning against, before continuing breathlessly. 'Don't worry, she told me your guilty secret. You're a policeman, a digger and delver into human folly, not a local flatfoot on his ponderous rounds. We don't even have one of those any more round here. We're more or less left to fend for ourselves, you know. Well now, you're here and we can defer to you.'

Jake decides to interrupt the torrent, if only for a second. 'I came here to escape being deferred to, Dr P—, er, Peter. And I might well need your help if I'm going to try and start a garden. I have no literally no idea about it. Livia sounds like an expert too.'

'Oh, the divine Livia, she would beautify any garden. I can say that, because I'm old and eccentric. The privileges of the marginalized. Not to labour an obvious metaphor, but it's a bit like a hedgerow: the beauty of being on the borders.'

'Do you bring everything back to hedgerows, Dr Peter?'

'I have a certain image to maintain.' A knowing grin splits his face. 'Though I am not quite the babbling intellectual I let myself be made out to be. But you're a keen student of social characteristics; you'd have spotted that eventually.'

'The one thing I learned in my old job is that everyone is putting on an act of one sort or another. Tell me about today's event.'

'One of the folk inheritances of rural England. It has probably been going on in one form or another for a millennium. The sort of thing that sends American tourists crazy with envy, and alleviates the daily tedium of life for local inhabitants like me. We get a chance to wander around on a late summer's afternoon, and then have an excuse to drink as well. Come on, we don't want to be late. I'll introduce you to our motley crew.'

They walk up the pebbled path, to the gate on which a pigeon is perched, its purpled chest swelling, cooing gently. Dr Peter pauses.

'My hero old Charles Darwin loved pigeons, you know? A publisher once suggested he remove reference to everything else in *On the Origin of Species*, and just write about pigeons, because, as he said quite rightly, "Everyone likes pigeons." Darwin loved barnacles, and worms too. His last book was on worms, which he wrote "just before he joined them," he said. I often think that he and I would have got on famously. Buried in the countryside, thinking about life and death.'

'And here I was thinking I was escaping from violence by coming to the countryside.'

Dr Peter puts his hand on Jake's arm, checking his progress forward. 'Dear boy, no. If Darwin taught us anything, it's that life everywhere comes from the struggle with death. You don't get one without the other.' His face is briefly serious, sepulchral even.

Back at the bridge, a crowd has gathered. Jake sees Livia holding the hand of a young girl who must be Diana, with long black hair, and summer-toned skin.

'I'll introduce you to everyone if you like. Sarah and the divine Livia, as we've established, you know. There's Clifford and Martin, skulking about the place like normal.' Clifford and Martin are very similar looking: middle-aged, wispy brown hair growing grey around the temples, in shorts, T-shirts and boots. The one on the left, Clifford, has a heart-shaped tattoo on his calf, half-buried beneath wiry hair. 'Their mother Mary is sitting on the bench; she'll go home as soon as we set off. But she takes pride, absurdly enough, in watching those feckless sons of hers.' Mary is old and wide, slack skin pooling around her neck and elbows.

A man wanders up to them, lean and tanned deeply by the sun. He is wearing a shirt half-open to the chest, flowering white hair. His sleeves are rolled up, his forearms muscular. 'And this is my friend, Mack. The most competent man in Parvum. Though that's not against especially tough competition. He doesn't talk that much, but I have never found that an especially significant obstacle to companionship.'

Mack has a placid and friendly face, and he shakes Jake's hand warmly. 'I'm the local jack-of-all-trades. Let me know if I can do any work for you in that big old barn of yours.'

'I might need some help in the tree-chopping and garden-clearing departments.'

'Sounds great. Let's get to it while we still have this lovely weather.' He wanders off to grab a drink of water from a jug Sarah has brought. Behind his shoulder, Jake sees someone he hasn't heard mentioned before: a tall, slender man with a ponytail.

He nudges Dr Peter, who is peering into the depths of the river. 'And that chap there?'

Dr P looks up. 'Oh, didn't Livia mention him? He's called Rose, which I presume is not his first name.' His eyes gleam with mischief. 'The two of them used to be the hot topic of our coven of intrusive gossips. We saw them driving together in his car; they went into Meryton once or twice.' Jake feels a prickle of jealousy. 'He doesn't have a regular job: he's a sort of roguish figure, part-time photographer I think, probably has some family money somewhere. He lives in a place a few miles off, an old farmhouse, not quite as grand as yours. You see, you've got him beat already.' Rose has just greeted two men and a woman of his own – and Jake's – age. 'That's the Meryton lot. There'll be a few more along in a minute. I told you there's not much to do around here, you know.'

By the time Sarah gathers everyone together, at a few minutes after the hour, quite a crowd has built up: some farmers and their families, a couple of taciturn fishermen who stroked up on a flaky white and green boat, two female teachers who have brought their own children along, and who all fussed over Diana.

Livia had come up to stand next to him, manoeuvring her daughter reluctantly with her. She was initially shy, hiding a bit behind her mother's legs. Jake felt huge and awkward, gangly and off-putting. He held his hand out to shake, and Diana giggled at him, pushing harder against Livia. Jake had wanted children for so long, it had been an unstated assumption that he would be good with them. He was kind and not too serious, he thought, he wouldn't be stuffy or formal. Just then he realized, though, that he didn't really have anything to say to a seven-year-old.

The crowd disperses, and Livia guides them across the bridge. 'There's a deserted old barn about two miles north of here. Sarah never goes more than that far away from the bridge to do her stashing; it's as good a spot as any to hide a bag of fake bones. Shall we go there? I've brought a picnic.'

Jake realizes he should have thought of food himself. Diana races ahead of them, talking loudly to herself.

Livia sighs, her chest rising and falling. 'Classic only child. She's very good at making her own world. I sometimes feel I'm not much of a mum, bringing her up in as quiet a place as this.'

'I've seen four kids crammed into a bedroom, living in fear of both parents, choking on exhaust fumes from a busy road outside. I reckon she might forgive you the tedium of paradise.'

'If this is paradise, then you do have low expectations of the future.'

'Just simple ones, perhaps.'

They walk in companionable silence, the path inclining ever upward to the apex of the hill. Perched atop, and silhouetted against the liquid azure of the sky, is the broken outline of the barn, one side of which has in some unmourned past toppled over.

Diana points to it, and shouts something incomprehensible that floats on the breeze. Livia waves. 'Come on, let's get some bone-finding done, before we get too philosophical.'

The barn is in the corner of a field, which is empty and open, its long grass pushed diagonally by the breeze. There is an orchard, a line of trees thick with foliage and weighted with fruit, planted on the opposite side. The three of them carefully explore the building, kicking through straw, peering into old barrels.

'Not here, Mum. We lose again,' says Diana, without much sadness.

'Never mind, we can at least have a picnic.'

They are just finishing when Lara and Nina, the two teachers from earlier, walk up to the barn, their noisy platoon of five children pausing at the top of the hill before starting to roll back down to the bottom. Squeals and laughs, the sound of happy carnage. The adults commiserate with each other about not finding the bones. Then Nina says: 'We're taking the gang to the brook on the other side of this field. We thought we'd go and look for frogs. I don't suppose Diana wants to join us? We can bring her back here in an hour or so, and all go to the Nook together.'

Diana is halfway to the other children already, before she turns around, an imploring look on her face. Livia goes through the expected dance of demurral and concession, and soon she and Jake are alone outside the barn, the only noise the whipping of the wind, and childish glee fading in the distance.

'So what are you really running from, Mr Policeman? Why would you come to this deserted spot?' He finds himself telling her, without really meaning to, an abbreviated history of his time with Faye, the love bleeding out, the pain of losing not-yet-children. And the eccentric legacy of Arthur, who she persists in calling 'King Arthur'.

'It's ironic, or something, that you're here because you couldn't have children; and I am here because I had one without really wanting to.' Diana is the product of a fleeting encounter at a house party: the man initially charming and witty, but soon domineering and drunk. 'I went along with him willingly enough, but I didn't really agree to sex from what I recall. And yet from this not-quite-rape I got something as wonderful and life-enhancing as Di. I thought I might resent her, but all that distaste towards her father was weirdly and instantly transmuted into love. He had no interest in sticking around, and is now on his second family, I think. But I was tired of explaining the non-relationship in our shared circle, so had to get away. There was an old vet's practice here going to seed, my inheritance helped me buy in, and here we are.'

'Here we are. I'm sorry about what happened to you.'

'Do you know much about the name Diana? The goddess of the countryside, and wild animals, and crossroads. She symbolizes energy and opportunity. I love the fact that my Diana could have been unwanted or burdensome, and instead is something elemental, a force of nature. I'd rather have her, whatever her sordid origins, than be left wondering.'

Jake nods. 'I tell myself that not having children was a blessing. I was in a relationship where we were living at sixty per cent, happy enough, but not really happy. Maybe the extra would have come from kids, but I don't know. Maybe I was destined for a monkish life, like our desiccated friend St Aethelmere.'

'From what I could see from the lake the other day, you're not quite in bag-of-dry-bones territory yet.' Their arms touch, electric, before they recoil, cautious.

He asks quickly: 'Do you fancy an apple?' They wander

down to the orchard, which is glutted with fruit, some rotting on the ground, some shining ripe and Edenic on the trees. The smell of decay and sweetness everywhere; the buzz of excitable flies. They munch and do not speak, until Jake darts forward and starts kicking at a pile of apples that looks a little too precisely arranged to be windfall. He sticks his hand in and pulls out a thick brown bag, with the word BONES stitched in gold letters. He waves it triumphantly at Livia. 'We've done it! We've got them! We've got to tell Diana!'

She leaps forward, and envelops him in a hug. He feels his hands accidentally brushing first against her left breast, then the cool skin of her thigh, before he manages to clasp her more neutrally, his arms snaking around her back. He wants the embrace to linger, and it does. Livia is not awkward, she simply pulls herself away while maintaining eye contact, her forearms resting on his chest.

'Come on, let's find her. I knew a detective would have an instinct for digging up bones.' They emerge from the deep shadows of the trees, the afternoon now on the wane, the sun less hot in their faces. They see a gathering of people at the barn, the frog-hunting group back from their expedition. Holding the bag between them like a trophy – it is pretty heavy, Jake notes – they run together, Livia shouting excitedly, he a little self-conscious, still something of an outsider.

In the fire

By eight o'clock, a big fire has been lit in the field-garden behind the Nook. Dusk is falling, the flames lick at the twilight. There is a barbecue and two open casks of local cider. People are clumped in groups, lying on rugs on the ground, children racing around, invigorated by the thrill of a party involving adults, the rare treat of being outside as the light disappears. Someone is playing a stripped-down version of 'Paradise City' by Guns N' Roses on an acoustic guitar. The bag of bones, which they had brought back triumphantly, drawing a crowd of disappointed seekers as they crossed the bridge and entered the village, has been placed on an earthen mound ringed with sticks. Some sort of primitive shrine. Jake and Livia are sitting with Dr Peter and Sarah, plates balanced on their laps, cups of the dangerously strong local concoction in plastic pint glasses.

Rose walks up to their group. He is swaying slightly, his face gleaming in the half-light.

'Congratulations, Livia!' He leans forward and pecks her cheek.

'To be honest, I got some help from a professional.' She nods at Jake, who stands awkwardly to shake hands.

'Ah yes, the newly arrived copper. I used to do some business with your uncle at that great pile of yours. I wouldn't do much investigating into everything he got up to, if you know what I mean.'

Jake squeezes harder, pushing into Rose's knuckles until they shift, his own face impassive. 'I don't know what you mean. No. But I'm retired now; just want to keep myself to myself.'

'And yet here you are, enjoying all the local attractions.' A brief glance at Livia. 'Don't worry, I didn't mean anything about Arthur. I'm just a man who has all the right connections. I'm easy to do business with.' Jake guesses Rose had helped with the appropriation of the electricity, which he is still a bit uncertain about.

'How is the old boy, anyway?'

'He died, a few months ago.' Rose must have known this, Jake reasons, if he had known who he was. He could see he was being needled; the bonhomie of the day, the feeling of happiness, his skin still singing with the effects of wind and sun, was being dampened. 'Well, nice to meet you.' He sits down and picks up his food, leaving Rose standing awkwardly. Nobody asks him to join the group. He pecks Livia on the cheek once more, waves at Dr Peter and Sarah, and walks towards the fire.

Livia leans forward. 'He isn't as bad as his first impression there. I had a thing of sorts with him a year ago, but nothing came of it.'

'You don't need to explain to me.'

'I wasn't explaining.'

Rose's arrival has poisoned the mood, Jake feels. All of

59

a sudden he is tetchy and irritable. He gets up and wanders over to the bag of bones, opens it. Inside, rattling together, are what appear indeed to be bone-like things: greyish white, differing lengths and thicknesses. He calls over to Sarah: 'What do you use for your fake bones again?'

Sarah finishes a piece of chicken: 'Oh, just some logs and sticks, to give the bag some weight.'

Jake hefts the bag in one hand, and brings it back to their circle. 'These don't look much like sticks to me.'

Sarah glances in, her face suddenly collapses into a frown. 'I didn't put them in there yesterday. I got some stuff from my woodpile like I do every year.'

The party is swirling around them heedless. Jake asks if they can go inside and look properly, and his three companions quickly put down their food and drink to accompany him. As he looks back into the gloom, he sees Rose's white eyes staring at him, like a startled fox, from the expanse of black beyond him.

Cold case

Sarah's kitchen, which is the room behind the main body of the shop, feels unduly bright after the fire-lit dusk. Jake drops the bag on the central table, then tips it over. Bones scatter across the surface, puffing dust, with one falling, slender like a twig, to the ground. He picks it up and tosses it into the middle with the others. They lie there, dirty white with brown patches, gnawed offerings.

'So first question: did you fill the bag with these?'

Sarah is pale and shocked. 'Absolutely not. This must be some sort of joke.'

'Second question: what are these bones? If I might ask my two nearly-doctors to take a look.'

Livia mock-grimaces, but steps forward, as does Dr Peter. She is the first to speak: 'They look human to me. I mean, in that they're definitely not large animal bones. Not cows or pigs or sheep, or anything that I normally come across. Not that I see too many decaying animal bones of any description. I'm babbling. Dr Peter?'

He is peering at what looks to Jake – who has seen

human remains before – like an adult's femur, which is heavy and club-like. 'Well my expertise is, as we all know so well, the hedgerow, so assume the appropriate caveats to anything I say. I did do some undergraduate anatomy though, and feel fairly confident they are human. The lower jaw bone over there and this femur especially, and that ulna Jake so casually threw into the middle. Plus, I think the top of the skull may have broken apart, but those curved bits look like something that should sit atop a human head. Jake?'

'They look human to me, and at least a few years old. So how did they get here?'

Sarah unconsciously retreats against the fridge, her hand pushed outward in protest. 'All I know is that I filled the bag with sticks Thursday afternoon, and cycled up to the orchard and hid it behind a tree.'

Jake leans forward: 'Did you check inside the bag before you left it?'

'I don't think so.'

'Did you leave the bag anywhere in the open before you cycled to the orchard?'

'Yes, it was in the shop. Quite a few people commented on it.'

Livia holds out a restraining hand. 'Jake, have you gone into interrogation mode? This is just a prank, isn't it? Some kids, or one of the farmhands. You're not back at work, you know.'

'I'm sorry; I'm not trying to be officious, but uncovering human remains, however old, is a serious thing. We have to report it. The police need to come, and see if they're what they call "bones of antiquity" or might be evidence of a crime. Look, I'm the last person who wants to get involved in anything. I'm running from the world, remember? I only came to the hunt because Livia asked . . . well because, well . . .' His voice trails off.

Dr Peter intercedes brightly: 'I know your motives are as pure as Galahad's. And I fear you're right. Someone knows we have them as well, so we would look suspicious if we said nothing. We should telephone the police in the morning. Jake, you actually found these relics, like the intrepid delver after truth that you undoubtedly were born to be. So you should be the one to do it.'

'I don't actually have a working phone.'

Livia smiles. 'Why don't you come and borrow mine? I'm not working tomorrow, and Diana is at riding school. I'll make you breakfast.'

Dr Peter rubs his hands. 'What could be more propitious than two young people conniving, respectably of course, over a corpse? Sarah, hand over the bones to the custody of our local veterinarian and allow these two stout citizens to perform their civic duty.'

Jake is pushing the bones into the bag using his knuckles. Not that he thinks there is much evidential meaning to be found, but out of practised habit. They walk out of the kitchen, now a complicit foursome, before Livia goes off to round up a reluctant Diana.

Rose sidles next to Jake: 'What were you all up to in there? I hope you're acting properly with our Livia?'

Jake looks into the middle distance, and speaks without making eye contact. 'As I said before, I'm just keeping myself to myself. I'm not keen on making any friends here.' He turns to look at Rose: 'Just so we understand each other.'

Breakfast and death

It is no more than mild when Jake walks to Livia's tiny cottage the next day. Chandler Lake was especially bracing this morning, and he wonders whether he will be able to keep up his daily swim throughout the autumn and winter. To Jake it is a challenge to his endurance, and an act of cleansing and invigoration. Maybe he is becoming as bad as all those wild swimmers on the subject. His new idea is to build a sauna on the lake shore: a place of expiation; the idea of hot and cold, inside and outside, dry heat and the dank depths of the water; the penitential search for meaning. He wonders if he will be too embarrassed to suggest it to Mack.

Livia's house is small and skew, built as if on an angle: white plaster walls, thatched roof, wooden beams the colour of chocolate. It has probably been there for centuries. Jake loves old buildings, especially out here. His own farmhouse is a happy mix of the historical and modern: the long part of the L comes from the eighteenth century, the stones of his kitchen bewitchingly smoothed by generations of footsteps. The other section is new, put in by Arthur at some point, damp-proofed and sleek.

Livia pokes her head out of the front door. She is inescapably, triumphantly modern in Jake's eyes, beautiful and incongruous in that space. Inside, the house is hearty and comfortable: a biggish living room with an open fireplace, a kitchen that is bright, and filled with childhood clutter, toys on the floor, pictures on the fridge.

'Food or police?'

'Let's get the call out of the way. Do you know the number of the Meryton station?'

Livia nods wryly. 'Amazingly enough, I still use the internet, unlike some desperate Luddites of my acquaintance. I've even typed it into this magic device I call a phone.'

Jake nudges a ginger cat from an old rocking chair in the corner, and sits down. It looks at him with a glance somewhere between boredom and contempt, its tail arching stiff like a punctuation mark, before it settles on a towel on the floor. Livia hands him her phone, and he makes the call. He is expecting to navigate quite a bit of bureaucracy, but the mention of human bones seems to startle things along. There is probably not that much serious crime in these parts, he thinks. He gets through to the chief inspector and fills him in on the find, before confirming his own identity as a former member of the CID. That information seems to speed things along further, and soon Jake is arranging for the evidence to be collected. He hangs up and warns Livia to expect someone in an hour or so.

'Well that gives us time for breakfast, at least.'

They eat together, bacon and scrambled eggs with thick

slices of homemade bread and local butter. They talk about policework, and bodies, and the grim reality of his former role. He tells her of his final case: a child murder – Shannon, aged six – that had gone unsolved for eleven years, before a DNA match had come along on a piece of clothing found at the scene. It was from a local teacher, who had been arrested and convicted of downloading images of abuse a decade after the original case. The teacher hadn't killed Shannon, but his presence at the murder location was a new and vital piece of information, and had led Jake into a horrific world of online conspiracies. His job had not been to force through a prosecution against a tainted suspect – though colleagues had been tempted – but to try to understand the true story of what had happened, however awful to imagine. In the end, there had been three adults involved, one a brother of the teacher: a collaboration of cruelty that could scarcely be fathomed. Jake's stomach has the familiar lurch as he explains it; he wants to avoid wallowing in detail, but wants to testify honestly to his experience too.

There is silence, and then he says: 'Sorry about that. I'm sure you as a mum don't want to hear this stuff.'

'I'm beginning to see why you're searching out peace, though. But I am not sure peace is your particular fate, or anybody's any more.' She pauses again. 'Did all this make you ever want not to have children?'

'The old "the world is too terrible to bring a life into" argument? I never agreed with that, because I always felt I could make my bit of the world safe enough and bright enough for a child. Like you do here.' He gestures vaguely. 'And as it turns out, raising a child wasn't our problem.' He wants to shift the mood of the room, which he feels has become too sombre. 'Anyway, you must have some tales of cows' bums and lambing to cheer us up. I miss my James Herriot books, you know.'

The caramel trickle of her laugh once more. The tone changes, and he listens to her tales of life as a vet, especially as a young woman in what is still rather a male world. But Livia doesn't complain, or even dwell on the difficulties; she is clearly in love with the natural world, and has found a way of marrying that viewpoint with an admiration for the artificial industry of agriculture. She finds bracing beauty in what he has only glimpsed: the flocks of sheep, scattered like dandelion fluff across the fields; or the patient, soulful faces of cattle, motionless apart from their twitching tails; the powerful snorts of horses nickering in their stalls. Hearing her talk brings the landscape into the room with them; it is like a mild enchantment.

A knock breaks the spell with a certain inevitability.

Livia opens the door, and a man – manifestly a policeman, as certain as if he were in blue uniform, swinging a truncheon – ducks his head and walks into the living room. Jake has come to stand in the kitchen doorway. When the man straightens, he is tall and thin and linear, like a ruler. His hair is pale grey, but he still has life in his hazel eyes, which twinkle in the morning sun.

'Livia Bennet?' Jake realizes it is the first time he has heard her surname. 'So that would make you Mr Jake Jackson, formerly known as Detective Inspector Jackson, infamous in certain circles in the Metropolitan Police.' He smiles to soften his tone, and shakes both their hands. 'Chief Inspector Gerald Watson at your service. I did a certain amount of my career in the Big Smoke, before

– like you both perhaps – I realized I could be of use in rather more beautiful surroundings.' He raises his hands as if in protest. 'No, I understand, you're no longer working yourself, Mr Jackson. And yet here we are: you've been out of the force for forty-five minutes, and you're already bringing a bag of human bones for expert inspection.'

Jake reaches down and hands him the bag: 'We opened it last night in a kitchen, to confirm what we had, but otherwise they have lain in this bag since I found them yesterday late afternoon.'

'Ah, the St Aethelmere Bone Hunt. How fortunate for us all that I'm enough of a local yokel to understand the tradition, so we don't need to waste time in explanations of otherwise improbable folklore.'

'Coffee, Mr Watson?' Livia is solicitous.

'That would be lovely, my dear.'

They all sit around the table, after Livia has bustled around preparing coffee, the aroma filling the kitchen with a cosy richness. Watson explains that there is a Special Branch laboratory and training centre in the county, which can be used to provide scientific analysis for any major crime scenes.

'Now I don't believe this is a major crime scene for one moment, but any time we have unknown human remains, we might as well move as quickly as we can. We should get gender and age, and hopefully a sense of a time of death, and we should know in the next few days. If I had to guess, I would say they came out of a graveyard as some sort of practical joke, maybe aimed at the new boy in the village, maybe just for general effect. But I'll get the process started now by taking this off your hands.

Would you like me to come back with the preliminary results, as a professional courtesy?'

Jake glances at Livia. 'I think we would both be fascinated. But I don't currently have a phone, so am a bit hard to get in touch with. Could you let Livia know when you know something?'

Watson pushes back his chair, and retracts his legs back towards his body. He has had them stretched out, his chin almost on his chest, as they discussed the case, and he creaks a little as he stands up. 'I will do.' He then speaks softly in Jake's ear. 'You know, you can never completely hide away from things, however much you try.'

'Well, chief, I've seen enough things to make it worth the effort. Thank you for taking a look at this personally. I'm sure it will be a prank, as you say.' Jake is not sure, though; far from it. His instincts are prickling, he is on edge and expectant, like he used to be in the past when he first got his hands on a case file. But he conceals his thoughts for now; he might as well wait for the lab work.

After Watson has left, Livia says she needs to pick up Diana. 'How am I going to get in touch with you? You know, when the police come back. I can't keep cycling up to surprise you when you're swimming nude in the lake.'

'I was thinking about it. It's not just me being a Luddite for effect: there is no phone in the house, and no signal either. How about this? You know the big beech tree, which is halfway between my house and yours?' Livia's cottage is on the outskirts of the village, on the edge nearest Jake's property. 'Well I can see it using binoculars from a certain point on my land, and look . . .' He points out of the window. 'You can see it in the distance too from here.' Livia rummages in a closet, and produces her own pair of binoculars. When she looks, the tree comes into sharp focus, halfway up a sharpish incline.

'Perfect. Now, whoever wants to speak will tie a bright piece of cloth to that tree. We'll call it Sherlock Beech. And the other will come along as soon as they can. What do you think?'

'I think it is absolutely ridiculous, including the name. So it's well worth a go.'

They part ways at the crossroads to the south of Parvum, after a short, self-conscious hug. Jake walks home shaking his head occasionally as if to clear it. What had started as a chance of splendid isolation is becoming more complicated by the day: the mystery of unearthed bones, and – what is it, really? – some connection with a beautiful woman.

Early autumn

The next day is brisk and sharp, the air clean like a tonic. Mack walks up to Jake's back door at just after ten. Jake has washed a week's clothes in Chandler Lake, and has some bread in the oven, an attempt at self-sufficiency, using a recipe Livia has given him. He is playing a Mahler symphony quietly on an old record player propped up in the corner. Arthur's love had been jazz, but Jake has uncovered all sorts of vinyls in the basement. Classical music, especially the lush romantic kind, suits him in the mornings. In the evenings, he still enjoys silence, or rather the noises of an empty house set adrift in empty land: creaks in the old wood, crackles from a fire, the call of a wild animal (the bark of a deer, or the gruff growl of a fox; the scratchy chuckle of a startled partridge), the insistent whisper of the wind.

Jake takes Mack to Agatha Wood, where he has been making a mess of tree-felling. Mack shakes his head. 'You're using the wrong tools here, that's the problem. I'll bring you some of my old ones, and get you properly started. Not that you need much firewood. I helped fill that basement corner last spring.'

'I thought I might build something. A sauna actually.'

'A sauna?'

'Yes. What, do you think it's a terrible idea?'

There is a longish pause, before Mack's face crumples into a laugh. 'Jake, why not? I was in the merchant navy for years and we sailed all around the Baltic Sea, and we used to go ashore every other week for entertainment, some of which . . .' He winks, before lighting a tiny rolled cigarette he has extracted from behind his ear. 'Some of which I won't tell you about, but there were plenty of saunas in that part of the world. A whole bunch of us would have them, and then jump in the sea afterwards. It was a fine feeling.'

'I thought you might think it was a bit ridiculous.'

'Jake, if I were you, I wouldn't care too much what people round here think, including me. A sauna is a comical one, no doubt, but I can see why you'd want it.'

'So, you'll help me?'

'For the right price, of course. And we'll need to get the wood from outside. You can't use this stuff, because it needs to be kiln-dried to get the moisture out. But you could trade some of your fresh wood, like this pine, because we'll probably end up using a similar sort of softwood. Let me have a think, but we could spend a couple of days getting the timber, and then I'll do the swap for the dried stuff with a feller I know. We can pay to get some of the pieces pre-sawn. Are you willing to do the labouring?'

'I am. I've never done that much with my hands.'

They are walking back alongside the lake towards the house now. Jake looks around him, the life bursting forth, the sheer thickness of the growth that threatens to be overwhelming, teeming, whether it be the reeds of the lake, or the trees dotted throughout the land, their boughs gnarled with age, weighted heavily with leaves that are starting their slow turn. The first blush of season's change.

'What about replanting? I'd like to plant more than I cut down.'

'That's good sense too. We could buy some cheap early-growth trees, and put them in that spot of land just by the side of the wood. But I was also thinking about what you said the other night on the subject of orchards.' Jake had forgotten this; it had been in the early, cider-inflected euphoria of the Aethelmere party. 'We could plant a beautiful orchard in the field adjacent to the western shore of the lake.' It was Velda Field he was talking about, Jake thinks reflexively. 'Some apple and pear trees, some good growers. What do you think? I could come a day a week, and leave you some work to do when I'm gone. I'll take care of the supply side. You just give me dinner and pay the bills, including for my time.'

Jake pauses to shake Mack's hand. 'It's a deal.' They get back to the courtyard of the house and stare at the long slant of ground running down to the lake. 'And how about some sort of garden here, for vegetables?'

Mack nods. 'The grass over yonder has been trampled down over the years, look. Even in this summer, it's all churned up. I reckon you could turn that over and have a big old vegetable patch. Maybe put some sidings down and raise it up a bit as well; I can bring some mulched compost later on. I'll leave you the spade and the hoe in my truck; I was allus lending King Arthur stuff.'

Jake walks him back to his car, Mack had driven over

73

the fields from the village, jouncing along in an old black and green 4x4. It has dirt around its wheels, and trails leaves and branches in the space at the back, so that it blends into the landscape when it is still.

After Mack has gone, Jake starts work, digging into the turf and uncovering a thick alluvial soil, coal-black and oozing moisture. It is hard going. Although his fitness has improved, it is a different sort of strength needed to turn the earth like this. His lower back aches and knots, his biceps twitch. After a couple of hours, he is grubby and sweaty, but he has marked out the beginnings of the area, and can now see how it might look when it is finished. It can be another part of a routine, he thinks, to come and do this every day. Funny how he wants that routine even now he has the chance to reject it entirely. Solitude requires busyness, he thinks, necessary occupation to still the restless thoughts inside his head.

Darwin's worms

A few afternoons later Jake is back at work, digging. It is still, the sky a bare slate, whitening around the edges. From the kitchen he can hear the imperial strains of Mahler's Fifth Symphony (he has decided to work through them chronologically; another example, he realizes, of self-imposed routine), and he is humming tunelessly. His binoculars lie discarded and disconsolate on the grass, and he has already walked to the edge of his land to peer up at Sherlock Beech. Nothing but leaves and branches, motionless and uninterested in him. He wonders if Livia has read any of the books he has given her, then wonders if a literary discussion would be a good enough reason to tie something to the tree.

He looks up, and weaving its way down from Velda is the bald head of Dr Peter. His course is typically erratic, and occasionally he darts to the edge of the field and into a hedge. Jake doesn't mind the interruption. Indeed, living here alone has introduced him to the curious sensation of welcoming brief human contact whenever it comes. Jake had always shrunk from neighbourliness, and revelled in the anonymity of city life. There was already enough distraction, enough noise and bluster in the very air he breathed. But here, his conversations with Sarah at the Nook, or Mack's arrival to discuss wood supplies, are all pleasant events in themselves. The mild joy of delayed gratification, the little jolts that come from sensory rationing.

By the time Dr Peter arrives, Jake has had the chance to sling on an old checked shirt, brew a pot of coffee, and turn the record over for the remaining movements. Dr Peter's head is gleaming, despite the lack of heat in the day, the few bits of white fluff over his ears plastered to his skull.

'The good thing about the sheer feudal scale of your property, dear boy, is that it is almost impossible to catch you unawares. There's no chance of me discovering you in flagrante, at least not indoors. No chance of a crafty ambuscade, as it were.'

Jake thinks back to Livia's arrival when he was naked on the pier, but decides not to mention it. 'I hope you weren't contemplating either, Dr P.'

'Far from it, my extra-judicial companion. No, it's a pleasant afternoon, good weather for a long walk, enlivened by an occasional foray into the margins to check up on things. You have a lovely supply of hogweed on the borders of your property, for example. Not much good to you, but sheep like it, and it achieves the inestimable benefit of scouring intestinal parasites from within them.' He waves his hands like a conductor, to illustrate the flamboyant aspect of scouring.

'Do you ever grow tired of hedges?'

'Oh of course not. What an unusual idea. No, hedges have been around for as long as there have been farmers, and they'll outlast us all if we don't spoil things too much. Even the word is old: people were making that sound to mean "the edge of a field" thousands of years ago. I love that. I feel part of a chain, a native history. I'm connected to the great web, as Marcus Aurelius once put it, though I don't think he ever made it as far north as this country. Now, as I'm here, availing myself of your hospitality, can I be of any help in that nascent garden of yours?'

He picks up a hoe, and deftly begins to turn the earth. 'I may not have your might, but I have a few years' more practice, I think.' They work quietly together, the music faint in their ears, punctuated by the accommodating noise of soil meeting metal. After twenty minutes, Dr Peter pauses to rub his back and stretch his arms. He has removed his tweed jacket and his red jumper, which countless washes has subdued to an inoffensive pink. He is wearing a greying vest, which reveals his lean figure, the skin starting to slacken perhaps, but a sense of persistent strength still visible.

'What did the police say about our bones?'

Jake pauses before answering. The question was a fraction too casual, too little ornamented by the baroque detail so central to Dr Peter's speaking style. 'They've taken them away. Apparently, there's a special laboratory somewhere near here, so they can get them analysed properly. Do you have any theories?'

Dr Peter sighs, and looks skywards. 'I'm sure you're familiar with the medieval belief in restless bones, refusing to stay buried because of some injustice that has been done to them, some violence unavenged.'

'So that's the view from the local scientist, then? Restless bones?'

'Aha, no, but it did feel suggestive for a moment, didn't it? I wonder if they've just been lifted from a dusty crypt somewhere – there are literally thousands of churches and chapels and follies in this part of the world – and put in the bag to shock everyone.' He resumes his digging with a glint in his eye. And then he exclaims: 'See how many worms you have here! I knew you would, we're in a very fertile, well-worked part of the country. Look here.' He walks to his jacket and pulls from his pocket a small paperback book, its cover coffee-stained and reattached with yellowing Sellotape. '*The Formation of Vegetable Mould Through the Action of Worms*. Darwin's last book; I mentioned it before. He says that worms "have played a more important part in the history of the world than most persons would at first suppose". Worms help preserve things like Roman villas, or the bones of their inhabitants. They move slowly and blindly, they make tiny changes to the soil around them, and yet over time they can fundamentally alter the landscape. Darwin went to Stonehenge and saw how some of those massive blocks had been partially submerged thanks to worm castings.'

'Am I getting a free lecture here, doctor?'

'You certainly are. I'm broadening your horizons, my dear boy. Small things make a difference, as I'm sure you know. Hamlet calls worms "your only emperor for diet", and saw them as a sort of memento mori, a warning to us all about the transitory nature of wealth and power: "A man may fish with the worm that hath eat of a king, and eat of the fish that hath fed of that worm." I quote from memory.'

Dr Peter is prevailed upon to stay for a late afternoon beer, but then hastens off into an impressively fiery sunset – the sky a molten red, bleeding down into the earth – so he might make it home before darkness descends. Jake takes his beer into the thriller library, and picks up a Cadfael book by Ellis Peters. He feels a yearning for some medieval mystery, that idea of unquiet corpses making themselves known. Had the good doctor spoken with the intent of planting that thought in his mind? Perhaps he is still too professionally suspicious; perhaps that might be a habit he has to break, too.

A case of identity

A couple of days – and several fruitless binocular exam-
inations – later, Jake does catch a glimpse of fabric whipping in the wind on the beech tree. It is a blue scarf, tied
at arm's reach from the ground on a drooping branch. Its
colour peers out from behind a leafy curtain, but it is
visible enough to attract the eye. Jake feels the catch of
elation in his stomach, and then tries to downplay it in
his mind. It is likely that Livia has been contacted by
police, and this is the only cumbersome way she can tell
him about it. It won't mean more than that.

Nonetheless, he marches to the village with a spring in
his step, listening to the melodic warble of unseen birds, the
occasional meek bleating of the sheep. It is late afternoon,
the bright countryside faintly muted by early shadow. He
knocks on Livia's door, which is opened eagerly by Diana,
her hands grasping upwards for the latch. He gives her a
warm smile, and she responds, before beckoning him in.
Livia is in the living room, reading a book. He peers at
the cover; it is from his Sherlock Holmes collection.

She closes it and smiles. 'Ah, my semaphore worked. Truly there must be a better way of getting in touch with you.'

'None that springs to mind, unless you don't mind me coming around at the same time every day.'

'Sadly, I am not here at the same time every day.'

'Mummy, is Jake in love with you?' Diana interrupts with a quizzical expression on her face.

Jake flushes and jokes to conceal his embarrassment: 'Give me time, Diana. I think I just really like her at the moment.'

Livia beams. 'Well that's good enough for me. Jake and I are friends like you and Phoebe at school.'

'Phoebe steals my paints sometimes.'

'So make sure you keep an eye on Jake while he's here.' Livia gestures to the kitchen, and they sit at the table. A radio is playing inconsequential pop music; a pot is bubbling noisily on the stove, scents of wine and meat. 'This is my famous, well to Diana at least, Bolognese. Do you want to join us for dinner in a bit? You will have to be gushing in your praise, though.'

It has been almost a month since Jake has eaten anything he hasn't prepared himself. He is still mainly subsisting on cheese, cold meat and fruit with the occasional locally grown vegetable thrown in. At night he often has a bowl of porridge – using the oats from one of the giant sacks in the basement – with cream and milk. He has calculated that a weekly shop at the Nook gets him extra provisions for decent enough meals for at least seven days, though he thinks he could survive without them. He enjoys the feeling of eating fresh food that has been produced with the minimum of intervention: apples squeaking in his mouth, just moments after coming from a tree; meat that has never left the farm until it is brought a mile or so to the shop, fresh or cured with local herbs; cheese made in cider barrels he has seen in the corner of a nearby farm on one of his rambles.

Livia points to a telephone note she has written. WATSON, BONES, 7PM. He nods. 'So I thought you could stay for dinner at six – we eat early, we rural folk – and then entertain Chief Inspector Watson while I put Di to bed at seven. Then we can talk a bit after she's gone down.'

'Sounds perfect. I haven't had an evening meal cooked for me for a while, so my standards are low.'

'This would be great even if they were high, I promise you. And I'm going to need a bit more gushing than that.'

Before dinner they play games with Diana, and Jake learns to relax a little. Not much is expected of him other than to be attentive, and to throw himself into her pursuits. They have a drawing competition to see who can create the best image of their house. Jake is spectacularly bad, which endears him to Diana. He is extravagant in his praise of her squiggly work, which also helps. And then when she goes off to watch TV, Jake helps Livia in the kitchen, laying the table, boiling water for the pasta. Domesticated life.

'Is this strange for you? I mean, being in a kitchen with people, not skulking on your own with your gloomy books and gloomy music?'

'I thought my lifestyle was more aspirational than that, all those shackles cast off, all those demands silenced. No, this is nice, but I have been enjoying the solitude too. My monkishness, I guess.'

'I often feel lonely even though I have Di. I miss conversation, even touch. Just being around adults. You must do, too?'

'I don't know what to say. I get contentment at home, I don't miss my old life very much. But I feel something like happiness when I'm around you in a happy home like this.'

'So you do need human contact.'

'I said you, not all humans.' There is a pause. The news comes on the radio, but so muffled Jake cannot hear the individual items. He realizes he has not heard a news story in more than a month, has no knowledge or real interest in what is going on in the country. He leans forward and turns off the radio.

Livia acknowledges the movement. 'I love your newslessness; I think it's rather charming. I read once in a book about Britain that on this one day in 1930 or some year like that the BBC news bulletin was totally blank. There was no news to report, so they just played music. Hard to imagine that happening again, isn't it?'

'Maybe just for me.'

'Anyway, that bulletin means it's time for dinner, so go and drag my daughter away from Peter Rabbit, and get ready to overpraise my Spaghetti Bolognese.'

They eat together, Diana and Jake competing to compliment the food in ever more extravagant fashion. She ends up snorting with laughter, her body trembling with scarce-suppressed convulsions, utterly unselfconscious, until Livia has to intervene to calm things down. They have local ice cream for pudding, before Diana runs off for a few last minutes of television. Jake and Livia drink coffee, something he never could do in the evenings when he was working, because he was always thinking of the next day's early start.

As if in reminder of his former responsibilities, there is a rapping at the door. Livia motions for Jake to get it, while she scoops up her daughter and takes her for a bath.

'Good evening, chief inspector,' she calls over her shoulder, as the door opens, and Watson begins the complicated manoeuvre of ducking and entering, which he completes in a series of awkward stages. He does not look comfortable until he is seated at the kitchen table, his long legs fully extended, his black boots twitching restlessly. He has a file with him, beige and covered with official stamps, which he flings casually at Jake.

'Take a look at our Jane Doe, as our American cousins would call her. Yes, we've had quite a lot of luck with the bone analysis. We can't rule out a crime, but can't exactly rule it in either.'

Jake runs through the file with a practised eye, picking out what seems to be the key data. The bones are definitely female, the intact pelvic bone proving that. There is some suggestion that she met a violent death, as one of the skull fragments showed pre-mortem lesions, indicating perhaps a blow to the head, together with a couple of fractures in the arms and legs.

'So how old are we talking here?'

'How old are the bones, or how old was the woman when she died?'

'Well, both would be useful to know, I'd have thought.'

'Let's take the second question first. The woman, our Jane, was around thirty-five years old when she died. A normal, pretty healthy young lady, around five and a half feet, no real evidence of chronic ailments left in the bone remains. But they're around a decade old, and appear to have been subject to some form of post-life curation.'

Jake raises a sceptical eyebrow.

'The phrase is not mine; it's from the wretched report. It looks like she had the services of an undertaker before being laid to rest. There is evidence of chemicals used in the funeral business. They then seem to have been cursorily washed before appearing in your bag.'

'Doesn't that take us into practical joke territory?'

'It does, but there is the skull impact question, and also the motive: why would anyone want to do this? Ah, Livia, you're back.' He fills her in quickly with the news, and she is thoughtful for a moment.

'So is the next move to examine all local deaths of women of a certain age from some form of impact, and see if we have an empty grave anywhere?'

Jake nods. 'What she said.'

'That is what our current "team" of one single harassed person is indeed doing. So it might take time. I thought you could ask around, see if anyone's memories can be jogged. We'll keep at it our end too, and you can be our people on the ground.'

'You want us to take on a case? I've only been retired for two months.'

Watson's eyes twinkle faintly. 'It would be highly irregular for me to commission you to investigate a crime. But this is not a crime yet, or . . .' He waves an impatient hand. 'Or only the middling offence of wrongful appropriation of remains. Second, we cannot investigate this properly without help, and I'm not going to get any from the county side. Third, I have always had a fondness for detective double acts: Sherlock Holmes and

85

my namesake of course, Rizzoli and Isles, Poirot and Hastings, Wimsey and Vane, Bones and Booth. That last one is a male cop and a female scientist, isn't it?'

Jake smiles. 'Bones and Booth are just in the TV series. In Kathy Reichs's books, the detective is a guy called Ryan. And I should warn you that Harriet Vane began as a suspect.'

'Nobody likes a know-it-all. All right, I'm mostly joking. But I would like you to keep your ear to the ground. And I would welcome any and all theories from you, Jake. Jackson and Bennet, the crime-fighters of Little Sky.' He chuckles to himself. 'I like the sound of that. The file is a copy for you. Livia, you call me if you get any intelligence, and I will do the same with you.'

They toast the idea with beer from Livia's fridge, before Watson takes his leave. Jake feels he should leave too, now there is a child asleep in the house, not wishing to overstay his welcome, or impose himself too soon. He sees perhaps a flicker of disappointment in her face as he stands.

'Shall we talk tomorrow? Are you free at all?'

'I'll be on my rounds all afternoon. I can stop off at the sheep field near you, where we first met, around three? Then we can work out a plan, partner.'

His journey back is circumspect, in the penumbral darkness of evening, but his mood is light as he thinks of the pleasure of a partnership to come.

Cuttings

In the morning, Mack walks up to the house and stands with a cigarette, the wisps of smoke curving wraith-like above his head. Today he and Jake are going to cut and sort some fresh pine to use in trade for the material needed for the sauna. Agatha Wood is thick with shade, and a note colder than the area that surrounds it. It feels like it is already beginning its inexorable retreat into eventual winter. There is leaf litter slowly mulching on the ground, the frenetic activity of squirrels leaping and squirming up and down the branches.

Mack and Jake work more or less in silence, Jake learning the trade of felling and hewing largely from hand gestures and imitation. They find a damaged tree, its trunk black and pitted, its surface a crater of hollows and excrescences. Mack picks up an axe and hefts it carefully in hand, weighing it as he does everything. Its handle is thick and bumped and marked with age. The blade is heavy but the edge is fiercely sharp. Jake notices a brown scar on Mack's wrinkled forearm. His skin is the consistency of wizened apple, the flesh tight around his frame with nothing to spare. The scar is more like a stain: it's round, about the size of a jam jar lid. The hairs have come off, and all that's left is a dark patch.

Mack marks out a line for the first cut, and they take turns – five minutes on, five off – slamming the blade into a notch, half with precision, half with a necessary anger. Jake enjoys the physicality of it. The lesson from tree surgery is that your initial notch must come on the side where you want the tree to fall. You have to weaken the body on that one side, and then cut again from the other, until it topples away from you, causing you no harm.

As he hews and sweats he feels his whole life is somehow more tangible, more based on sensations than it has ever been before: the pull of the axe in his hand, the taste of bitter black coffee at dawn, the scents of the forest, the sounds of the steel on wood.

They take a break after an hour, and emerge from the shelter of the trees to the bright light of the day. Jake has brought them milk in a bottle that has been chilling in the lake, and they both drink deeply. Milk moustaches, rubbed off quickly. Jake has arranged a dairy delivery from a nearby farm: they leave it, carefully packaged, in an outlying field once a week, and it has become one of his indulgences. The pure white of the milk, the top thickening into a yellowed cream, the fresh empty smell when he brings his face up to it.

Mack has been continually smoking since his arrival, a rolled cigarette either clamped to his mouth, or smouldering slightly behind his ear. He seems impervious to its heat and, Jake reasons, must be now pretty much incombustible, like a snake charmer immune to poison.

'Mack, have you heard about the bones we found, the real bones?'

'Jake, in a village, everyone knows about something pretty much as soon as you know it, sometimes sooner than that. The whole place is talking about it. Some even reckon that you did it as a trick, to make yourself the centre of things.'

'Did Rose say that? I've got a feeling he might not be minded to be too charitable to me.'

Mack holds up the axe in a surrender gesture. 'I'm not getting involved. Anyhow, you've become news of the week at least.'

'I don't mind that. But I am interested in the bones. I want to know how they got into that bag, and I want to know who they belong to. You might be able to help me.'

Mack exhales meditatively. 'That I might. Though I'm a bit too old to be involved in the news of the week.'

'So tell me this. Can you think of anyone who died several years ago, somewhere between seven and ten years perhaps? A woman, average height, in her thirties. Possibly from some sort of accident.'

Mack is circumspect. 'I'm not sure that I can. A few old folk died natural in that time, but nothing suspicious that would interest you.'

'It could have been a fall, or a farming accident, something domestic. Are you sure nobody springs to mind?'

Mack shakes his head sadly, and turns around to go back to work. They spend the rest of the morning, sweating and grumbling over the unflinching wood, and Mack turns down a lunchtime beer so he can go to arrange the trade with his local friend.

Later, Jake is sitting with his back against a rough stone

wall, having arrived at the sheep field early. He carefully positions himself to catch the afternoon sun, which warms his face and turns blood red when he closes his eyes against it. He rests his neck against the roughness behind him, worn stones that have stood unrelenting in this field for centuries, and allows his breath to come slowly and mindfully. He will have to see if Livia can help on this.

As he thinks of her, so he hears the noise of a creaking bike and slightly effortful panting. He pops his head above the wall, and looks down on her cycling towards him: mouth fixed in rictus grin, the top of her chest and neck gleaming in the light. She half falls off the bike when she sees him, and pushes it up the last few yards, her face as ever armoured in ironic smiles.

'Well that was an impressive entrance.'

She is now swigging lustily from a water bottle. He covertly looks her up and down, and imagines her without clothes for a second, an ignoble, exciting thought. They flop onto the grass together, which is thick and heathery, bouncy to the touch. He tells her about Mack, and his reluctance to talk about anyone in the area who has died.

'It's a shame everyone knows what we're looking for, in a way. I thought we might be able to proceed discreetly, but that seems unlikely now. Mack might indeed know something, but this is a pretty closed, cautious community. You have to earn your place in it. I'm not there yet, and I save their fucking animals.' He enjoys the rare profanity in her talk. 'We should probably talk to Sarah, though that is the equivalent of starting a parish newsletter on the subject. The other place would be the local paper: the *Shire Gazette*. It's a tin-pot affair, but the news editor is a friend of mine, the mum of someone in Di's class. I could ask her.'

'Good thinking.' Jake remembers that Arthur had always collected the local paper wherever he lived, because he enjoyed the occasionally intense ridiculousness of its form of journalism, its redoubtable sense of place, of self-importance, its reluctance to concede its own dwindling status in the world. Arthur used to send him clippings in his letters of stories and headlines that amused him, the minor absurdities of life: NARROWBOAT ON THE LOOSE, SEX BARN TO BE OLD PEOPLE'S HOME, APPEAL TO RETURN COAT TO MAN, and so on.

The *Shire Gazette* would now be primarily, he knows, a free website, garish with useless adverts, hard to navigate and determined to sell him things. And it probably won't go back to a decade ago in terms of its online archive. He has an inkling that Arthur had kept hard copies in boxes in the basement, though, which would be more useful.

'You talk to her. I'll look through the papers Arthur left in the house.' The accidental death of a thirty-five-year-old woman must have been news, even worth just a small article.

'I've made a copy of the file for you too, Jake. If we're going to do this properly, you need to have all the paper-work.'

He looks up to the sky. 'Are you vet-splaining how to do an investigation to a professional, albeit tragically early-retired, investigator?'

She acknowledges the point with a shrug and hands him the file. 'I have to go to pick up Di from art club. When are you free to talk again?'

'I'm always free. That's pretty much the point of my existence now.'

'OK, I'm free for an hour most days after my rounds. Let's meet here whenever we can at three. If the other one doesn't show by three fifteen, we put it off for another day. No pressure, no judgement.'

'And if the weather turns?' Jake looks at a sky, pale white but heavy with portent.

'Then we can do it in your library. I mean, do the case in your library. Oh, don't look so pleased with yourself.' She walks to her bike, and he watches her until she is a speck in the distance.

Filings

Night-time, the wind suddenly raised up to a howl, the fire spitting and agitated. Jake has dragged up to the library three huge, slightly sagging boxes of neatly stacked, yellowing copies of the *Shire Gazette*. The first is dated just over ten years ago, and Arthur seems to have kept every weekly edition since. Jake quickly and happily gets lost in local politics and controversies: there was a long-running argument about a bypass that would bring traffic through the valley, and was eventually abandoned due to opposition and lack of funding. There was a body of a young woman found, strangled and naked, propped up against a bus shelter in one of the villages near the county border to the south. This would have made the nationals, Jake thought. There was a huge investigation – Watson, he sees, featured prominently – but ultimately no conviction, and the coverage dwindled to sporadic updates and a couple of retrospective features. The victim was too young, sadly, to be of relevance now. There is plenty of coverage of farming issues, the price of milk and land,

93

and an indefatigable, almost perverse cataloguing of every fete, fair and event in the area. Some headlines distract him and would, he thinks, have amused Arthur: OUT-OF-DATE PASTY IS SOLD TO YOUNG MUM, PUDDLE SPLASH VICTIM VOWS REVENGE, FOOTPATH PROVES POPULAR.

Then, in the middle of a paper about a third of the way through the pile, he reads a short report headlined: FALL TRAGEDY STRIKES LOCAL FARM. In it he learns of the death of Sabine Rohmer, a thirty-two-year-old woman, who had been working as a fruit-picker and occasional shopkeeper at Smiths' Farm, which Jake knew was several miles away. The story told him that Sabine had been found at the bottom of the stairs by one of her colleagues, dead thanks to an apparent brain haemorrhage brought about by the fall. An inquest was expected to take place in the coming months.

Jake keeps flicking through the next few copies. There was a funeral announcement three weeks later, a public notice of the death and invitation to attend the ceremony at a church near to the farm. It is not clear if Sabine had family local, and none is mentioned. There is reference to her 'friends in the community' and nothing more. The inquest, when it came, was succinctly reported. Sabine had been a worker of good standing and impeccable character, originally from the Bavarian region of Germany. On the night in question she had gone to the local pub for a few drinks, but was not thought to have been grossly intoxicated. The landlord testified clearly to that, as did her drinking companions. Jake looks for names, and one leaps out: a Peter Jacobsen, local scientist. Jake circles the relevant piece of information on the page in bullseye-black: that must be the chattering, always-interested Dr P.

The coroner explored Sabine's mental status in the period running up to the tragedy, and was generally told by witnesses that she was hard-working and amicable. She had no current boyfriend, but had recently come out of a relationship, though there was no suggestion of rancour between the parties. The assertion was made by local police, and not gainsaid, that she had come home, having drunk if not actually been drunk, and fallen down the steps in the dark. The coroner was sympathetic in his concluding remarks – 'This was a kind and constructive life taken away simply by the capriciousness of fate, a fall in the night' – and promptly recorded a verdict of death by misadventure.

Jake keeps reading until late. There are other deaths, some involving women but of the wrong age, some clearly lacking any violent element. The case of Sabine Rohmer stands out as the most plausible. He stares at the picture the paper had printed: it is fuzzy and discoloured, but he can see the strong line of Sabine's chin, her dirty-blonde hair piled high on her head, the youthfulness still held captive in her body. And now she might be no more than a bag of unnamed bones, perhaps gathered up and passed around as a joke. She had been, like him, adrift in the middle of nowhere, no ties to a homeland, no grieving parents, no partner.

He shivers. His whole experience at Little Sky has been one of discovery, both internal and external, but it is also one of strangeness and, he thinks, sporadic sadness. He has given up life to come here. He has lost the chance at a loud, well-lit home, boisterous with youth, shouts and hugs and moments of togetherness. He is wealthy, in a way, but he is deeply, oddly alone.

Lightning cackles outside, illuminating the room for a flashy second, before it returns to its previous sombre hues. Jake glances around, and sees a sort of soullessness: another man's things, another man's house. And him gone too. Jake wonders if he has made a mistake, imagines the rain falling on the bedroom window of another house hundreds of miles away. The sorrowful truth is, in the end, there is nowhere he is welcome. Life with Faye, his police career, was not any improvement on this, nor was it really a potential place to retreat to. He is in a purgatory of inbetweenness. He drinks some of the whisky he has brought up from the basement, loudly plays some Mahler, feels himself wallowing, prey to self-indulgence, but is too far gone to do anything to stop it.

Rain day

The next morning he awakes, lying half off the main couch in the library. Jake's mouth tastes of vileness, sour with stale whisky; his head throbs. The room is a mess: piles of old newspapers, empty cups, books bent at the spine and strewn on the floor. He checks his phone, which he now keeps charged and uses like a digital clock. It is nearly ten. The storm has subsided but has left behind a bleak, gunmetal-grey sky and a grumbly feel. He drags himself to the lake, strips off his clothes and dives in, the shock of the cold water cleansing his skin, icing the previous night's excesses out of his body. After a few minutes, he grabs a towel and runs back to the house, and makes himself clean his teeth and tidy up. Soon the place is in comparative order and there is a fire roaring for comfort and company. Jake drinks sweet black coffee and feels half-human again.

The rain returns at lunchtime, growing steadily more persistent throughout the early afternoon. Jake puts on a waterproof sports top, and gets his run in, watching the lake pockmarked by drops, listening to the noises of the natural world muted in response to the downpour, the sound of little more than the endless fall of rain. He gets home, and steams in front of the fire, before dressing in his old pyjama trousers. A knock comes at the door. He hurries to check his phone, barking his thigh painfully on the table, and sees it is after three. Livia. He runs back to open the door and sees her standing, damp and slightly disconsolate, water trickling down the smooth contours of her face, runnelling to the floor to join the rest of the rain.

'I can't believe you came in this.'

'Neither can I. I was out in it anyway, so I was already soaked.'

'Have you thought of getting a car to do your rounds?' He talks over his shoulder as he guides her to the library, picking up an old hooded top and putting it on.

She stands in front of the fire, which Jake has prodded, a fierce, raging heat. 'I have one, a battered old Volvo. But I always try my best not to use it, as cycling around the place is the only exercise I get.'

'I wish I could drive you home later, but . . .'

'I know you have few possessions, outside your luxurious house.' She shivers, despite the warmth of the room. She has removed her coat, which is drying on a rack Jake has in front of the fire, but her jeans and jumper are soaked through.

He smiles briskly. 'I have always wanted the opportunity to say, "Let me get you out of those wet things," and now I have one.'

'I wouldn't recommend you trying it.'

Jake hands her a thick towel. 'Why don't you dry off

in my room, two doors on the left. There's clean clothes in the left-hand cupboard. Put them on, and we'll dry everything before you go.'

She snatches the offering with a bashful grimace. 'Fine, but keep out of your room when I'm changing. I don't want you barging in while I'm poking through your things; I demand privacy while I'm invading your privacy, thank you very much.'

Jake sits on the couch, smells the damp of the clothes and the smoke of the fire. He imagines Livia in his room, those smooth limbs, flashes of colour of her underwear, textures of skin and cotton. A vicarious proximity: she is in his space, about to put on his clothes. That is something to relish at least, even at a distance. The door opens and Livia comes in, bearing more wet garments. She is wearing a pair of his shorts – vast and baggy, showing off the slenderness of her legs – and an old checked woollen shirt. A bit of hair has fallen in front of her eyes. The clothes dwarf her, hanging off her body. And she has never looked more beautiful to him, as if the faint ridiculousness of the outfit only emphasizes what it conceals. He distracts himself by arranging her jeans and jumper before the fire. Steam rises from them, hissing. The logs spit uncharitably.

He points her in the direction of a coffee cup, which he has filled, and the newspaper pages he has extracted.

'Take a look at our possible Jane Doe.'

She reads quickly, and nods. 'She fits the timeframe definitely. And I'm interested to see our friend Dr P here.'

'I've been wondering about that. I thought we should speak to him about Sabine when we next see him. We also need to find out where she's buried if we can. There

99

are websites that do that, but they don't have every grave marked.'

'I'll check when I get home.'

'The other thing would be to go up to the farm where she died and ask. And wander around the place; we might stumble across a church if nothing else.'

Livia shifts, and pulls some of the spare fabric that has been caught beneath her bottom. 'These shorts definitely fit you better than me.'

'Thank God for that. So, are you free to do some investigating?'

'I'm working early tomorrow, and taking Diana out riding in the afternoon. But the day after I have off completely, and she's at school. So how about then? Come and meet me at my place first thing, and we'll get the Volvo out.'

Jake agrees, and they sit before the fire. Livia talks about all the books around them. She has enjoyed Sherlock Holmes, Jake is pleased to hear, and for the same reason he does: the neatness of the solutions, the cleverness of the detective, and that understated warm friendship between Holmes and Watson.

'I like the logical mind, I guess. And I like that you like it. But, here's a thing, Jake.' She rests her hand on his, he almost flinches at the coolness of her touch. 'I worry about you a bit, out here. On your own, surrounded by nothing but books, and all this nature. Are you sure you're happy?'

'Funnily enough I felt like shrieking last night. I did feel alone, and isolated, and anxious. But it passed. I like the simplicity of life now, and I like how you bring a bit of happy complexity to it as well.'

'Happy complexity? I'll take that. Come on, I better get

dressed. Turn the other way while I extricate myself from your baggy mess of clothes.'

He turns, as directed. There is a window twenty feet to his left, and it offers a blurred reflection of the room behind him. Does she suspect that? He watches; the dark flash of her skin, her body tottering as she pulls off his shorts and top. Her bra and knickers are white, gleaming. His mouth goes dry and he tries to think of something to say. She squeezes on her jeans, which are tight, and made even more so by the damp. She performs a pantomime of wriggling and tugging as she tries to manoeuvre herself in. Her stomach is flat, with just a faint puffiness above the waistband.

She shrugs on her top, and comes behind him. Her face is close to his, and she pecks him on the cheek. 'See you in a couple of days. I better get my bike. And yes, I did know the window was there.'

'Exhibitionist.'

'Hermit.'

The rain has stopped, a drying breeze emerges. There is a scarcely perceptible wiggle in her walk to the bicycle. The house feels a bit less stuffy, a bit less bleak than it did last night.

The cider house rules

Jake still feels restless though. As dusk starts its inevitable descent, he decides to see if anything is going on in the village. The Nook, he knows, closes officially at six p.m., but keeps open for drinkers for as long as they are around. He grabs a torch as he leaves. He doesn't lock his door, because there is pretty much nothing to steal in his house, bar his weed stash and the library sound system, neither of which is particularly accessible.

Outside, it is mild and dark. No longer that false light of summer which seems, he finds, to be somehow stored in the land and bounced around at night, making everything pale, washed with a meek kind of brightness. It is profoundly, unsettlingly black. The stars have been obscured by the thick swathe of cloud, the moon only a suggestion of looming light behind a dark patch. Jake doesn't mind: he knows the route across the land to the village by now, and he lets his torch play idly on the hedges and bushes as he goes, occasionally startling a small animal, whose eyes shine bright back to him before it twitches deeper into cover.

He walks past Livia's house, but feels he cannot obtrude himself on her again. Her curtains are not drawn, and he can see her through her living room window dancing with Diana, moving to a music he cannot hear. Joy and youth and maternal love, encased in glass as if in an exhibition. Sarah has packed up the outside wares of the Nook, but there is a light on, and he tentatively pushes open the door to the shop. She is wiping down a surface, her strong hands and wide forearms reddened by hot water.

'We don't often see you out at night, Jake. Are you here for a drink?'

'If you're offering one. I couldn't quite remember how it all worked, your pub-like service.'

'Well help me mop up, and then come down into the cellar. There'll be a couple of others along presently no doubt and we can have a bit of a drink together.' She hands him an old-fashioned mop, stained a dirty white, sopping with soapy water from a nearby bucket. He begins to clean the floor, with quick efficient movements, guiding the bucket with his feet every couple of minutes. Sarah watches him and then starts to tally up her day's takings. She closes the register and looks across at Jake.

'Are you still looking into those bones then?'

'A bit. The police are stretched, and I have some type of experience, as you know. Livia and I are doing the legwork for them.'

'I'm sure it's that legwork you're most interested in.'

'Sarah, how could you?' Jake has developed a sort of joshing relationship with her, like she is a favourite but formidable aunt.

Her face is wreathed in smiles, but there comes a pause.

'You need to take care, my old duck. This is a bad place to have a failed relationship. Though I reckon you'll never listen to a besom like me about that sort of thing. I'm old enough to know to keep my nose out of . . . well, friendships, you might say. The other thing I know about might be more useful to you. Bones should stay buried, and if they come up, I think you should put them back to rest. Why do you care where they come from?'

'Why should I worry about caring, Sarah? Maybe it's a harmless hobby, like digging up the garden.'

'It might be a damn sight more dangerous than that.'

'Are you warning me, Sarah?'

'Nothing so dramatic. Just looking out for the handsome arrival in these parts.'

Jake places his hand on her arm, which is rough and warm. 'I'm grateful, but I'm also stubborn sometimes. Do you know anything about a woman called Sabine Rohmer?'

She shakes her head, but seems about to speak. They are interrupted by a lusty rattle of the door, which sticks as it is pushed open, and the faint ringing of a bell. In troop two men, their big black boots clomping on the wet floor, leaving a trail of dirty footprints. They look into Jake's eyes but say nothing, and walk past Sarah down into the cellar. Jake is just pushing the door closed when Dr Peter springs in, his movements swift and scampering, like a rodent.

'Dear boy, what an unexpected pleasure. Are you playing bouncer tonight, or joining our merry symposium of thinkers and drinkers? Well, drinkers mainly. I do hope so. Just hold off pulling up the drawbridge for a moment, I saw some burly fellows a couple of minutes behind me. They looked thirsty enough. Sarah here, our hostess and patroness of the drinking cups, will no doubt agree you should stay your hand. Good evening, my dear.'

'Good evening, doctor.'

Dr Peter bows exuberantly and skips down the stairs. Sure enough, soon after him come three men: they are wearing thick work shirts and old corduroy trousers, like a uniform. They stoop as they enter and mouth almost silent greetings to Jake, then to Sarah. She smiles broadly at them, and directs them into the cellar. It looks like quite a party, an all-male party, apart from its host. Jake shuts the door and follows the landlady down the stone steps, once white-washed now darkening with age and repeated swabbing.

The cellar is large, and surprisingly airy. The guests are seated in a square on chairs arranged before some brown, ancient-looking barrels. A pleasant appley aroma is in the room. Jake sits down and Sarah stands behind him, making introductions: 'Dr Peter, you know, of course; and I think you have met Clifford and Martin from next door. Our last arrivals work at the big farm in these parts, Smiths', still known by the name of its old owner. That's Paul, Davey and Richard. The first two are brothers, the third their cousin. A close family like you get in these parts.' They nod warily. Jake's mind buzzes: it was Smiths' Farm where Sabine died. He resolves to try to keep a clear head and to learn what he can.

It will not be easy. Sarah pushes into his hand a flagon full of cider, the glass blurred and scuffed with age and the liquid chilled and flat, tasting slightly of sour fermented apples. After a couple of sips, he realizes it is strong as well. Sarah generally fusses over the party, pulling pints from the nearest barrel to replenish glasses, without waiting to be asked. She also brings out a couple of huge wooden platters of cured pork and hunks of cheese, accompanied by thick bread, oozing butter, and pickled onions so sharp they make Jake's eyes water. The food helps to soak up the alcohol, and is salty and rich and delicious. Jake soon falls behind most of the drinkers, who pour whole pints down their throats without apparently noticing. They do not seem drunk, though their faces become redder, their upper lips damp with sweat, and their speech – words already used sparingly, weighed carefully before being issued from their mouths – slower and more deliberate.

The conversation is stilted, but nobody seems to feel a sense of social awkwardness. Dr Peter soon becomes more animated, his movements more bird-like, a finch springing restlessly around its cage. He loudly confides to Jake at one point: 'Don't mind the manly taciturnity of our neighbours. They regard drinking round here as a more useful occupation than talking.' Offence is not taken, though moments later Clifford leans forward and places a heavy paw on Jake's shoulder. His breath reeks of vinegary onion and cider.

'Now then, what brings you into our quiet and happy little village?' He belches softly and rubs his chest.

'Haven't you heard the story? My uncle left me his place, and I've come to live in it.'

'Your uncle liked to keep himself to himself. Are you going to do the same?' The tone is quiet, but there is faint menace in his eyes. Jake has drunk enough not to want to pander, to defuse the tension. And he has been in more threatening places in his life than a country cellar.

'I certainly won't go where I'm not welcome. Unless you're saying I'm not welcome here now.'

Paul, the farmer, leans across and pulls Clifford back

gently. 'Nobody is saying that. We're a hospitable bunch, lads, aren't we?' There is a muted chorus of assent. And talk moves haltingly to weather, and a racing meet scheduled for the next week. Soon names of horses and stables are whizzing round, and Jake is content to let the conversation wash over him.

After a couple of hours, there is no doubt that most people in the cellar are drunk. Not fall-down drunk, but sleep-with-your-boots-on drunk. Jake has pretended to drink more than has actually passed his lips, and is ready to leave. He decides to take the risk.

'So, fellers, my uncle left me old copies of the local paper, and I've been reading them at night. I was sorry to see that a poor woman died at your farm. That must have been terrible.' He looks at the three farm workers, but keeps peripheral attention on everyone else.

Davey seems genial. 'Very sad. Just one of them things. Isn't that right Dick, lad?'

Richard has been quiet for the last half hour, pacified by the drink, but he lurches himself forward slightly and stares at Jake. 'Why are you talking about Sabine? What was she to you?'

Jake raises his hands. 'Just someone I read about in the paper, and I realized the coincidence in sitting with you boys from the farm. I thought I'd mention it.'

Clifford sneered. 'You thought you'd mention it. Well around here it's not good manners to bring up personal things from the past. I suppose ol' King Arthur talked to you about how he felt about her too.'

That was a new connection. 'Arthur only used to write letters to me by the end. They never mentioned her.'

Clifford's arm shoots out and grips Jake's bicep hard.

For all his languor, he is fairly strong. Jake knows enough about group situations to know he should not back down.

'Don't ever touch me.'

He breaks the hold with his left forearm, half-standing, pivoting to shoulder Clifford away from him, sending the older man falling to the floor. When Jake turns, Martin has risen and is glowering at him, big ham-like fists clenched, perspiration beading on his brow. He makes a grab for Jake's throat with both hands, thick hairs sprouting from beneath his sleeves. He is surprisingly nimble. But Jake shifts with practised agility to his right, and responds by pushing both hands into Martin's chest, hard, a shunt that sends the man falling. Nobody has been hurt, but two are on the ground.

Jake wheels and walks slowly backwards so the stairs are behind him, and he can see the whole room. Dr Peter has pushed his chair back to the wall and is sitting as if in a daze, an odd smile painted on his face. The three farmers have barely moved. Paul and Davey are calmly finishing their pints. Richard stares malevolently at him, but also remains in his chair.

Clifford and Martin get up. The latter's fall has turned one of the chairs into kindling, and he picks up a ragged length of wood. Sarah walks bravely between them, her face no longer sleepy.

'Martin Walbrook, put that chair leg down or you'll have to start walking five miles for your drink in the evening. Same to you, Clifford. We've always had a no scrapping rule at the Nook, and you know it. I think it is time Jake left too. There's no need to spoil a perfectly nice evening with roughhousing.'

Jake allows himself to be walked up the stairs, his body

pulsing with adrenaline. Sarah clucks and shoos him out of the shop door, closing it behind them. The wind has picked up, and the clouds have dispersed.

Sarah is angry. 'What did I tell you about letting bones stay buried?'

'I asked a couple of simple questions, like any curious person would do.'

'We don't want curious folk here. We like it quiet.'

'So here's the problem. If you all like it quiet, why is everybody acting so strangely when I mention someone's death? Why did I find dug-up bones in the middle of the orchard? I came here to escape, to move on. I'm not seeking trouble out. But I'm not walking away either. If something has happened, maybe I'm supposed to find it.'

'Or maybe, you're supposed to keep yourself to yourself like your uncle did.'

'Did my uncle know Sabine then?'

'There you go again, asking questions . . . Yes Arthur knew her, they were sort of friends, I suppose.'

'When I mentioned her name before, at the beginning, you were about to say something before the lads came in. What was it?'

'Just that she was a lovely, bright young lass, who died too soon. And that she was caught up in the business of that farm, that family, and it was a shame.' Jake starts to speak, but she shakes her head, ruefully. 'No, no good can come from us talking about this. Go home, Jake. Find some peace, find someone alive to give your energy to.' She nods down the road to Livia's cottage, enshrouded in darkness, merely the pale of the walls looming in the murk. She retreats into the shop and closes the door behind her with a tinkling thud.

Jake sobers up on the walk home. He has left his torch in the cellar, but his eyes swiftly become accustomed to the moonlit gloom. He deeply breathes the sweet air, can almost feel the trees and plants respiring around him. He should wallow in the peace of the night, but he cannot. The adrenal legacy of the confrontation. And the references to his uncle trouble him. Had Arthur known Sabine in some meaningful way? And what if he did? Jake still hadn't established with certainty if Sabine and the bones were connected at all. But he had an instinct that something needed to be uncovered here. He'd felt that before with cases, that sense of the ephemeral crying out to be given shape.

He realizes how little he knows about Arthur's actions and relationships in the last decade and wonders how much evidence, if any, he left in the house. Jake has been living there for more than a month, and has been in and out of most of the rooms, but he has not looked through the place properly, nor tried to trace the history of its owner. That's what he used to be, he thought, a tracer of history, a filler of story, a joiner of dots. Maybe he should do that with his own uncle first.

The lake swallows the sounds of the night as he approaches the house; it glistens and shivers, restless and alive, watery jostling of creatures he cannot see. The basic lesson of policework, of life: there is always more than meets the eye.

Searching

It is a big house, Little Sky, and quite a daunting place to explore carefully. Jake has been involved in property searches more times than he can remember: sometimes with absent owners, sometimes with a whole family standing mute, imploring with their eyes, humiliated as latex-clad hands finger and fluster their private possessions. Most people, he knows, aren't very good at hiding things. They simply rely on the camouflage of clutter, the sheer difficulty inherent in discerning the important piece of evidence amid all of life's numberless jumble. That is why the police in murder cases often use grid-searching, the division of a room into small sections that can be methodically worked through and worked over.

Jake is not sure he is up to grid-searching every room, especially with a home-brewed cider hangover. But he feels he should see what, if any, personal papers Arthur left on the property. He begins in the basement, which is warm and brightly lit. The furnace ticks noisily away on one side. In the corner where he found the back issues of the

Shire Gazette there are a couple of other boxes, which Jake sets aside for further investigation. He then starts on the main rooms of the house. There seems little to be learned in the kitchen and living rooms, nothing concealed in fireplaces or in the linings of cushions, but he checks anyway. After a couple of hours, with only the bedrooms left, he takes a break.

Last night's confrontation, though minor, has reminded Jake of the need to keep sharp in protecting himself. As part of his policework, he had been given periodic self-protection lessons, and had developed an interest in boxing. For the last few weeks, he has been working on setting up a small area for training near the house, and takes the opportunity to finish the job. He has almost filled the largest empty flour sack, over four feet in length, with damp sand, excavated from an old work site in the corner of the courtyard. He now takes some cushions outside and rips off their covers, exposing the spongy insides. He pushes fistfuls of the material down all of the sides of the sack, and ties it up with rope. He drags this now extremely heavy and cumbersome thing to the sentinel birch tree right next to the house. Throwing one end of the rope over the lowest branch, he manages to hoist the sack so the middle is slightly below head height. He winds the remainder of the rope back around the branch, and ties it fast with a thick knot.

The heavy bag does not move with the stiff breeze that is hissing through the leaves. Nor does it move much when he strikes it with a firm left jab, or the harder right-hand that follows. He feels the shock back down his arm, and the sting of his knuckles, and reckons this will work nicely as a part of his exercise routine. There is an old medical kit in the kitchen – a huge case which looks like it comes from a 1920s country house – and it is full of bandages. He finds the thickest and cuts two long strips of equal length. At the end of each, he cuts a line down the centre of a couple of inches, to act as ties. The resultant hand-wraps fit snugly, and provide a proper protection against the impact of the bag.

Jake brings his phone outside and sets the stopwatch running, timing himself doing six rounds of five minutes, with one minute rest. The thudding flurry of his punches, the heavy gasps of his breath, loud in the afternoon quiet. At the end of the sixth round, his lungs are screaming and he is streaming sweat, in his eyes, rolling down his body, darkening the ground beneath the tree. He pulls off his shorts and collapses into the lake for the cleansing shock of the water, before dressing and returning to the house.

His search soon peters out: there is nothing in the bedrooms, which are as impersonal as those in a holiday home. Old chunky furniture, the occasional fine art print, the faintly stale odour of disuse. Jake feels his arms throbbing, some pleasurable ache in his hamstrings, and he goes to the library. The room is quiet and inviting. He collapses onto the old couch and stares up at the reassuring volumes in their ordered rows. There is something about shelves upon shelves of books to gladden Jake's heart; they suggest an infinite amount of diversion, the endless scope for information, the sense that he will never be entirely alone, his life never completely lacklustre.

He is eyeing the main collection of English detective fiction, when he notices something unusual for the first time. The top three shelves, above head height, are set

113

about six inches further back than the lower shelves, as if there is a bulge in the lower part of the wall. That is possible, but unlikely, given that this is the newest part of the building, and would not have been warped by age or weather. The book at the end of the fourth shelf is also slightly unusual. It is bigger than the rest, thick and bound impressively in green leather, entitled *Sherlock Holmes: The Adventure of the Norwood Builder*. It is strange because that is the title of one story by Arthur Conan Doyle, but never a whole book. The mystery in it is about the apparent murder of an irascible man, who has actually faked his own death and framed the son of his former rival. He then conceals himself in a secret room, which Holmes spots by measuring the outside walls of the house and comparing the length of the interior walls.

Jake stands up, and cautiously pulls the book out. There is a faint whirring noise, and the block of shelves swings out on a hinge. In the space behind is a compartment, effectively a small secret cupboard. In it, there is a wooden box, long and thin, and made of mahogany, scarred with thick grooves made glossy with varnish. Jake opens it gently, and there is an old shotgun inside, which looks oiled and well-maintained. It is also loaded, and Jake closes the lid carefully. Beyond it is another box, filled with letters and various papers. The rest of the space is empty apart from a couple of white roses, which have dried and turned papery with time. He brings out the gun and the boxes, and swings the shelf door closed.

He leaves the gun on the kitchen table, and takes the other box down to the seat by the lake. It is late afternoon, and still warm enough, the air alive with insects. The dipping sun separates into a scattering of sparkling jewels on the tiny waves of the water. Glittering constellation. He stares for a moment at the play of the light, before he opens the box. He recognizes the first pack of letters immediately, because they are his, sent to his uncle over the years. The stories of his cases, triumphs and failures. The news of his life with Faye. The blithe optimism about his child-filled future, the long pauses between miscarriages, the mournful letters of self-loathing and searching that followed. These are snapshots of Jake's old life as much as anything else. He sets them aside carefully.

Beneath them is a pile of journals, carefully written in Arthur's spidery writing. Not long passages of prose, just sentence-long jottings, sporadic notes of an old man to his self.

Diary of a nobody

Jake reads until the light fades, the evening chill tickling his exposed legs. He then moves inside to the kitchen table and the welcoming warmth of the stove. Arthur used his journal to record little events at home, on the land or on one of his long rambles, which he called odysseys, most often abbreviated to 'ods'. A sample note might read: 'Today's ods: followed the river round for 10 miles before turning back. Breakwater lagoon at 8th mile: long reeds, blue bolt of Kingfisher, halcyon day.' He clearly spent much of his time reading, and for six months oversaw the construction of the extension to the house, built around his conception of the thriller library, a physical manifestation of his idea of disappearing into a world of books. Arthur had read Jorge Luis Borges's short story 'The Library of Babel', which he describes in the journal, and in which every possible book in the universe exists based on a combination of every possible letter of the alphabet. 'I want to disappear into eternity,' Arthur writes soon after his library is built.

Happily, he seems to find some comfort in occasional human contact, like Jake does. He goes foraging with 'Dr P – almost as learned as he thinks he is', goes searching each year for St Aethelmere's bones (without success), drinks his fair share of cider at the Nook. His friendships are all surface, though, 'like oil atop the still-like water', he says, drifting towards poeticism. 'I still like to go months without talking too much.'

One summer he comes across a woman, swimming naked in a quiet turn of the river. He writes about the 'shock of her white body, the dark tongue of hair between her legs, her unselfconscious dipping and splashing'. His odysseys become, for quite some time, stalkerish wanderings, hoping to recapture his moment of discovery.

Jake writhes in his chair as he reads, discomfited by this spectre of senescent lust. Arthur seems determined, driven by his lonely eroticism, and then one day – a few weeks after the first sighting – he sees her again, cleaning herself in the waters one hot evening when the air is thick with storm, angry at its own unfailing humidity. He makes a noisy, distant entrance onto the surrounding land, hollering a greeting as he comes, so she can cover herself on his arrival. They speak, politely and awkwardly. The final sentence of the entry reads: 'My siren is Sabine.'

After that point, their meetings become planned, though infrequent. Privately, Arthur still muses occasionally on the memory of her body, 'firm, cold flesh, reminder of youth'. She sees him, he notes, 'as substitute uncle or father, friendly and solicitous of her welfare'. They go on evening walks, searching for local birds, that elusive kingfisher, a goshawk 'of piercing eye and yellow-grey plumage,' a species, he notes, precariously balanced on the edge of extinction. They pick wild roses, entangled in a corner of a field, white petals deep as cupped hands. He clearly kept them as a memento.

Dr Peter becomes a regular companion, and evident third wheel. 'Dr P leaps out from bush to plague us once more', reads one entry, though later Arthur seems more accepting of the inevitability of his company.

As they come to know each other better, Sabine turns to Arthur for romantic advice, which both frustrates and titillates him. On desperate days, and now with a better sense of the schedule of her life, he returns to his solitary stalking, peering out at her in the river, imagining the icy water on her warm skin. Meanwhile, she has started a relationship with a man. 'Of all people, inevitably, it is Rose the Rogue, dark tempter of my pale Sabine.' Their love affair ebbs and flows, she is puckish with contentment, then miserable over perceived rejection. Arthur tries to steer her away, but the on-off romance persists despite his efforts. At one terrible point, he stumbles – genuinely it seems – across the couple making love outdoors: 'her white legs wide, him darting in, both too transported to notice me. What an old fool I have become. Love is for the young, after all.'

He mentions Sabine less for a couple of months, and Jake wonders if he has become philosophical about their friendship. The walks continue, more often with Dr P, without much glossing of detail. A couple of mentions follow that are musing and uncertain: 'Is she falling out of love; is something amiss?' Then there is one entry, stark and short beneath a black cross at the top of the page: 'The lightness has gone out of my life.' And there is nothing for more than two weeks. Then: 'Sabine falls, nobody sees, is that all there is?' His journal-keeping eventually returns more regularly. There is a note, three weeks later: 'Jake? Could he help look into death? Police seem so uncurious, satisfied.' And another two weeks on: 'I have to let Sabine go. Dr P disagrees; he believes she has been taken from us. What does he know?'

Arthur becomes more withdrawn from life as the years pass. He embraces the solitude, lets it clothe and shelter him. He notes with a sort of avuncular approval the arrival of Livia: 'New vet, new with child, exotic interruption in the tired village.' There is nothing, Jake is relieved to read, sexual in his interest. He admires her fortitude, leaves gifts for Diana. He begins to plan for his bequest to Jake: 'I know now that renunciation is the key to life. Embrace the little sky.' Much later, he begins to feel the pangs of illness: 'a heaviness inside me, blood when I cough, red on white'. He blames the cigars, which he tries to quit. He finds pain relief in cannabis – 'Rose, as ever, is reliably roguish; no doubt he takes his cut, but he gets me what I need' – first as something to smoke in substitute, then to drink in a tea.

Arthur decides to investigate Jake's life before confirming his legacy, and hires an investigator. For a year, the journal has few summative reports: 'Jake is the success I knew he would be. Has a gift for finding people's stories'; 'Jake promoted again, strong career ahead'. It focuses on his family life too though: 'Jake and Faye hospital regulars, no answer to the problem of miscarriage. Strain on relationship visible in public. He works late; she leaves early'; 'Home not happy for Jake – does he need the change?'

Jake flushes as he reads, tears almost beginning to form: that period of his life, everything such a battle, such a strain, such an effort for something that should be so natural. The way she looked at him as they failed. The way they stopped talking, they stopped sharing. Was it him, calloused and self-protecting from work? Should he have done more, fought harder, clung on?

He throws the journal aside, unfinished. It is black outside. He is on his own, like Arthur was, half-renouncing, half-subsisting in the world. He wonders if his desire – he can call it that to himself – for Livia is little better than Arthur's was for Sabine, something cramped and furtive, driven by impure longing.

And what of Sabine and her unquiet bones? Perhaps it is his allotted role to bring them peace, or that might be just the thought of a lonely man, solitary in the countryside's unforgiving black, seeking a purpose in a purposeless existence.

Cold comfort farm

'I can't believe how much I have to tell you.'

They are rollicking along in Livia's old black Volvo, which is roomy and comfortable, the fittings flecked with dried mud, smelling inside of the land outside. The lanes are narrow, tightly enclosed by thick hedgerows, dark green corridors, and they have seen no other traffic going the other way. Jake had arrived just after nine according to the old grandfather clock's ponderous chimes, and Livia was sitting in the front room waiting for him. The day is cool – each day now seeming a little cooler than the last; the long, slow grasp of autumn beginning its inexorable tightening – and she is dressed in thick brown cords and a long pale jumper. Jake is in shorts and a hooded top; his daily swims have more than acclimatized him to lowering temperatures.

He starts by telling the tale of his confrontation in the cider cellar. Livia nods ruefully. 'Sarah mentioned something when I popped into the Nook. She thinks you should have kept quiet. And I think she blames me a little bit for encouraging you.'

'Reactions like theirs encourage me, though. Why was everyone so defensive, so quickly? I was deliberately polite, vague even. And they jumped down my throat, almost literally at one point. But it did make me think: I don't want to make life difficult for you. You are a proper, valued member of the community, not a pale, suspicious loiterer on the margins.'

'You're not trying to ditch me, are you partner? I love a project and a problem.'

'Are you talking about me or the case?'

They laugh for a second, and then Jake explains about Arthur's diaries, which have been lingering in his mind.

Livia nods. 'This all happened before my time, though I half remember a friend of his being mentioned occasionally. That may have been her. I think we need to speak to Dr Peter soon; he clearly had some suspicions.'

'We first need to establish Sabine is involved in this.'

There is quiet, the crunching hum of the engine loud in their ears, the windows open so the occasional twitter of birdsong emerges at a higher pitch. Jake chooses his words carefully. 'What about him stalking her like that? I felt it was all a bit sad, and suspicious. If I'd been investigating, and read all that, I would have seen him as a suspect. The sexually ignored loner is a classic piece of profiling. Was he ever weird with you? The diaries don't suggest it.'

'He was always gentlemanly. Which now makes me feel a bit unattractive. And I don't think you should be too tough on your memory of him. A man on his own sees a naked woman in a beautiful setting, natural and unself-conscious. What would you feel? You can't tell me that you wouldn't feel desire? I sometimes think even I would, given the state of my life.'

'I can just about handle the thought of a naked woman in a lake objectively. I think if you throw yourself in, it will all get too much for me.'

A warm chuckle, his favourite sound. 'My point is that desire – lust, if you want to call it that – is natural, part of life. And yes it overwhelmed him, but he didn't do anything.'

'Unless he did do something and didn't write about it. I'd hate for that to be true.'

She pulls the car up to a layby and looks into his eyes, hers a darker, softer hue than the hedge behind her. 'Are you sure you want to take that risk?'

'I think I have to now.'

'And don't worry; I'll try to stop you becoming an old peeper if I can help it.'

'Just stay out of the river with no clothes on, then.'

The engine dies, and they get out, a firm breeze whipping their hair. They have come as close as the lane gets to Smiths' Farm. There is a broad tractor track on the other side, which leads eventually to the B-road going across the county border. But on this side, there is nothing much to see. It is a lonely spot.

'We should go across the farm, and at the other end by the road there's the farm shop. At the very least we might be able to speak to someone there.'

'What's our story when we do speak to anyone?'

Jake has wrestled with this unsuccessfully. 'Hello, we're a burned-out ex-policeman and a curious vet, half-authorized by police, trying to establish whose bones were discovered during a hokey folk tradition on the other side of the valley.'

'Well that should open things up.'

'No, I think we just need to shade the truth a little. We're helping to investigate the discovery of bones, and trying to establish where they come from. I think that's reasonable.'

For several minutes the point is moot, as they see nobody at all, and scarcely any living thing. A bird of prey hovers on the air currents above them, a dark scratch on the granite sky, wings tipping faintly left then right, and Jake wonders if it is a goshawk. He talks about Arthur's interest in birds, and Livia remembers going for occasional walks with him, a wise guide and enthusiastic giver of information.

'I'm good at avian anatomy, or at least the bits that I remember, but not good at the taxonomy.'

'That reminds me, are they not going to know you here as a vet?'

'No, look around you, this is arable land. There is corn, primarily. But a big market garden too. Look at the flashes of light over yonder. They're big greenhouses, full all the year around.' The two of them are coming to a stile and he holds her hand briefly as she clambers over it. She has put on green wellies, and is visibly in her element; she looks grounded by the land, part of its bounty. He is wearing his oldest trainers and looks something foreign, an invasive species.

He pauses at the side, looking at her closely.

'What are you staring at?'

'Just thinking how you look perfectly at home here, like part of the natural environment. Have you always been like that?'

They had talked of her background once or twice already: her mum, from the island of Trinidad, a baby of the Windrush generation; her dad, an Anglo-Irish doctor. She had been called all the racial slurs at school on occasion, which had been devastating, soul-aching, but she never felt she had been subject to persistent racist attention. The moments of hurtful disregard had come and gone. And as she got older, her sense of difference had become less pronounced. She had grown up in a big town, then gone to a university that attracted students from all around the world.

'The thing is I'm a chameleon. Almost anywhere I go around the world, I look like I belong: Mediterranean, Middle East, Asia, South America. I am a light-skinned Black woman, I have blood mingled from across continents. My mum always said it was a sign of strength.'

'But what about in the depths of the English countryside? You don't look like anybody else around here.'

'At the beginning, I had to put up with being called "exotic", in painfully polite fashion of course, but it was annoying. And God it used to wind me up when I was asked: "Where do you come from, really?" But you know I do love the land, and the animals, I do feel camouflaged here. I can't really explain it.'

'I have never quite felt I fitted in, too tall, too preoccupied. So although my family is English, or a sort of strange Scottish-English mix, I didn't ever feel much connection to home.'

'Don't you try to out-victim me, Mr Patriarchal White Man.' She grins, then puts a restraining hand on his arm. Up ahead is a gate at the end of a drive leading up to the farmhouse, which is big and Gothic, an ominous tower-like structure to one of its sides. A woman is standing, leaning against it, thick arms on flaking wood,

125

closely watching their progress. They walk up to her, gesticulating in a friendly enough fashion. The woman could have been engraved from sandstone. She barely moves even as Jake hails her, and waits until they are close before speaking.

'Who are you, and what are you doing on this land?'

'I'm Jake and this is Livia. We're helping police identify some human remains that were found not that far from here. We think they're of a woman who died in the last ten years. Somebody mentioned Sabine Rohmer to us, who worked on this farm and died in that period. We wondered if you could tell us something about her?'

The woman appears unmoved. 'I'm Joan. And I don't have time for gossip.'

She has time for standing motionless and inscrutable, Jake nearly says. 'This is hardly gossip. It's making sure someone's remains go back to where they belong. Did you know Sabine?'

'I did, I was sorrowful when she died, and I'm sorrowful now. But I told police everything I knew then, and that's the end of it. Her bones are safely laid to rest. If you found some, they won't be hers. And if you have no other business on the farm, I'll not be welcoming you in. The road is that yonder direction.' She sighs expansively, and waddles back to the house without looking back.

Livia and Jake look at one another, and head in the indicated direction. 'I must say, Jake, it's a privilege watching an experienced detective at work. The way you charmed her was extraordinary. It really feels like we're making progress.'

'We know that we're in the right place. She was never going to tell us much. Let's hope for better in the farm shop. I won't say "yonder" like you all do, but, look, it is just over there.'

The shop is a converted farm building, built from cast-off bricks of all hues from burnt orange to slate grey. It looks like a giant tabby cat preparing to pounce. Outside its open doors are banks of fresh produce from the farm: heads of corn, a lurid yellow clasped in thick green leaves; punnets of tomatoes; stacks of cucumbers, courgettes and aubergines. A picture of flamboyance. Inside, the shop is full of local milk, cheese and meat, and some rather chichi luxury products (bramble jam, chilli chutney), suggesting that there is some tourist-traffic-supporting trade here. Standing in the corner, in matching aprons, are a man and a woman. They are matching in other respects too. Jake has never seen two people of different gender look so similar: short brown hair, tightly curled onto their heads as if woven; stocky bodies, almost rectangular, with no sense of curves or bumps; thick black spectacles framing beady eyes.

Jake walks up to them, but Livia sidles ahead. Pushing herself forward, she says: 'Hello, it's David and Ruth, isn't it? You brought your cats in to see me last year, didn't you? Let me see, they were called Roy and Kelton, after Roy Orbison. Oh Jake, they're beautiful animals, such friendly personalities. How are they doing?'

Ruth speaks first, having scowled her twin brother into silence: 'They're just the job, now. No problems at all, veterinary. You were a tonic for them, and for us. You've not come to see them, have you? We used to have them in baskets here, but her ladyship said we couldn't. We leave them at home now, the little blighters.'

'Poor bastards.' David shakes his head, murmuring quiet invective to himself.

'No, I'm just glad they're doing OK. I'm doing a favour for my friend Jake here, who used to be a police officer and is now helping trace people's graves. You know, so loved ones who have lost touch know where to pay their respects. I said I knew some lovely people in this bit of the county, so I came along with him.'

They swell a little with pride, rocking on their heels as they try to look knowledgeable.

'Do you know where a woman called Sabine Rohmer is buried?'

Delighted faces; they do know the answer. Ruth speaks first again. 'She was the poor lass who died near on ten year ago, wasn't she? Fell down some steps. She was German, but couldn't help that, you know. And that's all so long ago, the war, isn't it?'

More mutterings, presumably of dissension, from David, which Ruth ignores.

'Any road, she was laid to rest not far from here. Church in Bluntisham, no more than a mile away. You can go and check.' She nods brightly.

David speaks audibly for the first time. 'Ruth, we're not supposed to talk about her any more. Remember, we was told it brought back too many bad memories to the area, and we're supposed to be all chipper and cheery now.'

That seems an unlikely task for them, especially David. 'Did you know her?' asks Jake.

David resumes a moody silence, but Ruth is undeterred. 'Oh yes, a lovely girl. Beautiful as the sunshine. And very popular too, everyone loved her.'

'All the men loved her at least.' This qualification from David.

'Well she couldn't help that. She was so interested in

everyone. Always going on walks with folk, or helping out here when we needed her. I was so sorrowful when she passed.'

The shop is still empty, and Jake wants them to keep talking, so addresses his next question to Ruth, whose face is open, her hands never quite still.

'And how did she die?'

David interrupts. 'You don't need to know that to find her grave, do you?'

Ruth raises her voice. 'Don't be so argumentative, David, I've told you a million times.' Calmer, again. 'It came from nowhere, her falling down from that tower like that. She was such a strong person, as strong and sure on her feet as a goat. We was all so surprised.'

Livia nudges Jake. Behind them, silent as snakes, three burly men have entered the shop. Jake recognizes Davey, Paul and Richard from the other night in the Nook. They stare levelly at the scene before them, not aggressive exactly, but tense and discomfiting. If they were animals, their hackles would be raised, their tails twitching in earnest.

Livia turns back to Ruth and David. 'Well, so nice to see you again, and I'm very glad the cats are doing so well.' Jake nods in agreement, and together they walk from the shop. The men move slightly to let Livia pass, before blocking Jake. He is expecting something like this, and has tensed his upper body, dipping his shoulder slightly to plough on through them, knocking them together so they nearly fall.

Outside, he doesn't have any time to speak to Livia before all three men barrel out of the shop, their faces flushed with anger. He notices that one of them, Davey, is clutching a shotgun against his body. He doesn't think it will come to that, but is suddenly well aware that nobody knows where they are. These men are naturally strong and resolute, but probably have not fought that much in their lives, certainly not against people trained in self-defence. Jack Reacher, in Lee Child's books, would not wait any longer and kick at least two of them in the knees, before smashing his elbow into the other's nose. Robert Parker's Spenser would make a wisecrack and then do something similar. So would Travis McGee or Mike Hammer, but would probably get knocked out themselves in the process, leading to the kidnap and general imperilment of their female assistant.

But this is not a book. These are not crooks, at least he doesn't know they are. Real life is messier, and more sedate. Jake is still weighing up his options, shading his way forward in front of Livia when she pushes past him.

'Good morning, chaps. We were just leaving. I know Jake has asked you about Sabine, and I know you know the police have asked us to help them, so there's not much more to be said. We'll head off. Come on, Jake.'

With that, she gives a merry turn of her hips, and strides down the track towards the road. Jake has little choice but to follow, and there is no point in lingering. He maintains eye contact until he is past the men, and then catches up with Livia, who looks across at him, her cheeks slightly darker, her chest heaving.

'Don't worry, we can cross the road and then double back to the car. It's quite a trek, but you look fit enough.'

They are soon out of sight of the farm and begin the process of circling around it. They enter a thick copse of trees, its exterior a forbidding bristle of elm and ivy. It is chill and dense, no sign of the sun. Livia clutches her jumper to her and shivers. They talk about the morning, and agree a plan to visit the church as soon as they get the car.

'Were you scared back there, Jake?'

'Not really. A bit apprehensive maybe about how it might play out. I thought you were exactly right in getting us out of there, however emasculating it felt. We do need to take care; there seem to be plenty of people who aren't thrilled with us at the moment.'

'I know. And they'll know we're going to the church, so we may not be out of the wrangle yet.'

'Do you want to drop me off and get home? I can have a prowl around the church, and report back. Not that you can't cope, obviously. Just that you work in this community. You have a daughter. You don't need this grief.'

Livia's response is hot, and determined. 'For all those reasons I don't want to leave Sabine's death unexamined. That would be wrong. I feel a kinship with her, I think. And I trust you already to look after me, and I'll do my best to look after you. If it gets too difficult, I'll let you know.'

Jake doesn't attempt to argue. They reach the Volvo and Livia drives to the church, which is ten minutes away along winding claustrophobic roads. It looms from behind a hedge, an old, forlorn building sitting squat in a grave-yard, hinting at the blight of death in the midst of the lush and living countryside.

A morbid taste for bones

The church dates back to Anglo-Saxon times, as do many in the area, and was unfinished by the time of the Norman invasion, which had led to some immediate alterations. Now, almost a millennium later, you can see the evidence of the culture clash in the structure itself. Conflict etched in stone. Jake loves ancient buildings, the coldness and heft of the material, the weight of the history, the sense that people had sheltered under this roof who were so unutterably different to him, but also in some respects similar: who loved and hoped and feared and felt like he does. Today he and Livia are interlopers, investigators, but also part of an invisible congregation.

They push back the gate beneath a yew tree, which may have been young when the church's foundations were being painstakingly laid. It looks like it has been fissured and wizened by lightning, its branches like ancient bones poking out in all directions. The graveyard is filled with stones, some old with legends impossible to decipher, palimpsests of a life. Others are new, suffering aesthetically in comparison, made from quartz and marble, too glittery in the gloom. Some are covered in weather-beaten photographs, dead flowers in scuffed jam jars, the occasional, mournful children's toy.

The church itself is gloomier still, its open door spilling the day's generous light upon the interior. To the left, high on the wall, is a window cut directly into the stone in the shape of a rose. It is rough-hewn and ragged, but still capable of arresting your attention. The other light comes in through dusty and dimmed stained glass, the stories it bears impossible to understand or even read now. There are a few candles flickering, desultory, the visible legacies of some people's moments of prayer. As so often in English churches, the modern clashes uncomfortably with the ancient: plastic foldaway chairs alongside ornate Victorian pews; a dehumidifier hums mournfully, its electrical cord snaking over a sixteenth-century dedication to some forgotten patron.

Jake and Livia's footsteps echo on the floor, which gleams with centuries of accumulated polishing. The over-whelming sense is of dotage, a building once powerful and magnificent, now allowed to dwindle into somewhat decrepit old age. There is a vicar fussing with prayer books in the corner: bald head half-obscured by carefully placed strands of auburn hair, a thick precise beard of the same colour. He is small and slight, a fastidious peacock in black and purple.

Livia walks up to him while Jake eases himself into a pew, which is as unyielding as any he can remember from the sporadic church visits of his youth. He can hear Livia's conversation, amplified by the stone that surrounds them. They agreed that she should present herself as a friend of

Sabine's, which is far simpler than the alternative explanation for them both.

'Excuse me, but I'm looking for a grave of someone I once knew. I was told she was buried here.'

'Hello, my dear. Let me just put these books down. I have no idea why we have so many of them, you know. I give sermons in three churches around here, when there really is only audience enough for one. I can't think of an occasion when a hundred and seventy people would like to join together to sing "He Who Would Valiant Be".' He deposits the final pile of books inside a cupboard and noisily shuts the door.

'Now where were we? Ah yes, your poor friend. Let me think of how best to help. You see, this is not strictly *my* church. Indeed it is not strictly anybody's church either. It is, like me, a relic of a different era.' He grimaces at the thought. 'We do funeral services, and there is still some space in the graveyard and crypt. When did you say your friend died?'

'I didn't. It was about ten years ago. Her name was . . .'

'Sabine Rohmer.'

The voice is clear and precise. Jake and Livia turn to see Dr Peter walking towards them, his movements jerky and imprecise, his leather bag bouncing against his side.

'Don't worry, vicar. These are my friends and I can help them find the grave from here.'

The vicar seems sad to lose his part in the conversation, but clucks off behind a curtain. Jake and Livia perch on opposing pews, and Peter stands in between them.

Jake is first to break the pause. 'How did you know we were here, and looking for Sabine?'

'Dear fellow, your quest for justice is as admirable as

134

it is unquiet. I was there, you remember, when you asked about her in the Nook. And I saw you and Livia on my walk this morning, going up to Smiths' Farm. And I know that Sabine used to lie here.'

'Saw us or stalked us?' asks Livia mildly.

'A distinction without a difference in practice, if you don't mind the homily.'

Jake shakes his head. 'More importantly, why do you say "used to lie here"? What do you know about the removal of the bones?'

'Let us proceed, as I believe your erstwhile colleagues in the police say, to the crypt for further examination.'

The vicar has disappeared, so they tramp down the old stone stairs without the need for further explanation. The light below is much the same as above. The sky is visible through two sunken windows on one side of the room, which feels old but not musty.

Dr Peter plays tour guide. 'I bet you didn't know, even with your extensive, ah, experience in matters homicidal, that crypts or mausoleums are still much used. They're not simple relics of the early modern period. This church did have tombs in its crypt from that date, before the rather archly efficient Edwardians cleared them all out and dumped them. Since then the surrounding farms have used the spaces as areas of rest for their families and, as we shall now see, their workers.'

Jake and Livia see a series of plaques set against the furthest wall. 'That's not actually a structural wall, you see. Behind it are a series of niches for coffins. Slightly macabre perhaps but no weirder than being prey to the worms in the soil outside.' Dr Peter nudges Jake. 'If we remember our *Hamlet*.'

He directs them to the plaque about a third of the way down, at about knee height. There is a metal door, a foot and a half high and a similar width across, in a deep navy blue colour. It has been locked down with six rivets screwed into place. The plaque reads: SABINE ROHMER, RUHE SANFT IN FRIEDEN. Jake inspects it closely, but cannot tell whether they have been tightened recently or ten years before. The whole place is well-maintained, buffed and gleaming, a contrast to the walls above them.

He turns to Livia. 'We've found her at least. The question is whether she's there. I am guessing, Dr P, that you believe she isn't?'

Dr Peter nods, sadly, and is quiet for the first time in Jake's acquaintance. Livia squeezes his wrist. 'Why don't you tell us what you think is going on?'

He straightens his back, and sniffs, before reaching into his bag. 'Why don't I show you?'

Jake stops him. 'I'm not sure about this. It's the middle of the day in a picturesque English church. We are, together, a burned-out ex-cop, a beautiful vet, and a fairly eccentric botanist.' Dr Peter nods at the accuracy of the labels. 'I don't think we should be desecrating a mausoleum. Livia, a sane view from you please?'

'I agree. Exciting though all this is, we have to do things properly. Dr P?'

'This is not exciting for me. It is deeply painful. But perhaps you're right. I have no objection to official action, provided I'm kept away from it. I'll tell you all I know, trusting you not to betray a confidence. Am I right to rest on that good faith?' They nod, unsure of any other response. 'Then let us repair to somewhere more convivial and airy, to sit upon the ground and tell stories of the death of friends. As Shakespeare nearly said.' Suddenly frail, he loops arms with his companions and together they walk back into the dimness of the church itself. They pass through the nave and out of the door, where the birds are chirruping their apparent approval.

Outside, Livia checks her phone, and sees it is past lunchtime. 'I have to go to pick up Di soon, so we better hear this now while I can. Then –' She looks meaningfully at Jake. 'We better contact Chief Inspector Watson.'

Dr Peter has sunk down on a mossy bank of grass at the edge of the churchyard. The nearby hedge is thick with nettles and dock leaves, screaming green at them. They join him on the ground, which is slightly damp and soft. Then, in a faltering voice, he tells them a short version of his tale, much of which they have already pieced together. The kindness and beauty of Sabine. Her friendships. Her love affair with Rose. And then her sudden, devastating death, the account of which makes his eyes moisten and his voice drop even lower.

'I told them that she would never have fallen, not Sabine. I told them that she was too loved by too many people, and that might have brought her doom. Nobody listened to me. Not the police. Not the coroner. Not even your uncle, Jake. So I plunged into my work, my heart fractured and sore, my mind never at ease. And then I heard of your arrival, Jake, and I thought there was a chance that a former policeman might take a look at this again. Fresh eyes. I have been coming to this crypt since it all happened. I talk to Sabine sometimes, and told her I didn't want to disrespect her, that she was beyond hurt. That German phrase means "rest gently in peace", you know. I wanted to help her rest. And my plan has worked, has it not? You are here, the police are interested again, or will be if you insist.' His voice trails off, the tears rolling down the tired lines of his cheeks.

Jake feels his choler rise. 'So you tricked us into all of this? Made us obsess about some bones of a woman who has already been laid to rest peacefully once. Committed some horrible act of grave-robbery, which we are now abetting after the fact. What the hell do you expect us to do?'

His voice has risen to an angry shout, which feels almost obscene in the grounds of this tired and tumbledown old church.

'I understand,' says Livia quietly. 'You want justice. But why do you think she has never got it?'

'I'll tell you, but first you need to tell me what you're going to do. I'm willing to go to prison for taking her bones if I have to.'

Jake is looking at Livia, and feels pacified by her attitude. 'Calm down, you old rebel,' he says to Dr Peter. 'Who says you need to go to prison? We're not here with official sanction exactly. Why don't I tell the good chief inspector that we have reasons, confidential reasons, to believe Sabine's bones are ours and then take it from there. We can then explore what really happened to her.'

Dr P swallows and forces a smile, taking Livia and Jake in either hand. 'You would do that for me? I would be extraordinarily grateful.' He sits, brooding, for a moment. He is crumpled like an old discarded suit, a cast-off scarecrow figure, neglected and pitied.

Making the case

Jake uses Livia's phone to call Watson, after a mild tussle over who should do it. 'I'm not just the glamorous, disposable assistant, you know.' They eventually agreed that Jake can afford the time to get entangled in any necessary procedure here, while Livia has a job to consider and, more importantly, a daughter, soon home from school.

Jake quickly gets through to Watson, and gives him an abbreviated version of the tale: his newspaper search, the reaction of the locals, the location of the grave. He makes no mention of Arthur's journals, or Dr Peter at all, except as a witness to the dispute at the Nook. The old man's eyes dance wide when he realizes he is not being involved. Watson immediately asks to come over to the church to speak to Jake, who agrees to wait. Dr Peter offers to escort Livia back to her car via a roundabout route, and so get a lift back to the village himself. She dislikes the concept of chaperoning, but does not object to the chance to hear more about Sabine from him.

They walk off, their noisy chatter, Dr Peter's lengthy

exposition on the mating and feeding habits of the hazel dormouse, slowly dissipating in the mild air. Some afternoon sun emerges to warm Jake's face, and he lies back on the spongy cushion of the bank, closing his eyes to avoid the glare. Half an hour later, a shadow looms across him, waking him from an easy sleep. He is stiff and slightly shivery, the sun now paled by scuffling white clouds.

He groans when he sees Watson's amused face. 'I'm happy to see it's you, chief. I seem to be wearing out my welcome in this charming area.'

'Then you need to start taking better precautions, sir. I could have been a far more dangerous figure. Now let's visit the crypt and we can discuss the case more. I've already disposed of the rather sheepish figure of the vicar, who has gone off to one of his other churches for the evening.'

As they walk back into the church, its roof now brazen in the gleam of the sun, Jake repeats much of his previous conversation. Watson listens, head cocked to one side like a gundog.

'Well I believe that all as far as it goes. But I think it doesn't go all the way to explaining your confidence that our bones and Sabine's are one and the same.' He holds up a placatory hand. They are now in the crypt itself. 'I appreciate you don't work for me, so don't have to share everything. I'm going to need something to justify the exhumation order we now need, but maybe I can pull together enough.'

'Have you found any alternative candidates?'

Watson irritably shakes his head. 'We barely got this one. Sabine's name was on a list of deaths in the age range, but we hadn't even got round to separating the women from the men. Without your legwork, we would be nowhere.' He sighs ostentatiously. 'The staffing perils of the rustic life.'

'I'd have thought you could get enough for an order on the strength of my original discovery of the bones, the correct gender and date range, and your interview with me about the local discomfort over Sabine's name. Which you can no doubt sex up as much as you need to. And no local family to be distressed either.'

'I'm not too worried, actually. It will take time, but I'm on good terms with the coroner, who I think will be interested. We'll need religious permission via the bishop's office, but the chief constable has his own relationship there to help us. After all, we're seeking the rest and return of unquiet bones, and I think the Lord – presuming of course that he or she exists – would smile on our aims. It will all take time, though.'

'Well time is one thing I have a lot of. And Sabine has none at all to worry about.'

'True enough. So, unless you have anything else you want to share, I'll get the thing started. Such a shame not to see Livia, so do pass on my very best regards.'

Together they climb up the stairs of the crypt and through the main body of the church. There is the creaking of old heating ducts, the mournful hooting of pigeons. Outside, half-silhouetted in the sun's glare, stands Joan, the woman from the gate, flanked by Davey and Paul. They are not smiling. Watson seems unperturbed, grinning affably and nodding, as if they are all neighbours, happy to share an unplanned moment in a busy day. But as the two men leave the grounds he tugs Jake's arm towards his car. 'Charming folk, no doubt, but I'll feel better if I drop you nearer your home, unless you're dining at Livia's . . .'

'The village road is fine, thank you.'

'And make sure you take care of yourself. I don't want to lose an unofficial copper in my patch if I can help it.'

Sauna

A week passes, autumn hastens yet further. Jake sees Livia with ever-increasing pleasure, snatched happenings on a couple of brilliant afternoons at the field where they first met. They talk about the case, and about other parts of their lives. They feel comfortable, their backs dampening the hot grass, watching the languid slide of the occasional cloud, pleased to breathe the same clear air for a moment. Jake then bumps into her one evening outside the Nook, when she is taking Diana to feed the ducks on the river. The water is black, audible rather than visible until they play the feeble light of their torches on its surface. The ducks are noisy enough, full of thumping wings and squawking, squabbling after the bread that Diana throws with careful precision. Jake and Livia do not speak much; he feels happy in her company, warmed at the hearth of her family, her love for Diana generously spilling over.

He walks them both back to their house, and turns, a joke on his lips, ready to leave. Livia stops him. 'Jake, it's been lovely bumping into you tonight, but I have to be careful. I have Di, I have my practice, and this point in the year is always really busy. I guess I asked myself the other day what I was doing wandering the countryside with you, trying to solve a crime that might not be real. I have to deal with my responsibilities at home before anything else can intervene.'

A flush of awkwardness spreads up Jake's body. 'God, I didn't mean to force my company or the case on you. I'd hate you to think of me as the strange loner who never knew when he wasn't wanted.'

'You could never be that. I just have to live here all the time, I have to make sure that bit of my life works, and I worry you're disrupting it in a way that I can't control.'

'Has anyone spoken to you about me, or the bones?'

'This is not about anyone else. It's about me and my priorities.'

'Well, thank you for being honest. I better let you go. Can you tell Watson that he should come and see me if he wants to let me know about the case? I'll find another way to stay in touch with him. Take care, and sorry again.'

She strokes his face silently for a second, and then closes the door. As he walks away, he has a keen wrenching in his gut, a sense of loss. He hopes she will call him back, but she doesn't. It isn't that he had a serious relationship with Livia; it is just that it was the main relationship remaining in his life, and he had cherished it. He wonders when he might see her again, especially if she takes steps not to bump into him.

He throws himself into work on Little Sky, and thinking about Sabine. He forensically rereads Arthur's journals, and gets nothing but the overwhelming sense of his loneliness, even as he is averring the value of his chosen life in the pages. As if Arthur were writing to convince himself, not for posterity. Jake also tries to gauge Arthur's level of attachment to Sabine, which undoubtedly had its sexual element. But many of the final entries are modest, avuncular even, the musings of an observer on the sidelines, reluctantly accepting he is no longer in the fray.

One entry lingers in his mind, a little, and comes close to the time of Sabine's death: 'Sabine and I walked for hours in the welcoming land. But glints and glimmers still bother me. Where do they come from, and what do they mean?' This is frustratingly gnomic, but could be the flash of a lens in the distance. Was Sabine being watched, Jake wonders, and by whom?

The other boxes he found in the basement contain painting materials, and a few partially finished canvases. One is of a blonde woman, nude but with her legs crossed away from her, her arms folded in front of her breasts. The peep of a ruddy nipple, a feathery tuft of pubic hair. Not crude, nor sexual, but created with something approaching reverence. Jake looks into Sabine's eyes, deep brown and searching, and wonders what happened to her.

One blustery morning, sputtering with rain, a mean wind wrinkling the surface of the lake and making the reeds bow down in its path, Jake starts building the sauna with Mack. They do not talk much. Mack because he never does, Jake because he feels a heaviness inside, a sense of rejection. They assemble the wood that Mack has had delivered, and begin the process of fitting it together.

When Mack does speak, it is out of the side of his mouth, the other side occupied with keeping his rolled cigarette from falling out. It smoulders persistently.

'To do this properly, we really should put down a proper

145

foundation. But I think if we create a solid base, and rest the wood on it, that should be enough.' They are effectively constructing a large shed, and then super-insulating the walls to hold the heat in and keep the damp out. Jake intends to use wood along with stones dredged from the bottom of the lake to heat it, and to install a light with a battery charged from a small bank of solar panels.

Carrying the pre-cut sheets of timber and working them into place is hard work, his hands stinging, the thin wincing pain of splinters on unhardened flesh. The frame of the sauna is soon up, a heartening new silhouette in the flat-tish landscape by the water. The next day Mack returns with tar paper for the walls and roof. They build a door from planks, using tongue-and-groove joints to slot the pieces together. The windows are small, fitted into a two-by-four frame, and hinged in case the sauna ever needs to be cooled quickly.

After two days of hard work, the thing is up. Mack fits the glass to the windows, and they build a small base for the inner stove using fireproof bricks he has cadged from somewhere.

They step back and close the door to examine their work. The yellowish white of the wood is attractive against the green of the fields, and the muddy blue of the lake. It looks snug, capable of weathering storms. Mack throws down his cigarette, crushing it into the earth with his boot. Jake can smell the fresh sweat of his body. Mack seems to be sizing up the place with satisfaction.

'I think you can varnish this, leave it a day, and then give her a test drive. I'd join you but,' a crackling wheeze of laughter, 'I reckon people might talk.'

Three days later, and both coats of varnish have dried,

the walls now browner, more earthy. At dusk, Jake lights the wood, lets the flames die until only red gleaming coals remain. He has brought some wet stones from the lake and drops them onto the smouldering heart of the stove. They sputter and steam. He shuts the door and lies naked on a towel. The heat is fierce, and soon he is bathed in sweat, thick droplets merging and running in manic patterns onto the fabric. When he sits up, flushed, he drips onto the floor below. The smell is of sweet hot cedar and pine. A scent of health, and penitence. He thinks about Livia, and wishes he had fought a little bit for their relationship, fought for the chance that it might even be love, or something approaching it. He feels a moment of despair, and then realizes he is becoming light-headed with the heat. He has been inside for about forty minutes, which is probably his limit for the first time. He opens the door, and there is enough light in the dying day to guide him to the pier and the lake beyond. He jumps in and feels the thrill of the water, the heart-stopping moment of shock, the embrace of the liquid cold after all of that painfully endured heat; it is somewhere between threatening and welcoming. He swims around limply, before heading back into the house. This is progress in his self-reliance if nothing else.

Washed up

The outstanding domestic issue for Jake is cleanliness, indeed maintaining his appearance more generally. He lives in a house that, apart from having no television, phone or internet, is functional and modern enough. He has light and heat and books and records. He has a fridge and freezer. But there are two tiny bathrooms, complete with flushing toilets and nothing else. Jake has looked for reasons in Arthur's journals, and it seems that the old farmhouse was late to running water. An outhouse had been destroyed because of rot and damage, and the one bathroom with an actual bath removed in the renovation process. Arthur had never installed a washing machine, at first enjoying the sense of rustic privation that came from washing his clothes in the lake, later as a sort of senile stubbornness. His last year or so, he had been aloof and a little wild, and probably, Jake thinks, not very hygienic.

There is also the problem of remoteness. Little Sky is not near any road. Visitors, such as they are, have to hike across unmarked land, or drive a Land Rover over bumpy and unreliable terrain. Getting anything installed, a shower or a washing machine, is not going to be easy. But it might be necessary, Jake reflects. He stands over the lake and looks at his shimmering reflection, honey skin tones flickering on blue. His shoulders have widened, his waist has narrowed, thanks to his training regime. His hair is now almost to his shoulders, his beard three inches below his chin. The late summer has turned his dark hair chestnut, with strands of unpolished gold. There are flecks of grey in his beard and on his chest. His skin has a flush of health. He looks like a castaway, which, he supposes, he is.

He's never been particularly vain. He wants to be liked, wants not to be dismissed by women, but has never developed very much swagger and self-regard. One of the things he had loved about Faye was the unselfconscious way she had flattered him: a surprise hug or stroke of the nape of his neck, a contented sigh, a whispered, needless compliment. He thinks he now looks wild, unkempt, perhaps even a bit eccentric, but doesn't seem to have the energy to mind. That said, he does not want to descend into strangeness, to become a sort of uncivilized curio. So he decides that his next project should be an outdoor shower, which can be built in the courtyard. The clothes issue can come next; perhaps he can get a washing machine delivered to the village and bribe someone to bring it home.

Meanwhile, the vegetable garden is coming on. He works on it most afternoons, with Mahler or Bach sorrowing gently in the quiet, the loamy earth becoming ever darker and more fecund-looking. He has turned over a large enough patch now, a black square emerging, uniformity amid the verdant chaos. He drags up some long offcuts of wood, to make a raised bed. The wood frames the garden, gives it a structure. Jake is just hammering the last piece into place, when he sees Dr Peter striding purposively towards him. No flitting sideways into hedgerows this time; he wears an air of thoughtful intent as he puffs his way up.

'Hail, fellow. I see you haven't been defeated by the horticultural challenge. I knew there was a naturalist beneath that tough exterior.'

Jake brings out coffee, which he sets on the ground. Dr Peter has already started digging the final corner.

'What do you think I should plant, Dr Peter?'

'Well autumn isn't absolutely the best time for planting, but there is much you can still do. I've been musing on your patch on my walk here, you know. So rare to get a tabula rasa, botanically speaking, if you follow me. I think we should have a section for late autumn harvesting from, say, here to there.' He gestures with a trowel he has picked up, scattering earth about him like a mole. 'We'll plant lettuce, and radish, and mustard leaf. Some hardy turnips and carrots to one side. And then in the main body of the garden we'll get you started for spring: some broad beans and peas (I like the name 'Aquadulce Claudia' when it comes to beans, you know, "Claudia's sweet water" in common parlance, God knows why); and then some onions and garlic too. That'll get the garden going, and then we'll really go for it in the new year.' He nods sagely and with evident satisfaction.

'Did you only come here for the garden?'

'No, I wanted you to tell me where we were in the Sabine investigation.'

'"We" are not really anywhere. And it isn't really an

investigation. They're going to open the grave once the order is approved, and then we shall see. They then might want to know from me who took the bones.'

'I feel sanguine that you would not, as you might say, shop a fellow gardener.'

'Not if you tell me everything you know about it, and convince me that there is something worth chasing here.'

Dr Peter sits on a wooden border, his boots scuffing the flattened grass, bony knees jutting against his old corduroys. 'I feel I do owe you that, dear boy. Yes indeed. Well, how to frame my story? I probably lost my head a little over Sabine, as did your uncle, you know. It wasn't as if we thought she would feel romantically towards a couple of old goats like us. But we felt protective towards her, and flattered by her willingness to be friendly in return. I often wondered why she was so generous like that.' He claps his hands on his thighs, energized for a second. 'Yes, that was the thing about her, she was generous above all else.

'Anyway, she was stuck in that farm. You'll have seen what it must have been like: the imposing matriarch, the three boys or rather men, who glower and fester, and stoop too close. They knew Sabine had no family, lacked protection, so they could work her hard, expect her to be on call for anything. Fruit-picking, shop work, cleaning. I think Arthur and I became surrogate uncles for a while, which was the best we could hope for.

'Then she met Rose, who soon swam into our waters, shifty as a shark. He was – is, I suppose – attractive and young and flattering. They started going to Meryton for dinner and the cinema, and were for quite a long time boyfriend and girlfriend. But then all of a sudden it was

151

souring. She stopped mentioning him, and started to lose that sunny bounce, that friendly effervescence she had. We didn't know what had happened. Two weeks later she was dead.'

'Is it not possible that she did simply fall? Occam's razor, you know, the simplest explanation.'

'You do have a philosophical bent for a flatfoot. Perhaps why you're now in the more respectable role of gardener. It is possible, but I don't feel it's likely. A young healthy woman, who never got drunk, all of sudden falls down off an old building and dies. I wasn't there, of course, but nobody seemed interested in investigating. The coroner said it was an accident. The police round here can't do much. But I believed she deserved the decency of our *interest*, of examination, and she never got it. Your uncle mentioned you – he was proud of you, you know – as someone we could consult, but it didn't seem practicable. And then time moved on, inexorably as it always does. Nature always ignores death in its pressing passage to onward survival, doesn't it? I think it was Virginia Woolf who said that "The very stone one kicks with one's boot will outlast Shakespeare."' He kicks at a piece of rubble on the top of the soil to make the point.

'Anyway, then all these years later, I learned you were living here and I thought I could ask you to take a look. But why would you, why should you? I'm just a blethering botanist. Oh I know how I'm patronized around here. The local wonk, the hedgerow bore. Why would you take me seriously? Well one evening I was visiting Sabine's grave and I thought of a means of inveigling you. That crypt is always empty and it wasn't too much effort to open her grave up. Not that it wasn't unsettling. But nature

152

and death are no strangers to me really, and I'm close to one and coming ever closer to the other. I opened the coffin, and saw her. The life seeped from her, just the carapace, the ossified remnants. Those half-bleached bones. The smell clung in the air, so I washed them outside, and then you know the rest. I'm sure I've committed some act of felony, but I refuse to be sorry.'

Jake is not angry. If anything, he is impressed, even moved. The power of friendship persisting after death. The refusal to let bones rest unjustly.

'I don't think you should be. And, look, I can't promise anything, but I know she meant something to you and to Arthur. And I used to pride myself on speaking for the long departed. Let's see what the police say, but I give you my word I will do what I can.'

Dr Peter's eyes are watery, and he suddenly looks rather frail. But they shake hands, as if a deal has been concluded; his is warm, and surprisingly soft.

Shopped

Jake stops by the Nook for his weekly provisions. He gets fruit and vegetables, which come, he notes wryly, from Smiths' Farm. He also picks up whatever local meat comes in: often it is lamb or chicken, but sometimes Sarah gets a delivery from the local poacher. Venison occasionally, but more often rabbit, its carcass peeled and wrapped, curled foetally in wax paper. Jake has dug a pit in the ground a couple of yards from the big tree next to his house. He fills it with charred wood from one of the house fires, with some fresh wood as well, and it becomes terrifically hot. Sometimes he puts in flat stones, which he dives for and collects from the bottom of the lake, and fries bacon and eggs. Or sausages and the local black pudding, which sizzle and sputter and give off thick, heartening scents. Other times he uses two sticks with natural 'V' formations at one end, which he has foraged from Agatha Wood, and spits a bigger hunk of meat across the smouldering ashes, like an entire rabbit, which shrinks and crinkles in the heat. Potatoes and root vegetables often lie, wrapped in cabbage leaves, wet from the lake, steaming in one corner. It is a pleasant, sustaining ritual.

Jake likes going to the Nook also, to stop himself becoming too introverted, and too silent. Sometimes the sound of his own voice surprises him, scraped from his throat, out of use like an old piece of machinery pulled from storage. Sarah has remained friendly, even become more tender in her attention as time passes. Not maternal exactly – her children have grown and gone – but concerned for his welfare. When not at the shop she spends much of her time watching cookery channels on her television, and is always foisting her inspired concoctions upon him. Today, she has a bowl of deep-fried clams ('clam popcorn'), and some potato cakes flavoured with local watercress. She hands Jake a platter, and motions him to one of the barrels in the corner of the room.

'I don't see you so much with Livia these days, Jake.'

'No, she thought I was taking too much time from her. What with Di, and her practice and all that.'

Sarah leans forward confidentially. 'You know she got warned off, don't you?'

'What does that mean?'

'Put it this way, a couple of the locals had a word with her to say that she needed their goodwill. A vet has to have the trust of the farmers to have any business at all. They said she'd lose that trust if she carried on messing around about old bones with you.'

Jake feels a pang of anger, and of guilt. He can imagine the position in which Livia has been put.

'I didn't know, no. Who was it?'

'I wasn't told. It was pretty much a community thing, it seemed.'

155

'Each time I hear about folk not wanting me to care about the bones, the more I think there's something for me to find out.'

'You don't need this either, Jake. You came here for peace, didn't you? King Arthur used to say that was the greatest gift he could give anyone. A chance just to be free.'

'Maybe peace is too lonely.'

'You could be social, I reckon, without becoming involved in solving a local mystery that might not even be a mystery. And that nobody wants solved.'

'Do you mean that? What if we have found someone who has been killed?'

'Nothing is going to bring her back, whatever you do. And it might drive away your friends, or folk who might be your friends.'

'Are you going to stop being my friend, Sarah?'

Her face softens, her eyes twinkling in the dusk of the shop. She grabs a handful of salty, spicy clams and crunches them in her teeth, which are unexpectedly white.

'Ah, well some of us are too old to worry about things. Plus, I'm a shopkeeper, ain't I, I have to look after a customer.'

On his way back, Jake takes a detour past Livia's house. Her car is out front so he knows she is home, and he thinks of her, ensconced in a warm kitchen, her family life compact, and undeniably present, reliable and solid, like a structure in itself. He examines his reflection in a window, shabby and windblown, and finds it hard to see himself fitting into that ordered, that modern domesticity. He walks away disconsolate, scuffling at stones in the path before he turns off just before the river to strike out for home.

He is putting away the shopping when he hears a knock on the door. It is Watson, raising himself up and down on his toes as he waits. He lifts an eyebrow of greeting and Jake welcomes him in.

They sit at the table drinking iced tea, which Jake has made using a recipe he found in one of his American detective novels, steeping it all day in a sunny spot. Watson takes off his thick waxed jacket, the same shade as the tree outside, and pulls out a file.

'At the very least it's good exercise coming to see you, Jake, though I discover that I'm not so limber as I used to be. In any event: to catch things up. We got the order, though with some – I have to say rather forcibly expressed – scepticism. And that scepticism was justified. We pulled out a skeleton from a coffin which you assured me had been desecrated and robbed. So I wanted to come here and see why you've made me look foolish.'

Jake is surprised. He is an old hand at reading people, and was convinced in the good faith of Dr Peter. And the news about Livia's warning has been further circumstantial evidence in support of his own instinct: there is foul play here.

'All I can say is that I'm more confident than ever that something isn't right here.' He decides to tell Watson about Arthur's journals, but that doesn't seem to weigh heavily in the balance. Watson is diplomatic, but firm.

'That simply shows that an old man, with rather mixed feelings on the subject, may have been suspicious. It doesn't tell me anything. You know that. I need a witness to the original grave-robbery.'

Jake has an idea. 'Have you examined the bones – the ones actually in the grave – properly?'

'No, I haven't. Why would I? There is a grave, it has bones in it, there can be no obvious grounds to do anything more.'

'Let me put it this way to you. I strongly believe – though I realize I haven't given all the reasons why – that the grave was emptied. You have a grave full of bones. That is important; that gives us an act to investigate. What if someone knew Sabine's bones had been taken, and replaced them?'

'You're now conjuring the idea of competing ghouls rampaging across this quiet patch of English countryside, engaged willy-nilly in grave-robbing. You might once have been a successful copper, Jake, but I worry you've become a fantasist. And you don't exactly look like a picture-perfect credible witness any more.'

'There's one way of proving that for sure. Test the grave bones. If they are of a woman of Sabine's age and dimensions, then you can dismiss me as a recluse and a half-wit, and we'll never speak again. But, chief, here's the thing: if they are the wrong bones, then you have proof that someone is trying to conceal something. And we go from a doubtful case to an active one.'

Watson sinks back in his chair, pursing his lips thoughtfully. 'The easier route would be for you to tell me why you're so confident. Do you know who took the bones originally?'

'I believe I do, but I have promised not to tell you.'

'I could arrest you for obstruction, I suppose.'

'You've just told me nobody believes there is a case to answer, so I can't be guilty of obstructing anything.'

Watson laughs in recognition, a homely sound. 'That's true. You know, Jake, I pride myself on judging people, but I can't make you out. You're young, and fit, and bright. But you're festering here, so much so that you're involving yourself in something that may turn out to be a spectre, a symptom of your own problems. So I think that on one hand, and yet on another I find myself believing you, and in you.' He pauses again, and slaps his hands on his thighs with a sudden, spirited movement. 'And if you believe in someone, I always say, you have to follow through. I'll get those bones analysed, Jake, not least because the terms of the order give me leeway to do so. But I will be circumspect in who I tell about this, and I caution you to be the same. And, whatsoever emerges, then you and I will have words with one another about how we have got here.'

Jake feels relief, and admiration. 'Chief, I think that's fair. And, for what it's worth, it's what I would have done in your shoes.'

Watson lingers to discuss gardening, and construction. The materials for the shower are visible from the kitchen window, and Jake explains what he is planning. Watson leaves with a wink, and a knowing glance. Jake's brain is tingling, the thrill of a case, of a chase, if this turns out to be one. As he sees it, somebody has worked out that Dr Peter stole the bones, that the grave was under examination, and that they could – maybe even had to – prevent any possible investigation by replacing the bones with someone else's. Such would be the actions of someone nervous about discovery. Such would – he has to think it – be the actions of a murderer.

Gone fishing

It is a warm morning, the first in a while. The rising sun an angry orange glare in the sky. Jake has found a couple of fishing rods in the shed by the lake and thinks it might be fun to try something new. There are salmon and trout in the river, he has heard, especially where it twists and ravels into the quieter backwaters. He can get bait from the Nook on the way there.

He breaks his walk at the sheep paddock, which he has been calling Morse Field. It was where he first met Livia and he sits for a spell, watching the animals mill and murmur, preoccupied with nothing. There is a sheltered corner by the stone wall, which clings to the warmth of the sun, and he is content to lie on the ground there, which has lost most of the morning's dew, his head pillowed on the springy turf. He is in jeans and clunky boots, a thick blue jumper with nothing on underneath. He wonders whether he should find a way of trimming his beard, which he scratches contemplatively.

A shadow falls across him as he stares into the middle distance. Livia.

'I hope you're not bothering these sheep. I get the blame if any of them start acting oddly.'

'I find them strangely soothing to watch. They don't seem to have much to worry about.'

'Other than erysipelas, scabby mouth, pulpy kidney, brucellosis, and so on. Plus the risk of being stunned to death and eaten.'

'They don't seem to let that bother them. That one there has been staring at the trough and defecating for the last twenty-five minutes.'

'I'm rather glad you weren't tempted to join him.' She laughs brightly. 'I'm so pleased to find you here, Jake. You didn't come and see me, even when I left the sign in Sherlock Beech.'

'I stopped looking, to be honest. I didn't want to be looming over you. And I don't want to make life difficult either.'

She sits down next to him, her waterproof leggings rustling, and nudges him over with a twist of her hip and thigh. The fabric is steel grey and glints in the generous light. Her brown hair is tied back austerely in a bun, which exposes her full face, green eyes flashing. A stray bit of fringe bounces gaily.

'That's my fault for making you feel like that. I was worried when we bumped into each other that night. If I'd not seen you until the next day, I probably would never have said anything. I cursed myself for it later, you know. I don't have many . . .' a pause, 'well, friends here, and you have been a real blessing coming to this place, a real, I don't know, happy event.' She rests her hand on his knee, and then gives it a gentle shove. 'And I can't believe you would take me so literally or seriously.'

Jake stares up at the sky for a moment. 'Livia, I know you were warned about me. Which means I'm probably touching a nerve, which means there's probably more to come when we get confirmation about those bones. I don't want to drag you into anything sinister or dangerous. I'm not always sure, especially, late at night, that I want to be dragged in myself.'

'That's just it. I don't have to be an amateur sleuth – that's the word your books use, isn't it? – and if you carry on your meddlesome ways, that's fine. I don't have to get involved. But that doesn't mean we have to stop talking to each other.' She leans her leg into his. 'It's a lonely old place if you've nobody to be close to. So, friends?'

She extends a hand, which he clasps. Her palm firm and smooth and cool. 'Friends.'

Jake feels a thrill of elation; there is no other word for it. He cannot think of a time when a connection has signified more. He knows it doesn't mean that Livia is talking about anything other than friendship, but friend-ship is not nothing; it is important and, he now realizes, life-enhancing, life-giving even.

'Deal. Before that, tell me who spoke to you. It might be helpful.'

Livia explains how she was finishing up at what she grandly calls her 'practice', two rooms at the far end of Parvum, when Rose came in. They hadn't talked much in recent months, apart from at the Aethelmere fire, and there was a certain coolness between them. He said that he was speaking for many in the area when he expressed concern

162

about the new arrival at Little Sky, the flurry of activity around the bones, and the prospect of police activity in the area.

Livia had said: 'I don't see why anyone should worry. It's just checking to make sure nothing untoward has happened.'

Rose placed his hand on hers, leaning his weight on it until it began to hurt. 'Well people are worried that you're helping that outsider cause mischief. And the sort of people I'm talking about are the sort of people who pay your wages, so you can keep yourself in luxury like this. Look, Liv, I'm just trying to be a friend to you. No good can come from you causing a problem here. No good for you or Diana.'

Jake interrupts. 'Do you think he was threatening her?'

Livia shakes her head, wrinkling her nose and wrapping her arms around her knees. 'Not overtly. But it was all so clear that my life would be made tricky. And I'm ashamed, you know. I'm ashamed it worked.'

'It's just being rational. You did the right thing. I wonder whether Rose is involved in all this, or just a representative of people who are, or just holding a candle for you and happy to stop you having your head turned by the exciting new arrival.'

'Don't get ahead of yourself.'

'I don't know, some people go for this sort of hobo chic. Let's agree to leave any investigating to me, but it doesn't mean we can't speak about it, does it?'

'Absolutely not. Tell me how far you've got.'

He quickly fills her in, and she sits quietly for a moment. He is thinking how much he would like to see Rose squirming on the floor, but also how little that would help things for Livia. As she leans back, she knocks into the fishing rods, which clatter against the wall.

'I didn't know you were a fisherman.'

'I'm giving it a go for the first time. Do you want to join me? Then we can be two clueless people next to a river together.'

'Speak for yourself. My dad was an angler, and desperate for his daughter to be one. I was thinking I could teach you. I can always bunk off for a couple of hours.' Her face gleams with mischief.

They stop off at the Nook as Jake was planning, and buy bread and cheese and a big glass bottle of local cider, as well as some bait. Sarah's eyes are smiling, but her face is as impassive as ever, as she leans against the counter and watches them leave. Livia says she knows a good spot two miles away, and they take their time, the air clean in their lungs, the light bright around them. The river bends and splits around an island, leaving a miniature lagoon, the water clear down to its muddy bottom, little glimpses of fish darting. They drop their things, and then Livia guides them up a steep incline. There, a spring is burbling greedily, rushing down into the surrounding fields where watercress is grown. She takes the cider and wedges it tight into the opening. Jake helps her; the water is so cold his arm is numb for a second.

They go back to the river, and Livia demonstrates how to bait the hook, him awkward and clumsy, the maggots roiling in sinister fashion, and then how to cast into the murmurous waters.

'There's trout here, even out of season, but we're not really allowed to keep them. Though you're in the land of poachers' rights now, so I'm not sure it matters.'

Jake pulls across a thick branch fallen from an old oak, its bark cushioned with lichen, and they sit on it together, silent for a few minutes, watching the floats bob in the water.

'So how are you surviving in Little Sky, Jake?'

'I mean, I don't feel happy all day, and sometimes I feel a sort of lurching inside, a sense of dread, like a ghost of old anxiety. But I look out at the land, my little piece of sky, and think I probably made the right decision.'

'What's it like to have such emptiness in your life? I was wondering about that, while I was waiting to see you again. Everything I do is built around Di, and a bit around work. I know my schedule every day. I have chores, pick-ups, washing, bathtime, Post-it notes and to-do lists. And you have none of that. Literally, in the case of bathtime.'

'And yet you're sitting freely with me in the middle of the day, unsuccessfully fishing.'

'I didn't say I worked especially hard. But you know what I mean.'

'I do, and I've never had that flurry, that clutter, that always-on part of life, because I never became a dad. And I worry maybe I'm shallow to be glad about that, and then I see a drawing on your fridge, or hear the shouts and squeals from a garden or a playground, and think whatever I do I'll always be the loser in life. Because my life is transient, unsticky; it will pass and that will be it. You have a focus, something to cling to and to cling to you. I guess nothing is perfect.' He sighs deeply. 'There's something profound for you.'

His float is suddenly pulled under the water, and he nearly falls off the log in shock, emitting a high-pitched note of surprise. Livia reaches over, almost helpless with laughter, and together they strike in the way she's taught him, fixing the fish upon the hook. He starts reeling it in, Livia making quiet mocking noises near his ear. She has let her hands rest on his hips for a moment; he can feel their clothes touching, the gentle breeze of her breath. The fish emerges on the hook, a squirming, vibrant thing, grey and sleek and spotted like a leopard, with a hint of pinks and yellows merging like oil in its centre. Jake is squeamish to touch it, which sets Livia off again, before she takes over and removes the hook.

'Not bad at all for a virgin. Do you want to knock it on the head?'

Jakes signals the negative. 'This is too nice a day for that. Let it go off and have a busy life with its rainbow family.'

The fish plops into the river from Livia's arms and disappears, wriggling for freedom. Livia washes her hands, and then stands straight, pushing the stray hairs from her face as she draws breath. 'How about some lunch?'

They find a sunny patch to sit, and Jake lays out the bread and cheese on their wrappings. They have no cutlery, so break off hunks, pushing the cheese into the fluffy white insides. It is salty and sharp, softened by the thick sweetness of the dough. Jake retrieves the cider, which is now breathtakingly cold, tasting of the orchard and faintly of rust. A heron swoops over them, gliding magisterially before landing on the water, its dignity slightly ruffled by the splash. It then stands sentinel before them, eyeing the water below. This all feels unreal to Jake, but the ground is firm beneath him, Livia's hand is soft when they touch as the bottle is passed. Her neck is long and brown and beautiful when she swallows.

She catches sight of her watch and snorts. 'I better get walking. I need to sober up a bit before I get back to work. Thankfully, it's just admin this afternoon, I think.'

They weave slowly home, arms brushing, which they both affect not to notice. Jake is determined not to do too much, not to make a pleasant situation awkward, not to scare her off. As they reach the village, she slaps him lightly on the arm.

'And next time I leave a message on Sherlock, make sure you don't ignore me. It's not good for my fragile ego.'

They hug farewell, Jake clasping her to him tightly. Their faces become close. He thinks of kissing her, but remembers his intention to take care, so he makes no move, content to stare into her eyes to see if he can somehow gauge what she is feeling. He watches the door close behind her, and exhales as if he has been holding his breath all day.

Police procedural

—

After the sauna, the shower is pretty easy to build, and Jake does much of the basic assembly himself, enjoying for the first time in his life the sense that he might be becoming more practical and self-sufficient. Mack comes to help with the plumbing, and soon water is gushing hot from the showerhead, which has been taken, Mack informs him, from an old Victorian watering can. A scalding shower after exercise is a luxury. And every day Jake stands for many minutes, steaming in the fresh air, feeling cleansed and calm. He buys some old-fashioned soap from Sarah, made in one of the towns at the end of the valley, and some shampoo for his hair and beard. Standards are rising, he thinks to himself. And the true joy of deprivation is the elevation of small pleasures: warm water feels better after the cold, friendly words resonate more after silence, a hot fire is comforting on a frosty night. Life should be as simple as that, perhaps.

As he comes out of the Nook one evening, a foggy dark poised thickly around him, he sees Rose standing with two men, their shapes backlit by a house lamp. Jake gets nearer and sees they are Clifford from next door, and Davey from Smiths' Farm. His heart beats faster against his chest, but he feels he should make his point. Rose smiles slyly as Jake comes up.

'Good evening, Mr Policeman.'

'Good evening. I'm not a policeman, but I used to be a very good one. Good at solving puzzles, digging up dirt, getting in the way. And although you might stop people round here helping me, you should know that I don't need any help. I'm pretty good at handling things on my own. Does that make sense to you all?'

His chest is swelling; he is making himself look big, he realizes, to tower over them. He pats Rose on the shoulder with the flat of his hand, staggering him back slightly. And he turns to the other two, inviting a physical response. They both look to the ground. Rose's face is impassive, and he says nothing as Jake walks away. But Jake hears him a few seconds later, as no doubt he is intended to.

'Just another weird fuck living in that house. I hope it doesn't get dangerous for him there.'

Jake stops, but then walks on. No point in things turning actually violent. He just wanted to set himself up as a solo operator, to give Livia some space. He gets close to the river, and is about to leave the road to strike out for home, when a car pulls up. Watson is driving, his long body folded in on itself in the car's small space, like a collapsed deckchair.

The window comes down. 'I called Sarah and she said you'd be on your way home. God it's inconvenient not being able to phone you. Even Poirot had use of a telephone.'

'I know. And Sherlock Holmes could always telegram. I am perverse.' Jake opens the passenger door and gets in.

'I can't even drop you home, because it's such a wretchedly long old hike from the road. Can I take you to a pub for a drink, then bring you back?'

Jake is momentarily nervous. He hasn't been around crowds of any sort for months now; he flinches at the thought of contact with others, of noisiness, and clamour, of proximity. People's breath and sweat, the exudations of life. But he cannot really refuse.

'Somewhere quiet at least. I've not been around people much.'

'You've been concentrating on a single person, rather than people, perhaps. Oh, ignore me. I'm just an old romantic at heart.'

'You certainly aren't your average copper, I'll give you that.'

Watson knows a pub on the outskirts of Meryton that is quiet. A smoky fire, the sweet, cloying scent of spilled beer, a pensive dog staring lugubriously out of the window. Thick, scarred oaken beams criss-crossing low ceilings. The landlord seems to recognize Watson – police relationships are always important in the countryside – and nods him into the snug, which is empty. Jake orders a lager, which arrives cold, condensation clouding the pint glass. Watson gets a Scotch and soda, and drinks a third off right away.

'So those bones were analysed a day ago. At first I thought they were Sabine's and we were back to square one. They are of a woman in her thirties. But we looked closer, thank God, and they're too old to be Sabine's, by fifty years at least. And they show little sign of a traumatic death, indeed there are quite a few signifiers of serious cancer having entered the bone. I went back to the crypt yesterday and found a nearby grave of a young woman who died in 1963, life "tragically brought short by a serious illness, now living painlessly with God". I'm getting it opened up to check. But whoever it is, it means that Sabine's bones have been removed and then replaced.

'The question is why? And by whom? The powers-that-be are inclined to dismiss it all as a practical joke, though our prediction coming true has stiffened their resolve somewhat.'

Jake takes a sip of his drink, which fizzes pleasantly. The room is quiet apart from the crackle of the fire, and the occasional sound of a car droning past.

'I know who took the bones. And he did it to make us investigate the death. He had nothing to do with replacing them. My working theory is that whoever replaced them wanted us not to investigate how Sabine died too closely, which makes me think there's something awry here. Are there prints?'

'We've taken a whole jumble of them off both graves. We'll keep them in case you get a suspect.'

'Am I going to be doing that then?'

Watson lets the pause linger. 'You know, I discovered something interesting from a procedural perspective. They changed the law a few years ago. Terrorism, probably, the reason. It normally is. Anyway, I'm allowed to make use of retired police officers in good standing at my discretion, and that of the chief constable. So how about that?'

Jake takes a longer sip, froth catching the hairs of his moustache. 'I don't really want to go back into harness at all. I mean that. I'm not cleaning myself up, or part-nering off, or attending health and safety lectures.'

'I understand all that. This would mean that you have delegated authority to ask questions and to make a report, if needed. I can give you temporary identification.' He slaps a laminated card on the table, Jake's pre-wilderness features staring back up at him.

Jake picks it up and taps it on the table in front of him. 'I'll take this and carry on ferreting around. I'm committed to doing that for my own pride in any event. Let's meet once a week, somewhere I can get to on foot.'

'Let's say Wednesday evenings at seven, where the road meets the river. You have my mobile too. I know yours no longer works, but I am sure you can get in touch if you have to. I'll begin the slow process of confirming Sabine's bones, by DNA if possible. And I'll speak to the folk who looked into her death in the first place, though it seems there wasn't much work done on it. What are you going to do?'

'Take another look at the farm where she died. Ask some questions, provoke a reaction or two.'

'Be careful. You're on your own out here.'

Jake does realize that. On the one hand, Little Sky is remote, in the black depths of the countryside at night, hard to find and explore; on the other, it is sprawling, difficult to defend, and easy to come quietly upon. It is not something he can worry about too much, he reflects. Renunciation, as a philosophy, must also mean a disavowal of fear, the setting aside of worrisome lingering on the potential for harm.

As they leave the pub, Jake idly picks up a copy of *The Sunday Times* from a nearby table. The splash headline

172

is virtually meaningless to him, and he realizes it is the first news he has seen in a very long time. He doesn't miss it, or even feel compelled to find out more. What was it that Livia had told him? About that time in 1930 when the BBC said there was no news. He feels like that all the time now. His world is all that is within his own grasp and no more: he has food, exercise, emotion, even professional curiosity. He needs no more news than that.

Watson drops him in the pitch, almost purpled, black of the country night. It takes him a moment to acclimatize himself, and then the moon peeks forth from behind a gauzy cloud. It is full and richly pale, still generous in its haughty effulgence, enough to guide him home. When he arrives, he takes the keys he had found a few weeks before and – for the first time – locks up the front and back doors. He feels self-contained, protected for the moment.

Weed

After lunch the next day, Jake decides to visit Dr Peter, to let him know that things are progressing, and to try to get some more information about Sabine and her life. On the way, he takes an old mauve towel and ties it to Sherlock Beech. He wants to spend time with Livia again, for all sorts of reasons swirling in his mind. He hopes she will come to see the changes he has made to Little Sky; he feels proprietorial for the first time.

Dr Peter's house is large and ramshackle; thrown up at some point in the last couple of centuries, it sags and twists like a piece of old linen. The roof is thatched, and the front was once whitewashed, but is now a dirty grey. To its rear is a small labourer's cottage, huffing a cloud of smoke from a redbrick chimney. It is a model of concision and order, care and attention, and contrasts starkly with the larger building and the surrounding gardens. Jake remembers that Mack lives close by, and senses his effortless competence as an influence on the cottage.

As he is walking up the drive, Dr Peter emerges from

his house, as always like an animal from a burrow; small, fast movements, looking out and back in again, patting his pockets and murmuring to himself. He waves cheerily to Jake, and darts towards him.

'Dear fellow and member of the Watch, so pleased to see you. I was going for my constitutional, but that can be deferred, if not disregarded altogether. Can I invite you for a drink? At this time of the day, I often have some homemade dandelion and burdock; I'm sure I can tempt you.'

Jake can remember that taste from his youth, part sweet and part medicinal. It had been fizzy at least, which had always set it apart as a treat. As he is recalling it, Dr Peter springs back inside and re-emerges with a tray of a peculiarly ugly floral design and two beaded glasses of a plum-coloured concoction.

They sit at a picnic table in the middle of a messy lawn, the grass lush and healthy, intertwined with a profusion of wildflowers and what look to Jake like weeds.

Dr Peter notices his attention. 'I can't abide a manicured garden. It defeats the point of having a garden at all. You cannot discipline nature if you truly want it to thrive. We must remember our Hopkins.' He closes his eyes and recites in a ponderous tone:

'What would the world be, once bereft
Of wet and of wildness? Let them be left,
O let them be left, wildness and wet;
Long live the weeds and the wilderness yet.'

Jake is half-listening while also examining the table, which has been beautifully made and varnished to a chocolate hue. Dr Peter gives it a resounding tap. 'Mack's work, of course. I know he's been helping you up at that giant pile of yours. He's quite the craftsman, thank God. I'm not sure what I'd do without him living so close.'

Jake takes a sip, and prevents himself from wincing. His adult palette is rather less forgiving than his childhood one was. He tells Dr Peter about the case, that the police are becoming more interested, and of his own deputization of sorts.

Dr Peter becomes animated at once. 'Splendid, splendid. You are a modern Gawain, stoutly accepting a quest whatever your personal feelings.'

'I thought you said I was Galahad, but I'm not sure I know the difference. You can help me, Dr P. Whoever replaced the bones did so because they wanted to forestall the investigation. That means they knew the original bones had been taken. Who did you tell?'

Dr Peter takes in his hands the wisps of white hair above his ears, and twirls them meditatively. 'I confided in nobody fully. But I think Sarah knew. And I think at least Davey from the farm suspected: he wasn't far away when I came out of the church, and could have seen something. My worries about Sabine were not exactly a state secret at the time.'

'Was there anything pointing to murder, or to a possible suspect?'

'She had just fallen out with Rose, of course, so there is always the spurned lover theory. I just had a terrible feeling about that farm, and it got worse towards the end of her life. She became quiet and distracted in the last couple of weeks. I wonder if something happened to her there.'

'I was reading Arthur's journals, and he said he saw some glints in the distance during one of their walks, and I wonder if she might have been followed. That ring any bells with you?'

Dr Peter is thoughtful for a moment. 'I don't think so. But we all know that the countryside conceals danger with invisible ease. But I can't recall anybody following her. Apart from your uncle of course.'

'Do you think he could have meant her ill?'

Dr Peter is sipping his drink meditatively, and puts it down with solid authority. 'God, no. I knew him very well, and I knew his feelings for her, not least because they mirrored mine so closely.'

'Do you know he stumbled on her naked swimming, and tried to repeat it?'

A faint smile. 'I'm not sure any of us in good conscience could deny that particular pleasure. Arthur had lustful thoughts, I'm sure, but was a gentleman throughout.' He hems awkwardly, then leans forward. 'Did he mention me at all in his journal?'

Jake pauses to consider the polite response. 'Only as a scholar and a friend.'

'And occasional gooseberry, I imagine.' Jake concedes the point with a nod. 'No, we were united in our regard for Sabine, and our sense that all was not quite well around her.'

'But you have no actual evidence of anything?'

'Dear boy, if I had, I could have made my plea direct to the police, and saved this rather macabre dance of speculation we've been indulging in.'

'Well, can you keep your ear to the ground, and let me know if anything occurs to you?'

'Of course. I shall be the determined helpmeet, the amateur sleuth, the Wimsey of Caelum Parvum.'

He and Jake spend the next hour or so talking of other things, primarily books they have both read. Dr Peter's thirst for knowledge is seemingly insatiable, and he is a very generous companion when it comes to sharing what he has learned. The afternoon is beginning its inevitable wane, temperature dropping, the light fading, as Jake gets up to leave.

He is mooching thoughtfully, wandering down the lane outside of Dr Peter's house, when he notices someone a hundred or so yards ahead, who drops in and out of sight as the pathway twists and turns in its infuriating way. Jake recognizes the insouciant lope, the longish black hair of Rose, whose name, he notices, keeps coming up whenever the death of Sabine is discussed. He idly keeps him at a distance, tracking him without trying, until he comes to suspect that Rose is heading towards Smiths' Farm.

Clouds bustle together promptly as if late for a meeting, and a slight drizzle starts to fall. Rose is now increasingly lost in the murk, until he decides to switch on his torch and head off-road up towards the land around the farm. Jake follows the wavering beam with relative ease. The ground is soft and his footsteps make no sound. All that can be heard is the hooting of an owl, and the restless scamperings within the hedgerows. Rose has bypassed the farmhouse and is looping his way around to a bright light on the other side. It is, in fact, a series of bright lights, emanating from three vast greenhouses, each one as big as Jake's own place.

Jake crouches behind the final hedge before the ground descends towards the structures. He watches Rose go into the middle greenhouse, and emerge ten minutes later, carrying a large knapsack, which clearly has something heavy in it. He then makes another stop in the furthest building, before effortfully slinging the bag onto his shoulders. He picks up a bike, which had been leaning against a wall, and wheels it past Jake, his eyes darting around the whole time, a look of pained concentration on his usually sanguine features. Jake remains ducked-down, securely concealed in the gloom where the light doesn't quite penetrate. He waits five minutes, counting the seconds, before raising his head again, and feels – with an instinct that has become honed by his recent isolation – that he is alone once more.

The whole thing strikes him as somewhat suspicious. Rose doing something in the farm alone at night. There was something furtive in his movements, cautious, especially at the end. As a policeman, Jake would need a warrant, and probable cause about a crime, to go and look at these greenhouses. As a semi-official police consultant, is he similarly restrained? The trick, he concludes, is not getting caught, and – as he is here – he decides to have a poke around.

He gives himself no more than fifteen minutes' searching time, and sneaks forward to the middle greenhouse. Inside it is light, and hot, the noise of electronic machinery burbling in the background. There are large soil beds in front of him supporting stout tomato plants, and behind them beans and peas. The smell is of fecundity and plenty. But there is something else there too, a cloying sweetness. Jake walks past the beds to another door. The greenhouse is in the structure of a giant triangle, with the roof descending at an angle, so this second room is smaller and more enclosed.

He pushes at the door, and the smell becomes recognizable: inside is a jungle of cannabis plants, writhing and twisting around each other. There is so much profusion it makes him feel heady. He grabs a leaf and sniffs; it is strong stuff. This explains Rose's circumspect attitude, and also perhaps his role in the local economy. He is not sure how it helps his theories around Sabine's murder, though.

Jake is puzzling over this as he pushes his way out of the greenhouse, his jumper damp under his arms. The brisk evening refreshes him and he pauses silhouetted in front of the light, as he breathes deeply. Only then does he notice that Rose is standing, leaning against his bike, watching him closely.

'What are you doing trespassing here?'

Jake's pulse is racing, but he remains outwardly impassive. He has a degree of moral advantage, given the cannabis plantation he has just discovered, and is determined not to be faced down by a drug dealer.

'Just nosing around. I told you I was going to be looking into what happened to Sabine. She died here, so I thought I'd have a poke about. And then I discovered your little market garden project back there.'

'You have no right to be here.'

'Let's just say I don't think you'll be calling the police on me. Are all these greenhouses full of weed? That's quite a big operation.'

Rose looks uncertain for a second, unsure whether to defend or attack.

Jake walks towards him. 'The thing is, I'm not bothered by weed-growing. I have no crusade to fight there. I want to know about Sabine. You know the police are thinking of reopening an investigation into her death?'

Rose gulps visibly, before trying to put confidence into his voice, which rings out loud enough in the night. The drizzle has stopped, and the breeze has dropped away.

'Why would they do that?'

'For one, her bones were dug up and placed in the bag for St Aethelmere's Day, and then they were replaced in her grave by someone, or some people, who didn't want that to be discovered. So there's some sort of foul play going on. Every time I ask about her I get evasion, or awkwardness, or threatening behaviour. And you told Livia – who you must know has no real involvement in any of this – to back away from what I'm looking at. You see, you've got yourself a problem here, my friend. I could tip off the police, get you arrested on the drug distribution, and then let them lean into you on the old murder. Or you could talk to me now.'

'The drug threat is a bluff, and we both know it.' Jake wonders if he could really be confident about that. 'But I'll play along. I had a great time with Sabine. We were close, and then she became withdrawn and then it ended. Sadly, but not with a fight. And then she was dead.'

Jake tries to read him, but his face is in shadow, his voice pitched at the same arrogant lilt as before.

'You're not wanted here, because you're a copper and that could be bad for business. This is a big operation; you think that comes with a casual attitude to police interest?'

'Is that why you warned Livia off?'

'I warned her off because you're bad news, and no good can come from you stirring up trouble.'

'Who told you to warn me off?'

'It doesn't matter. Why should you care about Sabine

anyway? Only that fool of a doctor really thought there was something wrong.'

'Well, it looks like he might have been right. Why else were the bones removed and replaced?' Jake is careful not to imply Dr Peter's involvement here.

Rose shifts the weight of his pack, clenches the handlebars of the bike and starts to walk away. 'Who knows? This place is full of jokers. They have to mess around because it's so boring round here, as you'll have seen.'

Jake stops the bike with one hand, and pushes it to the ground, where it lands with a thud. He draws his face close to Rose's, sees the dark stubble on his cheeks, his eyes a sickly yellow, coffee and cigarettes on his breath. His body is taut with tension, narrow but firm, like a strung longbow.

'I try not to make threats. But if I hear of Livia being spoken to like that again, I'm coming after you, and snitching this whole operation.'

'I get it, I get it. You're into her. So was I, mate, for a while.' He raises his hands, placatory

'Like you were into Sabine?'

This provokes something. Rose grabs Jake's top, and pulls him closer. 'Listen, I was into Sabine. She was a lovely girl. I want her to rest in peace, and if you think she was killed, I won't get in your way. I have business that I need to take care of, that's all.'

Jake gives him a shove, determined not to concede the physical edge. 'Well remember this, I'm working with the police on Sabine. I don't want to have to notice you and your business, but if I have to I will, and you'll be sorry.'

Not the snappiest curtain line, but it will have to do. He shoves him again, into the bike, and Rose staggers and

182

puts his hand on the floor behind it to keep his balance, ungainly flailing. But he doesn't say anything else and, with as much dignity as he can muster, mounts and cycles into the nothingness of the night.

Chickens

Jake sleeps deeply and late; it is mid-morning by the time he finishes his exercise. There is still some rain in the air from yesterday, and the cobbles in the courtyard wink brilliantly in the watery sun. The clouds are mossy and white, untroubled by much breeze. Jake stands in the shower, his chest and arms lathered with soap suds, hot water cascading upon his frame, legs red and tingling from the exertion, his skin tight from his dip in the lake. The shower's door reaches to just below eye level, so he can look out across the courtyard to the lake and beyond. His long hair is now slicked back onto his neck, his beard trapping droplets of water and letting them fall more slowly.

His heart leaps when he sees the tottering figure of Livia on her bike. She is dressed casually as normal, blue jeans, walking boots, and a jumper dress that tapers in just a little at the waist. She dismounts, her face wry and pointed.

'I thought if I waited this much later, I'd manage to avoid catching you naked again. I bet you leapt in the shower just as soon as you saw me in the distance.'

'And yet look at me chastely concealed by this Victorian screen, my modesty carefully protected.'

'Well keep your "modesty" to yourself at this time of the day, thank you very much.'

'I won't ask if it would be different at any other time of the day. I'm just glad you came.'

He gestures for a towel, which is just out of his reach. She makes a show of looking the other way as she hands it to him. It is old and scratchy.

'I saw your mauve sign in Sherlock Beech, so waited a day to keep you keen, and bustled over. "Mauve" was Nabokov's favourite word, you know.'

'The *Lolita* guy? No, I didn't know that.'

'He was a bit more than "the *Lolita* guy", but never mind. Serves me right for sharing literary quips with someone who just likes stories with bloody murders, and implausibly smart and athletic men solving them.'

Jake has wrapped the towel around him, and is precariously making his way barefoot across the cobbled ground, wincing as he goes. Livia looks at the shower, which is steaming, beatific, in the morning sun. She notices some sodden clothes draped over the wooden walls.

'Please tell me you're not still washing your clothes by hand. You're like Crocodile Dundee when he goes to New York.'

Jake calls over his shoulder, 'No washing machine; you know that. And Nabokov to Crocodile Dundee in two minutes: you do have a broad cultural palette. Come into the kitchen and have a coffee.'

She watches him go through the door, he can feel her eyes on his back, the towel tight across the ridges of his haunches. When she gets inside, he has jeans on but

185

unbuttoned, and no shirt. He can tell she is appraising for a second the thick dark mass of hair beneath his stomach. He pats it self-consciously. He pulls on an old jumper, with a hole in one of the arms, and fastens his trousers.

The coffee machine is bubbling and filling the room with its welcoming smell, a deep draught of roasted beans which they both pause to inhale. Jake tells her about his surprise meeting with Rose, and the drug discovery. She thoughtfully bites her lip.

'I knew he dabbled a bit in dealing. It was one of the reasons we would never work. Not that I'm square or anything; just it didn't fit in all sorts of ways.'

'I think only square people use the word "square". But I can see how the weed would make him cautious of me, and willing to warn me off, even putting aside the Sabine situation. He also said something about her changing before they split up. Arthur noticed that change in her in his journals.' He picks one up from the kitchen table. 'Look, here, just before her death: "Is she falling out of love; is something amiss?" I thought maybe Rose had upset her, but perhaps something happened outside of the relationship. You know him, do you think he's a killer?'

'No, I wouldn't say he is. But I don't trust him, and my skin crawled when he came to see me the other day. I think he might be a bad man, but why would he kill her? Why would anyone?'

'There might be something about that farm. I should find a way of getting back in. Oh, that reminds me, I wanted to show you this.' He slides his police ID card across the table. 'Watson wanted me to have some sort of official standing, to act as a consultant of sorts. What do you think?'

186

'I like this young, fresh-faced hunk, especially when I compare him to the hairy beast in front of me. Are you sure you want this?'

'Not really. I do still want the peace, the little sky, not the broad horizons. But I also want to help Sabine. Not that she'll ever know. I want to give her some sense of an ending, a narrative that means something even if it is tragic. I probably sound mad.'

'Not at all. Well, not totally.' She drains her cup. 'Come on, show me all your improvements, or are you just proud that you finally have a shower?'

They wander the grounds for an hour. It is mild, and the birds are in full throat. He shows her the wood-cutting operation in Agatha Wood, and the plantation of replacement saplings. The orchard has been staked out in Velda Field, awaiting the arrival of the apple and pear trees. And the vegetable garden has been planted: tiny shoots peering up from the dark heart of the earth, freckles of green and white against the browns and blacks. The smell is of ancient soil, of permanence. It is vitalizing. They both pick out a couple of weeds and throw them on the floor, their roots surrendering in the air.

'And here is my proudest achievement . . .' Jake leads her to the lake and shows her the sauna. Inside it smells of clean wood that has been fired and faintly scorched. 'You're more than welcome to use it, I mean, you know . . .' He stutters. Is it possible to offer to share a sauna in the middle of nowhere with a beautiful woman, and for the invitation not to carry some sort of sexual overtones?

Livia opens the door and lightly jumps out. 'Jake, when our relationship is ready to take that crucial next step, I'll let you know.' He can't quite gauge how much or little she is joking.

She looks at the waters of the lake, rippled and blue-black, little rises and swells. 'Do you really swim in that every day? I'd be so worried about being that cold.'

'You should try it. It feels great when you come out.'

'It's when I'm in that I worry about.'

'Promise me you'll try it once. Just once.'

'You'll know you've got inside my head, if you ever see me in that bit of water.' She picks a coil of hair from her face, which is suddenly illumined by a break in the clouds, her skin a glinting, golden hue. 'Is this the end of your schemes, or do you have more?'

He gently grabs both of her arms and sits them both down on the bench by the lake. 'I wanted to ask you something.'

She frets for a second.

'Can I get some chickens easily, and do you think it's a good idea for me to have them?'

'Chickens, you say. I'm your chicken advice lady, am I?' Is there a trace of disappointment in her voice? 'Well, you've come to the right place. I know plenty of farmers who will sell you a cockerel and a few hens. Where will you keep them?'

'I saw a programme on TV once, where they built some chicken houses on poles, with ramps coming off them, so foxes couldn't get up at them.'

'I can get you chickens, my dear. When will you build the chicken fortress?'

'In the next couple of days, hopefully. We have plenty of wood.'

'Always glad that you have wood.'

'That was beneath you.'

She digs a playful knuckle under his ribs. They catch each other's eye and smile, both prolonging the stare. A heron skids into the water behind them, and gives a guttural call. The moment has passed.

'Is that bird following you?' complains Jake. She doesn't answer and they both look at it. Thin and magisterial, supremely indifferent to them. Jake wonders if it can be the same heron from the river when they were fishing. If they could get to both places, so could the bird, he supposes.

Livia stands up to leave. 'I'll tie a sign in Sherlock Beech when we can go and get the chickens. Say the morning after I put it there? Maybe at the weekend, because it isn't possible for us working stiffs just to drop everything and do things. Diana will come as well, as she loves the baby chicks.'

'That sounds perfect.'

They walk back to Livia's bike and she leaves, his eyes glued to her body until she fades all the way into the landscape.

Night thoughts

It is three a.m. Jake is sleeping in a tight curl, his legs poking out the bottom of the bed, his covers clutched to him as if in self-protection. He wakes, unsure whether he has been disturbed by a noise or not. Three o'clock in the morning is the bottom of the abyss of the night. The creatures of the day are not yet awake, while their nocturnal cousins have ceased their rustlings and snufflings. Even the moon has concealed itself in cloud. There is no sound he can hear, but his senses are tingling. Then he thinks he hears the soft slide of a foot on the cobbles outside. He gets up, the heat of sleep dissipating instantly as it is touched by the cool of the hour. He is naked, and feels vulnerable, but doesn't want to make any noise dressing.

His bedroom door is open, and he prowls out, his bare feet the mildest tap on the smooth floor. He walks down to the kitchen, which is full of looming shapes rendered unrecognizable by the night. Outside, a subdued and solitary lamp casts a long shadow, fading into black. He waits.

There is no more noise. He checks both front and back doors are locked, and brings the shotgun box down from the kitchen cupboard. He takes the gun out carefully. It feels substantial in his hands, a weighty reassurance. He sees he looks slightly ridiculous as he passes a mirror, his long, slender, ghostly body, the dark line of the gun, the taut parts of his chest, the still slight puffiness below. He makes himself silently tour the property. Nothing seems out of place, nothing seems disturbed. It feels empty apart from him.

He takes the gun back to his bedroom and puts it in the box, then under his bed. He tries to calm his racing heartbeat, to soothe the pounding in his head. He thinks of Livia and their walks together, tries to replay their journeys through the quiescent countryside. The calm of all that colour. But his mind keeps drifting back to Sabine, and the question of her murder. It stops him sleeping, and he reluctantly rises, wrapping himself up in a warm brown robe. In the kitchen, he starts the coffee machine and the bubbling noise seems to break the night's truce, its concord of silence: outside a bird hoots, leaves flutter and shush in the tree, he can hear the faint honk of geese at the other end of the lake. It is not dawn, but the day is stealing a march on the night.

Jake does what he always used to do with his cases: rereads his material, including the inquest report and the thin file Watson had left him. He gets out a pen and paper and tries to set down what he knows.

Sabine: worked on farm for years. Kind and warm, well-liked. Oppressed by owners. Relationship with Rose, ends with her becoming withdrawn. Him or something else? Fall

unlikely, because she wasn't drunk. People in the pub with
her: Dr P, two local women, the three men from the farm.

**He makes a note to himself to visit the scene when he
can. He drinks a gulp of coffee, which is strong and sweet,
warms him through.**

Rose: involved in drug-dealing, falls out with Sabine.
Not present in the pub on the night of murder.
Suspicious and slippery, but seems to have liked her.
Name keeps cropping up.

The farm: Joan, the matriarch figure, supposed to
be domineering. Wanted all talk of death scotched by
workers. Three men: living at home, big and threatening.
Davey was there that night. He and Paul at church when
Watson came. Drugs come from farm: who is the boss?

Clifford and Martin: two more at home with mum.
No obvious connection to Sabine. Both angered when I
mentioned her death.

Dr P: in some form of love with Sabine. Stole the bones in
the first place - any motive for that other than to find
the killer?

Arthur: in love with Sabine. Stalking her.

The bones: Dr P takes them. Someone must have seen
that, and then replaced them. Why? Unless to stop the
interest. Who knew?

One last note: How do we know for certain she was
murdered?

Sheep

Jake stretches a kink in his neck, and decides to go for an early run. The sky is a lurid combination of pink and peach, the clouds a strange and patternless swirl. It is cold, and his breath steams as he jogs. The same route he always takes, the grass flattened into a path from the remorseless press of his feet. Jogging is penance and healthful pain, a self-imposed ritual of testing routine. He resolves never to slow his pace, never to make his latest run easier or gentler than his last. He loops around the lake, through the fields on the upper side (Bosch, Wimsey and Velda). Wimsey is his least favourite, as it rises and falls, testing his stamina, and comes at just past the halfway point. He always feels at his strongest, though, as he emerges from it, through a gap in the hedge, the sweat now flowing, the day breaking around him. He sees the silhouette of a hawk above his head, a pompous committee of crows just behind him, jawing and bobbing, the beginning of the buzz and thrum of rural life. He makes himself increase speed as he descends back to the house, quicker as he hits the path by the lake, eyes now bloodshot with sweat, lungs beginning to tighten with strain.

He picks up the pair of swimming goggles he always leaves by the pier, and disrobes quickly, to keep the heat in his system, make the coldness of the plunge a soothing pleasure. And then the lake envelops him, icy velvet, the shock driving thoughts from his head, his only focus his breathing, the stretch of his muscles and the blank sheet of water ahead. As he reaches the far side, his hands touch the silky silt of the ground and he stands for a second. A huge gulp of clean air, and then he swims back, the home straight now, the euphoria you get when your daily offering, your appeasement of the physical fates, is nearly done.

Jake has showered and dressed when he sees it. He had left for his run earlier from the back door facing the lake, and now happens to walk to the front of the house. There is blood smeared on the door, crudely, a thick sweep of maroon. He knows dried blood well. Beneath it is the corpse of a sheep, its head half-severed, eyes staring open, the wound already doted upon by insistent flies, yellowed tongue lolling obscenely. Nobody else is around. Jake approaches carefully, and can smell the death in the air. There is blood on the floor, but not much, and Jake suspects the body must have been brought here already killed. Which is quite a feat, when he thinks about it, given how isolated he is. The land is grassy and lush, and doesn't take much of a trail, but Jake follows a line back towards Poirot Point, his keen eyes noting flecks of red clinging to blades of grass. He sees more on the path that runs away from his property, and follows the occasional spatter until he hits a large field. He knows the road that brought him here is only a mile or so away. And, in the field, there are thick tyre tracks, pretty fresh, the moisture still there in the crushed blades of grass. A 4x4, Jake reasons, driven off the road; the sheep then carried to his house sometime in the night.

He can only take this as a threat, of course. But who from? It might be Rose, who is the last person he confronted. And it could be the same person who replaced the bones, the same person who might fear investigation into Sabine's death. Jake jogs back down to the house, his legs sore from his run. He wonders if he had disturbed the intruder, which is why the message had not been more pronounced; perhaps a lusty smear was all there was time for. It looks like someone had dipped a thick stick into the sheep's blood and used that, as he quickly finds the likely tool, its first four inches reddened and sticky with dried liquid.

Jake remembers a course he had taken towards the end of his time in the police called, euphemistically, 'Emergency Fieldwork'. It was given to senior officers who might end up working on emergency or crisis cases, such as live terrorist incidents. The purpose was to train them how to function without back-up, to make logical jumps, use heuristics – intuitive short cuts – to advance a case forward. Most of this was mental, but some of it rested on how to improvise in the field. As a result, he knows how to check for fingerprints without a forensic team.

He runs inside and grabs some cocoa powder, a clean toothbrush, thick Sellotape, and the reverse of an old print made from black card. He imagines himself, at night, trying to spread blood on the door, and tries to work out the probable spots where a hand may have been pressed against the wall. He pours cocoa on those parts he thinks most likely, and carefully brushes away the excess. The first three attempts produce nothing, but he scores on the fourth one: like magic, a whorled image emerges, which he carefully transfers via the tape onto the black card. He will give it to Watson to see if anything hits when it is checked.

There seems little else useful to do, so he takes the carcass and buries it deep in the ground away from the house. The first grave he has ever dug, a sad memento mori. He then scrubs the stain until it has almost gone, but a final ghost line remains, a mark of what has happened. He is standing, wondering what to do, when he is hailed from the other side of the house. Mack, coming to build the chicken pens.

Jake quickly moves to intercept him before he turns the corner. He feels exposed, not quite ashamed of the security of his home being breached, but not quite confident in talking about it yet either. The old handyman is standing by the sentinel tree, his brown face in repose, a small cigarette smouldering in his sinewy hand.

Leading him amicably by the arm, Jake takes him to the paddock nearest to the house, and they form a plan for the build. Jake's idea is to have three chicken houses, raised up eight feet high on sturdy poles, with what amount to ladders coming off them at an angle. The idea is that the birds can roam freely in the day, then retire at night away from the foxes, and come down the ladders in the morning. They have already shaped the wood on a previous day, so the main task is carrying and fixing it all into place.

It is hot work, and Mack accepts a cold beer, and some

196

ham and cheese, at noon. By three, Jake's head is heavy with lack of sleep, but they are nearly finished. Stout, simple structures, which they raise into position with ropes before filling in the holes around the pilings. From a distance, it looks like a village in miniature, something out of the Dutch lowlands, built to survive regular floods. Jake wonders if Livia will approve, and be amused. He shakes Mack's leathery paw as he heads up to his vehicle, which is parked on the edge of Velda. They agree to tackle the orchard as the next job of home improvement.

Resurrection

It is Wednesday, his otherwise defunct phone reminds him, and Jake walks to the river to meet Watson. He brings with him the fingerprint, carefully preserved on the black card, which he puts into his shoulder bag. He is early, but the evening is already there, the water is languorous, sliding idly away from him. There are no boats passing by now or, if there are, they are hidden by the gloaming. He hears the humming purr of an engine, and Watson pulls up and parks, facing the river. It is chilly enough outside for Jake to welcome the car's comfort, and he pushes the passenger seat back to give himself some room.

Watson puts the radio on, which is playing some mild and inoffensive classical music. One of Jake's future projects – and he sees now that life will become a series of projects, of self-improvement or -expansion – is to learn about music. He still finds jazz baffling and discordant, has embraced the lush headiness of Mahler, and wants to fit together all the different pieces in the canon, so he can understand it more. Like everyone, he thinks, he knows the major names, but vanishingly little about them or how they relate to each other. Does he prefer Brahms or Beethoven, and why? It is an inadequacy he feels keenly.

Watson seems unconcerned by the niceties of musical appreciation and asks him for a progress report.

Jake first explains what happened with Rose, and the presence of the drugs operation. Watson raises an eyebrow: 'You didn't flash your credentials, then? I'm glad. As a policeman, you wouldn't be allowed to barge in. As a curious individual, it's your own lookout. We can't go after the operation based on your illegal actions, of course, but we can find other grounds to take more of an interest. Drugs mean money means power and the need to maintain order. Could that have led to Sabine's death?'

'Perhaps. I need to get to the crime scene at some point. Can you arrange that?'

'We could ask their consent, which I'm sure won't be forthcoming, so we would need a warrant. This case hasn't been formally reopened, remember. You might need to find us something else to go on. Do you like Rose for this?'

'I don't. But I'm not sure. We still haven't fully confirmed that a murder took place at all.'

'What I can tell you is that we have checked the dental records in Germany, and our bones are definitely her, which means we can prove the original desecration. Though you already know who did that. And the replacement bones were indeed taken from the nearby grave from the sixties. But that doesn't take us to a murder investigation.'

'We need someone who knew what happened to her in that last couple of weeks before her death. Let me look into that. Because someone is certainly starting to feel the heat.' Jake pulls out the card, and explains where the fingerprint has come from.

Watson takes it from him thoughtfully. 'We'll run this, on the quiet, and see what we get. I take it you don't want to make a formal complaint?'

'Sadly, vandalism and animal cruelty might not energize the arm of the state enough. Could you send me a note with any hit you get on the print? I've realized I can use Arthur's PO Box still, and so anything you ever need me to see you can send a copy there ahead of this meeting.' He gives him the address on a slip of paper.

'Are you scared, Jake?'

'Not really. This is the bit I was good at, worrying away at a problem. And I have never felt, you know . . .' He searches for the phrase. 'So light on my feet, if you see what I mean. I have no baggage, no connections. I'm comparatively healthy and strong, and, I don't know, untethered. I feel like I can't be threatened that much really. I don't know, that might be crazy.'

'It might. You still don't want a knife in the dark coming for you.'

'If it does, I intend to be ready.' He laughs with a confidence he doesn't entirely feel.

The radio changes to a piece of music Jake does recognize: it is from Mahler's Resurrection symphony, an appropriate enough motif in the circumstances. That thing about being untethered has been nagging away in his mind. Most days he does feel lighter, fresher, unmoored from the weight of normal life. Just occasionally, the sinking feeling enters his stomach, the sadness over lost opportunity coupled with loneliness, the feeling of flayed nerves such that every sensation registers as pain or sadness. He doesn't want to explain all this to Watson, but mulls on it, as the banks of strings and brass rise and fall, the music filling the car.

On the walk back, he tries to plot his next move. The shape of what has happened is there to be traced, he feels; he can sense the beginnings of the outline. He just needs a break, a moment to clarify and connect things. He unlocks the back door when he gets home, alive as now he must be to the possible presence of intruders. He stumbles over a brick placed in the middle of the step, and sees it is securing a note that has been carefully folded beneath. He switches on the light, a sudden blinding glare, and locks the door behind him while he opens it. It comes from Dr Peter, a scrap of a notebook, the words in fountain pen with beautiful copperplate handwriting, the loops and lines like something from the nineteenth century. It reads:

My dear Jake,
    Come to find me as soon as you can. I have been sleuthing to the best of my ability, and am building a story for you. Shades of Titus Andronicus and poor Lavinia, alas, if your Shakespeare is good enough. I shall explain if not: 'Complots of mischief, treason, villainies / Ruthful to hear, yet piteously performed.'

It is signed with an exuberant P, the long stroke like a downward dagger on the page. Jake wonders what he might mean. He has no knowledge of *Titus Andronicus*, bar the title, which he had seen on posters at some point outside a theatre in the city. He will have to ask Dr Peter to explain, and he resolves to see him as soon as he can. The house is secure, and quiet, and he slinks off to the library to hide himself in a book.

Stories

Dr Peter is not at home the next day when Jake calls, or the next, and Jake leaves him a note, asking him to come to Little Sky whenever he can. He spends an hour in the Nook, nursing a pale beer from a local brewery that Sarah has started to sell. He asks her about the people of Smiths' Farm.

'I want you to take care not to wrangle me into owt, Jake. I'm not sure I approve of your nosing about, and I certainly worry for you about it all.'

'I'm not asking you to do anything. Just tell me who these folk are.'

She pulls herself a drink in a pewter mug, and settles her considerable haunches on the old armchair she keeps in the back room for quiet moments, her feet resting on a pile of old newspapers.

'The woman who runs the place you've met. Joan. Not someone I'd care to cross, or to spend an afternoon on a picnic with neither. She was married to a big old brute of a man, black beard longer than yours, a dark temper. He used to terrorize the kiddies there. The two sons, Paul and Davey, had a terrible time of it. Working on the farm all day when they wasn't at school, shouted at and beaten up. You should have seen the bruises on their bodies when they went swimming in the river with the other children, their legs all welted and blotchy. Nobody said anything. The dad had a scowl that could curdle butter.

'Richard, their cousin, came to stay when they was a bit older. He lost his parents, I think. Not a lucky family. He is quieter than the other two generally. The dad, now, he died of a heart attack near enough twenty year ago. Was sorrowed over by nobody bar Joan, I shouldn't think.'

She takes another meditative sip.

'Now I should know, but when your feller goes, you have to either sell up and try to manage, or put your very all into being the boss. Joan, credit her enough, did just that. The farm is bigger than ever, and the boys always have money to spend. But she is no kinder a soul than her husband, and they have been shaped, if you like, by that.'

'It doesn't sound much fun for other people there.'

'I would think that "fun" is not a word that would get much recognized on the farm. Rose does OK with them, but he does business with everyone. And those twins who work in the shop, well they're a bit wanting anyway. Just glad to have a job to pay for their cats, I should think.'

'And Sabine?'

Sarah tips her chair back, belches silently. 'Ah, I thought we might be getting to this. Look, she was too bright for that place, too sunny somehow. But she stuck it out, she was as game as the rest of us. It ground her down in the end; before she died she was like a wraith. Oh, it used to sorrow your uncle and the doctor. And then she died, and worrying about it seemed, well, pointless.'

'Do you think she died naturally?'

'I don't know, Jake, and I don't see how you're going to find out. You need to make sure you don't get sucked into the meanness of that place. You don't need to, you know.'

The bell to the shop tinkles gently as the door swings open. It is Clifford and Martin from next door, stooping and taciturn, their boots clunking on the floor in unison. Like Jake, they seem too big for the shop. An imperceptible bow to Sarah. They ignore Jake almost entirely, the tension from their previous confrontation palpable. Clifford speaks, his bulging forehead wrinkled, his hands restlessly moving, clasping and unclasping.

'Mother wants us to pick up the hogget from the other day. We've made space for it now.'

Sarah wordlessly goes to the back room freezer. Jake looks across at them, curious. 'Where did you get that from? I could stand to get some meat back home, and I like a bit of lamb.'

'There was a slaughter the other day. A few days' labour for us, and a carcass or two in return.'

Jake stares at them both, trying to look for any sign of shiftiness around him, any sense they might have been involved in bringing that sheep to his door. But they are impassive, their faces a blank, no hint of the warmth of any feeling. Sarah drags in the meat, a whole young sheep, and Martin picks it up effortlessly and hoists it over his shoulder.

'Much obliged, Sarah,' they both say, formally, and in turn. The door closes, and Sarah resumes her position on the chair, wiping her chapped red hands with an old scrap of cloth.

Jake raises an inquisitive eyebrow. 'Another pair of mummy's boys.'

'They'll not thank you for that. But you're right, I suppose. Family's important here. And we always say you don't stray from home unless you're running from something. That's why we're suspicious of strangers: Livia, though she's making headway because of how good a vet she is; Dr Peter; your uncle, and of course you, Jake. People say that you must have done something pretty bad, if you ended up here by yourself, going feral.' She glances at his thick beard and long hair.

Jake ponders this for a moment. 'It's no secret that I could leave my old life without much regret. But I did nothing worse than abandon a dwindling relationship.' Was that all, though, he wonders. Would a normal person be sitting here, in this old curiosity shop, an eccentric hostelry in a village of desperate eccentrics, or would they be struggling on in the city, worried about promotion, fretting over a social life, locked into a relationship that had been nurtured over the years? It was a nagging fear of his.

'What's their excuse for staying with their mum? Is Mary a monster?'

'No, she kills with kindness that one. Those two boys are bone idle, always have been. They do labouring stints for pocket money, or payment in kind like that there big lamb, but Mary's pension and that of their dad, who passed a while back, is enough for them to get by. Once you get your house here, there's not much to spend on bar food and a drink or two. They're here because it's the easiest option.'

Jake drains his drink, and pats Sarah on the hand. 'Always a pleasure to spend time with you, my friend.' She looks away, embarrassed by the affection. He can always rely on her for local intelligence, but he needs something more, to speak to someone closer to Sabine. Perhaps Dr Peter had been doing his own investigation like that, and where has he got to anyway?

On the road

Jake is slowly walking homeward, the sun setting poster-paint pink in the corner of the sky, the river reflecting the remaining light like a pool of shattered glass. He pauses, as he often does, to drink in the air, fill his lungs fit to burst. Then he hears a shout.

Loud sounds always appear perverse in the depths of the countryside, especially on a balmy, gentle evening, and this one jolts him utterly. He looks around. The noise returns, and he recognizes the articulation of his own name. It is Livia, rushing towards him from one of the fields to the left of the path. She is powerful even in distress, he thinks, her body in control of itself. She bursts through a gap in the hedge, a hunted deer, and falls against his body.

'Are you OK? Christ, what's happened?'

She winces, out of breath, and sits him down on the edge of the road, the grass flattened by tractor wheels, the ground baked firm by the summer that has gone past. He waits. She leans forward, her heart racing wildly, chest heaving. She sucks in air to calm herself. Jake shuffles his body in slightly awkward fashion; his consoling hand shifts restlessly between gripping Livia's arm and patting her shoulder.

'So what happened to you?'

A gulp. A pause. 'I was walking home after my rounds, pushing the bike. Not really thinking of very much. It was what, an hour ago, a quiet early evening, and I was going to get a bath before Diana got dropped off.

'A 4x4 came past, loud and sudden, and I moved the bike into a little run-up to an old gate. I didn't get a glimpse of the driver or the make.' That vanilla trickle of a laugh, self-deprecating. 'And no, nor the registration number. I'm not a character in one of your books, you know. Anyway, I thought nothing much about it. I kept going, with half an eye skywards, looking for that goshawk. I had seen a shape ducking and dipping just above the treeline, and I didn't want to miss a glimpse.

'All of a sudden, two hands gripped my arms, like talons. And I felt this lumbering presence behind me. A man, obviously; had some sort of scarf around his face. The smell of leather and a fairly ugly aftershave. Then this voice.'

She shudders, and he strokes her gently.

'He told me to keep my nose out of Smiths' Farm. That this was my second warning, and the next would be less gentle. He said they know how to hurt people who meddle.

'I felt paralysed. My body froze, like it was a traitor to me. I hated that I couldn't do anything. But I just couldn't. He lingered his hands for a second, and then pushed me down into the ditch. I landed with a thump, face in the muck. Not hurt at all. Just scared. After a moment of wrangling with my timid self, I scrambled up the verge, and nobody was there. Just the sound of a car heading off in the middle distance. Then I realized I could cut across the fields to see you, and there you were, mooching about like normal.'

Her eyes are clouded, milky with angst, and he can sense the deep frustration, a coil of white heat, within her.

He speaks quietly. 'So we can assume the first warning was through Rose. Now this. Do you have any sense of who the man was?'

'It wasn't Rose. I know his, well, you know, smell and feel.'

'Quite. One of the other three from the farm?'

'It could be. The voice was a gruff whisper. It was a local definitely, but I don't know much more than that. It was pretty shadowy by that time, and he kept me facing away from him. I wish I'd turned around, I wish I'd done something.' She slaps her hand against her thigh. 'I hate being fucking weak.'

'There is nothing weak about being ambushed. Nothing at all. I've been jumped before, everyone has. I remember lying in a ball, curled up, on the grass of a park being kicked in the head.'

A wan smile. 'Thank goodness it didn't damage your looks,' she says.

'It did damage my sense of self-worth, though. Really. There are few feelings worse than impotence. Don't make a joke. Feeling feeble in the face of strength, especially when it comes unfair, from nowhere. So your reaction is exactly as it should be.'

'But what does it *mean*? Does this take us anywhere?'

'A couple of places, but not exactly clarity.' Jake pauses to think. 'The farm is both Sabine's home and a drug business. Either one could be the reason to provoke some-body to warn you off.'

'Or maybe both. We reckon that Sabine knew about the drug business, probably through Rose. Maybe she was getting in the way.'

'Maybe. It's a solid theory but, like everything in this, there isn't much to back it up.'

'I have bruised arms, and pride, as evidence.'

'Well there is that.'

They sit in silence, the hum of the evening around them, soothing white noise. Jake wants to hug her, but doesn't want to intrude too much into her personal space, so pats her once more. She grips his hand in fond retort.

'I'm so glad to have seen you. And now I have to get back home before Diana does.'

He wordlessly stands and by tacit agreement accompa-nies her to her house, the road deserted, lights flickering on in the distance as night falls. His hand is on the small of her back briefly. It is damp with sweat, and he can feel the waistband of her trousers. She leans into him as they approach her front door.

'You're a good man, Jake, but I don't know what we've got ourselves into.'

'Me neither. Would you recognize the man again?'

'I'm not sure. I might recognize his smell, but who knows? I was going to tell Watson about this, but I don't think I really have anything concrete to say. Some amateur detective I've become.

'The best detectives always get ambushed at least once. And often wake up the next morning, bound and impris-oned, subject to the evil cruelty of their assailant. So you're doing pretty well, all things considered.'

She pats his chest. 'You're good at consoling me. Now thank you for walking me home. I can still grab that bath if I hurry; and you can return to your mooching.'

The thick, scarred door closes, and Jake moves off once more, his face furrowed in thought.

Chickens part 2

Sunday morning, rain spitting and seething at the window as Jake opens his eyes. Yesterday, Livia had sent the signal from Sherlock Beech, and he feels excited to see her. By the time he gets to her cottage, the day has settled into a gentle, maundering damp, the sky pregnant with billowing grey cloud.

'Chickens!' shouts Diana as soon as he walks into the front room. 'You're so lucky to be getting them. My mum says we don't have the space.'

Livia walks in, looking a fraction embattled. She is wearing denim dungarees over a military green top. 'We've had a bit of a falling-out on the subject, haven't we, madam?'

Jake crouches down and looks Diana in the face. Her eyes are like her mother's, but a paler green, like Coke bottles in old American movies.

'Well you're lucky to have a cat. I'd love one of them. So how about we make a deal? I can come and stroke your cat when I like, and you can come and help me look after the chickens whenever you like. And, you can even name one of them. What do you think?'

She nods brightly, and runs to get her coat and wellies. His knees crackle as he stands up. He is getting old, he thinks.

With Diana out of the room, he raises a questioning eyebrow to Livia, who responds with a grimace, then a smile. 'I'm fine after my little incident. Thank you for being there for me. I won't forget that.'

Jake starts to say something, but is stalled by Diana's return so hurriedly changes the subject.

'Livia, can I ask a favour? On the way back, can you stop by to let me pick up my post? I'd totally forgotten I had Arthur's PO Box still, and Watson might have something for me.'

'No problem, at this rate you might make the twentieth century at some point this year.'

Diana gets to choose the soundtrack for the car journey to the farm. 'It's the only way we get any peace,' Livia half-apologizes as a Disney audiobook intrudes on the airwaves. They talk over the brightly voiced sounds anyway and it is nice, Jake thinks, once you get used to it. They jolt along an ill-paved lane up towards a big house, fields either side of them full of cows dolefully cropping the grass. Livia clearly knows her way around and hails the farmer, a woman in her thirties tinkering with a piece of machinery. She introduces herself as Jess, and they tramp over the muddied and scuffed concrete towards the sound of sporadic clucking.

'Why do you want to have chickens, Jake?'

'I think I'd like to have some things to look after. I'd quite like the eggs. And I have a lot of space, so reckon

213

that they might have a good life. Are they good enough reasons?'

He explains his set-up of the raised houses in the big field. Jess nods. 'I think that will work. The two breeds I'm giving you are good fliers, wiry little devils, and can live semi-wild.'

At the farm, the chickens have the run of the big old barn, straw bales stacked like children's bricks, and a patch of land outside. He can see hens fussing and pecking at the ground; spasmodic, precise movements, indifferent to their presence. He gets Diana to pick out five hens, and a cockerel with dark brown feathers, its wattle a festive, strident red, full of strut and swagger. The attempts to corner them all are predictably farcical. Shrieks and leaps, explosions of feathers. After half an hour, and the expenditure of a lot of energy, the birds are shut up in travelling containers, which they hoist into Livia's car.

On the way back, Livia stops off to let Jake pick up his post from a storage building. It is one of the services Arthur had set up in perpetuity in his will. His allotted container is full, predominantly of junk. But on the top is an envelope with the local police stamp visible, and Jake grabs it. He quickly throws away most other things, circulars and fliers. And there, sitting innocently atop some gaudy shout of advertising, is a letter with the address written in Faye's familiar, careful style. It is a stab in the stomach for a second. Jake picks it up, tucks it behind the police letter and heads back to the car. His effervescence has been dulled, and he tries not to show it.

Back at Little Sky, they park the car, which has bounced across some of the upper fields and taken them close to what Diana has already called Chicken City. She has also named all of the chickens, after her favourite characters from Disney films. Jake, who named his local landmarks after fictional detectives, can hardly complain. So he now has Ariel, Elsa, Beauty, Jasmine and Tinkerbell. He tried to object to the last one, but was overruled by Livia. Diana calls the cockerel Beast, to go with Beauty. She seems content around Jake. If she feels awkward about the absence of her own father, she never seems to show it. He is just a defined absence in her life, something to be displaced and ignored, something for others to fuss over, but never her.

Jake and Livia heft the boxes to the middle of the field, and open them. The chickens do not move, stunned by their unaccustomed journey. Livia explains that they need space to adjust in their own time, so they sit on a blanket, watching. Diana sips a juice Livia has given her, and stares resolutely at the boxes, willing there to be action.

Livia turns to Jake: 'What was the letter that has bothered you?'

'You are direct, aren't you? I thought I'd hidden it, and my reaction.'

'You did from a seven-year-old, but not from me.'

'It's from Faye. I guess I had begun to put her out of my mind. And now she's back there.'

'Do you want us to leave, so you can read it?'

'I don't want you to leave, no. But let me open it to see what sort of letter it is.'

That is the point, he thinks. Is it a declaration of undying love? A tirade of resentment and scorn? Some big announcement he needs to know about? He snicks the opening apart with a fingernail, and scans the two pages. It is not angry or passionate, but simply a declaration that she wants to get divorced. She is dating, it might not be serious, but she wants the freedom. She is moving on. He can understand, but still feels an ephemeral sense of disappointment and rejection. He doesn't want her to keep wanting him, but is somehow still sad that she profoundly does not.

A rueful smile. 'A request for a divorce. Which is fair enough. Not too big of a deal.'

As he speaks, two chickens cautiously poke their heads out, and then in a big flurry jump forward. Then another, then two more. Finally the cockerel, chest puffed and curved like a sail made big by the wind, joins them with fake nonchalance.

'See,' says Livia, 'it's possible to get used to change.'

The birds' eyes are wide as they try to gauge the extent of their new home, and Diana throws feed to encourage them. After an hour, they have all been coaxed in and out of the houses, leaping down the ladders as if they have been doing it all their lives. Livia pats Jake on the chest with one hand, and with the other starts manoeuvring her tired child home. A few seconds later, Diana runs back and extravagantly cuddles Jake's legs before scurrying back to her mum. His first ever hug from a child, he thinks, on the day his marriage ends.

That night, he sits by the fire with a glass of wine and reads Faye's letter properly. She is considerate and thoughtful, hoping that 'the experiment' is going well. She doesn't give any details about her new relationship, but talks a little about her job and their friends. She asks him to come and sign the papers in a few days' time. He is amazed how little he feels tugged back home. It is like a message from a world he doesn't recognize, and can't quite bring back full-coloured and furnished in his mind. The request for divorce should not be complicated. He has already renounced their shared assets informally, and is happy to concede all at the formal end of the marriage. Arthur's solicitor, the questioning Krunkle, had shown him the scale of his inheritance in cash terms, and there is no need for him to fight for anything further.

He feels a little empty, something incomprehensible echoing inside him. But divorce also feels normal, like the sign a thing has been completed. Perhaps this is the only way it could have ended. Perhaps rightness requires no further emotional wrangling. He was in the wrong place there, and he should be nowhere other than here.

He drafts a note back in modest, gentle tones, his own handwriting a puckered scrawl, indicating that he will cooperate with the process, and make a visit to the city on the suggested day. He ends by wishing her – and this is heartfelt – a happy future in a world that is no longer his.

Watson's letter is more immediately pressing. The finger-print Jake discovered is not on the system, but is the same as one of those retrieved from the crypt. Predictable perhaps, but the beginning of an evidentiary chain: the person who replaced the bones is still trying to warn him off. The problem is he doesn't feel he has got much closer to establishing who that person is.

Acts of black night

It has been a few days since Jake has seen Dr Peter, and he is starting to get concerned. He goes back to his house, which stands obdurate and unresponsive when he knocks. But the door gives a little, and swings open to his gentle push. He enters tentatively. Quiet. The insistent ticking of a clock the only noise that disturbs the peace until Jake starts calling Peter's name. No response comes. He walks down a hallway, which is dim with dark green wallpaper, the echo of his steps on stone flooring. There are bookshelves, waist-high, along each wall, volumes spilling out of them, squeezed together in apparent disorder. Fiction and non-fiction. Beautifully bound text books of country life butting up against spy novels by Len Deighton and John le Carré, some tattered paperbacks by Agatha Christie and Dorothy Sayers, and the complete works of Gerald Durrell in the editions Jake remembers from the dining room shelves of his childhood home.

The door at the end is open, leading into a kitchen, which is empty and clean. Dishes have been washed and stacked, a notebook with some pages torn out sits forlornly on the table. Jake doubles back to the other door leading off the hallway. Out of habit, he has touched nothing, and he uses his knuckle to push it open. It gives a moan as it swings, and he walks into a big living room. More bookshelves, a sofa, a large grandfather clock.

And there on the floor Dr Peter, facedown and sprawled, his blood almost black in a pool around his head, his white hair on the left side turned a dirty red-brown.

The sight hits Jake hard, a kick to the guts. He feels the throb of sorrow and anger, the surge of heat inside him, part energy, part guilt, part some atavistic version of fear. Death is always shocking, however often you have come across it. And your body treats it as a reminder of the sensation of being alive: the thump of your heart, the glistening spread of sweat across the brow, the tingle of your extremities. A readiness to fight or flee. Added to this is Jake's sense of affection for the man, who has become part of his new life, almost part of the scenery and landscape itself.

He approaches and gently feels for a pulse. Dr Peter's skin is rigid and cold. A figure of such endless twitch and movement now permanently stilled. Jake wants to preserve the crime scene, but pauses to look around the room. It has been little disturbed. Dr Peter had fallen towards the mantelpiece above the fire, as if he had turned away from his assailant. There is no sign of forced entry, there is no sign of fight. This usually suggests the victim had known the attacker.

Jake retreats and, using his sleeve to cover his hands, pulls the front door shut. Outside the natural world chunters and busies itself regardless. Smoke is coming mournfully from a nearby chimney. It is cold enough for a daytime fire. He walks the ten minutes to the Nook, and explains briefly to Sarah. She sags against the wall, and then leads him to her phone. Twenty minutes later the police come screeching from Meryton, blue lights flashing. Watson's car is close behind, and he grabs Jake, who is waiting outside the house.

'This is appalling news. You're going to have to tell me everything you know, and you're going to have to do it now.'

'Do you want to go and see for yourself first? And then we can talk.'

Jake goes to sit on the picnic bench, and watches with practised eye the establishment of the crime scene: the taping off, the forensics, the removal of the body. He feels bereft for a moment, and another hot flash of guilt. Did he underestimate the threat? It was hard to tell. Dr Peter had been the one to lure Jake into this, not the other way around. His blitheness, his lust for knowledge, his desire for fair treatment of a long-dead friend, had ended here in this bloody quietus.

Watson comes to join Jake. 'Poor old bugger. You're going to have to give a statement about how you found him. But tell me first what he had to do with our Sabine investigation.'

Jake explains Dr Peter's involvement in the initial removal of the bones, and the reasons why. And he shows the note he had received from him, which Watson reads and then bags carefully. While he is doing that, Jake borrows his notebook and makes a rough copy of the text. 'What does this mean, the references to *Titus Andronicus*?' Watson asks.

'I was going to ask him that. And now we'll never know. But our best line of investigation leads us back to Sabine, surely. He has been silenced because of his interest in her. We find her killer, we find his. And vice versa.'

'If the connection holds.'

'The alternative is that this murder, in the middle of a nowhere village in the middle of nowhere in England, is a coincidence. And I don't buy that.'

Watson is quiet for a moment. 'Nor do I. Come on. I'll drive you to the station so you can give your statement. I'll be running this investigation, and I want to get your information in the front and centre of it.'

Jake spends three hours at the station, drinking tepid, watery coffee to stay alert. Watson drops him back in the centre of the village afterwards, and he walks to Livia's house, his head bowed.

She opens the door in tears. 'Oh my God, Jake, I've just heard.' She sobs into his shoulder, her head against his chin. He squeezes her close. In the background, he can see Diana watching television and he gives her a reassuring smile. She gets up and walks to them: 'Mummy told me that Dr P died and it is very sad.'

Livia smiles through her tears. 'And mummy is just having a quick cry about it. Go on, you watch television, and I'll make some hot chocolate.'

She and Jake walk to the kitchen together, her hand nestling in his. She heats some milk and pours it over chocolate powder, then takes a small mug out to Diana. Then she sits at the table, dabbing her eyes with a tea towel.

'I just keep thinking of him, so lively and active, nipping in and out of places, and now he's dead. And you saw the body, you poor thing. Are you OK?'

'Sadly, it's not a new sight to me. But I feel terrible. I just wish he'd never got involved in all this.'

'So he definitely was killed because of Sabine, you think?'

'Who can say anything for definite? But, yes, I reckon he must have been. He was doing some snooping, which I guess I encouraged. Poor old sod. He sent me a note, saying he had learned something.'

Jake shows the copy of Dr P's note to Livia. She is silent as she reads it. The sounds of happy shrieks from a children's programme in the living room.

'You're better-read than I am, does it mean anything to you?' Jake asks.

She sniffs, and thinks. 'I've heard of the play, but I don't really know anything about it. I have a Complete Works somewhere, wait a second.'

She leaves the room and he watches her through the door, running her finger along an old mahogany bookcase. She is in pink pyjama leggings and an old T-shirt. He smiles at the thought of their fellowship of scruffiness. Then he hears a small yelp of self-congratulation, and she brings a thick volume in with her.

'I won this at school for coming top in my class when I was thirteen. My dad made me get it. I have never done more than flick through it.' She hands it to him, and he frowns as he checks the contents for *Titus*. He is no scholar, and worries that none of it will make sense to him.

Livia sits down and looks him direct in the eye. 'Jake, do you think you should walk away from all this?' She drags her chair closer to his, places her hands on his knees. They are brown and slender, like perfectly shaped and fired clay, hints of pink beneath the fingernails. 'Actually, of course you should walk away. You've done your bit: this is all going to get investigated properly now. Sabine. That farm. Dr P. What more can you do?'

'Well I can probably help, can't I? I'm almost certainly more qualified than anyone within a hundred miles of here. And I am in it whatever now. I feel I have to get this sorted, because otherwise what sort of peace is there going to be for me, or for anyone? I mean, you've been grabbed and threatened for Christ's sake.'

He realizes something, and sighs deeply. 'So I should back away from seeing you for a little bit. Who knows what will be provoked now? I can't be responsible for any harm coming to you.' He places his big, ugly hands on top of hers, a forest of intertwined fingers, and drops his voice a gentle octave. 'I don't want now to be the time to talk about how I feel about you, but I like you, Livia. I think you are . . .' He struggles for the word. 'Just magnificent. I think about you all of the time. I want to see you and hang out with you. I even want to garden with you.'

He has been staring at their hands, and looks up to see her reaction. There is a half-smile beneath some tears.

'But you have a life and a daughter, and might not see me that way, and I don't want to push anything. And anyway now is not the time. Let me walk away and try to finish this, and stop you from getting hurt.'

His voice trails off. She squeezes his hands, and nods. 'Jake, I want to see where our thing is going, too. But I can't risk Diana. There is too much violence around this; it terrifies me. That fear I felt when I was grabbed the other day, it lingers. And I can't be close to someone else who then might go on to make her lose a sense of security.

223

I can't believe this is the second time I'm trying to distance myself from you. And we've only known each other three months.'

He nods and tries to make a joke. 'I'm quite the catch, you know: hairy, jobless man about to get divorced by post.'

But he feels deeply sad inside, an ache of longing. It all seems so unlikely all of a sudden, so overwhelming: he sees he has been secretly using Livia as the foundation, the fount and origin, of his newfound contentment. His life, his new routines, the quietness, the acceptance of nature, all of that pleasure was based on the unspoken precondition that there was this person who kept appearing to bring joy, and excitement, and beauty. And physical connection: those fleeting touches, his hungry imagination about what her thighs would feel like around him, her lips when they kissed. Instead, he is a just a shabby man sitting in her kitchen, while her child – the true focus of her life – watches television, and a murder inquiry involving him is picking up pace. Love feels ridiculous, if anything, in such a place.

They lean forward in a hug of mutual consolation. He feels her inhaling deeply, wonders what his scent seems like to her, remnants of woodsmoke from the fire, perhaps, the heathery odour of outdoors, the decaying sweetness of drying sweat. Hers, for him, is the cherry of her perfume, and the bright clean smell of her skin beneath. He tastes salt from her cheeks, as their faces press against each other. Then he stands, pats Diana on the head as he passes, and heads for home. The light is fading with him as he goes.

Sauna part 2

Another evening, Jake sits in the sauna, obsidian night outside, the single light inside burning like a beacon. He knows he is seeking some sort of ritual, a washing of his sadness through his system. He has built the heat up to a level that feels hectic on his skin. His breaths have to be short and quiet because the air is too hot for his lungs. He is limp, wallowing in the sensation of physical defeat. After half an hour, he can take no more, and lurches forward to push the door open.

It holds against his weight. He stands up and gives it a shove, but the heat overwhelms him for a second. He can feel the thud of his pulse in his head, his vision blurs maroon, and the sweat pours even more from him, sopping his flesh. His knees buckle. He crouches on the floor, where the air is slightly cooler. With one hand he shoves again. No movement from the door. He is trapped.

He can feel panic rise in his system, acid in his throat. He remembers once reading in a file somewhere about someone 'sweltering' to death. He whispers the word 'sweltering'. His tongue feels dead in his mouth. His towel is now soaked through from the moisture on the floor. He pushes the door a fourth time, to no avail. He stands again and throws his whole bodyweight against the door. The wood burns hot against his skin and he is forced to crouch down again. Two problems crowd his mind: first is the issue of the heat, which could, he feels, kill him at a push; the second is, even if it doesn't, he is locked in a small room with nobody likely to check on him for days. He has already drunk the jug of iced water he always brings with him. The peril of self-isolation.

It is hard to think clearly. If anything, the sauna hasn't yet reached its apex temperature. It is almost unbearable for him to climb to the top level. He gasps when his skin touches the wood directly. But he wants to get at the windows. He pushes at them and they do not fly open but yield enough to suggest that they have been secured less effectively than the door. He pushes again but is too weak to shift them very far. He can feel a sort of blackness welling around his eyes, his mouth dry and metallic-tasting. He drops to the floor again, retching. He lies there for five minutes, conserving his energy. Then up, teeth gritted, survival instinct surging, he reaches into the coals and picks up one of the burning-hot stones, the pain jolting down his arm, holding it only long enough to throw it through the glass. One of the windows shatters, and he can feel the breath of air coming in. His hand throbs. He forces himself to wait again, crouched on the floor naked and gasping, while the temperature drops. He wonders why he hadn't thought to use the towel to touch the coals. Was he losing his mind due to the heat?

Gritting his teeth and wrapping his arm carefully in his

towel he clears out the glass. He can see someone has pushed logs from the outside woodpile, thick and mossy and heavy, against the centre of each of the windows, and two more against the door. Pushing his arm through the hole he can just reach it to knock it to the ground. He opens the whole window easily now and carefully squeezes his body out. A piece of stray glass embeds itself in his stomach as he falls to the grass, which is dew-drenched, cold and welcoming.

He sits up. All around him is black. He pulls on his discarded clothes, which are thick and dark and help camouflage him. His sweat has dried tacky all over his skin. He wonders if the person who did this is still around, watching and ready to pounce. He forces himself to lie still, to allow his mind and body to attune to the environment around him, before he pads back towards the house. He can sense no movement anywhere.

A thin trickle of blood collects in his belly button, but he is fairly confident the cut is not immediately threatening, and it distracts from the pain in his hand. As he performs one circuit of the house, he sees what could be a light moving away from him up to Poirot Point, but it is too far to chase and is soon enveloped by the darkness.

Inside nothing seems to have been disturbed. He takes the gun from his bedroom, and performs a search, his nerves jumping. Quiet persists. He locks the place up, and goes to the library, stopping off to grab some ice from the freezer, and the medical case. The blood has dried on his stomach, the hair there is matted. He pours some brandy on the hem of a clean T-shirt, and cleans the cut. It stings, and a small amount of blood bubbles up. It should be fine. He looks at his hand, which is angry and red, the outline of the stone clear, the edges starting to weep a clear liquid. He grips a handful of ice, and then secures it awkwardly with a bandage, holding it in place with his teeth as he does it. He remembers as a child reading about the medieval trial by ordeal, the people ordered to put their hands in boiling water or to grab burning coals. He had always tried to imagine what that would feel like, the scorching of your own flesh. And now he has an idea.

He has a shot of brandy to help quell his shaking, an agitation that has been rising over the last half an hour. The fear itself stings and is shameful in his mind. Cowardly. The booze doesn't help, which figures: alcohol only works in detective books. He has read about it so many times. The shot to warm you through or soothe your raggedy nerves, the necessary jolt, the pick-me-up habit to get you through the day and the job. The trusty bottle, sheathed in brown paper, in the desk drawer. But not for him.

He finds a blanket and curls up, breathing slow and deep, letting his muscles relax, seeking to find a peaceful equilibrium. He must have fallen asleep at some point, because he next notices that dawn is coming. The dark thinning into grey. His wounds ache. The ice on his hand has melted, the bandage painfully pressed against his palm. He gingerly peels it off, and sees he is lucky: there are two or three small blisters, but nothing much to fear but the pain. He stands up and stretches carefully so as not to reopen his cut stomach, and takes a deep draught of water. The sham detective revived by water not booze, he thinks.

He spots Livia's copy of Shakespeare's plays, and wriggles himself into the least painful position he can find on an easy chair beneath a lamp. *Titus Andronicus* comes early in the collection, and he starts reading, almost instantly bemused by a scene of military proclamation and baffling names. Dr Peter said this, he remembers: '*Shades of Titus Andronicus and poor Lavinia*.' He doesn't know if Dr P meant Titus, the play, or the man, a big general who is successful at the beginning before a whole, bewildering series of miseries is visited upon him. 'Poor Lavinia' is his daughter, raped and mutilated, which doesn't sound like Sabine. Jake almost casts the book aside, wondering if the eccentric academic had just been that, eccentric to the point of folly. But then he notices something: Lavinia is assaulted by two brothers, Chiron and Demetrius, abetted by their mother Tamora. A family guilt. A mother and two brothers: 'away with her, and use her as you will, / The worse to her, the better loved of me,' says Tamora at one point. Which even he can understand.

A mother and two brothers bearing the guilt, he wonders. Joan and Davey and Paul at the farm, brutish and violent. Or Mary and Clifford and Martin, less entangled, but still part of the same small world. It is thin stuff, though. He wonders what Dr Peter had discovered, or to whom he had spoken. Jake thinks he should at least share this with Watson, even if it does not go anywhere.

The day has broken as he has been reading. A pallid sun washes into the room, and he tidies up, disposing of the bloodstained material, stashing the gun in a cupboard in the kitchen. Then he showers, with one hand dangling outside, his body turned away from the warm jets of water to protect the weal on his stomach. He was right, he thinks, to push Livia away; he is no safe person to cling to at this point.

Renunciation

That afternoon, Jake is clearing up the glass outside the sauna when Sarah comes up, on one of her rare consti-tutional rambles. Her face is red with exertion, her eyes twinkling. She coughs to signal her arrival, and leans forward to give him a tentative hug.

'What happened here, Jake?'

Jake describes being trapped, pointing to the big heavy logs, but downplaying the risk slightly. Sarah sighs, her lungs faintly crackling. 'I hate to say it, Jake, but you've got to stop bringing this on yourself. This is a wild part of the county. You saw what happened to Dr Peter, didn't you? I could help, you know. Let it be known you've given up your interest. Are keeping your head down. Whoever is doing this would leave you alone.'

Jake looks at her age-softened features, like a statue modelled with a caressing hand. 'That would mean you are talking to the person, or people, doing this, Sarah. So who might that be? Someone who comes into your shop?'

'You know how things are. One person knows, everyone

knows. I don't know who's creeping up on you, and I certainly don't know who took the doctor from us. I shall be sorrowing for him for a long time. But if I speaks to people about you, it will become known around the place and that cannot but help.'

Jake feels suddenly tired of it all. Perhaps he should let it go. Or at least let it be known that he is tending in that direction. He nods. 'I'll tell Watson I've had enough. You can speak on my behalf if you wouldn't mind. Come on, I'll walk back with you. He might still be at Dr Peter's house.'

'Good lad. I know you don't like backing down, and nor should you. But there are other things in life than mysteries, and more important people than the already departed. You're a tough bird, Jake, you know. I shouldn't have thought of throwing a smoking rock with my bare hands.' She shakes her head.

'A clever bird would have used something other than his hand to pick it up, of course.'

'Aye, that's true and all.'

They walk across the fields to the river. Sarah is quiet as if conserving her breath, but occasionally throws out observations about the flora and fauna. The sheep in Morse Field are all tightly clustered in one corner, mumbling and pawing the ground. 'The weather's going to turn, I reckon. I think there's one last bit of heat before the cold weather sticks. You can enjoy yourself for a spell, even if you stay out of the sauna.'

Watson is sitting at the picnic table outside Dr P's house when they walk up. Sarah nods, and trudges off to her shop, her shirt clinging to her back, the flip-flop of her feet loud against the warm concrete of the road.

231

'You only just caught me, Jake. What happened to your hand?' Jake had left a loose bandage on while he was cleaning the glass, just to stop the blisters popping. He talks through the adventure of the night before, and his reading of the Shakespeare play. Watson listens intently.

'Jesus, Jake. I think Sarah's right. You need to walk away. I'm happy to take back that consultant role, and leave you to it. And you should come and formally report that sauna incident.'

Jake shakes his head. 'I can't see the upside in a formal report; and I'd rather you all focused on Dr Peter. I'll let Sarah spread the word, and you can too, if you like. But I'm not going to be driven off the field just yet. We're getting somewhere. Someone is getting rattled. So I'll do my thinking and prodding, and share everything with you. You can say I'm off the case, now that it's a murder inquiry. But let's keep speaking. What do you know about Dr Peter's last movements?'

'I trust you, Jake, you know that. But I hope you know what you're doing.' He pounds his thighs decisively. 'Well, I suppose no blame can be attributed if two former colleagues keep chewing the fat, can it? I'm building a timeline for Peter, and I'll get a copy to you. I'll leave it with Sarah tomorrow. Is that good enough?'

'It is indeed. You're a good man. Any leads?'

'Not much to report. Nobody heard anything. A single blow and a fall wouldn't make enough noise anyway. The initial view of the doctor is that it happened at about eight-ish the evening before you found him. That's why there was still rigor in the body. It was a dark night, not much moon. Anyone could have come in and left without being seen.'

'I think we have to assume he knew his attacker. No forced entry, no defensive wounds, and it took place in the room you'd take a visitor.'

'I agree. But that just puts the whole area under suspicion. Everybody knows everybody. And that's before we even dig a bit deeper into his past.'

'Did you find a murder weapon?'

'No, which means the killer took it with him. The pathologist thinks it was a heavy, metal object, like a spanner or wrench. Hard to wield, but deadly when used with force.'

'It suggests he brought it with him, I guess, to do it. Someone who knew him, who had decided to shut him up.'

'That's definitely our working conclusion, Jake. I don't need to tell you how we think.'

'What do you make of his own theory about Sabine? The mother-brother thing?'

'I shall bear it in mind, but it's pretty weak, I should say. Your statement about Smiths' Farm means we can get a warrant for the greenhouses, but I suspect they'll have been cleaned out by now. Sabine isn't a priority, but it's there at least to be considered.'

'That seems to be her peculiar fate, doesn't it? Overlooked and undervalued, except by a couple of old men who probably should have known better, and now are no longer here to keep the flame burning.'

Watson gets up to leave. 'You and I both know, Jake, that some mysteries never get solved, however much we might like to hope otherwise. You look after yourself now. I don't want to be setting up a crime scene over in Little Sky.'

Jake walks him to his car, and then goes through the village. Livia's house looks empty, her car not parked in the front. Jake is not much interested in company other than hers, and makes his way home, the clouds clearing above his head, and a hazy blue emerging in the heavens around him. Perhaps Sarah is right, perhaps the weather is turning. It is light enough when he arrives, a little foot-sore, beside the lake, and looks down towards his house. And then at the man, a bold line in black, a blemish on the landscape, standing unmoving in front of it.

Cold comfort farm part 2

It takes Jake ten minutes or so to get within hailing distance. He walks past the chickens, who at this time of day seem content to do little more than meander around their field, pecking at worms and slugs and the corn Jake leaves out each morning. They have been a pleasurable addition to life at Little Sky. He can very faintly hear their clucking and fussing from his bedroom, a sound of preoccupation and contentment. The cockerel does greet the morning, as Jake had always read it would, with a brassy stridency, but never quite so loud as to disturb his slumber. They are a little corner of self-contained society, just reliant upon him enough to be a pleasant obligation, not quite bothersome enough to become a burden.

The man has sat down at the table in the courtyard. His dark coat is pulled up around his ears, a shock of black hair sprouting from the top of his head. As Jake approaches, he recognizes his visitor: it is Richard, the cousin from Smiths' Farm. He stands awkwardly as Jake arrives, and defensively holds out a hand. He is big and gangling, his long arms hang well past his waist, his shoulders wide and strong. His clothes are old but clean and functional: dark denim jeans, a brown shirt and brown, heavy boots.

'Pleasure to see you, Jake.' His voice quiet, the feathered lilt of a local accent.

'Richard, isn't it? What brings you here? And can I get you a drink?' Jake feels he should be hospitable, anything this man might tell him could be useful.

'I wouldn't say no to a beer. My stomach thinks my throat's been cut.' He gives a stiff smile, and sits back down, his pink hands worrying at each other. Jake goes inside to fetch drinks. The kitchen is warm and bright and quiet. He puts on a record to mask the noise of his movements – Samuel Barber's String Quartet, which has the famous adagio he has grown to enjoy – and pulls the gun from its cupboard above the sink. He checks it is loaded and leaves it, nestled in the box by a table near the door. He gets two big bottles of local craft beer from the fridge, and two pint glasses, and takes them outside. Richard hasn't moved position. Jake pours the beer, which has the colour and fragrance of honey, and they both take a deep drink.

'So what can I do for you, Richard?'

'Are you still interested in Sabine Rohmer?'

'Yes I am. The police are now looking at everything since the death of Dr Peter, and that includes what may have happened to Sabine. Dr Peter certainly was asking questions about what happened to her, and someone has silenced him. So that makes me want to find out, yes. Do you know what happened to Peter?'

'Only that he got done over in his own house. He allus

236

had been interested in Sabine, though. At one point, he was never out of the hedges near the farm, ready to pop up to say hello to her. He was a harmless old goat, I think. Sabine really liked him. Well, she was so nice to everybody.'

'Including you?'

'Oh ah, yes. God yes. See, it was not a happy place, that farm. My uncle, used to be called Black Paul by folk on account of his thick dark hair and that temper of his, ran the place like an army barracks. He was desperate to make a bob or two, or more. That's how he got into the drug growing: at first a few plants, then producing the stuff wholesale. I know you know about that. Rose told me. But when Black Paul was alive he would make everyone's life a misery: the two lads, who were his, got a lot of it. Shouting, criticizing, as well as the physical stuff. I got a bit. And Sabine saw how miserable it was for everyone.'

'Did he hurt Sabine?'

'Not physically. He would rubbish her work, and when he'd had a few he'd talk about her, crude like. Maybe slap her backside. But Joan was always watching, and wouldn't let him get up to any nonsense. She was always about as frightening as him. Then he died, and we all felt that things would get better. But they didn't. Joan took over, and was as mean as a snake, just as her husband had been. And the boys, Davey and young Paul, they got more power, and started behaving just like their dad. Sabine was trying to get out. She started seeing Rose and thought about leaving the farm. I thought about leaving too, but neither of us made it.'

He is talking to Jake, but staring into the middle distance, his glass emptied in two gargantuan swallows. Jake gets him another beer, nurses his own.

'Were you jealous of Rose?'

'No, well not much. Sabine was never that interested in me, and I'm not exactly much of a catch. She collected people who just liked her: me, the doctor, your old uncle that as built this place.' He looks around appreciatively.

'Why did it end with Rose?'

'She told me she wanted him to take her off the farm, to live elsewhere. She wasn't no naïve little girl. She knew he was involved in the drugs. But he was free, he had money, he was her route out. The thing was, nobody wanted her on the outside. She'd seen all the family business for so long. So the boys put in the word to Rose: end it, or get pushed out yourself. He ended it.'

'So who killed her? I guess that's why you're here.'

'I don't know, I swear. All I know is that she wanted to leave, but was stopped. And then she ended up at the bottom of those stairs.'

'Your cousins, then?'

'They rightly are mean enough. Dirty fighters, allus have been. Davey was a bit queer on Sabine, though. Got close to her, would talk to us about her hair, or a bit of her body he'd seen.'

'Why are you telling me this, Richard? We've barely spoken and now you're doing down your own family to me.'

Richard nods, and says nothing for a moment. 'True enough. But I've not had an easy life in that place, and don't figure that I owe them all that much. Whatever happens I'm going to try and get work elsewhere. I'm a pretty useful farmhand now, and there's still demand for that. I reckon the police are going to shut the drug thing down, and that farm is going to all of a sudden make a lot less to go around.'

Jake thinks of other things he can ask him. It is the first chance he has had to have an open conversation of sorts with anybody close to Sabine and her life.

'What about the brothers in the village, Clifford and Martin? Were they ever around?'

'They were around like everybody is around. They sat and looked at Sabine, like we all did. Like the doctor and your uncle did. But I don't know much more than that.' He pours the dregs of his glass down his gullet, so as not to waste any of the precious liquid. And lurches upwards into a standing position. Jake guesses he is in his forties, and has had a hard, physical life. 'It's a long walk back. I wanted to get to see you and tell you what I know. It's up to you if you do anything about it.' They shake hands again; Richard's is firm, thick clusters of fibrous hair on each knuckle.

As their faces come close, Jake looks into his eyes, surrounded by careworn lines, tired-looking. 'What about Livia, the vet?'

'What about her? Somebody said you were sweet on her. No drama from me about that.'

'Who warned her off from meddling in anything to do with the farm?'

Richard lets go of the handclasp, and raises his palms in a sort of supplication. 'I never did anything to Livia.'

'I didn't say you did. But somebody got Rose to tell her to back off, and then someone grabbed her the other day.'

Richard is thoughtful for a second, scratching both sides of his head. He sighs. 'It could have been Davey or, more

239

likely, Paul. He's the person that runs most of the drug business, under Joan's orders of course. I knew that they weren't happy with you getting close, and they didn't much like the cost of moving the weed to another set of greenhouses.'

'Did you ever hear them say anything?'

'Just that they were going to back you off somehow. Not because of Sabine, or at least they never mentioned her in front of me.'

Jake thinks of the sheep's blood on the door: was it part of a pattern, along with the grabbing of Livia in the wilds?

Richard lifts his hand in a farewell salute, walks away with a shrug, and is absorbed into the landscape. Jake slowly finishes his drink after he has gone, staring at the sun setting in the lake in front of him, a palette of sanguinary colours, set against the solid dark of the water. Wisps of cloud amid the iridescence. He can hear the hoot of an owl. If he waits until the dark has all but claimed the light, he knows it will emerge from behind the trees; impossibly large wings, brown on the top and daringly white beneath, powering itself across the fields with a sort of indolent strength. Its head is so small all you can see, even through binoculars, are those M-shaped wings, which beat faster when it hovers over a creature cowering in one of the fields. Then a sudden drop, a strike, and soaring once more complete with prey. Nature red in tooth and claw, Dr Peter had said once, when he told Jake that he had a resident barn owl in the wood. All that death amid our daily life.

He wonders if Peter had said anything about Sabine to any of the residents of Smiths' Farm. He will have to wait to see if Watson comes up with anything when tracing his final movements, and whether any queries around the farm itself produce something. He checks his phone, on charge by the door, and it is Wednesday in three days, so he can speak with him then. Feeling wistful, he rolls and smokes a small joint as the spectacular sunset washes over him, enjoying the liquid feel of the colours. And then he carefully locks up his property as he goes inside.

Small town

The next day is the day Faye had proposed for their divorce meeting. A trip to the city feels like an unwanted mission, a disruption, or rather an irruption into the new life Jake has created. But perhaps it is all the more necessary for that. He has been concerned he has become too comfortable with remoteness, too cushioned by the distance that comes with nature. He needs to be able to withstand sharpness and rough edges, as the events of the last few days have taught him. He worries – out here in the lonelier, wider expanses – about developing a sort of agoraphobia, that fear of busy meeting places. He wants to confront the tingles and lurches of anxiety inside him, rather than let them build and dominate his thinking.

He packs some water and some nuts, along with a hastily selected, thick novel (one of the later Robert Crais books featuring Elvis Cole and his taciturn, enigmatic partner Joe Pike; another double act who hit first and asked questions later), and heads towards a place on the other side of Parvum where he can pick up a bus. Its service is erratic, but good enough, with patience, to get him to a connecting train station. It is an early start, the lingering darkness slowly dissipated by dawn's hesitant arrival. It is not warm, but the trek takes a couple of hours, sweat mapping a jagged continent of dampness on his top.

The bus stop sits astride a small hill, a verdant view on all sides, wildness battling and losing against the controlling forces of agriculture. The road darts away towards the horizon, the town invisible, but a clear gravitational pull nonetheless, concealed behind blousy white clouds. Jake sits on the turf next to a windblown, moss-stained marker, and reads quietly. The breeze buffets him, dipping then returning, nudging him like an overaffectionate animal.

After an hour or so, the bus appears at a sedate trundle, huffing its way up the incline. It is blue and grey and old, the smell of petrol sweetly toxic in the air as it hisses to a stop. Jake sits at the back and closes his eyes to the affront of the ugly orange upholstery, as he tries to ignore each judder and bounce, the vehicle heaving itself around the twists and turns, pausing every few minutes as if for breath.

There are few places that feel more deserted than a small country train station. The tracks stretch out in both directions, the wind whistles tunelessly through, the buildings are locked up, the posters tattered and out of date. A sense of emptiness and abandonment. And then all of a sudden the thunder of a train's arrival, all bluster and dash, purpose cleaved out of the lonely air. Jake gets on board, and moves to the furthest end of the carriage, away from the only other fellow travellers he can see, a bored family whose young children are squalling listlessly.

It is a steady build-up of human proximity over the course of the morning, culminating in his arrival in the city, a press of humanity in all of its guises. Noise everywhere. The intrusively loud public announcements, the screech of steel on rails, the rising chatter from unfamiliar faces. Jake's size and apparent wildness ensure that his neighbouring seat remains unoccupied, but soon he is made uncomfortable by the crowding of the carriage. And then in the station, a huge Victorian vault, which hungrily absorbs the chatter of the throngs, he notices he is closer to more people than he has been in months. His heart races, his mouth dries.

He moves to the street outside and feels a little better. His phone has burst back into life during his journey, the blurts and bleeps of rediscovered connection. He had removed most of the apps, including email, so it is mainly texts and WhatsApp messages that are appearing, most of which can be easily ignored. The freedom of summary deletion, that sly movement of a finger rightward to consign something to electronic oblivion. He arranges to meet Faye at a bar near their old house, her own messages brisk and efficient in return.

He has some time to kill, so heads to his old office building, a nondescript, century-old shell that has been inexpensively knocked about and extended to meet modern requirements. The guard at the desk remembers him, and welcomes him with warmth and restrained inquiry. There are rules about who can enter, but they are always bent for returning police officers, the force a sort of dysfunctional family that always looks after its own.

Jake heads to the research floor, a warren of rooms filled with stacks of files, and boxes of evidence, for cases from around the country over the last few decades. It is the nation's crime repository, mouldering and growing every year. But it houses the people – searchers, they are called internally – who are experienced in the more modern forms of information retrieval as well.

Jake knocks on a door, confident in the knowledge that its inhabitant will be behind a cluttered desk, eyes pressed dangerously close to a computer screen, her dark skin bathed in a queasy green electronic light. He is right. She looks up, her face crumples into a smile, and she waves him in.

They hug, her glasses pushed up against her head. She is wearing a thick blue cardigan against the room's air-conditioned cool. She has a soft, biscuity smell on her clothes.

'Aletheia, it's so nice to see you again. I knew I'd be able to find you here.'

Her devotion to duty is well-known and celebrated. Aletheia lives with her elderly mother, and caring for her takes up all of her non-work time and most of her money. The rest of her mental energy is poured into her job as a searcher, and she has become indispensable to a handful of senior detectives who know when to turn to her.

Her voice is deep and mellow, like a well struck drum. 'Well, you're quite a sight to wash up here again. I'm not sure we've had anyone as healthy-looking in this place since it was built.'

'I don't know, you look as well as ever.'

'I note the qualification, Jake.' She pats his arm. 'And I can see you've been out in the open rather than working, so you must tell me why you're back in my office again.'

Jake had spent hours here over the years on different

cases, using Aletheia's bloodhound skills to find traces of people's lives. She is an expert in picking up the electronic spoors of existence, the myriad occasions on which an individual leaves a mark on either official records of the state, or – less legally, but just about deniably – on private or commercial sites. Aletheia never leaves the office, about eight feet square of gloom and dust, nothing to see or hear bar the relentless thrum of the computer, where she pieces together connections invisible to everybody else.

Jake tells her a semi-abbreviated version of events, omitting his personal feelings and assessments. Aletheia, eyes closed, flashes a white grin.

'We can talk about your involvement with Livia another time. She is a big silhouette in your story, so must mean something to you. But not I think relevant to the matter at hand. So who are you interested in? The two sets of brothers? Give me an hour and I'll see if there's anything, but I wouldn't get your hopes up. My work is always more successful in an urban environment. I'm a glutton for connectivity, as you know: cameras, and websites, and rapid transactions. That doesn't seem to be a big feature here.'

'I can give you three hours. I need to go and get divorced in the meantime.'

Aletheia nods understandingly, aware of some of Jake's past history with Faye. 'That will be more than enough. It's good to see you again, Jake.'

He decides to walk to meet Faye, a considerable distance by city standards but now his only, his unthinking way to travel. Yet the sheer hecticness of his surroundings shocks him. The endless crush of cars, hooting at any perceived delay on his part. The sudden shriek of an unnecessary siren. A blare of music through open windows. Other pedestrians stopping him getting into his stride: the groups of girls arm in arm across a pavement, the spread of families with their recalcitrant toddlers, the many people shuffling and pausing to look at their phone mid-step.

Space is a luxury, he thinks. Not just for a house, but for each moment of your waking life. He had lived in this place, cramped close to others, compressing himself into the smallness of whatever was available, without feeling the strain of it, without recognizing the shrinkage. But now it all seems so unbearable. The tyranny of proximity.

Jake arrives at the bar in a lather of perspiration and discomfort, and welcomes the air-conditioned calm of the interior. It is not incredibly hot, but the city's stuffiness, the way it holds onto whatever heat is there, feels oppressive after his months away. There is an empty table in a corner beneath a smear of modern art, flanked by two overstuffed armchairs. Nondescript music hums in the background. A group of men in suits bray obstreperously. Television screens silently scroll through the day's news, the eyes of the presenters imploring futilely for attention. He orders a cold lager and watches the door for Faye's arrival.

He has lost much of his tactile memory of her. He can no longer summon up the scent and feel of her skin, the heft of her waist in his arms, the texture of her lips. But she looms familiar when she arrives: coppery hair brushed bright, gentle tan across her lean body visible beneath a pale dress patterned with small flowers. They hug, a model of platonic restraint, before she steps back to appraise him.

'God you look wild, Jake.'

He is used to his appearance now, his image shaped by the outdoor lifestyle. Faye pinches his upper arm. 'And you seem so fit, as well.'

'The joys of wild swimming, you know.' As a way of breaking the ice, he explains his new routine in the mornings. Funny, he thinks, how he needs to conjure up friendly subjects to relieve the potential awkwardness. And sad that the awkwardness is there, a hanging presence, an indictment of where their relationship has settled.

Faye orders a beer too, then pulls out a sheaf of papers from her bag. 'We're both lawyers. Well sort of. So let's get this formal bit out of the way.'

He skims and signs; and the marriage is ended. All of that happiness and anger and planning and frustration and hope and despair. All of that intertwinement. Dissolved with the scratch of a pen.

He looks up. 'This is not where I thought we'd get to.'

'Of course not. But we gave it our best, and just because it didn't work doesn't mean it was a failure. We love each other, we never disrespected each other. We weren't a fit in the end.'

'Do you think if we hadn't lost the, you know, babies . . .' As hard as ever to think of the right term: foetus sounds so impersonally clinical; a term too slight to bear the weight of what they went through together.

Faye holds up a forestalling hand. 'No good can come from us thinking like that. I don't let myself dwell on that. One of my new things is forward thinking, not letting myself be held back.'

They talk for an hour about their lives, but are, Jake sees, now simply skating on surfaces, neither one seeking to understand deeply the other's circumstances. There is far too much politeness in play, the true sign of newfound unfamiliarity. They have no common cause any more, no reason to keep speaking. She can see his new life is not a failed experiment. He can see that she remains what she always was: a beautiful, successful woman able to move on to the next thing.

Jake pays the bill and walks her outside. She buries her head in his shoulder for a second. He can feel a tear prick his eye. They kiss, their mouths brushing, their faces so close he can inhale her beer-sweetened breath. She walks off without looking back, and is absorbed instantly into the city.

Back in the office an hour later, Aletheia is pushing sheets of paper across her desk in his direction.

'I warned you, big man, that this would be slim pickings. As far as I can tell, there is little official interest in that part of the world, or in these characters. I found one reference in an internal Home Office briefing about drug farms, but you seem to have stumbled on their existence yourself. And these names – Clifford and Martin Walbrook; the Smith family on the farm – produced only a couple of minor things. Paul has an assault conviction, now wiped from his record. A fight over a woman that left the victim with a broken nose. And your man Clifford was picked up on a prostitution sweep back in the nineties, and one of the girls nearly pressed charges. He wasn't very gentle with her, as I'm sure you can imagine. It's not clear just how bad, except she doesn't seem to have gone to hospital at least.'

'What happened?'

'Well, you know how it was then. She did a runner

from the police, the case sat on file, folk figured he might have learned his lesson with all the humiliation. He tried to give a fake name, which is why the computer picked him up now. Someone somewhere had to take the trouble to find the right one. Look, here is an image from the file: an amused copper wrote that his mum came to get him from the station. Men, I tell you: pathetic.'

'Not all men,' says Jake automatically. A standard joke in the department, from people who saw the worst of the gender on a regular basis. 'And what about Sabine?'

'I could get access to some of her immigration papers. She had started the process of naturalization, but let it lapse before her death. No trouble to anyone, no problems, no major mark on the record.'

A double tragedy: the innocence of a lost life and the simplicity of the unentangled victim made tracing her fate even more difficult. If it hadn't been for Dr Peter, it would have been as if she had never existed.

'Any help to you?'

'It keeps Clifford in the "possible" team, I suppose. And I'm not surprised about the violence connected to Paul.'

'Are you even sure there's a crime here?'

'You know me, Ally, I get an idea in my mind. Even without the murder of a kindly old man, I was sure something untoward was happening, or why would I have been complicating things in my new simple life?'

'Don't make me answer that. I find clues about people's physical behaviour, but I reckon I could offer plausible psych evaluations as well.'

Jake rests his head on the back of the seat and holds the stale office air in his nose. His former habitat, but something that suddenly feels somehow unhealthful. He needs the broad vistas again, the free, deep breath in his lungs. He takes his leave of Aletheia with friendly regret and starts the long, inconvenient journey back to where he calls home.

Wild swimming part 2

Sarah had indeed been right about the change in weather. Summer seems determined to have its final fling. The next day dawns clear and bright, the sun no longer just a hint in the sky but a blazing presence. Jake spends the day chopping wood, cleaning out the chickens and getting the place in as much shape as he can. There is something pleasingly incomplete about this existence, the work can never be truly finished, subsistence is always an ongoing task. Peter's Garden, as he now thinks of it, is beginning to show signs of life: there is a crop of mustard leaf, and two lines of radish, already ripe for eating. The mustard has shot out of the ground, spreading itself urgently, an insatiable mess of green. He has nibbled it, and it is delicious: peppery and tangy, with a hint of lemon. It requires almost no looking after, and seems determined to cover the whole ground if he lets it.

The orchard is due next week, so Jake hikes up to Velda and starts digging holes. He has a piece of rope, which he uses to make sure the trees will be equidistant, three lines of apple trees, a line of pears, and some plum trees in the corner. That is a lot of digging, and the day ends with plenty left undone, but Jake again has the satisfaction of seeing a shape forming that had hitherto not existed except in his mind.

He feels tired by mid-afternoon, but has had an idea he wants to try. There are a couple of main points of entry to his property: one the approach from the river, going past Morse Field; the other from the road closest to Poirot Point. Jake thinks he should try to do something about security. He has been saving empty food tins since his arrival, out of necessity. There is no rubbish collection out here, which worried him originally. But it is amazing how little refuse he now creates: the food he buys locally has no wrapping, and the bottles of milk and beer he gets are all reusable. The far corner of Peter's Garden is a compost heap he and Mack have fashioned out of wooden offcuts to frame a large container. In it go food scraps, coffee grounds and weeds. When he lived in the city, everything felt like it created an unchecked flow of waste: he and Faye, despite just being the two of them, used to fill bags and bags of the stuff. Even their recycling, dominated by the almost-daily arrival of unneeded clutter and comestibles from Amazon, towered, toppling in the weekly boxes.

But cans are difficult to dispose of in the country, and he has been washing them and storing them in a sack in the basement, waiting for a chance to take them for recycling. He grabs the sack, and walks up to Poirot Point, the afternoon still clinging on against the onset of the evening.

After the stile that marks the entrance to his land there is a narrow neck of ground enclosed on both sides by hedges, before the fields open up to offer the first glimpse of the house. Jake sits atop the stile, pushing individual holes in each can with a screwdriver. He can hear the sheep in the fold above, the hum of bees nearby. When he has a pile of cans prepared, he threads a piece of wire through each of them, and then attaches the wire at just above ankle height to a shrub at each side of the opening. In the night-time, it will be invisible, and the noise will be audible as far down as the house. He does the same across the path, as it emerges from the stream just past Morse Field, with less confidence. This is much further from his house, and there are numerous routes possible for someone to approach the place. But he feels he has done something to advance the cause of security, and that itself is satisfying. An encouraging feeling to go to bed with.

He wakes to another glorious morning, a sunrise hungry for another day of heat. His run leaves him sticky and flustered, and his first dive, naked, into the lake is like a ritual cleansing, the fresh water a soothing balm to his skin, the light bouncing like scattered jewels on the water. He gets his head down, swimming past the island, his eyes staring vacantly at the dark bottom, his front crawl powerful and efficient. As normal, he shifts to breaststroke as he approaches the far side, his head emerging from the water back into the warmth of the morning air.

And then he sees her. There is a pile of clothes on the beach about fifty yards away. And coming towards him, lithe as an otter, is Livia. Her hair is up, and she is swimming breaststroke, her hands cutting the glinting water, the spray hitting her face. She is still in the comparative shallows when he reaches her. A shout of joy sticks clinging in his throat. They stand, thigh deep in the chill liquid, hands clasped. She is naked and breathtaking. Her smooth skin trickling water, pinpricking the surface of the lake. She looks at him, his own skin slightly red from exertion, his broad shoulders and strong arms thickened by the swim. They hold each other. She is pressed against his body. He feels her flesh, firmed, almost rubbery from the cold, her pointed nipples pressing into him. She feels the muscles of his chest, hears the flustered beat of his heart.

He breaks the silence. 'I thought you said you'd never come in here.'

'I actually said that coming in here would show how much you're inside my head. Well you are. I know that now. What better way to show it.'

He rests his hands on the curve of her bottom. They are both shivering slightly. Her arms now have goose-bumps, and he traces them gently with a finger. Her beauty in the water is almost overwhelming.

'Can you swim with me back home?'

She looks back at the beach. 'I forgot to bring my towel, now I think of it. We'll have to walk back for my clothes later.'

So they plunge in together. She is a powerful swimmer, her body beautifully poised as it pierces the water. Each movement thrills him, each movement reveals another part of her: her long neck, her smooth arms, the dip of her breasts, the strong line of her back. Water droplets caught like pinpricks of light in the glare of the sun. And she is anatomizing him in return, as she will tell him later: the curve of his triceps, the bulk of his thigh, his long hair plastered onto his back as he rises from the water. They get to the pier, and he shoves her up first, yet another

255

touch to thrill to. Then he gets out, and grabs towels, one big thick one to wrap her in to still her shivers, the other to tie quickly around his waist. Holding hands they hurry inside. The light is splintering through his bedroom window, warm and inviting. The towels drop. They stare hungrily. And then they come towards each other once more.

The lady in the lake

After they have made love, Jake and Livia sprawl in the patch of light, the sun picking out the green in her eyes, giving a coppery tint to her dark pubic hair. They had clung to each other ferociously, desperately and joyfully. It was all they had both imagined it would be. Jake can feel her drying on him, the weight of her flank against his arm, her cherry scent once more.

'What made you come to see me?'

'Lust, obviously. And just a sense of how wrong it felt to not see you. I know I need to worry about Diana, and our safety, and your safety. But, fuck, I also want to live a little too. I haven't felt like this ever. Coming to the lake was all such a not-me decision, but it seemed to be such an obvious decision too. And a thrill when I stripped off and jumped in that freezing bloody water. I just wanted you like I have never wanted anybody.'

'Me too. I almost started shaking when I finally got to see you naked.'

She looks down appraisingly at her body. 'Not bad, I

suppose, for someone nearly in her forties.' Her skin is now warm to the touch, her stomach slightly soft, tan lines revealing an enchanting milkiness to her breasts and bottom. 'And you were probably shaking from the cold.'

He hadn't been. For one of the few times in his life he had felt enveloped by the moment. Not analysing or over-thinking, just giving himself over to the sensation. He feels himself stirring again, sensing the freedom of two people, joined by lust, and something more than lust, alone in a house in the middle of nowhere. He rolls over, kisses the tip of her nose.

'We better check just once more to see if we're really compatible.' Her hands descend, her eyes twinkle.

Later, Jake makes lunch. He had started the firepit before his run, so it is still smouldering effectively. He grabs two steaks from the fridge, rubs them with garlic-infused oil, scatters rock salt and pepper, and then drops them on the sizzling stones. They take barely two minutes to cook, the flesh charring almost instantly. He serves them with a salad made from the mustard greens, some radishes and a couple of tomatoes from the Nook, dressed in more of the oil and a bit of local cider vinegar. He grabs a bottle of cider from the fridge – 'Not as cold as when we had it at the river,' he recalls as he holds it up to Livia – and they eat on an old purple rug in the sunshine. He is wearing just a tattered pair of shorts, she is in one of his shirts, which gives him tantalizing glimpses as she shifts position.

'That reminds me. We need to go and get your clothes at some point.'

'It's a beautiful day. I can wear something scandalously short of yours, like this shirt, and then get dressed on the other side of the lake. There is luxury in all this land, isn't there?'

'More even than I can appreciate now. If we didn't have all the last few days hanging over us, we could be free.' The wealth of space, as he thinks of it. He has already told her of his visit to the city, the formal ending of his marriage.

She strokes his thigh. 'We can never be totally free. It's dangerous to think that. I have Diana and my job. And I love both. Freedom even for you is a fantasy you should take care not to believe in.'

She is right, he thinks, in a sense. His new life has had most obligation, most of the need for social interaction, removed, and yet still he is here now with her, deliberately tethered, moored once again.

'What we do about us, now that there is an us? I still don't want you involved in the investigation, and you're right not to want that either. You know,' he raises his hand to point behind him, the land generous and overspilling, greens and yellows bathed in the benign rays of the sun and framed by the azure sky, 'all this paradise, this big mass of land, is less secure than ever. One day I hope I won't be thinking about murder, but that day is not now.'

She already knows about the sheep's blood, of course, and now he tells her of what happened in the sauna. She rests her finger on the scab on his stomach, less angry now, blending back into his body.

'You have to get to the bottom of this to get any peace. For both our sakes. I see that now. You carry on, and I'll see you as I've been seeing you. I'll come over when I can. We'll leave each other signs on Sherlock Beech. And you can make occasional visits to the house. Diana likes you, but she has no idea about what a relationship for her mum might mean.'

'I don't need any promises or commitments, just a sense that we have some sort of possible, I don't know, story together.' He kisses her, tasting salt and apple. They listen to the crowding quiet of the empty grounds, the occasional cluck or coo, and nothing more.

After a few minutes, she looks at his phone. 'I've got to go back in a couple of hours. Will you escort me?'

'Of course. I have my meeting with Watson anyway. There's still so much we're both missing.'

'I wish this didn't have to have involved Dr Peter.'

He talks her through what he knows now: Richard's tale, Sabine's desire to get out, Rose being forced to end the relationship. Apart from the discovery of Clifford's prostitution record, they feel the direction of blame is pointing towards the Smith family, especially the two men Davey and Paul. That might be what Peter was implying in his note. But it is not proof, it is barely an argument. That is what now has to be constructed painstakingly, he thinks.

They walk back towards the village in the dying light of the afternoon, summer's final moments stolen from autumn. Livia moves lightly over the trampled grass of the path, barefoot, his shirt rucking bewitchingly as she dips and rises. They hold hands like the young lovers they are not. At the beach, Livia pulls on her clothes, some pale pink knickers, denim shorts. She rolls up her vest, and hands it to Jake to carry, as she has decided to leave his shirt on. She then steps into some green flip-flops, and walks to a clump of reeds. Just behind them is a small package, wrapped in brown paper.

'I got you a present, just in case my body wasn't enough to lure you.'

He opens it, and it is a book: *The Simple Art of Murder* by Raymond Chandler.

'Last time I was here, I couldn't see it in your library, and thought you'd like a bit of theory about detective novels.' She has written a message at the front in black pen, her handwriting neat and precise:

'Down these mean streets a man must go who is not himself mean, who is neither tarnished nor afraid.'
On the day it first begins, love from your lady in the lake.

He closes the book, and hugs her close. Her voice is muffled against him. 'Obviously I wouldn't have given it to you if you'd turned me down.' They walk together through Morse Field, the sheep dotted all over in a pattern-less sprawl. Livia gives them a proprietorial gaze. Jake recalls Sarah's prediction about the weather changing, and how accurate it has proved.

Livia wipes her forehead delicately. 'I can't believe I didn't get a chance to use your shower, now that you mention it. And me being so sticky this afternoon as well.'

'There's always a next time. But,' the shadow of a thought hits him, 'we do need to be careful. This is still a tricky time for us, and I don't want you drawn in.'

They agree to steal their last kiss before they get to the lane by the river. It is lingering, her hair fired by the setting sun, the sparkle of something unknown in the distance, the noise of the flowing water nearby. They look up: the heron is swooping over them, and they hear the beating pulse of its wings, before it is extinguished by the horizon.

Timelines

It is no great hardship to wait for Watson on an evening like this. Scents of late roses and hot grass mingle in his nostrils with notes of cherry perfume and the dwindling sour-sweet tang of sex. Jake is trying to work out his next steps, and how he is going to determine what happened to a woman a decade ago when everything about the crime has been passed over and almost forgotten. Perhaps the better idea is to work the Dr Peter end of the case, on the grounds that his killer is either responsible for the murder of Sabine or is very close to the person who is.

He is staring intently at the water, shambolic choirs of flies seething and swarming incessantly. He doesn't hear Watson's car arrive, and starts when he sits down, clutching a file.

'For a former copper, Jake, you seem to have no awareness of people getting close to you. I could have been anyone.'

'Don't be silly. I could smell the Scotch from here.'

But Watson is right: Jake has a certain blithe disregard

to his surroundings, and he needs to shake it. He suddenly feels that he is now responsible for preserving something, for maintaining something special, and he has to take more care of himself. He is no longer quite the shaggy loner in the farmhouse; there is a thing greater and more fragile in his life to foster and cherish.

If Watson guesses that Jake's life circumstances have changed – and he is, Jake thinks, a canny and nosy old man – he does not let on. 'Why don't you report anything you've learned, and then I'll tell you what we've got, which isn't much.'

Jake explains his conversation with Richard, as Watson stretches out thoughtfully, his feet bending some reeds back towards the water.

'More and more points to that family again. We looked at the greenhouses, following your statement, and they'd been cleared out, those rooms at the back. I've no doubt about the existence of the drugs, though, those rooms were oddly spotless and disinfected. I reckon the stuff has been moved to another hothouse somewhere, this county is lousy with them. I questioned Joan, and she stonewalled, stared at me with those fierce eyes of hers and refused to answer questions. The sons seem dumber, I fancy my chances with them, but I need something to go at first.'

'Does the Clifford record change anything, chief? Is he more than just another creepy, maladjusted man-child?'

'He's been no trouble to me in my time. But nor have the Walbrooks. Nor has Rose, for all his seediness. Perhaps they've all been acting suspiciously, and I've been dumb. The bumbling rural copper, so beloved of your novels.'

'What about Peter's last movements? What do we know?'

263

Watson hands him a sheet. 'I left a copy of this at the Nook, but you must have been too busy to pick it up.' A faint smile plays across his lips, swiftly swallowed when he catches Jake's eye. Jake looks down at the printed paper: it is a list of sightings of Peter based on local canvassing. Peter had been at the Nook for a lock-in the night before, where he was drinking with Davey from the farm, Clifford and Mack. Sarah was in and out of the cellar all night and couldn't recall anything especially suspicious. The day of his death, Peter had been seen striding through the fields by a farmer on his way to make a delivery, and, later, with a swarthy, slight man with dark hair, talking animatedly on the path not far from Smiths' Farm.

'Was that Rose?'

'Yes, he admits that. I spoke to him myself. He denies the drug claims, of course, but says he did speak to Peter, and about Sabine. He says Peter was buzzing around the place, trying to trace what had happened that night when Sabine died. Rose told him what he told you about the end of their relationship, so he seems to be consistent in his story at least.'

'What about the forensics around Peter?'

'We have no murder weapon, though a wrench of some sort is still the most likely. No fingerprints anywhere that we can tie directly to the murder. A crime committed in the dark depths of the night, with nobody to witness or record it.'

'It seems the only thing in our favour is someone is trying to sabotage the investigation, and me personally. I wonder . . .' Jake stops and weighs up his options for a moment before plunging onwards. 'I wonder if our only hope is to draw them out, get them coming after me, to break cover somehow. We then get something to work on, rather than these endless dead ends.'

Watson is quiet. 'Is it worth that, Jake?'

'We have to bring this to a head and whatever peril I'm in, I'm in whatever happens next. I am seen as a meddler. Maybe people will think I've pulled back, but will they want to make sure?'

'They'll know that attacking a former policeman will bring the full weight of the force on them.'

'They might also feel that they have left too few other clues for that to matter.'

'I want you to think about this, Jake. Our last idea was to get you out of this, not draw you back in. Now you seem to want the opposite.'

'The funny thing is I do want to be left alone. But I want peace. I want to swim in my lake without thinking about someone lurking in the woods. And I want Sabine and Peter laid to rest too. I feel I owe them both that. But you're right, let me weigh it up before I decide what to do.'

They sit meditatively as the dark draws round them like a shawl, each wondering how to unearth what is being concealed from them.

Heavy weather

The next day the heat breaks. A dawn comes of mizzling rain and chill winds. The shower's steam is blown sideways when he stands to warm himself. Jake dresses carefully and paces around the house, a coffee in his hand. He has unearthed some of Arthur's old records from the seventies, and is playing them, thick amplified guitars, wailing singers, effortful lyrics. All that expended energy is oddly soothing. He has *Toys in the Attic* on by Aerosmith, and sits to reread all of his case notes since all this began.

The one thing he knows he should do is return to the farm and see where Sabine died. The crime scene is always the most important place in any investigation, and he has never examined it. He locks up carefully, wondering whether he should indeed lie low for a while. Content himself with snatched ecstasy with Livia, and hope that other people solve the problem. But even then he cannot be sure of an eased mind, of peace. He already wonders if there is someone crouched in the drab mist outside, watching him with malevolent intent. He doesn't want to spend his life looking over his shoulder.

Visibility is pretty low, the rain now squalling, blustering into his face as he walks, head slightly bowed to the ground. The lake is slate grey, pockmarked with raindrops, austere and uninviting. The walk is a long one, as all have been since his arrival. He is used to that rhythm in his life now: the remorseless pacing at one determined speed, the stretch of the hamstrings, the hot sting of the feet. He gives himself up to it; it is steady and predictable. He can feel the dead weight of the ground, hear the restless swish of the trees and hedges. There are ruts in some places, now filled with water, thick churns of mud. The rain beats down on his coat – his one waterproof item, a sports top designed for outdoor running – and makes broad damp marks on his jeans. His boots squelch as he goes.

Smiths' Farm has the sullen silence of all buildings in the rain, peering out into the green damp, looking like it has been washed up and discarded. Jake comes to the farmhouse and looks through the window. There is a light on, and a small fire mournfully stuttering in the corner of the room. He is about to knock, when a hand descends on his shoulder, spinning him around. It is Davey, and behind him, water soaking her black dress through, his mother Joan.

Jake weighs them up carefully. 'Hello, both of you.' Joan inclines her head and says nothing. 'You know why I'm here, probably. I'm still interested in the death of Sabine Rohmer. You've had plenty of time to talk to me, and you've not done it. I want to know why?'

Joan manoeuvres herself past him and opens the door.

'Why don't you come in, policeman, it's far too grim a day for us to be outside anyhow.'

He follows her in, Davey behind. Joan motions him through the living room, where the fire is surly, losing a battle with the damp, to a warmer kitchen, heated by a huge black stove that dominates the room. She pours three mugs of thick milk from a steaming, cream-coloured ewer kept warming at the stove's corner, gives one to Davey and looks enquiringly at Jake.

He takes it, feeling his pinked fingers tingle as he holds it to his chest. Joan perches herself on a stool by the stove, which leaves the kitchen table for Jake and Davey. They sit at opposite sides, their feet almost touching in the middle.

'So why are you here mithering us?' Her eyes are small, coal-dark, and beady.

'I just want to know what happened to Sabine. Nothing more. I don't care about your,' he reaches for the euphemism, 'side-business. I care about Sabine.'

Joan snorts into her drink. 'You've never met Sabine. Though I have to say that she could attract men while she was on this earth, so I shouldn't be surprised that she has carried on afterwards.'

'All I know is that she meant a lot to some people, and now someone else is dead because of caring about her.'

She smooths out the fabric of her dress with small, controlled movements. 'That old fool was always poking around the place. How do you know he was interested in Sabine's death?'

'Because he told me. And because every time I've mentioned it someone looks nervous.' He turns to Davey. 'Are you nervous, Davey? Did you like her? Were you jealous of Rose getting to touch her whenever he wanted?'

Davey glowers back and says nothing. He looks to his mother like he is asking permission to speak. Jake looks across to Joan too. Her face is expressionless.

'Can I see where she died? I can't see it can do you harm either way.'

Joan stands up slowly, gestures with her head for him to follow. Davey remains slumped in his chair, his face impassive. They walk through the house, which has the wintry feel of neglect outside of the main rooms, the walls pale with peeling paint. They emerge from a back door into a courtyard. To their left a tower rises out of the side of the building, three storeys high. Coming from the top floor is a flight of stone steps down to the ground. They are brown and crumbling, and look desolate in the dimness.

'We call that tower the Folly around here. And it's part of the oldest section of the house, more than three hundred years old. Sabine used to stand at the balcony on top. That's where she slipped and fell.'

'What's in the tower?'

'Sabine had her room on the ground floor, and the top two are storerooms. She often liked to stand on the balcony and look at the land. She was always talking about her love of the land.'

'Can I climb it?'

'Be my guest, policeman. Just you make sure you stay upright.'

Joan waits for him at the base, and he climbs up carefully. The steps are mostly solid, but some dampened brick has sloughed off with age and moisture. At the top there is a small viewing platform. The countryside spreads out before him, a giant patchwork of muted pastels, the clouds hanging thick and low. Joan looks up at him, and he leans on the rail.

'Why would she come up here in the dark?'

'It was about nine when she died, and it was summer, it would have been light enough.'

Jake remembers the police report. No evidence of struggle, no damage to her body apart from that caused by the fall. So either she was with someone she trusted, who somehow threw her off the building, or she fell. Or there is one other option: she threw herself. His stomach lurches as he looks down to the ground, imagining the impact of the concrete, the hardness shattering the bones as they landed. He sees Joan's scowl of impatience but is transfixed to the spot. Despair can send you over the edge. He has seen that before. But, why, if the truth was suicide, would someone need to cover it up? What might have driven her to a silent leap into certain, crunching, eviscerating oblivion?

He walks down the stairs carefully, a hand on the railings, which are cold and slick with rain droplets. Joan has folded her arms, big pink slabs, and is looking at him.

'Do you think she jumped, Joan?'

'She fell is all I know. I can't tell why.'

'Something changed in the couple of weeks before she died. What was it? Was it Rose, was it one of your boys? Did you ever see anything?'

Her voice is controlled, coiled with serpent menace. 'I see what I see in my own house. Now it's time for you to leave.'

He is getting soaked through. He troops back into the house. Davey hasn't moved. There is mud on the floor where he has been kicking it off his boots. He doesn't look up at Jake or respond to his farewell.

Jake waits until Joan catches up with him, her awkward gait rolling her into the room at no great speed.

'One other thing. Somebody made a grab for Livia the other day. And it was either to do with Sabine or with your drug business.'

A petulant harrumph from Davey, who continues to look disconsolately downwards.

'Joan, can you tell me anything about it?'

'I'm telling you nothing. But I'll tell you again that if you leave us alone we'll leave you alone. You and yours, if you understand me.'

'And if you understand me: anything happens to Livia, any threats, any sense of grief at all . . . and I will come here and tear this place to the ground, ruin your home and hurt your entire family.'

Joan nods. 'That seems to be the situation.'

'Make sure your other son sees that too.'

Jake walks back through the miserable house, pushes open the front door and heads back out into the rain. It is afternoon, but it feels like night already.

Scoop

On his walk home, Jake skirts Parvum, keeping to the sides of fields on a series of well-trodden paths turned plashy in the downpour. The relentless drumming of the rain is beginning to irritate him. His thoughts jump around, trying to work out what is bothering him most about the plights of Sabine and Dr Peter. He comes close to Sherlock Beech, and sees a scrap of fabric hanging down, pink and sheeny, torn from a nightdress. There is also a card propped in the crook of the branch, sopping with water. He carefully opens the envelope: *Come at 5pm if you get this. I want you to meet someone.* The ink is running and soon the message is rendered illegible. Jake has no way of knowing the time, but guesses it must be approaching late afternoon. The sky is scowling, turbid with thick grey clouds that darken the day. He decides to see if Livia is home, and doesn't mind him coming early.

There is a light in her window. The street empty and silent. He knocks and she comes to the door, wearing green leggings and a long cream jumper. A flash of smile, abrupt like lightning. 'Well, well, glad you got my message. You poor thing, all bedraggled in the rain.' She leans forward, her tongue darting out to touch his ear. 'As they say, let me get you out of these wet things.'

She draws him into the house, which is bright, and busy with childish clutter, and warm and welcoming. Jake looks at the clock, its pendulum rocking with calm persistence. It is five minutes to four o'clock. He kisses Livia, one hand on her shoulder, the other on the small of her back.

After a minute, she pulls away. 'I have to get Di from school, so why don't you jump in a bath while I'm gone. Your clothes can dry by the fire, and I still have your shirt from before. I'll be back in half an hour, and then my friend will be here. I mentioned her a while ago: Joanna, the journalist. I thought she might be useful in working out what happened with Sabine.' She is bustling and efficient as she puts his wet shoes to dry in the corner. 'I know, I know, I'm not getting involved, but she's nearby and I told her you were interested.'

'Having another person tell me I don't have much of a case can hardly hurt, I suppose. And she may well have picked up something we haven't thought about yet. You'll just have to tell her to be gentle with my fragile male ego.'

'When you meet her, you'll realize that's not very likely.'

Livia guides him into the bathroom, which is big and echoey. An old-fashioned white tub stands on porcelain feet in the centre. She switches on both taps and soon a thunder of running water can be heard, a fug of steam rising.

'There's a bit of a knack to getting the temperature right. Now, let me take those clothes.'

With a sly, lubricious expression, she helps him pull

off his two tops, which are damp and cling to him. She undoes his jeans and tries to push them down, but they catch on his thighs. He squirms and helps her shuck them off, taking his socks with them.

'I'll leave your underwear, my dear, for you to put on after the bath.'

She rests her hand against his stomach, tracing how the hairs there connect with those below. Then she pulls down his boxer shorts and places them on the chair by the door. She looks back appraisingly, her eyes wide and hungry, a curl to her lips.

'I do like objectifying you like this, Jake. I can't tell you how much I want to stay and deal with that thing you're pointing at me, but you're going to have to wait, I'm afraid.'

She leaves for a moment, and comes back with his old shirt, which she has washed and dried, and places on the chair. 'I'll be home with a child soon. So get clean, and beat that down, and wear this. We'll have to find some other time when we can have a bath together.'

'I'll hold you to that, I promise.'

He hears the slam of the front door, and turns off the taps. There is a mountain of sweet-smelling foam and he sinks through it gratefully. It is his first bath in more than three months and he wallows in the luxury of it. He finds some shower gel – something green and minty and strong – and washes himself carefully all over. He shampoos his beard and his hair, and then completely submerges himself in the water. That wall of comforting silence when your ears are filled with no sound. He emerges, spluttering and feeling clean. He spends the next five minutes emptying the bath, and drying himself and the surrounding area, which is wet with his splashes. Then he puts on his shorts and the shirt, and waits by the fire, picking up the Sherlock Holmes stories he had given to Livia. When he sees the twin lights of her car poke into the room as she parks, he pulls his damp jeans on, so he is in an acceptable state to receive them when they come through the door.

They enter, animated, the happy chatter of mother and child. Diana doesn't seem surprised to see Jake, and gives him a jaunty wave, before coming close to show him her latest artwork.

'You're still much better at drawing than me, I see,' he says. She beams, and goes to the kitchen.

'Only one piece of fruit before dinner, lovey.' Livia sits down next to him on the sofa, their thighs touching, and gives him a quick, surprise peck on the cheek. He is wary of being too affectionate in front of Diana, and senses that Livia is not entirely comfortable. He rests his hands on hers for a moment, and that has to suffice.

'So Joanna has worked at the local paper for ages. I said that you were interested in Sabine's death, and she wanted to help. I think she may have been suspicious about something at the time. She'll come for an early dinner.'

'That's great.' He lowers his voice. 'And I know we want to take things slow, especially around Diana. So I'll go whenever you give me the push.'

'How gallant.' She moves her hand up towards his crotch. 'No sleeping over, but we may be able to sneak something on the naughty side after Joanna goes.'

It is a promising thought, and he pauses, before mirroring her pecked kiss. Jake then helps Livia cook dinner: marinated chicken thighs, sweetcorn and jacket potatoes. The chicken, she explains, is a recipe of her mother's: a little bit of Caribbean that has come with her. It smells fragrant of thyme, garlic and Scotch bonnets.

'The rest, as you see, is more English. Actually, is there anything more English than jacket potatoes?'

Jake doesn't mind, he still relishes the novelty of a family meal. And the corn is fresh, picked and shucked that day, a violent yellow, tingling with sweetness. They boil it for just a minute, before smothering it in salt, pepper and butter.

Joanna arrives just before dinner. She is in her early forties, pale and thick-waisted, with mousy hair down to her shoulders. She is dressed in jeans and a jumper, and carries an outsize brown shoulder bag, from which he can see papers poking. She has laughter lines around her eyes, and is warm and friendly to Jake.

He asks her about her job.

'It's always interesting, just about, even in these days of clickbait and no subeditors. Though most people think journalism comes straight out of the devil's bottom hole, and most national journalists think local journalists are desperate hicks who wish they could be promoted to somewhere sexier.' Diana half-chokes on a mouthful of potato and salad cream. 'Sorry, Livia. I shouldn't have brought bottom holes into it.' Diana snorts again. 'But you know what I mean, Jake. You used to work for a despised institution like the police; not everyone respects it and it sometimes makes you a little unwelcome at parties.'

'And I thought we were going to sit here and tell war stories about how vital to society our contribution has been.'

'Absolute nonsense, of course. Now Livy here is useful: you can't have a rural society without a vet. And Diana is going to be something marvellous, I can tell. No, you and I are the bottom-feeders, Jake. Sorry for bringing bottoms into it again.' She takes a sip of wine. Jake is drinking water with lime cordial, along with Diana, who enjoys the fact they are sharing the same type of drink.

'I started out as a reporter, which is where I might be useful later, actually. And it was lovely. I had my little Mini. I'd get tips about goings-on all over the shop and head out, file a story on my laptop, and then eat my lunch on some bucolic hill feeling like a Brontë sister, before meeting farmers or whoever for a drink in the late afternoon and a talk about local politics. I got paid bugger all, sorry, Diana, but just loved the job, the chance to get to know an area properly. Now I've been promoted to news editor and assistant editor, two jobs rolled into one. And I spend my day overseeing a website that tries to get as many clicks as it can about a sinkhole or a traffic accident, marshalling a team of two people to rewrite agency copy written by someone with no connection to the community. Once a week we chuck most of it into a paper that hardly anybody buys except for the old or terminally bored, paid for by ads that are getting less common every year. Soon we'll just be a website with annoying pop-up demands to sell you some sort of tat, a series of local announcements, ripped-off national stories, and the odd court copy we have managed miraculously to write ourselves. Still, cheers all.'

Jake tells her about the headlines he used to be sent by Arthur. 'Oh thank you very much indeed, always good to patronize the local paper, chaps, I get it. I probably wrote some of them myself. Let me think: "Girl with eyepatch called a pirate by teacher". That was one of mine. Or: "Drunken man threw crisps in dry cleaners and shook fist in bakers". Or: "Budgie to squawk at funeral". And "Man stole woman's pants for 17 years". Serious story that.'

Jake and Livia are laughing hard, as is Diana. Joanna rolls her eyes in mock-anger, and drains her glass.

They play charades over coffee and ice cream, Joanna leading the way with her rude rendering of *The Untouchables*, which renders Diana limp with laughter on the floor. Then Livia bustles her to a bath and bed, and leaves the two others to talk. Joanna pulls out a pack of Marlboro Red.

'Livy, can I have one of these poisonous things while you're tucking Di safely away?'

'You will anyway, so I don't know why you're asking.'

'True enough. Never ask permission, just apologize after. The journalist's code.' She winks at Jake. 'Now, let me get my stuff together.'

They move to the living room, which is warm, the fire rasping with every gust of wind outside. Joanna explains that she had covered the death of Sabine at the time, which meant she reported the inquest, and spoke with some of Sabine's friends for background.

'I ended up writing a longer version of the story they used in the paper, so I've brought that for you.' She hands him over a sheaf of typed paper, slightly yellowing with age, a coffee stain visible on the cover sheet.

'Why are you helping me, Jo?'

'First of all, I love Livy like a sister. She looked after my kids when I was ill, and she is just a wonderful thing

278

in the world. And I can see something in her eyes when she talks about you. Personally, I like my ex-coppers a bit more straightforward, and a bit less hippy, but there's no accounting for taste. Second, I was serious when I said about how much I loved being a reporter. I did get immersed in stories, and there was something not quite right about what happened to Sabine. Of course, the coroner was satisfied, and I got distracted with the next thing – probably man shouts at pothole or something – and it went away. But I remember her picture, that young face with a kind smile, and wondering why she ended up dead at the bottom of some stairs.'

'Did anything particular strike you as odd?'

'Just that there were a lot of men all around her, and most were weird when I spoke about her to them. Defensive. Clammed up quickly. And that something seemed to have happened to her before she died, but nobody could say what.'

'I've found something similar.' Jake tells her an abbreviated version of his experiences, including his visit to the tower in the farm.

'So you think she might have been driven to suicide?'

'It's certainly a possibility. But what drove her, and why is someone trying to cover it up?'

'If you can connect Sabine and this dead doctor, you'd have a hell of a story. "Deaths a decade apart shock sleepy village" and all that. I could even write it and sell it to the *Mail* or somewhere. Just to reassure you that I'm not the first altruistic journalist in existence.'

'I don't mind, so long as we get to the bottom of it. And, of course, I don't want Livia mentioned.'

'Who's being overprotective and patriarchal about me

now?' Livia emerges from Diana's bedroom, blinking from the dark inside, her face softened and maternal.

Joanna lights another cigarette, and waves her empty glass hopefully in Livia's direction.

'There's one other thing that might help you. Back then I was constantly trying to get serious features in the paper. My naivety has worn off, needless to say, but I did some work on the problem facing women in rural areas. All the talk about harassment and assault focuses on big cities when you think about it: you know, dank underpasses, neglected tower blocks, tube stations late at night. But look at us in the countryside: no lighting, isolated cottages, pubs in the middle of nowhere. So I started digging around for cases of assault that had been reported but never solved, and boy were there a lot of them. The piece got spiked in the end, and I never really proved anything, but you can have my notes. If you're looking for something bad that happened to Sabine, it could have happened to someone else. What do you think?'

'I think you're a great woman, especially for a journalist. Let me go through all this, and I might come back with questions.'

'Yes, Livia tells me that you have no phone or internet, and you communicate by garments in a tree, so I'll wait with rapt attention for you to make contact. Perhaps a smoke signal, or a compliant pigeon, or a trained collie will follow me home one morning. "What's that, old boy, Jakey is stuck in the old mine?" and all that.' She gives him a file, about half an inch thick, and tells him to look after it.

'That's some of my best work in there, you know. Not that those braindead dickheads on the paper saw that.'

She slaps her thighs lustily, and rises from the sofa. 'Now I'm going to toddle off home before I get too drunk, and so you two can have a good bonk while the innocent child is asleep.' Livia escorts her to the door. Joanna turns as she leaves. 'I hope you're as good a man as you seem, Mr Jake, that's all I'll say.'

Livia closes the door, and leans against it, eyes closed in mock-embarrassment. 'She's great, isn't she?' She walks forward, pulling off her jumper. Then pauses to remove her leggings too: a lengthier, and delightfully awkward process in Jake's eyes. His breath catches, the flickering light of the fire plays across her skin. 'Now about that bonk . . .'

He follows her into the bedroom, and they shut the door. The noises they make are muffled through the rest of the house.

Digging in

One in the morning, cold and clear, and Jake starts the walk home. Livia had said he could stay, but he could also see in her eyes that she was worried about Diana waking up to find a man in her mum's bed or at the breakfast table. He waggles his torch around as he walks, a thin streak of light in the black. He never fails to appreciate the depth of the silence at night, or the darkness. It feels like oblivion. Nothing seems to be moving in the air as he approaches the river, which he can sense more than he can see, something not-quite-black snaking out away from him, faint shush of flowing water.

Out of nowhere, the huge growl of a revved engine, blinding bright lights, his shadow suddenly stretched out before him. A car ten yards away, bolting forward bull-like, on the charge. He has no time to think. He can feel the instant proximity, the throbbing pressure of its immense weight as it swerves towards him. He throws himself into the ditch beside the road, leaping in desperation, heedless of where he might fall. The car passes by him, so near it almost scratches against his clothes. The papers he was holding scatter upwards. His descent is quicker, he slams shoulder first into the unseen ground, hot pain in his face as twigs snag against it, his body coiling into the dip at the bottom where the rain has softened the ground to a sludge that absorbs his impact. He is immediately on his feet, changing his location in case the car reverses into the ditch to crush him. He ducks down and half crawls half runs in the same direction as the vehicle, which is now performing an emergency U-turn just before the road becomes the river. It roars back, the centre of the universe, but he is flat in the depression, his dark clothes part of the unseen landscape. His eyes are up: all he can see is a big 4x4 screeching away, loud as obscenity, its number plates obscured by smeared mud. The noise ebbs slowly into the nothing. The night is still again.

He lets out the breath he has been unconsciously holding, checks himself for injuries. There is a thin smear of blood he can feel on his face where the tight coils of the hedgerow, the tiny tough twigs at its base, snagged him. His shoulder throbs a bit, but his landing had been soft enough to stop him breaking anything. Three months of exercise have left him much lighter on his feet, he reflects, much less fragile physically. He spends ten minutes trying to recover all of the papers he dropped, most of which have landed near to each other. They feel damp and he hopes they are still legible. His hands start to shake as reaction sets in. He feels the chill more than he normally does. Another attack on him also means his assailant knew he was at Livia's. He is drawing her into danger every second he spends with her.

And what about him? He has now been attacked twice,

both times in ways that could have left him seriously injured or worse. It means he must be close to something, but it also feels like he is trapped, so enmeshed in the problem that escape to safety and solitude is now impossible.

He takes care in his approach to Little Sky, which was once such a haven and now feels more like a fortress. There is no sign of disturbance, the chickens are silent in their houses. Nothing stirs as he makes himself pause, crouched in cover, to wait five minutes so he can survey the place fully before he goes to the door. His friendly owl hoots from an invisible point. No movement. He goes in and locks up.

The papers are damp, and he lights a fire in the living room, and spreads them out in front of it. Then he goes to the library to distract himself with a book, his heart too wild for sleep. Eventually he calms himself, and sprawls on the couch as the grey light of the pre-dawn slinks slowly across the room, his eyes closed, his breath becoming steady.

The next day, it takes a while for his body to feel normal, and he has to stretch before he exercises. Mack arrives mid-morning with a trailer full of trees for the orchard planting. The rain has been completely driven off by the stiff breeze, and it is achingly bright, the sun's rays falling with more light than heat, small white clouds scudding fast across the sky. Each breath is a tonic of clean air, a chance to swell the chest and drink it in.

Jake spends a couple of solitary, pleasant hours planting. It is not arduous work. The ground is soft and giving, the trees bed down with minimum effort. And an orchard is springing up around him like a gift. It is too late for fruit this year, so this also strikes a note of confidence, of forward thinking. He is, he realizes, still emotionally equipped to furnish a home, to prepare for a future. That must mean something.

By lunchtime he is done: three lines of trees, mere saplings now, tottering even when the breeze runs light, but setting down roots, forging thicker and stronger connections day by day. Jake looks around carefully, as he now must do, and locks up the property. The chickens are taking in the sun, their brown feathers glinting as they strut. He takes with him some bacon folded into his last bit of homemade bread, something to keep him going.

The Nook is empty of customers, so he asks Sarah if he can use her phone, an old-fashioned, cream-coloured device hanging off the wall in the kitchen. He calls Watson and tells him about the car incident, quietly and calmly. Watson's reaction is loud and concerned, and Jake agrees to meet him, this time by the church at the far end of Parvum. Jake has been going there occasionally on his walks: it is smaller than the one in Bluntisham where Sabine was buried, less architecturally distinct. But it has been quietly, humbly serving the religious needs of people for centuries, its medieval interior ripped out and painted over in the Reformation, leaving a space that is calm and restful. It is mostly locked up except on Sundays, but Jake likes the bench in a sunny corner, which is always quiet. There's not much reason to go there in the week, which makes it attractive enough to him.

Sarah has clearly been listening, because she is staring at him as he hangs up. His face flushes hot with sudden anger.

'I know, I know. I shouldn't be doing this. But I am

sick of the stress of it all. You can have your little gatherings with these silent, cryptic guys, who don't want newcomers and don't want change, and you can tell them that I'm not backing down. For fuck's sake, Sarah, don't you care that Peter died?'

She gingerly approaches him, and enfolds him in a surprise hug. 'I miss Peter, the daft old stick, every day. And I wasn't going to tell you to stop anything. You can count on me in my own little way to help you, you know. I want this over. But I don't want you hurt, and nor that lovely lass either. I know what I know when I see you together, and it gladdens my heart. But at the moment you seem to be stumbling this way and that and not getting anywhere.'

'I don't know. I'm beginning to see something. I think Sabine didn't fall and wasn't pushed: I think she jumped. And I think someone must have driven her to that, and didn't want anyone to look into it. I think someone bothered her in that farm before she died. Maybe it was one of the brothers, maybe it was someone else. But I'm going to find out one way or the other, or what peace will any of us have? Especially Livia.'

Sarah digs him in the ribs. 'I knew you were soft on each other. What can I do?'

'Just let me use your phone sometimes. And maybe tell one of your gatherings that I'm getting close to working out who caused Sabine's death. And let me know any reactions that stand out. Meanwhile, I'll go and tell Watson where I've got to.'

'Just keep your eyes open whatever you do.'

Good advice, he thinks, as he steps on the road to the church, happily empty of cars for the moment.

286

Crayfish

Watson is waiting for Jake on the bench, his head, as ever, seeming distant from his body which stretches out away from him like a piece of bubblegum pulled to breaking point. They shake hands, and Jake sits at the opposing end of the seat. Meetings on benches remind him for a second of Faye, that part of his life as remote as someone else's history. He wonders if he will ever see her again.

'You don't look bad for an almost hit-and-run victim. No chance you're overdramatizing just for effect, I suppose?'

'Go and look at the road. You can see the tread marks where it skidded, and the U-turn did a bit of damage to the greenery too.'

'I'm not going to doubt you. So what more do you know?'

Jake explains his theory of Sabine as a suicide, and his conversation with Joanna. 'I haven't had the chance to go through her notes yet. What with the keeping alive thing I've been prioritizing. But I will, and something may jump out to fresh eyes. What about you? Where is your investigation going?'

Watson sighs, lugubrious. 'Not in any positive direction. There's not much physical evidence we can work on. We did look through Peter's things, and there was little to find other than observations of the natural world, and this.' He pulls out a piece of paper. 'It's the beginning of a note he was writing at some point, we presume, that day or evening. Some pages of a different notebook had been torn out, perhaps by the killer. But this had fallen down behind the kitchen table.'

Jake takes the note. It had never been finished, and ended in mid-sentence:

Dear boy, we must speak. Since my last note, I realize that we must look closer to home when

'Does that mean anything to you?'

'Well it could mean that he found out something about Sabine that happened where she lived: involving one of the brothers perhaps. Or it could mean closer to his home, someone in the village. Or even my home, but I don't know who that could be other than Arthur. It's another thing that suggests Peter was killed because of the questions he was asking. God, I wish I'd had the chance to speak to him.'

Watson's lips are pursed. 'Do you need to do something about your security?'

'I'm keeping things locked up, and I have good lines of sight in the day. At night, I should probably stay locked inside, I guess.'

'No reason to be out and about, is there?' Watson smiles

broadly. 'Oh, I'm enough of a policeman to draw conclusions about you coming out of a house at one in the morning, your mind on something other than a nearby car . . .' He pauses as two crows stalk the ground in front of him, their piercing calls a harshness in the soft afternoon. 'I shall say no more. You can always call me if you get anything; I'll come running. Now, can I drop you anywhere?'

'I better tell Livia what happened, now that I think of it. Can you drop me there?'

Livia has left a note on her door: *Gone crabbing, back at 4.* She often had concerned farmers come to her house if there was an emergency, so she tended to tell people where she was. Jake had left the church at after three thirty, so he thinks he won't have long to wait. He doesn't. He is leaning against the side of the house, out of the wind, when the happy cackling of Livia and Diana reaches him before they do, laden with buckets and bags.

Diana runs up to him, face flushed by the weather. 'Jake, we caught so much! It's amazing.'

Livia opens the door, and then takes the two big buckets to the kitchen sink. Jake and Diana follow, her clutching at his hand in excitement. 'Diana, you know so much more than me, I thought you could only catch crabs at the seaside.'

'We call it going crabbing, but we're catching cratefish.'

Livia looks up. 'Crayfish, lovey. The river is teeming with them, Jake. We have a couple of traps we fill with rotten fish, which draws them in. She's called them "crate-fish" since she was little. And they're amazing to eat, if you want to stay.'

'Stay, stay!' Diana is keen. 'Because mummy has promised to ask you something.'

'OK, how could I refuse? But I have to get home straight after. Can I talk to mummy first?'

'Not before she asks you the question.'

Jake looks across at Livia, who is cleaning crayfish, her fringe falling over her eyes. 'I said I would ask if we could come to see how the chickens are doing, after school tomorrow. I said you might be busy, and we could always do it another day.'

Jake is torn. On the one hand, he thinks he shouldn't have them anywhere near him. On the other, he thinks that in the day they will be safe enough: he has only faced danger in the dark, on his own.

'I'm going to say yes.' A squeal erupts. 'But I need to talk to mummy first. Can you go and do me a picture that puts my drawing to shame?'

Diana darts off with a delighted expression. Livia dries her hands on a towel.

'Do I need to be worried here, Jake?'

'Not exactly.' He explains what happened last night.

'Oh, thank God you're OK.' She rushes to him and clutches him tightly. She feels reassuring in his arms, her body snugly fits his.

'So I came over to warn you to be careful.'

She strokes his arm. 'What did Watson say?'

'He told me to be careful. Which I am being. The house is locked up tight, and in the day I can see for miles. So I think you're safe for a visit in the afternoon, but you shouldn't stick around. And I'll be gone from here before dark tonight too.'

'Are you scared?'

'I'm scared of losing our chance at something. I feel more concerned about my life because of you. But I have to think I'll get to the bottom of this, or the police will lose interest and the danger will go with it. I just want to be wary until then.'

She raises her head and kisses him hard on the mouth, her tongue finding his with urgency. He pushes the hair from her eyes, which are shining green as a cat's. He kisses her nose and her forehead. She grasps the front of his shirt. 'I'm glad you think there's something to lose here. Because I feel it with all of me.'

She looks up at him, he is lost in her gaze, and then over at Diana, who is getting up from her drawing. Livia backs one pace away.

'Well let's see what the artist of the family has done.'

The late afternoon passes happily. The crayfish are smooth and chunky, served with bread and Livia's take on a hollandaise. Jake leaves while the sun is low in the sky, the colour of egg yolk, but casting enough light to make shadows on the ground. Nobody follows him as he walks carefully home.

No country for
young women

Joanna's notes have dried into stiff sheets, and apart from the odd smear of roadside dirt are completely legible. The next day Jake sits with a steaming coffee and begins to read. For all her drollery, Joanna is, he can see, a fine journalist, diligent and thoughtful. Her unpublished feature takes as its subject the problem of solving rural crime against women. She explains what it must be like to be the victim of domestic abuse, stuck in an isolated homestead, the husband a surly drunk, silent and uncommunicative during the day, an unremitting votary of booze-sodden self-pity and violence at night. The demeaning remarks, the twists of the wrists, cruel slaps, sudden punches and pinches. The slobbering, stinking entitlement towards sex, untender paws coming through the nightclothes when the room is black.

All rape, she argues, is a scarcely reported crime wherever humans congregate, but in the countryside, away from street lights, and sympathetic colleagues, and places to escape, it becomes entirely hidden away, not discussed or explored. Jake thinks her point is expertly proved by the fact this thesis was never even published. Joanna talked to women anonymously, who shared their stories, often with initial reluctance and then towering anger: the teenager who used to walk two miles to and from a village pub to earn money as a waitress, and gets forced into a car to be defiled in an isolated barn; the wife whose back and legs are so bruised by pummelling during her husband's impotent attempts at sex it hurts her to dress in the morning. Joanna also looked at the records of sex-linked crimes that had actually been reported. The vast majority were unsolved. Some due to recalcitrant, unco-operative, terrified witnesses. Some because an assault out of nowhere, the blinding pressure of someone forcing you to the ground in the darkness, does not leave much evidence in its brutal wake.

This was all written in the months after Sabine's death, which itself does not feature in the account at all. But in the years immediately preceding and following there were several examples of unsolved assault cases, which Joanna sought to chart and connect. One woman reported the time a man pulled her into his big car, as she completed her daily walk at dusk. She thought he had been watching her for days to observe her routine. She had seen glints of a camera or binoculars on various occasions, little flashes of light from the depths of the landscape she had always discounted and ignored. She never saw his face, as he wore a sort of neckerchief around it and forced her to face away from him, head pushed against a window. That neckerchief appeared again in another case two years later, twenty miles away: a woman who always went fishing early in the morning, alone, as a way of finding peace in the world. That was permanently ripped from her: her little favoured patch of land and water forever tainted by the horror of cruel force and violence, appearing out of nowhere in the early glimmering of the dawn.

Jake feels overwhelmed reading this, and there are other cases too. One clue that appeared and went nowhere was the tattoo on the left arm of an attacker. Two women noticed it: it was small, and dark, and looked like a dagger or a sword, something sharp and pointed. It never produced a viable suspect. Whether or not there was a serial rapist in the area a decade ago – and Jake is inclined to think this should have been investigated more thoroughly – the idea of sexual predation as a factor in Sabine's life is far from impossible. Joanna has included clippings of all the inquests into deaths from violence in the county in the last two decades, and Jake skims through them: names of some places nearby he can recognize, but an unremitting torrent of detail he cannot adequately process as well.

Down by the water

Jake puts the papers to one side and goes for a run. It is another clear day, and he feels strong as he follows his familiar route. He can now do his five miles in just over half an hour, his legs thick and tireless, his wind always good. The progress of exercise – the more you do it, the stronger you get – is one of the great discoveries and certainties, he thinks, of his new life. He has never been fitter, never more in tune with his own body. Today, his mind is fevered with speculation about Sabine and Peter, and he doesn't take the path back home as normal, but keeps on running to the river, then along it. His heart is pounding, the sweat is flowing and then steaming from his body in the brisk air. After a couple of miles, his back begins to tighten and he stops to stretch. The grass around him is bejewelled with dew. The leaves on the trees are continuing their slow transformation with the season. A festival of colour surrounds him, from stubborn green to mustard yellow to deep maroons, the hue of bruises.

A couple of hundred yards ahead, Jake notices someone

fishing, bent forward over a rod and line that arcs into the water. Nothing seems to be biting, and the man is staring, still, into his shimmering reflection. It is Rose, and Jake thinks this is a good opportunity to talk again about Sabine. He runs up to him.

'How's the drug business?'

Rose does not move his head. The river drifts soundlessly on. Jake squats next to him. 'I want to ask about the last two weeks of Sabine's life. She was trying to get away from that farm with you, and then you turned her down. Was she devastated, is that why she killed herself?'

Rose turns to look at him. 'Kill herself? Is that what you think happened?'

'I think she either jumped or was pushed, and the first is just as likely, if not more likely, than the second. Killing someone and leaving no evidence is pretty hard to do.'

'So you're saying I drove her to her death?'

'I'm saying that there's not normally just one reason someone kills themselves. Did anything happen after you broke up?'

Rose is silent, then spits into the water, before speaking in a curious monotone, as if trying to protect himself from excess emotion.

'She wanted to get out of that farm. But it wasn't possible. You might think that it's just hicks here, but the drug business is the same everywhere. Nobody gets out, nobody weakens the circle. And I was into her, but I wasn't no – have never been no – knight in shining armour. It couldn't have lasted, so I ended it. She was sad, but it was like she had seen over into the horizon, and was going to find another way out without me. She wasn't broken. And then all of a sudden she was. The light went out in her eyes. She couldn't look at me, or anyone. She avoided all the men who used to hang around her: your uncle, the doctor. She stopped going into the Nook. A couple of days later, she's dead.'

'Why didn't this come out in the inquest?'

'Who would say owt? Anyone connected to the business wanted it hushed up, and nobody knew anything for certain.'

'So what did you think, even if you weren't certain?'

'I thought the family had put the fix in hard to her maybe, or something else had happened, someone had got tough with her. She was strong, you know, but she wasn't tough like you have to be round here. All this green, all this prettiness, the quiet of the river, it gets you thinking one way, and then you realize it's a hard place to make a life sometimes.'

'Nature red in tooth and claw.'

'What's that?'

'Something Dr Peter said to me once. He was always suspicious about her death. And that's what killed him in the end.'

Jake stands, his body is getting cold, his joints stiff. Rose looks up at him, his face less aloof than before. 'What are you going to do about it?'

'First, I'm going to get running before all my muscles freeze over. And then keep going at this. You could have talked to me before, you know. You didn't have to have this code of silence.'

'You're a copper. I'm a drug dealer. What we gonna do?'

Jake turns to leave. Rose holds up a hand to check him. 'Are you with Livia now? I don't mind. She's someone tough enough to live here, but all the same I wouldn't mind someone looking out for her.'

'Were you involved in warning her off working with me?'

'I was the first time: I was politely asked to speak to her. Then I heard Paul had gone out to threaten her later, and told him I thought he shouldn't bother her again. He listens to me sometimes, but he sometimes follows his own ideas too. He likes getting close to women, especially women he can't have.'

'Was he like that with Sabine?'

'Of course. But he wasn't on his own with that. There's a lot of lonely, desperate people round here. Shit, I'm sometimes one of them. But these men that still live at home, frustrated, a bit unsure of themselves as men, they are terrible with women: the boys at the farm, those two big hefty fellers at Mary's place. I had to warn Paul off Sabine more than once before we got together, even by threatening to tell Joan that he was going to damage the business.'

'I wonder if he did something to her?'

'It's possible. But you know the old men were almost as bad. Your uncle, even the old doctor, wanted more from her than she ever would give. After we stopped seeing each other, even for that short time before her death, she seemed more harassed than ever.' He is silent, his shadow bobbing on the water, looking up at the horizon steepling away from him.

Jake gives a small gesture of farewell, his stride hesitant and awkward, the lactic acid in his muscles making them sting, wincing pain. Rose has returned to his position, watching the water drift by, becoming more remote by the second.

Afternoon assault

It takes Jake a while to get the blood flowing again, all the pleasure in his own strength gone, the seeping cold entering his bones. He decides against a swim, and instead leaps into the lake simply because it is part of the routine, a pointless test of his own toughness, before climbing out soon after. The shower warms him through, and he heats up some broth for lunch. Parsimony in the kitchen is another self-imposed part of his structured life: taking the leftovers and making them last. The smell is of rich meat, bones and vegetables; it is restorative and soothing. It returns the sense, somewhat slipping, that this is a homestead, a place of sustenance, of sustainability.

After lunch, he is at the Nook to use Sarah's phone. She discreetly gives him some space, and he leans against her fridge, which buzzes away in the background. She has left the number for Smiths' Farm on the side and he calls it. It rings three times and a man answers gruffly, the old-fashioned way by simply listing the number. Jake didn't think people did that any more.

'Is that Paul?'

'It is.'

'This is Jake Jackson. We met at the Nook, and I know you're interested in what I'm doing. So I want to meet up with you. I reckon we have plenty to talk about, but I'm mainly interested in what happened to Sabine. Will you speak to me?'

The silence runs long, the throb of the fridge motor the only sound.

'Why should I?'

'Because I'm tired of pussyfooting around. I know you warned off Livia, and I want to know what you're scared of. And I'm not going anywhere. You can talk to me and tell me your story or I'll keep coming back and back until I work out what's going on.'

Another pause. Jake can hear the rasp as Paul scratches his stubble near the receiver. 'I'll meet you in an hour. The old barn near where you found them bones is quiet. We can speak there.'

An interesting choice of location, Jake thinks, but sees no reason not to agree. Paul hangs up the phone abruptly and Jake heads out, giving Sarah a friendly smile as he goes. Her eyes follow him absently, a perplexed look on her face.

The day is blustery, clouds skid above his head, banks of leaves rustling with a rising and falling like the ocean in his ears. A sea of trees. Jake remembers the route he had taken with Livia and Diana, the silhouette of the barn soon on the horizon, black and misshapen against the creamy sky. When he gets there, the whole field feels empty, the orchard in the corner below still mostly cloaked in its summer garb and heavy with fruit. Cider scents drift up to him.

He looks down the ridge where the river can be seen in the distance, sparkles of light on grey. When he turns around, Paul is standing at the entrance to the barn. He is in his work clothes, pastel and shabby, his face set still as granite. Jake walks back towards him and raises his hand in greeting.

Paul mirrors the gesture, but his hand is not empty, it is holding a long knife, a butcher's blade that glints and gleams. He is still a few feet distant, but a sudden lunge could place Jake firmly in harm's way. Jake turns to edge back down towards the path, when he sees coming up from there Davey, similarly armed, his expression fixed and determined.

Jake brings his other hand up, conciliatory, and tries to weigh up his options. He doesn't quite think they will simply attack him, but being wrong on that score would be hard to recover from.

'What are you doing? I just came to talk.'

Paul moves closer, Davey pauses in Jake's peripheral vision. 'Well, we want to make sure you listen.'

'I'm a polite sort of person. I don't need blades waved in my face to listen. Put them down, and we can just talk like normal folk.' He figures his main option, if it comes to it, is to disarm Paul, and then use his weapon against Davey, but it is fraught with risk. Jake had seen knife wounds often in his career, the deep puncture marks haloed with angry bruising, the red swell of pulsing blood, the disbelief on a victim's face as the life drains helplessly from them.

Meanwhile, Paul has inched closer, within striking distance. His arm is wavering with tension. Jake can see his cracked lips, his tongue darting. He may be tough and violent, but he clearly has not often been in this situation.

'Keep still, copper.' His voice is scratchy with the strain. Davey is shifting his feet, but has advanced no further.

'I'm happy to. But how do you think this is going to end? You could kill me, but I've looked into the eyes of killers and neither of you look like you have it in you.' A dangerous statement, but Jake believes it. These are not killers in cold blood. In a moment of rage, perhaps, but not like this.

Paul brings the knife tip close to Jake's chest. He can feel the pounding of his own heart, see the reflection of his shirt on the breadth of the blade. A quiet afternoon for an assault.

'Just shut up for a minute, will you. Keep it shut. Don't get us angrier than we already are. We lost money on the greenhouse move. We lose money when our customers worry about police interest. And we don't much like losing money.'

'I've told all of you before. I don't give a shit about the drugs. But I am interested in how you protect the business. Did Sabine know too much about it? Is that why she had to go?'

'Sabine knew about the business, and had known for years. She wasn't no saint. She took a bonus every year from it; she didn't love it exactly, never got her hands dirty, but she was no problem. If anybody got to her, it wasn't us.'

'Why should I believe that?'

'I don't care if you do believe it. I care what you're going to do next.'

Jake isn't quite sure what to believe now. He has been drawn all of this time to the strange family at the heart of this isolated farm. These dour, cruel-looking brothers, now wafting their sharp metal towards him. The heartless matriarch. The illegal business.

'I care what you're going to do. I've had narrow misses at home and on the road, with someone keen to shut me up.'

Paul nods. 'I heard about them. Not much goes on around here in private, as you may be learning. But that wasn't us. We're more upfront in our warnings.'

'I can see that. Though coming armed to a friendly chat isn't exactly upfront.' Jake pivots back to Sabine. 'How do you think she died?'

The knife has been lowered fractionally so it hovers over Jake's stomach. Davey moves forward, and opens his mouth to speak. All of a sudden a shriek pierces the quiet, the wail of a police siren. Bright lights just behind the hedge, and then the tall figure of Watson striding forth towards them.

The two men lower their blades, but do not move. Davey's head is bowed.

Watson's chin juts forward as he approaches. He is in uniform, black against green. Behind him stand two constables, burly men whose uniforms do not quite fit. His voice is as loud as the siren.

'Everyone take two steps backwards immediately. And you two put down the blades.'

They comply quickly, Paul turning to Watson as he does so. 'Chief inspector, kindly of you to join us. My brother and I were just here to trim the apple trees, and meet our new friend Jake.'

'From where I stand, it looks like you were using the blades as weapons in a threatening fashion. Which I don't need to tell you is illegal. Jake, have you a complaint to make?'

Jake shakes his head. 'No, chief. These folk weren't much of a threat. Davey was about to tell us a theory about what happened to Sabine.'

Paul has moved to stand next to his brother. 'No, Jake, he wasn't. We keep our opinions to ourselves round here, don't we, chief inspector?'

Watson is not smiling. He is upright, and taut, a blade in his own right. 'Well you can both listen to my opinion, chaps. The force has its eyes on you now, your whole family, and any extended business activities it might be involved in. And Jake is – in my eyes – part of the eternal brother-hood of policemen, so if anything happens to him, or those close to him, I will do everything in my power to come after you. Now leave the knives on the ground, and get out of my fucking sight before I decide to arrest you anyway.'

There is ice in his voice, all trace of amiable warmth departed, and the two men sense he is not to be challenged further. In surly fashion they troop down towards the path, eyes on the ground, avoiding the expressions of the two constables who are smiling broadly at them.

Jake lets out a breath. 'Thank you, chief, I'm grateful. It was Sarah who called you, I imagine?'

'A fine woman. She was worried about you.'

'I think I was talking my way out of it.'

'I don't disagree, but better not to take the risk.'

The two men are standing at the highest part of the field, the shadow cast from the barn engulfing them, a breeze rising against their faces. Watson pats Jake's arm. 'Did you get anything out of them?'

'Just that they've been after me before, and they want

me to stop nosing around the farm. I reckon because of the drugs, which I can't help noticing you're not prosecuting them for.'

'The only evidence I have is from an illegal entry from a disreputable-looking former copper.'

'Fair point.'

'Do you think they might have done for Sabine?'

'They say no, but why would they admit to it? They are violent men used to getting what they want.'

'The world is full of them.'

'It keeps people like us in business. Well, used to keep me in business, at least.'

They turn, and head down the hill. 'Where are your burly colleagues?'

'They'll keep an eye on our friends. Make sure they do head back home like good boys.'

'But they can't keep an eye on them permanently.'

'They cannot. Let's hope they don't have further business with you, Jake.'

The sun drifts behind a cloud, and the shadow spreads out like a stain across the whole of the visible landscape. Jake feels the sense of desolation keenly for a second, and shakes his head to try to escape it.

Chickens part 3

When Jake gets home he flicks through more of Joanna's notes, this time for the story around the Sabine inquest. Joanna had talked to the cousin, Richard, who, Jake can see, was trying to suggest something dark at the heart of the farm. 'She was such a sunny character, a lovely woman, someone who drew people to her. And that's hard to sustain here. It's a place where life is hard, and it was hard for her. But she fought to make sure you never knew it.' Joanna read this as a tribute, not a testimony to be examined.

Dr Peter is there in the notes too, but in his role as confirmed local eccentric, talking in baroque metaphors, exuberant references to the natural world. Joanna could sense some intensity, but one without purpose or use to her. Arthur is another, a distant figure, anxious to stay aloof, not be involved. 'Sabine was *loved*,' Joanna noted at one point. 'Too much perhaps?' She had the idea of talking to the people who spent the last hours with her, in the pub, and the notes from those conversations were the next to come in the file. Jake is about to plunge ahead, when he hears the cheery hallooing that denotes Livia's arrival. He puts the papers down and goes outside, shrugging on a thick shirt as he goes. The afternoon remains cool, but it is dry, the sky enclosed in on them, pale grey in one single expanse.

There is colour and movement in the field ahead. Diana is in a magenta cagoule, white jumper and blue jeans. She is leaping as she walks, fermenting with excitement. Livia is fractionally more sober in appearance: jeans, a dark blue T-shirt and a thick grey cardigan. She walks with her arms folded, five yards behind, throwing out occasional words of encouragement. He waves expansively, and they see him. Diana's words float across to him: 'IT'S CHICKEN TIME!'

He laughs, and heads up to meet them. Diana shoots past towards Chicken City, which allows him a moment to embrace Livia, warm and lithe, scents of crushed fruit, hair dampened by the air and the faint hint of perspiration. 'I nearly stopped you coming, you know.'

She grips his waist, pinches slightly. 'Jake, we live here, and walk these fields all the time. I can't keep her locked up any more than I would want that for myself. I'm more worried about you than you should be about me. You're the troublesome outsider, you're the threat.'

He has come to a similar conclusion himself: he is a much greater focus for confrontation than her. There are all sorts of reasons to take things slow with Livia, but she is in his life whatever else might happen, and it is something he has to make work. The longer-term issue is always going to be around Diana, now gambolling up to the chicken houses, so free and so happy. Would he be a

307

welcome presence in her life? Or an unnecessary addition, a drag on her mum's attention, an unwanted excrescence to the sort of insular relationship that only a broken family can produce?

Jake and Livia have fallen into step, hands seeking out each other, the teenage tingle of newfound connection. 'What are you thinking about?'

'Diana. Whether she might not want us to happen.'

'Don't overthink it. She likes you. She'll get plenty of time to get used to you. And we'll take things one stage at a time, no need to rush.'

'I see we rushed pretty quickly to the extravagant orgasm in bed stage.'

'Speak for yourself. I was the model of chaste propriety, if you remember. We spent several hours on several days before I jumped your bones. This is the countryside, you know, temptation is everywhere, and there aren't that many other distractions.'

They walk on up to the field, the thick, heathery grass snagging at their boots, before sitting on the rug Jake had laid out in preparation. Diana is slowly climbing one of the ladders to get a look in the chicken house. There is squawking and fussing, homely sounds.

He tells Livia about the confrontation with the brothers, then Joanna's work, her theory about predators, the possibility he is building in his mind that something happened to Sabine that toppled her, both literally and figuratively.

'You can't prove that very easily, can you?'

He shakes his head. 'No, I can't. But cold cases are always just stories in the end. You have to find the narrative that makes sense, that links up the bits you do know about. Things don't happen randomly, or at least things like death don't. There's a chain of events, like in a detective book. You just need to find a way of reading them. That was always my theory when I was on the job, anyway. Maybe it's nonsense.'

'It makes sense to me. You're talking about the pathway to diagnosis, and, though I might not know much about detective books, yet, I do know about building a diagnosis. You see, doctors get to talk to their patients, get how they're feeling spelled out to them. Vets don't. We have to read the signs: is that cow not eating because of a big horrible cancerous tumour, or because there is poisonous ragwort in the field? We weigh options, do a differential between each one, and settle on a story that makes sense.'

'That is exactly the same for me. So here is the story as I see it: Sabine's spirit is strong, but slowly beleaguered by life at the farm. The drug business is something nobody talks about, but it brings a shadiness, unsavoury characters. The cruel bosses: Joan and Black Paul, then the brothers. The men who stare at her, talk about what she might look like naked, undermine her and threaten her well-being. So she wanders far and wide, spends time with older guys who are less of a threat, whose admiration for her is palpable, but safe. She swims naked where she thinks she won't be seen, she takes joy in the natural world around her. Then she meets Rose, and they have an exciting relationship, a bit of danger, sex, satisfaction. She almost falls in love, but her sensible head tells her that he's not quite the one either. He's enmeshed in the drug business, he's weak when it matters. He is not a route out. They split up. She is damaged, but still strong in the head.

'Then something happens to her from person or persons unknown: some criminal act of violence, some possession

309

of her, abuse, a rape possibly. And she is defeated, she realizes that she cannot get out, that her attacker is part of the community, and will always be around. So she jumps; her final act of courage, her final bid for freedom.

'Fast-forward a decade: one of those old men, who connected with her at a level he probably never fully realized, remains agitated about what happened, and decides he cannot allow it to lie, allow some hidden injustice to persist. So he drags me in, brings some external attention on a community committed to tamping down insurrection and questioning. I start making waves, Peter starts his theorizing again. And the person or people who escaped the attention before fear it might come to fruition this time. And so they first try to make the bones look like a hoax, just a bit of fun. But we keep going, the forensics support us. So Peter has to die and I have to be warned off.'

He has been speaking without pause for a couple of moments, the narrative solidifying in his mind as it spools forth. Livia shivers in the breeze. 'So who did it, who is to blame?'

'That's the problem: there's no evidence. I have criminal activity at the farm, and some people who are certainly capable of appalling acts. Then I have a guy like Clifford with a record of sexual misconduct. I even have two old men who seemed to have an obsession with Sabine. I have the thread of events, just not the guilty parties.'

'Did you know, my love, that the word "clue" comes from the Greek word for a ball of thread? The idea is that you follow it to get out of the labyrinth.'

'How do you know that?'

'My dad was obsessed with etymology. He used to bore

310

us all rigid when we were kids, but now I'm so glad he did. It's like a secret code to the world, something not everyone gets to crack.'

Jake leans over and kisses her, his stomach fluttering. He examines her face with abiding pleasure: her autumnal skin, the arch of her eyebrows, the generous curve of her lips. He is startled by a shout from above.

'EGGS!'

Diana has found two in the second hut she visited. Livia and Jake run beneath the structure, and she tosses them down to him. He catches them, overacting how precarious his hold is. The eggs are warm to the touch, a piece of perfect natural design, stable and strong against the world. They take them to the side of the house and fry them in an old pan on top of the firepit, the shared childish excitement of eating something that has just been produced. Jake also cooks steaks and some heads of corn, which go blackened and smoky and sweetly delicious over the flames.

The shadows begin to lengthen, the temperature to drop out of the sun, and Jake is desperate to ask them to stay in this rambling house that is so superfluously big for one. But he doesn't want to rush the relationship or bring the scantest sense of alarm to them. The late afternoon has passed in a welter of happiness, in a sense of homely security, which only serves to remind him that this is not actually his family, and this is not actually (or quite, or yet, he thinks) his way of life. Little Sky in the daylight is bright and bold and welcoming; in the evening, it is shadowy, filled with places of dark concealment, possible threat.

Diana is picking up the dirty plates and carrying them inside when she points to a figure in the distance. She shouts and waves, her face open and generous. 'Mack! We found some eggs.'

He has parked in his usual place in the field, and he is carrying a pane of glass. He approaches with his customary wariness.

'Glad to hear it, young missy. Jake, I have the glass for the sauna. I'll fit it in a jiffy, and can take the ladies home if that would suit them.' He marches towards the lake, his toolbox clanking against his legs with each stride.

Diana is keen to go in the big car, and Jake can tell that Livia has not been looking forward to a long walk with a tired child. She waves her thanks to Mack, and takes Diana to the lake for one last look at some geese that are serenely bobbing near a clump of reeds. The descending sun has dyed the surrounding water bloody. After ten minutes, Livia heads into the house while Diana crouches outside, knees almost touching her cheeks, throwing stones at an old piece of pottery. Inside, Jake is washing up, plangent notes of trumpet whispering from the record player.

Livia slips behind him, runs her hands up his body. He tenses instinctively. She reaches up to nip his earlobe. 'It's not far from getting dark, so we'll jump in the car with Mack and leave you all the tidying up. And then I'll hang a sign on Sherlock when I have a spare afternoon. Should be tomorrow or the next day. Make sure you come running.'

He turns, and dabs some foam on her chin, before they kiss, expressively and luxuriantly.

'Mum!'

Diana is in the doorway, silhouetted against the setting sun, hair alive with the pinks and reds of the sky.

'Just saying goodbye to Jake, lovey.' Livia moves smartly

312

to grab her daughter's hand and marches her out of the kitchen to the courtyard.

'I'm seven, I'm not stupid, you know.'

'We'll talk about this later. Bye, Jake!'

'Bye, Jake! Kissy kissy kiss kiss!'

He hears them meander down to the lake, giggling and joshing. At his window, he sees them get into Mack's car, the headlights suddenly bright, setting the twilight into relief. A gentle roar of the engine, and the vehicle jounces merrily over the hill. They are away from here by dark at least, he thinks.

Filings part 2

Jake spends a while clearing up, and then turns over the record, Mahler Symphony 9, and resumes his reading. Joanna has included a full, un-subbed version of her article covering the inquest into Sabine's death. It is clear that nobody sought to examine the victim's mental state very much, and the lack of any physical evidence at all makes the rejection of murder a formality. Joanna lists the names of those who had been with Sabine in the pub before she died: Dr Peter Jacobsen, Richard, Davey and Paul and a name he has not seen before: Jim Macdonald. Jake walks across to his cuttings file from the local paper, and sees that the name had been omitted from the published report, presumably by accident.

He begins to feel the flutter in his stomach, half excitement, half concern. He goes back through Joanna's other reports and initially sees nothing to startle him. But, tucked away in one set of notes about the rape of the waitress, is a 'list of people who saw her leave the pub'. A series of unrecognizable names and then this: John Macdonald.

Are they two different men? Or is it the same person, coincidentally near the scene of two crimes committed within a couple of years and about ten miles of each other?

Jake rereads the cases once more. His mouth dry, his face wrinkled into a sneer of fixed concentration. His mind is racing. The man with a tattoo, the man who observes before pouncing, the man who nobody notices or can name. Macdonald. Mack's arm, his skin brown and tight, man of the land, the circular scar that looks less like a cut, more like something has been cut away. An old tattoo that became an identifying brand. The man who lives closest to Peter's home, who spends his days given free run of Little Sky, who is part of the landscape, silent and watching. The man with a big powerful 4x4. The man who has just taken Livia and Diana away in it.

Jake lurches to his feet, his heart pounding. He puts on his boots and a thick, dark jumper, sticks a torch into his pocket. Then he grabs the gun box from the cupboard. What is he going to do? He has very little to go on here, nothing approaching proof about Mack. He can't just walk up and shoot him. Mack's departure with Livia doesn't mean he is going to do anything. But Jake fails to reassure himself. He grabs the dried white roses, which Arthur had kept with the gun, and places them into the box, the petals sticking out. It looks like an impromptu gift at a distance. He shoves it in a knapsack, and puts it across his shoulders to free up his arms.

Dusk has deepened meanwhile, and the world has become dark grey, wolf-coloured. Jake sets off at a lope, and makes direct for Parvum and Livia's house. Across Morse Field and down to the river he runs, his gait shambling and unmeasured, his mind aflame with thoughts of

315

Livia. The river drifts past invisible, as he meets the first lights of the village. Livia's house is unlit, and he looks inside through the window at a room empty of everything but messiness. Life is lived here, vibrant and jumbled, but not now. He feels a deep sickness in his stomach.

His next move is to go to Mack's cottage. He rushes in its direction down the empty lane, and then halts himself about a hundred yards away. He cannot blunder into this, he realizes. He creeps past Peter's house, a big, shapeless patch of darkness, nothing stirring inside. There is a single light glinting in Mack's place, and Jake crawls along the ground beneath the window. He peers in: the room is empty. A drowsy fire smoulders in the corner. Jake can hear nothing other than his own pulse hammering in his ears. He makes himself breathe out slowly, he has to keep control over himself if he can. Where are Livia and Diana? Where has Mack taken them?

He suddenly thinks that they may have stopped at the Nook, a treat for Diana. The most likely location, in fact, for a mother and child. He edges back from the cottage, his feet sticking in the clay-like soil, and jogs into the centre of Parvum. The Nook is lit, and Jake looks through its main window and listens. He can hear a childish snort, then Diana's familiar giggle. He opens the door softly so as not to ring the bell, and pads halfway down the stairs to the cellar. He sees Mack's thick and dirty boots, his legs stretched out from him. Livia is mock-seriously telling Sarah off for bringing out ice cream at this time of night. A wave of relief washes over Jake, and he is about to make his presence noisily known, when he thinks of that empty cottage, the small light in the darkness. If he is right about Mack, there might be evidence, something that ties him to Peter or Sabine, or any of the other women. The police have never even thought of him as a suspect, much less looked around his home. Now might be the only time to do it.

Before he can convince himself of the folly of the enterprise, he gently turns and tiptoes out, closing the door quietly and then jogging, determined now, back up to Mack's cottage.

Double act

Jake dredges up some nerve and lifts the sash window. He has spent ten minutes circling the place, checking for the easiest point of entry. Mack clearly likes some fresh air in the evening, and has opened the window a couple of inches. It is stiff, but yields to Jake's shove with a low moan that penetrates the stillness of the night. He is motionless for a minute, counting heartbeats, to check whether anyone has been disturbed. There is no movement anywhere. A bird coos in the garden, but it is a sound of comfort, not of alarm.

Jake lifts himself in, and topples over into the room and against a table. A loud clatter, then more silence. He nurses a barked shin for a second, before beginning his prowl. He has given himself no more than thirty minutes, or until the church clock strikes seven. The room he finds himself in is a modest dining room. Everything is clean and tidy, there is a sort of military efficiency behind the person who lives here. Table gleaming in the torchlight, one place set with knife and fork, a photo on the side: Mack as a young man with his merchant navy friends.

They are standing on deck in vests and cloth trousers, the sun must be glaring savagely just outside the frame, their eyes are almost closed, their grins rictus. Jake looks closer: there is some sort of marking on Mack's arm, but the image is too blurred to be sure.

He edges out into the hallway. There is a kitchen to the left, and to the right a living room where the fire is whispering and shifting. Jake tries there next, and the light is bright enough for him to switch off his torch. More signs of order, a compulsion for efficiency. A bookcase of gardening books, unthumbed and mainly decorative. A small television in the corner, no pictures on the walls. Monastic. Jake's attention is drawn to the table, on which an expensive digital camera rests, an anomaly in the homely, unsophisticated setting. He turns it on.

The hard drive is missing, but there are a few images on the camera itself. He skims them: one series of Livia and him kissing by the lake after their first time together; another series featuring an unknown woman walking down a path, her face gleaming with sweat, her skirt rucked up as she moves. Some pictures focused in on the dark patches under her arms, some on her long limbs pinked by the sun.

Jake puts it down and is about to continue the search when he hears a loud noise. The presence of someone in the dining room. Before he can move, the door swings open and a dark figure enters, torch swinging ahead of him. Jake prepares to defend himself, is readying to spring, when a familiar voice rings out.

'Hey, man, it's me. Don't go leading with any punches.'

It is Rose, his blue-black hair tied in a bun, his body clad in black overalls.

'What the fuck are you doing here?'

'I might ask you the same question. You know, you have a bad habit of breaking and entering, especially for a copper.' Rose pats his arm in an overfriendly fashion. 'I've been thinking about Sabine, and those last two weeks, and how she withdrew herself, and how I did nothing to help her. I was coming to see you via the Nook, and saw you running in this direction. And I remembered that last night, her flinching anytime Mack came near her, and him smiling in that quiet way of his. You said someone had done something to her, and I thought he was more likely than the brothers. So here we are. Drug dealer and policeman. Friends at last.'

Jake tries to seem unworried by the intrusion, conceals the faint tremor in his hand. 'I wouldn't go that far.'

'Do you think he raped Sabine and killed Dr P?'

Jake nods. 'And maybe others. It's all circumstantial stuff, though, and I could be wrong. Why don't you get out while you're still almost on the right side of the law?'

'I've never had much truck with keeping on that side. I think I owe it to Sabine to stick with this.'

'All right, seeing as you're here, you might as well help. I think he's been taking photos of people – victims, whatever – for ages, and people like him tend to keep a collection. Where would it be?'

Rose pauses, rocks back on his heels. He is standing in the shadowed corner of the room, the whites of his eyes brilliant in the black. 'This is where your local drug-dealer knowledge becomes invaluable. All these cottages have a cellar, and there's normally a trapdoor somewhere. Look, help me move this rug.'

They pick up a tattered old bit of fabric, and Jake rolls

it and stores it in the corner. 'The clock is ticking. Neither of us want to be caught doing this, so let's hurry up. Can you open it?'

Rose is already lifting the latch, it slams open with a crash, revealing some stone stairs heading into darkness.

'Well now that you've woken the neighbours, let's go and make it worthwhile.'

Rose puts a hand on Jake's arm again. 'The one neighbour is not exactly going to hear it any more, is he?'

'I take the point. So let's be quick about this.'

'Fair enough.'

Jake goes first, his torch dipping restlessly as he walks down. He waits for Rose to catch him up. 'OK, it's hard to search in the dark with torches, so let's stick together and look for cupboards or any places he might have stashed things.'

Rose walks away as Jake is speaking. 'Rose! Rose!' Jake's hissing is loud and spittle-flecked.

The light comes on, revealing a large, dry, ordered room. Rose is standing by a switch. 'Admit it, you need me. This isn't the first local cellar I've been looking for stashes in.'

In the corner of the room is a brown mahogany cupboard, full height from floor to ceiling. It is padlocked shut. Jake turns to Rose: 'We can either leave this and sneak out, or smash this lock and give us no real wriggle room or deniability.'

'It's like you said to me back on the farm: I can't see a police complaint coming against us. We've come this far.'

Jake sees an old poker in the corner by the furnace, and jams it behind the lock. He twists viciously, a loud crack rings out, and the door is open. What they see inside catches their breath. Photos upon photos, strung on lines of string like Christmas cards. Each line a different woman. Some of the images have aged, are yellowing in the corners, and the women can be dated by their clothing. Big hair, shoulder pads, blousy dresses. By Jake's reckoning, those must be forty years old.

The images near the bottom are clearly from the last couple of years. Old and recent, they form a familiar pattern: long-distance at first, the subject alone in lonely places, on moorland paths, or a deserted beach, emerging from a wood, fishing by a stream. Most are fully dressed, but occasionally some are more compromising: a naked swimmer; a woman caught short and relieving herself behind a bush, legs wide apart, knickers stretched taut. Then more focused close-ups, the photographer clearly moving in, the minute details visible: the strands of hair blown across a face, the shade of some lipstick, individual parts of the body – calves, buttocks, neck – itemized and anatomized. The images on the far right turn Jake's stomach: trophies after an assault, the victim facing away, their clothes dishevelled and torn, their intimate parts exposed.

'Jesus fucking Christ.' Jake can hear Rose breathing next to him. 'That swimmer is Sabine. Look what happened to her. The dirty fucking wretch.'

'Have you got your phone on you?'

'The wild man of the woods wants technology now, does he?'

'Just shut up and take as many images as you can of what is in this cupboard. Trace a whole line from beginning to end.' Rose's face distorts in disgust. Jake can sense his anger, his loathing, rising up and connecting with his own. 'Don't touch anything. We'll want prints, if we can get the police here.'

'Should I call them?'

'Not yet. We're technically breaking and entering, so we need to get away first. I'll need to work out privately how we justify what we've done.' All the time, Rose has been clicking with practised ease, his phone taking image after image, a pictorial history of sad and violent obsession. 'Done. Let's get out of here.'

Rose leaps up the stairs, two at a time. Jake closes the cupboard as best he can, then kills the light. He climbs the stairs more cautiously. He can't see Rose when he gets to the top.

Then he can. Lying on the floor where the rug had been; thick, dark blood pooling around his head, staining the pale floorboards. And standing over him, impassive as a statue, is Mack, who is now pointing a gun directly at Jake.

Endings

Mack has blank, dead eyes, fish eyes, staring boldly. He motions with a slight twitch of his gun for Jake to stand next to the wall. Rose is motionless. In the gloom Jake can't quite see if he is breathing or not. He looks back at Mack, who is rolling a cigarette in one hand, a homely gesture Jake has witnessed over and over again during their time working on the house together. Then Mack's silences were mild and companionable, even though there was always a distance between them. Now he is aloof, dangerous, frightening.

Jake tries to unsettle his eerie calm. 'I can't see this working out for you now, Mack. There's too much mess around this. You should have left those bones alone. It would have been seen as a prank, or Dr Peter would have owned up to it. Now look at you.'

'I kept telling *you* to leave it alone. I warned you. And yet I knew you'd be trouble.'

'That's why you were watching me. I remember the occasional glimmer of light hitting something in the distance.'

'I like watching people when they don't know I'm there. I even caught the end of your skinny dip with the delicious and dark vet. Just didn't have my camera ready. I can remember what she looked like though. Every time I close my eyes.'

Jake's muscles twitch, but he knows he can't move yet. A shotgun blast, even in the night, would attract no attention and Mack knows that. Mack could kill him, clean up and be gone, in the wind, to start again in some other deserted spot.

'What are you going to do?'

'I'm going to have to shut you up. Come with me.' He walks up to him, pushing the gun barrel into Jake's stomach, giving it a twist. 'Turn around, walk out the door.'

Jake turns, feels the hard end of the gun pushed against the small of his back, stumbles slightly.

'Move.' Mack's voice is soft, devoid of emotion. But Jake thinks he must be suffering from the stress he is concealing: his whole life has evidently been one of control, power exercised alone, in the margins, keeping watch and then pouncing. He has been camouflaged in the country-side, lurking safely and quietly. He has been in command, without challenge. This whole house is a temple to that sense of order. Jake's presence is messing it up, and Mack must feel that almost as a pain.

'This isn't the first time I've had a gun pointed at me, you know.' Technically true, but both other times Jake had been part of a team responding to a hostage situation, and he had been wearing protective gear, following a set procedure. The sense of peril there was different, and much less pronounced.

'Shut up, and walk.'

'Why did you kill Peter? What did he know?'

'He told me he'd changed his mind about Davey and Paul. They were too clumsy and brutal. They could never have slyly killed Sabine, and they convinced him they didn't care enough about her to have bothered anyway. And he remembered I had been in the pub that night, that Sabine had tried to tell him something about me, something small, but that had nagged his mind. He was about to bring me into it. So I stopped it.'

'You didn't stop it. You murdered him. You brought even more attention on it. You've lost control, you're no longer running things. And if you kill me, it will be worse. I'm an ex-copper, working with the police, who know I'm investigating all this. Something happens to me, there'll be more questions, more mess. Your moments on the margins are over.'

'Shut your mouth. I know what you're doing, trying to panic me, but it won't work.' The first trace of excitement and unease in his voice.

They are walking along the lane in almost complete dark. The faint smell of woodsmoke in the air. Hedgerow rustlings. The hoot of an owl. Mack's cigarette is in his mouth, he has one hand holding the gun pressed against Jake's back, the other holding a torch, which swerves and bobs as they walk.

'Where are we going, Mack?'

'We're going to visit the vet, Jake.'

'No, I'm not going to do that.' Jake stops in the road, the gun jabbing against him painfully.

Mack puts his head just behind Jake's, his voice a whisper. 'If you don't, I'll kill you now, and then force her onto her front to give me pleasure. You can imagine that,

Jake, can't you? You've been there already, haven't you? You can see why I might want that.'

Anger and despair rise in Jake's throat like a sickness. He weighs his options: he could make a run for it, dive for the shadows, go for his gun. Mack seems to sense this. He drops his cigarette, and holds Jake's side with one hand, twisting the skin as he goes. It would not take him long to pull the trigger. And then what? Would Mack escape to parts unknown, or would he let the yawning, empty aloofness of the dark night absorb the blast, wait for the silence to return, and then make his way, filled with lust and vengeance, to plunder Livia's home?

That seems, terrifyingly, more likely. Jake's feet take him mechanically forward, his pulse throbbing again in his ears. Rose might wake up and sound the alarm. Rose might be dead, his blood thickening and cooling on the floor in Mack's cottage. Jake looks around for any sign of assistance, any sign of life. A single passer-by would change the situation, force Mack to do something that Jake might exploit. But the night is black and empty. Streets are deserted in this part of the countryside at this time of the evening. Nobody is coming to help.

They are approaching Livia's house. Mack pushes the gun harder against Jake's back. 'Knock on the door and walk us in. I can shoot and run at any time, remember.' Jake knocks, willing it with all his might to stay obdurately shut. It opens. Livia's face is split with a smile, as Jake stumbles in. It turns to horror, a pain he can read in her green eyes, when she sees Mack behind him, gun in hand.

He puts his finger on his lips. 'Let's not wake the little missy just yet. I've no inclination towards hurting children, never had. Let her dream peacefully, while the grown-ups talk this over. And don't hold anything against young Jake here: I said I'd kill him if he didn't bring me along, and he wasn't quite ready to leave you open to callers without him.'

Jake is still trying to plant some doubt in his mind. 'You've brought more people into this, Mack. You're losing control. Remember when it was just you and the woman, whoever it was. You were in command. She was the prey, and you were the hunter. Now, there's more people who know about you. You should run. You're losing it.'

Mack turns and, before Jake knows it, has clipped him above his eye with the gun. An explosion of pain in his head. Blood runs down his cheek. Mack's movements were controlled, unhurried, and yet Jake barely saw them coming. Livia gasps, and moves towards Jake. Mack stops her with a gesture, and then pulls off the neckerchief he is wearing around his neck. He puts it over her head, her wide eyes bulging with fear and fury.

'Put this in your mouth, and tie it tight, so you stay nice and quiet. The next time I won't be asking. Now let's sit down and I'll work out what's going to happen next.'

Livia does as she is told, then slumps on one end of the sofa, while Mack motions Jake into a chair. He knows he needs to keep talking. 'See, you're having to work out what to do as you go along. That's not how you operate, Mack. I've seen it before. You're a planner, a fixer. You don't know how to handle this.'

Mack's voice is raised a little, half above a whisper. 'Will you shut up, Jake. Or I'll take it out on the lovely Livia. You see, I already know what she looks like stripped, I know about those suntan lines, that little patch of hair.' He rests his hand on her head, as he paces past the sofa.

'I haven't got her full smell yet, but I will, you know, I will. Stand up, Jake.' Jake reluctantly rises to his feet. He is still wearing the backpack carrying the gun, but can see no immediate way he can get to it.

'So here's what my *plan* is, Jake.' Mack spits out the word with relish. 'I'm going to be gone soon: out of the door and out into the wilds. You're right: the run has been coming to an end. I've tried to fight it, but I always knew this day would arrive. I know where I can get to where nobody will look. I had that in mind all the time, see. That was my emergency planning. But do you know what, Jake? You're not going to know what happens between now and my departure. Livia will know. But not you.' He slams down the gun on Jake's head, as hard as he can, as hard as he did with Peter and Rose. Jake falls to the floor in a heap, unmoving. He feels for a moment paralysed, his brain a fog, the rest of the room a muddy blur of sounds and shapes. He is aware of what happens next, but powerless, utterly enervated, incapable of movement.

Livia chokes out a scream, and Mack is on her, that speed of his, so controlled and surprising. His face is close to hers. He grips her shoulders and raises her to her feet, turning her to face the wall.

'Start stripping, or I kill you, then the little one really will have nobody to look after her on these dark nights.'

Tears are falling down Livia's cheeks. She is wearing her home clothes: black pyjama trousers and one of Jake's shirts over a small pink vest. She starts undoing the buttons, her hands fumbling. She is breathing through her nose; the gag must be making her nauseous. It must taste how he smells, the sweetness of cider, the sourness of the unwashed male. How he is going to smell the next time he comes near her.

'You can take your time, missy. There's nobody to disturb us, after all. And I only have to be gone before light. I don't mind taking off the scantier items myself.'

The shirt falls to the floor. She takes a look over her exposed shoulder. Mack is standing, gun in one hand, tongue moistening dry lips, his own breaths short and excited, like an animal's.

'Come and stand in front of me, Livia. I normally don't get a chance to talk to the women I love, because I have to hide who I am. But we're past that.'

She moves to the middle of the room, and he sits down behind her, swivelling her to face him, one hand on her hips. His head at her navel. Her only hope is surely to keep him talking, to allow for something to intervene. Her face betrays her fear, her eyes flicker towards the door of Diana's bedroom. There is a palpable grief seething through her: in her mind must be an image of her daughter, lying curled in bed, clutching a toy, surrounded by soft pastels and pinks, in warm, cosy sheets, dreaming innocently of days in the bright sun to come. She shakes with impotent rage and hate, her muscles twisted and tight.

Mack pulls her forward, gripping the waistband of her trousers, so she is leaning over him. He looks up, and tugs down the gag, then lets his hand rest on her visibly beating heart. Her vest is flimsy and his eyes linger on the outline of her breasts.

She looks him in the eye. 'You don't love these women, Mack. Whatever you get away with doing to them, it's not love.'

He shrugs, philosophical. 'I call it love, which is all that matters. And you're going to call it love, because how you treat me is going to affect whether you get out of this in one piece, with one daughter still. Do you understand?' He runs a thick finger with a trimmed fingernail across her collarbone. 'I think you'll do anything to love me.'

He suddenly stands, and swivels her again, pushing her towards the bookcase by the wall. He is short for a man, but strong. His mouth is against her neck, forcing her down towards the top shelf. She holds out her hands to brace against the wood. Her body tenses, stiff as rictus, and she pivots her hips back into him. She picks up a glass candle holder in her right hand, smashing it down towards his head. Thick blue glass, an ugly ornament, but it fits perfectly in her hand. Mack has swift reflexes, and he just avoids the full impact, the glass crashing against his shoulder, drawing blood. He has staggered but is not falling, blood on his cheek, and on her hands. He still has the gun, and now passion in his grey eyes. He points the weapon at her, its end quivering slightly.

'You're going to regret that, my love.'

But behind him Jake has risen, his own head now clear. One of the lessons he had once learned in hostage training was how to take a blow to the head. 'Don't make them knock you out. Fall with the hit, soak some of it up, twist your temple away, stay conscious, stay alive, but let them think they've hurt you.' He is in pain, but he barely notices it. He has been watching and waiting for a moment of distraction, and this is it. Mack turns to him, his once-impassive face now a mask of surprise and fear, and Jake puts all his weight behind a left hook, a perfect punch he has been storing his whole life. It connects with Mack's jaw, shattering bone, the crunch audible across the room.

Mack falls, his body limp, the gun out of his hands, dropping on the ground with a thud.

A moment of pause, the quiet somehow thicker after the noise, the ponderous tick of the clock continuing its steady patterning. Jake and Livia run to each other, grasping for reassurance, clutching with a sense of love and the celebration of safety. There is blood everywhere: above Jake's eye, on the other side of his head, on Livia's hands. It smears across her face as they kiss.

'Mum, what's happening?'

Diana in pink and blue nightclothes, wide-eyed at the scene of carnage before her. It brings Jake back to reality. He squeezes Livia. His voice is rasping, staccato. 'Livia, take Diana out of here. Get to the Nook, and call Watson from there. Get an ambulance to Mack's cottage. Rose is down. Mack hit him. He was helping in the end. I'll keep things safe here.'

Livia grins fiercely. Her face streaked with tears and blood. She has never looked stronger or more beautiful. She squeezes his shoulders, touches his nose then his cheek, and runs to her daughter, enveloping her in a hug.

'Don't worry, my little lovey. Something bad nearly happened, but mummy and Jake stopped it.'

Diana's face is distorted with shock. Livia strokes her hair. 'It's all nice and quiet now.'

'Why is Mack on the floor, where did all this blood come from?'

'Don't look at it. Mack tried to do something mean, and we didn't let him. So we're OK, we're OK. Let's go and tell Sarah what's been happening, and let Jake clean things up here.' She looks over Diana's head back to Jake, who is leaning against the side of the sofa.

He sags further, suddenly exhausted. 'I'm sorry it came to this.'

'So am I. But there has to be an ending, unless all those books you've got have been lying to us.'

She escorts Diana out of the door, closing it behind her. Jake moves Mack, unconscious, onto his front. He is still breathing, shallow desperate gasps, and Jake thinks he will live. He tears a strip from his shirt, and binds Mack's hands tight behind his back. He shrugs off the backpack and pulls out the box containing Arthur's gun. He carefully lays the dried roses on the table, then removes the gun and hefts it in his hand. He points it at Mack. There is a mirror on the wall behind him. He sees himself: wild-eyed, shaggy beard, two separate cuts oozing blood, his body jolting with fear and adrenaline and the joy at seeing Livia safe. So this is what renunciation looks like. This is what comes of seeking the quiet life.

Mack moans, and wriggles slightly. Jake sits, cradling the gun and watching him, waiting for the blare of lights and noise and people. That next part will not be quiet, he thinks.

Beginnings part 2

A week later, Jake is sitting in the sauna. It is mid-morning, the rain is falling, blown almost horizontal by a blustery wind that rises and drops like a scolding voice. It snaps at the window, which had been fixed by Mack on the day he was arrested. The whole structure, like several parts of the house, bears the marks of his craft, his presence engraved into solid material, unyielding and unmoving. But Jake is determined not to be swayed by metaphysics. Mack is gone, and will not return. His physical legacy is unimportant. The things he helped build still work, are still worth having.

That night, Watson had walked through the door an hour after Livia left, his advent heralded by a cacophony of sirens and a blinding flurry of flashing blue lights. Jake had been sitting motionless, emptied of anger and passion, staring at the prone figure. Mack had started to writhe more vigorously a few minutes before the police arrived, unable to frame any coherent words through his mangled jaw. Jake could see the pain in his eyes, the despair of a cornered animal, the rage of the suddenly disempowered. He felt no pity.

Watson brought with him some uniformed police officers, who robustly hauled Mack up to his feet, and escorted him to a police car. They would stop off at the hospital on the way to get his jaw looked at. One of them would be stuck waiting outside a room for a time while he healed, while the case was built against him. Mack suddenly looked old and pathetic, no longer the hard, practical man of the land. Watson, avuncular, sat next to Jake on the sofa, and patted his leg.

'Well this is quite something, and no mistake. I stopped off at Mack's cottage to seal it, and the paramedics saw Rose. He's unconscious but still alive, so that's something. Why don't you tell me what I'm going to find out when I look around his place?'

Jake took him through everything from Joanna's notes to Rose's unexpected arrival to the violent contest at Livia's house.

Watson whistled through his teeth. 'There are all sorts of problems with this, of course, but I think we'll be able to steer through them. That cupboard will give us plenty to go on. It's a good job that I formally withdrew your role as a consultant, so your presence is just a minor crime on your part, which we'll no doubt find a clever way of overlooking. Meanwhile, let's sort this place out so Livia has a home to come back to.'

Jake got some ice for his head, and gave a formal statement, while various functionaries milled about. He then went to the Nook to check on Livia, who was sitting in Sarah's kitchen, Diana asleep and peaceful on her lap. She was restless, wringing her hands, biting her lips.

When Jake held her tight, he whispered that he loved her.

She responded with a nod and a squeeze, but her eyes were absent. 'I just keep thinking of the man you brought into our house. What could have happened to Diana. How awful it would have been for her.' Tears were streaked on her face.

'I had no choice, you know. He said he would have killed me and then come after you anyway.'

'I know. I'm being unreasonable, but you led him in, he could have devastated us. I just want to get home and in bed and clean. Can you walk us there on your way back?'

Jake sensed a barrier suddenly flung up between them, the insidious creep of blame and responsibility. Livia was loyal to Diana above all else, and he had been the one who brought danger upon her. He spent the walk home afterwards cudgelling his brain, wondering whether he could have just dared Mack to do his worst, and kept him from the family, kept them safe at all costs. Had he played the part of a coward or a hero? He wanted to believe he had understood the odds, stayed alive and in one piece, and was there to get them out of it at the end. He wanted Livia to believe that.

The next afternoon, Watson came to pick him up for more interviews at the station. The early forensic news was good: Mack had left the wrench that killed Peter in his car, washed clean but still bearing some tell-tale marks when closely examined; his cellar contained images that put him close to the victims of a number of unsolved rape and assault cases. Some would have preserved DNA evidence that could now be linked to him. It had been

Mack's fingerprints found in Bluntisham church, and at Jake's doorway. He had been worried that his guilty past was catching up on him.

Watson was philosophical. 'The way this will work is that we'll present a whole raft of possible cases to the CPS, and they'll want to focus on the slam-dunks: the murder of Peter, the attempted rape of Livia, at least one of the other rapes. Mack's lawyers will want a deal, given the scale of criminality at stake. I reckon there'll be a bargain, and no victim will have to testify. He'll go away for a long time.'

Jake remembered the strangling he had read about in the *Shire Gazette*, which Watson had investigated and never solved. He asked whether that could be attributed to Mack.

'It's too old now to know for sure. The victim isn't among the photos we've examined, but that doesn't necessarily mean anything. I think the murder could have been an example of his plans going wrong, so he wouldn't have kept a record. He's not admitting to it. Not that he's talking much about anything with that knock you put on his jaw.'

Jake shrugged. 'Ironically, the other thing he won't face justice for is Sabine. I don't think he killed her anyway, but he drove her to suicide. Still, her memory has been avenged. Peter would be satisfied.'

'And it's thanks to him we got to this point. If he'd left those bones resting, none of this would have happened. He gave up whatever life was left for him, but probably stopped some other women's lives being ruined. Sabine's death has meaning too now, God rest her.

'You did a good thing, Jake. This guy was not on our

337

radar, could have carried on for years, random attacks, destroying lives. I'm conscious of my failure as a copper here: I should have found something that led me to him. And I have to live with the fact I didn't. You've done something for this community, and you've helped me.'

Jake laughed bitterly. 'I'm not sure everyone will see it that way. And I'm not sure Livia will forgive me for bringing all that so close to Diana. She would have been better off keeping away from me, as she thought herself once or twice.'

'I'm old and romantic, as you know, so I won't agree with you. Give her a bit of time, that's all she needs.' They shook hands. 'Any of this get you tempted to go back to work, go back to civilization?'

'No, I still want my peace and quiet, I want my narrow horizons. I think.'

Peace and quiet had followed. Livia had left him a note at the Nook, saying that she and Diana were going away for a few days, to recuperate and restock, get away from memories of that scene. It was signed with love, but who knew what that meant. Jake had resumed his habitual routine: the hard exercise in the cold, the manual labour, the quiet nights by the fire. The orchard – which he called Wolfe's Orchard, after the Rex Stout detective – was well-tended, the chickens looked after. He longed for little other than Livia.

Joanna got her story in the *Mail*, and was a minor hit on radio and television news broadcasts. Jake gave her some quotes, and for a couple of days had to dodge curious journalists sent from national newspapers and broadcasters to talk to the figure who helped to catch the man accused of serial rapes across the decades. Little Sky was too hard to find for most of them, and he locked himself away in the library from the others, music playing loud, buried in some books, refusing to speak.

It is peaceful and quiet in the sauna, just the hissing of the fire, the racing of the heart. Sweat pools around his stomach. Inside it is roiling with regret.

Sarah had come the day before, cautiously approaching Little Sky, as if she felt unmoored this far from her shop. She had brought news of Rose's recuperation: a terrible concussion, but nothing more. He had enjoyed being on the right side of the law for once, had felt the pleasant tug of the heroic. He was avoiding journalists too, though, in case they examined his affairs too closely.

Jake and Sarah drank coffee companionably: this elderly lady, full of quiet resolution, and this straggly, wild-looking man, full of questioning self-doubt.

'I'll always speak up for you, Jake,' she said, 'and so will Rose now. Though who can speak against you? We harboured a snake here. We let our daughters and sisters and wives live in danger, and that's gone.' She patted his hands. 'Livia will come through, you can see that.'

He is not so sure now. Everything had seemed so clear in his brain: his desire for Livia, his pursuit of the answers or justice or whatever he had been seeking. But perhaps one had come at the cost of the other. He shakes his head, scattering droplets of sweat from his beard. He has been in the sauna long enough, the painful tingle in his memory of the time he was once trapped here. He opens the door, walks through the icy rain and into the icier water of the lake. His body can handle the temperatures now, and he gently strokes his way up to the far side, where the beach awaits, barren and autumnal. Where she had left her clothes that time.

As he pauses before turning back, he peers into the distance, where he knows Sherlock Beech is standing, hidden by the hump of land and the low-lying cloud. He wants not to check for a message, to live his self-reliant life, needing nothing more. Cursing to himself, he plunges back into the wintry water and furiously swims back, as if by flurry of muscle he can expel his fears.

Later, he is warmly dressed and walking, drawn towards any place from which the tree is visible. The rain has stopped, but the ground is soggy and the air pregnant with damp. He looks through his binoculars and for a moment sees nothing but murk hiding an arboreal shadow. Slowly the mist clears and there is the tree, ancient and heedless. It will outlive life and love, but today carries a sign of something current and in the moment, a forlorn pennant fluttering. Jake hastens towards it, recognizing that fabric from a nightdress Livia owns. There is no note, and he fast-walks to Parvum, his mind warring between hope and fear of the finality of a considered rejection.

Livia's house is empty, a note on the door refers to some farming emergency. Does she mean for him to wait? He goes to sit in the churchyard, the place where he first met Peter, that hot, distant day when the bones had been discovered. Such a lot has happened since then. The rain returns, a steady, disconsolate downpour. He walks back through the village, waves through the window to Sarah but doesn't stop to talk. There is still no answer at Livia's door, and he starts his sodden march homewards.

He is just reaching the river, when he hears her calling his name. He looks back. She is running towards him, hair flat on her head, waterproof leggings rustling between her thighs as she moves. She calls his name again, and he starts walking towards her. Before he knows it, she is in his arms, and they are spinning, her mouth crushed against his, so he can feel the shape of her teeth. She pulls back, her songbird throat heaving. Her voice is urgent.

'You know you said "I love you" and I said nothing. That was unforgivable. But I want you to forgive me. I love you. I have loved you since the first time we sat on a blanket and talked. I love you because you're odd, and live in a big weird house, and have a lake and a sauna, and a long beard. I love your big, awkward body. I love you because we fit together. I love you because you swim in the cold and shower outside and wash your clothes by hand. I love you because you listen to me, and love me, and will love my Diana. I love you because you've never had the warm messiness of a family, and I have that ready and waiting for you. I love you because you came here to hide, and when it mattered you didn't. But if you want to keep hiding, I want to hide with you.'

She kisses him again, this time more tenderly. His eyes are moist with the rain and the emotion. She holds his hand, and draws him back to the road. 'Come on,' she says, 'let's both get out of these wet things.'

At the bank of the river stands the heron, indifferent to the damp and its surroundings and the people walking away. A moment later, it rises, beating its wings with power and precision, and soars off into the grey.

EPILOGUE

A winter day. The sun an angry crimson, the air dense with cold. Jake is walking the land. There is a fire burning at home, he can smell the woodsmoke on his clothes. Livia and Diana are coming to stay for the weekend. They don't live together yet. He has bought a second-hand washing machine, which Rose helped him carry home and install. His clothes now smell a little less of the lake.

The family is still just part-time. Livia has work, Diana has school, and what does he have? Peace at least, some moments of happy solitude. And the sense of something more to come. The sky hangs heavy above him, like a cocoon. He cannot see much beyond the smallest of horizons, and that feels enough for him.

ACKNOWLEDGEMENTS

My debt of gratitude starts with the hundreds of authors of crime novels I have read since I was a child. They have given me solace and enjoyment at all times of my life, and continue to do so. Like with rats in London, I am never more than six feet away from a thriller at any point in my day or night. I have relished the privilege of contributing to the genre more than words can say.

Lots of people have helped me get here. My agent Cathryn Summerhayes didn't want to read the manuscript of this, my first foray into fiction, in case – in her words – 'it was rubbish'. She did it anyway, and hopefully it has been worth it. She remains the least rubbish agent in the world.

HarperCollins is such a fine publisher, and I am hugely grateful to everyone there, including Charlie Redmayne, Kimberley Young, Julia Wisdom and Angel Belsey. Liz Dawson has been a publicity marvel, and I benefitted greatly from social media guru lessons from Maud Davies and Olivia French. My thanks go to my editor Kathryn Cheshire, who has been marvellous, and to Rhian McKay for all her work on the copyedit. I have enjoyed discussing point of view with both of them enormously.

Thanks must also go to early readers of the book, including Jeanette Sanders (my novel-addict mother-in-law), Xand Van Tulleken and David Shriver.

My parents allowed me to read grown-up novels when I was too young for them, and have been an inspiration and support ever since. I'm happy to say that my own children have caught the reading bug, and the eldest two have great ambitions as writers as well. Nelly, Teddy and Phoebe are the main reason I do everything that I do.

But final thanks, as ever, must go to my wonderful wife, Nadine, who stubbornly refuses to believe anything but the best in me, and remains every day the greatest thing that has ever happened in my life.

Keep reading for a sneak peek
at *Death in a Lonely Place*, the next
book in Stig Abell's atmospheric
series following Jake Jackson...

PROLOGUE

You can see it, if you like, as a thick sheaf of papers, a breeze flicking curiously through them, each page another account of a crime committed, a life ruined, someone's thoughtless desires satisfied without challenge or recourse to justice. Or maybe – this being the twenty-first century after all – it's just a screen endlessly scrolling, a narrative without apparent end, information heaped upon information, case running seamlessly into its own sequel.

And, if you are a quick enough reader, you'll learn of all sorts of examples of human misery connecting back to one group of people, too shapeless to appear visible as an organization, too consistent in their application of power to be dismissed as the product of coincidence.

Their range of activities, their productivity, is as much of a defence against scrutiny as a sign of their continued success. All of these examples of crime, of hurt and grief, are so numerous as to make them hard to link together, to join up into a picture. Until now they have never been connected.

To the family missing their youngest child, snatched from their negligent care, there is no glimpse of a pattern, no chance to see how their own devastation had its origins somewhere else. It is part of a figure so intricate that it cannot be perceived in close-up, particularly by those blinded by despair.

We're talking of the husband and wife, who wake up that morning with normal grumbles and gripes about life, but confident – without even thinking about it – that their world would be intact by evening's close. Then their son disappears, and their world is ended. If you were to catch their eye, weeks and months after the snatch, when hope had burned down to nothing more than an ember, you would always be able to see something – an emptiness, an absence – that they could never conceal. Part of them, maybe a light, maybe their soul (if you believe in that sort of thing), gone forever.

You don't want to imagine the feelings, or the fate, of their son himself. No sane or humane person would. Someone too young to understand the adult world in normal circumstances, now grabbed from outside their home, hustled into a van, drugged and baffled, and then who knows what follows? You don't want to read what happens next, the thought is too awful, you think immediately of those closest to you, already replacing the true victim with an imaginary version from your own family. His plight now a bit diminished, the inherent selfishness of empathy. You turn the page to another story, hopeful its horror will be less.

And maybe it will be. Children always make tales of cruelty worse. Take instead the two business rivals, scrapping over some mining territory in China. It is not edifying, it is morally wrong, it is catastrophic in its own way. But you can read on at least. One man decides – the actors in these appalling dramas are often, but not always, men – that he cannot defeat his opponent through conventional means. So he pays for someone to arrange his ruin: drugs planted, allegations of inappropriate behaviour, hitherto exemplary accounts discovered to be tainted by fraud. The framing is brilliantly done, drum-tight, no possible means of wriggling free. His family deserts him, his losses mount incalculable, and he ends it all with an antique shotgun blast through the mouth one day in the office that is about to be taken from him.

The page might turn again. Two cyclists lying crumpled at the side of the road, limbs cast at impossible angles, blood smeared on the tarmac. Or again. A woman sobbing outside a beautiful city house, the exterior white as marble. Light rain falling, running into her tears. A business card drops from her grasp and is washed down into the gutter. If you're quick you can see the elegantly crafted writing on it, though the words won't mean anything to you. Yet.

Chapter One

A cold wind scurries beneath the half-door as Jake stands in his outdoor shower staring at the familiar, now wintry landscape. A record is playing loud: maundering sounds escaping from his kitchen along with the steamy warmth of his house. There is ice on the cobbled courtyard in front of him, hard as iron, treacherous to negotiate in bare feet. The winter here grips you painfully tight, he thinks, it imprisons you, it makes you think of airy summer days like they are a story from someone else's memory.

Melancholy thoughts, and Jake snorts them from his nose along with the running water, rubbing his cheeks hard, and washing the soapy suds from his long hair and thick beard. Everyone feels gloomy in the winter. The days short and sullen, the sporadic splutters of icy rain, the nights starting early and then lingering, reluctant to concede the space to the morning. And what has he really to feel low about after all? His muscles tingle from his daily exercise, his head feels clear, his very own land stretches out before him into the pallid and sightless horizon.

It's no fun, though, switching off the shower and tiptoeing into the house on a day like this, an old towel wrapped around his hard middle, the frigid air clinging to the rest of him. There is quite a lot to cling to: he is tall, too tall he often feels, almost six and a half feet, and in the last two years his body has become broad and lean, with sinewy hillocks of muscle.

He cowers naked in front of the fire in the back living room for a moment, spinning slowly as if he were roasting, before he shrugs on his thick hooded top and pyjama bottoms. He remembers seeing Livia in front of this same fire for the first time, almost eighteen months ago, her rain-soaked clothes steaming, his own thoughts restless with curiosity and desire. At that point, she had been someone beautiful and inaccessible, a surprise that had brightened his existence from their first accidental meeting in a sheep field (he a city slicker clomping about uncertainly; she a local vet, who seemed as much part of the countryside as the meadow flowers beneath their feet). Livia still looks good in his clothes, he thinks, an old shirt hurried onto her body after a night-time shower, or lazily ahead of a morning's pottering in the vegetable garden.

The record finishes. It is Ravel's *Pavane for a Dead Princess*, slow piano echoing in the bleak. Jake goes to stop the hiss, and pours himself a coffee, carefully stirring in thick, dark sugar. He sips and feels warm inside for the first time. On the table in front of him is a postcard from a policeman, announcing that he will be visiting today at 11 a.m. Jake has no phone, no internet, and is miles from any postal route, so is a hard man to make an appointment with. He still loves that in the main. He now gets any relevant mail routed to the local shop – called, in a twee attempt to appease tourists, the Jolly Nook – in the nearby village of Caelum Parvum, and tries to remember to collect it once a week. The policeman, Chief Inspector Watson, knows Jake and his strange way of life, but also knows that Jake will always make time for him. They became close during a murder investigation, following the death of a local woman, and have stayed in complacent touch ever since. That particular period is still fraught in Jake's memory: the investigation had spiralled, an innocent old man – another sudden friend of Jake's – died, and together he and Watson had discovered a pattern of violent sexual assaults in the area dating back decades.

Jake has a few moments before Watson's arrival and tidies in a desultory fashion. Clothes drying above the stove go into three baskets, one each for him and his two regular house guests, Livia and her daughter Diana. He frowns for a second. The arrangement still feels temporary, and he wants it not to. But he and Livia can't quite agree on what permanence should look like, or whether a newly nucleated family like theirs can really prosper in such a place of awkward solitude.

Jake had been given his home as a legacy from a dying uncle, a gift to help him renounce the world and its entanglements. Little Sky – a glorious farmhouse, half from the eighteenth century, half newly designed, set in countless acres of land – had lured him from the city, as Uncle Arthur had intended, become a haven, a soft pastel expanse of peace, a world entire of tumbling fields and ancient hedges and deep loamy soil. The windy shudder of banked trees often the only sound to Jake's ears. The welcome of natural quiet. But it asked the insistent question still: was renunciation, complete rejection of all that is ugly and necessary and modern, ever fully possible? He reckons he doesn't seem to be making that good a job of it.

The sounds of stamping outside the door seem to answer the question once more. Jake can hear muttering, imagines the fussy removal of gloves, the inefficient search for pockets to put them in.

He opens the door ahead of any knock. 'Good morning, chief.'

A wizened face wreathed in smiles, nose reddened by that unforgiving wind, grey hair poking unruly from beneath a black woolly hat.

'Jake, my boy, delighted that you're in. I didn't much fancy an immediate tramp back across your fields.'

'I got your note right enough. And you know I tend not to have many other places to be.'

'I did know that. But strange things can happen around here. And who's to say that your lovely companion hadn't lured you away somewhere.' Watson was fond of Livia, whom he had known before Jake in her role as the local vet, a figure of warmth and positivity.

Watson walks past Jake into the kitchen, the heat embracing him instantly. He leaves his boots by the stove to dry, and in stockinged feet – a lurid red, Jake notes – pads across to one of the two nearby armchairs. Jake had soon realized, in a rural winter, that much of life can be conducted in the kitchen, near to food, and heat, and boiling water, so he has made the room – which is big and clean and welcoming – as comfortable as possible. He still spends most evenings in his thriller library, though, which has its own fire, and the palpable comfort of thousands of books as well.

Watson is long and thin as a poker and extends his legs so his feet are almost touching the stove door. He sighs exuberantly. 'Oh, but that's better. I thought my toes were going to fall off out there for a moment. It's not civilized, you know Jake, living somewhere that you can only visit by walking. It's like something from the Victorian period.'

Jake smiles and pours coffee. This is a version of a conversation the two had been having since the beginning of their friendship. He grabs another record from his kitchen stack, which totters awkwardly on a table in the corner and which he is always meaning to arrange more carefully. More piano, he thinks, and selects something by Liszt, his *Ave Maria*, then dips the volume so the sorrowful tinkling barely rises above and through the sputtering of the wood in the stove.

The two men, at ease, talk of this and that, the weather, the season, some of Watson's more routine work. The latter leads Watson where he wants to go, and he pauses, sits up and clears his throat with some unease.

'Jake, I know you're not one for talking proper shop, but I did want to see you for a reason.'

Jake had figured as much. He had been a detective himself in another life, a past that now only barely intruded into his present. A good one too, a cold case expert, a weaver of fresh narratives from old, broken threads. He had been rescued – as he sometimes saw it, when he bathed in the greenness of the lush land around him, or closed the door on an icy night for the comfort of a solitary fire – from a life of metropolitan crime. Arthur had made his new life possible, had given him not only the house but the chance to narrow his horizons, embrace peace, avoid the murk and pain of lives shattered by violence.

Jake winces slightly, shifts in his chair. 'Knowing your lack of athleticism, shall we call it, I was fairly sure you hadn't come here for the exercise. What do you want to discuss?'

'It's a grim one, I'm afraid. A child snatch, something more or less inexplicable, happened maybe fifty miles from here.' The county Jake lived in was long and broad, filled for the most part with farms and tiny villages, and Watson's jurisdiction was almost unmanageably large. 'I've been working it these last few weeks and, you know at this point the trail is cold and the prospects bleak.'

'Parents?'

'Of course we've looked at them very carefully. But nothing suspicious. It was an IVF baby, a girl called Laura, the love of their life who arrived when they thought they couldn't have children. Now five, from all we can tell a happy and cared-for girl. I know that doesn't mean much, and we've both seen it mean nothing, but there's literally no evidence that they have done something here.'

The stove grumbles, and some wood dislodges itself. The record comes to an end, and Jake reaches forward and flips sides.

'What do you want from me? You can work this as well as I ever could, and I'm not a copper anymore, as we established last time.' A wry smile for them both, an acknowledgement of what had happened in the past, and how that inquiry into murder, suicide and spate of historic rapes had been solved mainly by Jake acting free from the restraints of official investigation.

'Oh, I know all that. But there's one piece of evidence.

It may be nothing, it may not even be evidence. But it's nagging at me, and I thought you might help me understand it. I even broke the rules a bit and brought it with me.' He reaches into his pocket and withdraws a transparent bag, which contains nothing more than a small, tattered business card in the corner. He hands it to Jake, who looks at it circumspectly. One side is blank, the other has two words in black and bold, printed with careful calligraphy: *NO TABOO*.

Don't miss Death in a Lonely Place
by Stig Abell. Out April 2024.